PRAISE FOR

'Endlessly inventive, with a fresh delight on every page, *Nevermoor* rewrites the genre of the Chosen Child Novel. This is a special book' – David Solomons, author of MY BROTHER IS A SUPERHERO

'*Nevermoor* is the most magically mad book I've ever read. It's one of my favourite books ever!' – Zac, age 9

'This magical debut novel is a dazzling and engrossing feat of imagination' – DAILY EXPRESS

'Utterly mesmerising from start to finish, a masterful piece of storytelling, full of wonderful characters and world so rich in magical detail you'll think you've actually stepped into it' – Claire Fayers, author of THE ACCIDENTAL PIRATES: VOYAGE TO MAGICAL NORTH

'*Nevermoor* is wunderful!' – Sonny, age 12

'Written with a wonderful deadpan humour and sharp dialogue, this is a must for the next Harry Potter generation' – DAILY MAIL

THE
HUNT FOR
MORRIGAN
CROW

A BOOK

JESSICA TOWNSEND

Orion
Children's Books

ORION CHILDREN'S BOOKS

First published in hardback in Great Britain in 2020 by Hodder & Stoughton

This edition published in Great Britain in 2021 by Hodder & Stoughton

1 3 5 7 9 10 8 6 4 2

Text copyright © Jessica Townsend, 2020
Illustrations copyright © Hannah Peck and Beatriz Castro, 2020

The moral rights of the author and illustrators have been asserted.

A CIP catalogue record for this book is available from the British Library.

ISBN 978-1-5101-0386-3
WTS ISBN 978-1-5101-1022-9

Printed and bound in Great Britain by Clays Ltd, Elcograf S.p.A.

The paper and board used in this book are made
from wood from responsible sources.

Orion Children's Books
An imprint of
Hachette Children's Group
Part of Hodder and Stoughton
Carmelite House
50 Victoria Embankment
London EC4Y 0DZ

An Hachette UK Company
www.hachette.co.uk

www.hachettechildrens.co.uk

*This book is dedicated with love to Jo Laurance
and her friend Mrs Miller, the original cabaret duckwun.*

CHAPTER ONE

Unit 919

Winter of Two

On a glossy black door inside a well-lit wardrobe, a tiny circle of gold pulsed with light, and at its centre was a small, glowing W.

Come in, it seemed to say with each gentle beat. *Hurry up!*

Morrigan Crow finished buttoning her starched white shirtsleeves, pulled on a black overcoat and carefully fixed her gold W pin to the lapel. Finally, she pressed her fingertip to the shimmering circle and, just as if she'd turned a key in a lock, the door swung open on to an empty train station.

These quiet, still moments had become Morrigan's favourite time of day. Most mornings, she was the first to arrive at Station 919. She liked to close her eyes for just a few seconds, listening to the distant rumbling of trains in the Wunderground tunnels. Like mechanical dragons waking from slumber. Ready to carry millions of people all over the city of Nevermoor on a complex tapestry of tracks.

Morrigan smiled and took a deep breath.

1

Last day of the autumn term.

She'd made it.

The rest of her unit began arriving, shattering the peace and quiet as the remaining eight doors were flung open up and down the platform – from Mahir Ibrahim's ornate red door at one end, all the way to Anah Kahlo's small, arched, unvarnished wooden one at the other – and the tiny station filled with chatter.

Hawthorne Swift, Morrigan's best friend, arrived in his typical morning state – unbalanced by armfuls of dragonriding gear, grey shirt not quite properly buttoned, unbrushed brown curls sticking out at wild angles, blue eyes sparkling with some mischief he'd either just dreamed up or just committed (Morrigan didn't want to know which). Archan Tate – who was always impeccably mannered and dressed – took half of Hawthorne's teetering pile of kit for him without a word and gave the badly buttoned shirt a discreet nod.

Cadence Blackburn was the last to make it this morning. She ran in with seconds to spare – thick black braid whipping behind her, long brown limbs taking great strides – and arrived just as a single, slightly battered train carriage chugged into view, trailing puffs of white steam. Painted on its side was the familiar W symbol and the number 919, and hanging halfway out the door was their conductor, Miss Cheery.

This was Hometrain, a mode of transport and home-away-from-home exclusively for them, the 919th unit of the Wundrous Society. Inside were beanbags, a lumpy old sofa, piles of cushions, a wood-burning stove that was always lit in winter and a ceramic polar bear biscuit jar that was rarely empty. It was one of Morrigan's favourite and most comfortable places in the world.

'Moooorning!' the conductor shouted, beaming from ear to

2

ear and waving a handful of papers at them. 'Happy last day of term, scholarly ones!'

Miss Cheery's role as Unit 919's official 'conductor' was an interesting one – part transport operator, part guidance counsellor. She was there to smooth a path through their first five years as members of Nevermoor's most elite and demanding organisation. The Wundrous Society was made up of extraordinary people with extraordinary talents, but most of them were too absorbed in their own extraordinary endeavours to pay much attention to the Society's youngest inductees. Without their conductor, Unit 919 would be lost in the wilderness.

Miss Cheery was the only person Morrigan knew who utterly lived up to her name: she was pure sunshine. She was fresh linen, birdsong at twilight, perfectly cooked toast. She was all rainbow-coloured clothes and impeccable posture, deep brown skin and enormous smile, and when the light shone through the edges of her cloud-like halo of curly black hair, she made Morrigan think of an angel . . . though of course, she would never say anything so cheesy out loud.

As their designated grown-up, the *one* thing she probably ought to have had was a bit more decorum. But 919 liked her exactly as she was.

'Last! Day! Last! Day! Last! Day!' she chanted, kicking her legs out from the train door in celebration, before it had even come to a halt.

Anah shouted back in a fretful voice, 'Miss Cheery, that is NOT safe!'

Miss Cheery responded by contorting her face into something comically terror-stricken and flailing her arms as if she was going to fall out – and then actually falling out on to the platform when the train suddenly stopped.

'I'm okay!' she said, jumping up to take a bow.

The others laughed and applauded, but Anah turned to glare at them one by one, pink-faced, her blonde curls swinging dramatically. 'Oh yes, very *funny*. Except who'll be expected to stop the bleeding when she falls on to the tracks and snaps her tibia in half? I bet none of you even *knows* how to splint a leg.'

'That's why we have you, Anah.' Archan smiled at her, his pale cheeks dimpling, and bent down to help Miss Cheery pick up the scattered papers with his free hand.

'Yeah, *Dr Kahlo*,' added the brawny Thaddea Macleod, nudging Anah in the side and nearly knocking her over. (It was a gentle nudge by Thaddea's standards, but sometimes she forgot her own considerable strength.)

Anah made a face as she straightened up, but seemed somewhat mollified by Thaddea's use of the word 'doctor'.

'Miss, what's . . .' Archan was staring at one of the papers, frowning in confusion. 'Are these new timetables?'

'Thanks, Arch. Help me pass them out, will you?' the conductor replied, waving Unit 919 on to the train. 'Come on, everyone aboard or we'll be late. Francis, put the kettle on please. Lam, hand round the biscuit jar.'

Hawthorne gave Miss Cheery a puzzled look as she handed him his timetable. It was the last day of term, and they usually only received new timetables once a week. 'You gave us these on Monday, miss. Remember?'

He dropped into a beanbag while Morrigan settled on the sofa between Cadence and Lambeth, scouring her own timetable. As far as she could tell, it was identical to the one she'd been given at the start of the week: there was Tuesday's workshop in *Undead Dialects*, and Wednesday's master class in *Observing Planetary Movements*, followed by a class in the Sub-Five espionage wing called *Cultivating and Handling Informants* (that had been Morrigan's favourite lesson of the week so far – turned out she was quite good at spy stuff).

'I *do* remember, yeah,' said Miss Cheery. 'Despite my advanced age of twenty-one, Hawthorne, my decrepit brain *does* still allow me to reach into its vast memory bank to the distant past of four whole days ago.' She smiled, raising an eyebrow. 'These are *new* timetables. Please note where today has been updated.'

Morrigan skipped to Friday's column and, spotting the difference, asked, 'What's *C&D*?'

'I've got that, too,' said Hawthorne. '*C&D*, Level Sub-Two. Last class of the day.'

Mahir put his hand up. 'Me too!'

There was a general murmuring and comparing of schedules, and the scholars found they all had the same class. Mostly their timetables were individualised – tailored by Miss Cheery to help each of them develop their unique talents and work on their weaknesses – and it had been a couple of months since Unit 919 had had any lessons together as a group.

'Miss, what does *C&D* stand for?' asked Francis Fitzwilliam, sounding slightly worried. His brown eyes grew large. 'Does Aunt Hester know about this? She says she has to approve any changes to my timetable.'

Morrigan raised an eyebrow at Hawthorne, who made a face back at her. Francis's family went back several generations in the Wundrous Society, on both sides – the famous Fitzwilliams and the admired Akinfenwas. His patron – the Society member who nominated him for admission and therefore had a stake in his education – was his aunt on his father's side, Hester Fitzwilliam. She was very strict and, in Morrigan's opinion, a bit of a cow.

'And she says I'm not to do anything that could put my olfactory instrument at risk,' Francis went on.

'What about your old factory?' asked Thaddea.

'My nose,' he clarified. 'What? Don't laugh – a chef's sense of smell is his greatest asset.' He nervously pressed on the end of his light brown, gently freckled olfactory instrument.

'No need to worry about your schnoz, Francis,' said Miss Cheery, with a mysterious sort of half-smile. 'But I can't tell you.'

Nine eager faces shot up to look at her, their interest immediately piqued.

Hawthorne sat up straighter. 'Is it . . . Climbing and, um . . . Doing . . . something?'

'Nope. Solid guess, though.'

'Camouflage and Disguise!' said Thaddea. She twisted her long red hair into a topknot and rolled up her grey shirtsleeves, as if keen to get started immediately. 'We're going to learn evasive combat techniques, aren't we? *Finally*.'

'Costumes and Drama?' was Mahir's guess.

'Ooh! Cats and Dogs!' Anah clapped her hands, bouncing up and down on her cushion. 'Are we going to play with cats and dogs?'

Miss Cheery laughed at that. 'Lovely thought, Anah, but not quite.' She held up her hands for quiet. 'Now everyone stop guessing, please. My lips are sealed. I am a vault.'

Anah's shoulders slumped in disappointment, and she passed the biscuit jar on to Mahir.

'*Lef'selah*,' he said, which meant *thank you* in Jahalan, one of the thirty-eight languages he could speak with native fluency. Lately he'd been teaching the rest of the unit what he considered the 'important bits' of his favourite languages – mostly how to ask for directions, *please*s and *thank you*s, insults and rude

6

words. (More rude words than anything else, Morrigan had noticed, though that might have been because Hawthorne kept making requests.)

'*Hish fa rahlim*,' was Anah's glum response as she bit into her biscuit.

Mahir looked up at her in mixed shock and amusement, and Morrigan's mouth fell open.

'What?' Anah said through a mouthful of custard cream.

'That's not "you're welcome", if that's what you meant to say,' said Mahir, trying and failing not to laugh.

'Oh, you *know* I'm no good at languages.' Anah made a petulant little huffing sound. 'What did I say?'

Mahir, Hawthorne and Thaddea shouted the vulgar translation in gleeful unison. Anah's face turned bright red, Miss Cheery looked scandalised, and the rest of the unit didn't stop giggling for the rest of the journey to the Wundrous Society.

It was a wrench to leave the cosy warmth of Hometrain when they arrived at Proudfoot Station. Huddling close against the wind, Unit 919 waved goodbye to Miss Cheery and dashed for the dubious shelter of the Whinging Woods.

Wunsoc – the Wundrous Society's one-hundred-acre campus, in the heart of Nevermoor – had plummeted into winter earlier than the city outside its walls. It was now several weeks deep into a cold snap that could freeze the snot from a runny nose. The mysterious 'Wunsoc weather' phenomenon meant that Nevermoor's days of drizzle were more like days of pouring rain and sleet inside Society grounds.

In fact, whatever the weather outside Wunsoc, inside was always just a little bit *more*. If Nevermoor was having a mild thunderstorm, the sky over Wunsoc was black and electrified, flashing like a disco, and to walk across the grounds was to risk becoming a lightning rod.

Today they felt the cold bone-deep, but it was made more bearable by a weak showing of winter sunlight and the knowledge that as soon as their last lesson was over, they'd be leaving Wunsoc behind for two weeks of festivities. Morrigan couldn't wait. There was no place like her home, the Hotel Deucalion, at Christmas. She'd been dreaming of eggnog, roast goose and spiced chocolate rumballs all winter long.

To take their minds off the chill, Unit 919 spent the long walk up to Proudfoot House making increasingly outlandish guesses about what *C&D* might be.

'Ooh – what about Creation and Destruction?' Hawthorne's face lit up as he thought of it. 'Maybe they're going to turn us into ALL-POWERFUL GODS.'

'Or Chanting and Dancing,' said Lam.

'Or Chips and Dip?' said Francis.

They all lost the plot at this last, hopeful suggestion, but even through the shrieks of laughter, Morrigan didn't miss the sound of someone hissing *Wundersmith* as a group of older scholars overtook them on the woodland path.

She was used to it now, but it still made her flinch. Almost two months had passed since her secret was revealed to the entire Wundrous Society. Sometimes, when Morrigan needed courage, she thought of Elder Quinn's words: *She may be a Wundersmith, but truly from today onwards, she is* our *Wundersmith.*

Most people at Wunsoc had the kindness and common sense to heed the High Council of Elders and accept Morrigan as one of their own, even if they weren't thrilled to have such a 'dangerous entity' among them. There were some who still took every opportunity to make her feel unwelcome, but it didn't matter much. Morrigan was getting better at ignoring the whispers and glares, and knowing her unit had her back helped a lot. Over the last year Unit 919's loyalty had been tested to its limit. There had been a time when Morrigan felt she would always be an outsider, but now she *knew* she belonged.

Cadence had heard the whisper too. Without missing a beat, she called out, 'Bite your tongue,' and a second later there was a cry of pain and a muffled, '*Ow!*' as the perpetrator obeyed. She smirked sideways at Morrigan, who shot back a grateful smile. She couldn't help feeling a *tiny* bit pleased; there were benefits to having a mesmerist for a friend.

'I saw that, Cadence,' said Anah quietly, coming up beside them. 'You know we're not supposed to use our knacks on other students.'

Cadence groaned and rolled her eyes. 'And *you're* not supposed to be a boring cry-baby who's constantly telling everyone what to do, but here we are.'

Anah scowled at her. 'If you do it again, I'll tell your Scholar Mistress.'

As she stomped up the path ahead of them, Cadence muttered to Morrigan, 'I liked her better when she couldn't remember who I was.'

If Anah really *was* inclined to tell the terrifying Scholar Mistress for the Arcane Arts, Morrigan thought she'd have her work cut out for her. She'd been trying to speak with Mrs Murgatroyd herself for weeks now, but it was proving impossible. Every time she saw her in the halls of Proudfoot House, she seemed to get lost in the crowd, or even worse, to suddenly transform into her School of Mundane Arts counterpart, the awful Ms Dearborn. It had happened so often lately, Morrigan was beginning to wonder if

Murgatroyd was deliberately avoiding her . . . or if Dearborn was trying to interfere.

Until about six weeks ago, Morrigan had been a greysleeve – a scholar of the Mundane Arts, just like Hawthorne, Anah, Mahir, Arch, Francis and Thaddea. Overseen by Scholar Mistress Dulcinea Dearborn, the School of Mundane Arts was the largest of two educational streams in the Wundrous Society, comprising three departments: the Practicalities on Sub-Three, Humanities on Sub-Four, and Extremities on Sub-Five.

The School of Arcane Arts was much less populated, but still had its own dedicated three subterranean floors, deep beneath the red-brick five-storey building of Proudfoot House and only accessible to Arcane scholars.

They were much harder to navigate than the orderly Mundane floors. They weren't divided into three departments so much as countless covens, workshops, clubs, labs, top-secret mini-societies and top-*top*-secret guilds dedicated to various esoterica – none of which seemed to acknowledge their own existence, or each other's. There were an awful lot of locked doors and unanswered questions in the Arcane school, but in the past six weeks Morrigan had learned to simply go where her timetable sent her and nowhere else – certainly not, for example, down a mysterious fog-laden hallway that hadn't been there the day before. Detours like that were guaranteed to make you late for class.

Dearborn had been *furious* to learn that Murgatroyd had swiped Morrigan from the Mundane into the Arcane Arts. Not, of course, because she had any warm feelings towards her – just the opposite, really. Dearborn didn't think she should be in the Wundrous Society at all; she couldn't tolerate the idea of Morrigan learning anything more than the absolute bare minimum. It would be *so* like the icy, silver-haired Scholar Mistress, she thought, to sabotage her education from afar.

'You're being paranoid,' Cadence said when Morrigan mentioned it later that afternoon. They were lurking in a hallway on Sub-Seven waiting for Lam, so they could all head to their final class of the term together. 'Anyway, why would you *want* to talk to Murgatroyd? Personally, I try to avoid it as much as possible.'

Morrigan found that *most* people tried to avoid the unsettling Mrs Murgatroyd as much as possible, and with good reason . . . but she still preferred her to Ms Dearborn.

'Look at this.' She sighed and held out her timetable, pointing to that morning's roster of lessons. '*Peering Into the Future. Finding Your Familiar*. Yesterday it was *Opening a Dialogue with the Dead*.'

'You said you loved that class! You love spooky stuff.'

'I did,' she admitted. 'I *do*. I just don't know why Murgatroyd keeps putting me in all these weird subjects, when she's the one who said I should be learning – ' Morrigan paused, glancing around to make sure nobody could overhear. She lowered her voice a little – 'the *Wretched Arts*.'

A brief look of discomfort crossed Cadence's face. She knew as much as Morrigan did about the Wretched Arts – which was to say, not very much at all.

Morrigan knew the Wretched Arts were the tools of the so-called 'accomplished Wundersmith', and that she'd have to learn how to use them if she was ever going to understand what it really meant to *be* a Wundersmith. She'd picked up a few little scraps, and she'd been practising them on her own. But there was only one other person in the entire realm who could properly wield the Wretched Arts . . . and it was an uneasy feeling indeed, to have something so important in common with *him*.

'I just mean . . . I'm not a clairvoyant!' Morrigan went on.

11

'Or an oracle, or a sorcerer, or a witch, or . . .'

'Yeah, I know, you're a mighty Wundersmith. Dry your eyes, mate,' Cadence replied quietly. She spotted Lambeth emerging from her transcendental meditation class in her usual daze and waved to get her attention.

There weren't nearly as many Arcane students as Mundane, but with teaching staff, graduates, academics and researchers, as well as visiting members of the Royal Sorcery Council, the Paranormal League and the Alliance of Nevermoor Covens, the Arcane halls were usually busy. Today they were filled with junior and senior scholars celebrating the end of term, in ways that most of them were strictly forbidden to do so outside the School of Arcane Arts. Illusion scholars could practise their craft anywhere in Wunsoc, because illusion – in the words of Murgatroyd – was 'a bunch of tediously innocuous trickery'. (Morrigan thought this freedom was wasted on the illusion scholars, because they mostly used it to gross people out, creating false images of dog poo and scurrying rats in the hallways. Even Hawthorne, who loved grossing people out, was unimpressed with their efforts, declaring them 'unimaginative in the extreme'.)

But if a junior scholar was caught practising – for example – sorcery or witchery anywhere outside of the Arcane floors, they'd almost certainly regret it. Some of Murgatroyd's favoured punishments included cutting the arms off winter coats, shaving eyebrows, and dangling people by their ankles over the side of the footbridge above Proudfoot Station.

In the Arcane halls, however, nothing was off-limits.

This afternoon, in some sort of bizarre end-of-term celebration, a group of sorcery scholars had stolen a case of unlabelled elixir bottles from the Witchery Wing and were shaking them up, daring each other to drink them, and howling

12

at the results, either with laughter or pain. One of them burned her throat breathing piping hot steam for a solid minute, one burst all the capillaries in his eyeballs, and another fell deeply and publicly in love with the first inanimate object he laid eyes on – a fire extinguisher.

'Lam, hurry *up*, will you,' Cadence groaned as she saw their friend dawdling several metres behind.

'Stop,' Lam said, holding up one hand. Morrigan and Cadence both halted instantly, just before they reached the intersection of two long hallways.

Lam was a gifted short-range oracle . . . which meant she had visions of the future, but only the *immediate* future – mere moments ahead. Unit 919 had realised by now that heeding Lam's warnings often helped them avoid some minor disaster like stubbed toes or spilled tea. Sometimes it even saved lives, as Morrigan had learned last Hallowmas night, when she'd deciphered Lam's cryptic predictions and shut down the illegal Ghastly Market – just in time to save Cadence and Lam from being auctioned off to the highest bidders.

If Morrigan hadn't figured it out, someone would almost certainly have paid a lot of money to steal Cadence's knack from her . . . but Lam's fate could have been much, much worse. Because their friend *Lambeth Amara* was, in fact, the Princess Lamya Bethari Amati Ra, of the Royal House of Ra, from the Silklands in the state of Far East Sang. She'd been smuggled into the Free State illegally from the Wintersea Republic to trial for the Wundrous Society, just like Morrigan – but unlike Morrigan, her family had been in on the plan, and if their treason against the ruling Wintersea Party was ever discovered, they could face execution. Nobody in the Republic was even supposed to *know* the Free State existed.

13

Unit 919 had vowed to keep Lam's secret. There were certainly others out there who knew – Lam's patron, of course, and Miss Cheery and the Elders. A few wretched people who'd escaped the destruction of the Ghastly Market and scurried away into the night. But there was a feeling in Unit 919 that if they buried the secret between them and never said it aloud, they could protect Lam from anyone who might wish her harm.

Cadence heaved an impatient sigh, looking at her watch. 'Lam, we *really* need to—'

'Wait.'

SPLAT! Bzzzzzzzzz . . .

Morrigan and Cadence watched in horror as, farther down the corridor, one of the boys from the Sorcery Department sprayed a shaken-up elixir bottle all over a passing senior scholar. The older girl was engulfed by a wave of black tarry liquid which, on contact with her skin, turned into . . . *bees*. Angry, buzzy bees that swarmed to her as if she was covered in pollen. She ran down the hall, shrieking and trying to bat them away, while the sorcery boys chased after her and tried to help, half laughing and half horrified.

Lam finally lowered her hand.

'Carry on,' she said, sauntering past Morrigan and Cadence with a very *I-told-you-so* look.

Morrigan hadn't ever had a class on Sub-Two before – although she went there most days as that was where the dining rooms, kitchens, and the Commissariat were. The rest of Unit 919 was already waiting outside the assigned classroom when Morrigan, Cadence and Lam arrived.

'Crime and Donuts,' said Hawthorne, turning around to face the others as he held out an arm across the door, barring their entry. 'That's my final guess. Anyone else? Last chance.'

'Oh, just *open the door*,' Thaddea groaned, pushing past him.

The room was small – maybe a quarter of the size of a regular classroom – and empty. It was also very dark. Morrigan felt around on the wall as the group made their way inside.

'Where's the light switch?' she asked.

'Ow! That was my *foot*, Francis, you klutz.'

'Sorry, I didn't see—'

BANG. The door swung shut behind them, and the group fell silent.

'Where's our teacher?' Anah whispered in a voice that shook a little.

'Shh,' said Lam quietly. 'Watch the wall. It's about to begin.'

CHAPTER TWO

A Carefully Manoeuvred Sequence of Events

A few silent seconds passed in the darkness and then the wall came to life with vivid, moving images. Morrigan blinked into the sudden brightness.

They were watching a projected film of a night she remembered well.

Nine children were lined up outside the Wundrous Society. A huge, elaborate tapestry made of real flowers covered the gates and twisting green vines formed the words:

Come in and join us.

The members of Unit 919 stood dumbstruck, watching their past selves of a year ago and wondering what this new strangeness was all about. Most of them, anyway.

'Does my hair really look that fluffy?' Hawthorne whispered in Morrigan's ear.

'Yes.'

He nodded. 'Cool.'

'What're we meant to do?' asked the on-screen Thaddea. The on-screen Morrigan peeked sideways at her, looking smaller and more intimidated than she remembered feeling.

And then something happened in the projection that made Morrigan's skin turn instantly to gooseflesh, all up and down her arms. Something she didn't remember.

She felt a hand grip her wrist as Cadence came close and said, 'What . . . are *they*?'

Even if Morrigan had known the answer, at that moment she couldn't have made her throat form words.

The nine unwitting members of Unit 919 stood outside Wunsoc at midnight on Spring's Eve, excited and expectant, waiting breathlessly to begin their new lives as members of Nevermoor's most elite organisation.

And all the while, behind them, crawling out of the darkness, were dozens of . . . Morrigan didn't know what they were. Monsters, she supposed.

They were dark-scaled creatures, fleshy and many-limbed, not quite unnimals but barely human. They crawled on the ground, pulled along by powerful forearms, and dragged long, muscular tails behind them. Their strangely humanoid faces were angular and wide, their eyes as black as their scales, glittering like beetles.

Morrigan had never seen anything like them in her life. They were like an experiment gone wrong. Snakes turned nearly human . . . or vice versa. Even looking at them on film, she felt a visceral, primitive urge to *run*. Yet she was frozen to the spot.

'Is this a joke?' asked Anah. Her voice was high-pitched and tremulous. 'Is this some sort of horrible joke? Because it's not very *funny*.'

She turned and ran for the door, but found it was locked.

'This isn't FUNNY!' she shouted again.

The rest of 919 instinctively drew closer together, watching in creeping horror as the snake-like creatures slithered up behind their on-screen counterparts. If Morrigan hadn't lived this night herself, if she didn't know how it ended, she'd be convinced she was about to watch herself and her friends get attacked and eaten by monsters.

It didn't happen, of course. Seconds before the prowling creatures would have reached them, more figures came out of the darkness – human figures this time, sorcerers in black Wunsoc cloaks – and silently herded the beasts back into the shadows, wielding firelit branches and swinging strange smoking talismans.

Improbably – *impossibly* – the Unit 919 of the past hadn't noticed any of this. Their eyes were fixed keenly on the gates as they creaked open, inviting them into a secret world of opportunity and adventure.

All except Lambeth, Morrigan noticed. She watched her carefully on the screen. Lam stood at the end of the row of children, peering back into the darkness, her eyes wide with terror.

'You never said anything,' Morrigan said quietly, turning to look at Lam. The light from the projection illuminated her face. 'Why didn't you *tell* us?'

Lam's chin trembled a little. 'I . . . it just . . . seemed kinder not to.'

The nine children marched eagerly into the grounds of Wunsoc, all but Lam oblivious to the danger behind them.

Morrigan exhaled in relief, looking at Hawthorne and Cadence in the dim classroom, and they stared back at her in mute bewilderment. At last, with the gates shut behind them and the monsters no longer visible, it felt like some air had returned to the room. Then an amplified voice spoke over the footage, and they all jumped in shock.

'I suspect you are all wondering why you're here.'

Morrigan knew those brittle tones. It was Elder Quinn.

Gregoria Quinn was one of the High Council of Elders, the three most revered people in the Wundrous Society. The High Council was elected by all members of Wunsoc at the beginning of each Age, to lead and govern them until the next. Morrigan could see why Elder Quinn had been chosen for this honour; she may have been small and frail and very, very old, but she was a formidable woman. Her fellow Elders – Helix Wong and Alioth Saga – were nearly as impressive, Morrigan thought. (But not quite.)

'For many years,' Elder Quinn's voice echoed around them, 'the Wundrous Society has had one mission. One unified, secret purpose, expressed in two discrete yet equally important tasks. We call this purpose, for want of a grander title, Containment and Distraction.'

'So . . . not Chips and Dip,' whispered Hawthorne and, absurdly, Morrigan had to clap a hand to her mouth to suppress a hysterical giggle.

'Shh,' said Cadence, elbowing her in the ribs. '*Look.*'

Elder Quinn spoke while the footage continued – of an inauguration night that was entirely different from the one they had experienced. And yet it *was* the same night.

Morrigan remembered marching up the drive to Proudfoot House feeling a little nervous, perhaps, but not afraid. She remembered seeing the cloaked Wundrous Society members holding candles, perched high in the dead fireblossom trees that lined the drive, and feeling strangely comforted by their presence. She remembered thinking that the hard part was over. That she'd got through the trials and into the Society and everything was going to be easier from then onwards.

She'd been wrong, of course. But it wasn't until now that she knew precisely *how* wrong she'd been.

Behind the nine new scholars, jumping down from the trees, the figures were not members of the Wundrous Society. They weren't even human . . . just doing a good imitation of it.

'What in the Seven Pockets are we watching?' breathed Arch.

The figures seemed to unfold from their vaguely human facsimile, shifting into what must have been their true form: enormous vulture-like creatures, hunched and haunted-looking, with yellow eyes and great, hook-like talons.

Morrigan couldn't believe she and the rest of the unit could have been so oblivious.

'*Run*, for goodness' sake,' Arch whispered to the projected Unit 919, quite pointlessly. Morrigan understood the impulse. She wanted to shake her past self, to force that other Morrigan to turn around and see the danger.

Because it wasn't just the things slithering from out of the shadows and perching in the trees. There was more, so much more.

She'd believed – they had *all* believed – that the splendour and spectacle of their inauguration was meant to be a celebration of their success.

It wasn't a celebration, she realised now. It was a distraction. A series of precise, choreographed distractions designed to direct their line of sight to exactly the right place so they missed everything else happening around them.

The marching musicians accompanying them up the path to Proudfoot House had distracted them from the human-sized vulture things crowding in behind them.

The sparkling, iridescent rainbow archway had blinded them to the fact that every window in Proudfoot House had begun to *bleed* – thick, oozing rivulets of red dripped down the brick walls like something out of a horror story.

The trumpeting elephant caught their attention at the bottom of the marble steps just as a team of Wunsoc members conducted a thousand-strong army of spiders to skitter across the shoes of Unit 919.

None of them had noticed a thing.

And when they'd looked up in awe to watch their nine names burning across the sky in dragon fire, they'd missed perhaps the most extraordinary sight of all: a platoon of trees at the edge of the Whinging Woods had drawn up their roots from the ground and were marching – slowly, very slowly – on Proudfoot House, like an ancient arboreal army of the damned.

It was ghastly to witness, and yet . . . it was extraordinary. Even through her horror, Morrigan couldn't help feeling astonished at how she and the others had done exactly what they were supposed to do, without having the *slightest idea* they were supposed to do it. They'd looked just where they were guided to look, turned where they were meant to turn, at precisely the right moment for precisely the right amount of time. It was like watching herself perform and perfectly execute a ballet she'd never rehearsed for.

'Whoever did this is twisted,' said Mahir.

'No.' Morrigan shook her head. 'Whoever did this is a genius.'

'You have passed your fifth and final trial – the most important test of all, the test of loyalty – and are about to begin your second year as members of the Wundrous Society,' Elder Quinn's voice rang out again, over footage of the scholars following their patrons up the marble stairs. 'In proving that you are worthy of our trust, you have opened the door to deeper knowledge and greater responsibility within our ranks.'

Morrigan grimaced. They'd passed their fifth trial only six weeks ago, and the memory was a sour one. The test of Unit 919's loyalty to each other had come in the form of blackmail. They each had received an outrageous demand to fulfil, or their anonymous blackmailer would reveal to the rest of the Society that Morrigan was a Wundersmith – a secret the Elders had ordered Unit 919 to protect, or else face exile from Wunsoc for life. It had been Morrigan's biggest source of misery all year long, and not only had it turned out to be a test . . . it was a test contrived by the Elders themselves.

The most diabolical thing – even now, she couldn't think of it without grinding her teeth – was that in order to pass the test herself, Morrigan had to reveal herself as a Wundersmith. So now everyone in the Society knew the truth anyway.

Well, she thought bitterly. *At least we passed.*

On the projection, the doors of Proudfoot House closed behind Unit 919 and their patrons. The projection cut out. They were surrounded by darkness again.

Elder Quinn's imperious voice continued, filling the room.

'The first and most important of these new responsibilities is for you to witness the truth about our beloved city, and to see your rightful place within it.'

Morrigan felt the skin on the back of her neck tingle. She had an urge to say, *No thank you. I'd rather not witness the truth about Nevermoor. Not today.*

'To understand your future in the Wundrous Society, you must know our past,' continued Elder Quinn. 'The Society was founded for a very particular purpose. Until just over one hundred years ago, our entire mission was to support the work of nine

22

people. Those nine – elevated and exalted above all others – had a mission of their own: to serve, protect and improve the lives of the citizens of our realm.

'They were the Wundersmiths. Nine human beings gifted beyond all others, chosen – many believed – by the Wundrous Divinities themselves, the ancient deities who were once said to have watched over our realm. In exchange for the powers they'd been blessed with, the Wundersmiths would dedicate the entirety of their lifetimes to mastering their craft, and using their power wholly in service to others. And when their lifetime was over, each of those original nine Wundrous souls was – so the story goes – reborn in another, who would take their place, serving the realm with the guidance and support of the Wundrous Society. On and on the cycle went, one generation replacing another, never forgetting who they were: human representatives of the nine Divinities, here to do their work.'

Was that true, Morrigan wondered? Was she just the latest version of one of those original nine Wundersmiths, reborn in the body of Morrigan Crow? A copy of a copy of a copy? It sounded made-up, the kind of fantastical detail you'd find in mythology books.

'But eventually,' Elder Quinn continued, 'the Society failed in its mission.'

Morrigan felt a flicker of discomfort. Even in the darkness, she could feel eight pairs of eyes upon her.

'The nine Wundersmiths became subjects of worship and devotion, even *fanaticism*. We allowed them to believe *themselves* divine, to set themselves above ordinary people, and so some of them became corrupt and careless. Dangerous. Power-hungry. Many would say evil.

'Finally, one among them decided his time had come. And so,

he toiled in secret to build an army of monsters, legions of his own vile creations, and he tried to lead his fellow Wundersmiths in a crusade against the crown.

'He failed, of course. He was exiled for his crimes and became the man we know as the last Wundersmith. Ezra Squall tried to conquer and enslave our city. We have not forgotten. We will not forget.'

Morrigan felt sick. She wanted to cover her ears or run away, but she also felt an irresistible compulsion to know more.

'The Wundrous Society's purpose now is to protect Nevermoor – and the greater Free State – from the corrupt and dangerous creations of Wundersmiths past. From the chaos that still thrives here. The chaos we ourselves allowed into this city, through our weakness and our failure to act in time.

'We must right our past wrongs,' boomed Elder Quinn's disembodied voice. 'We must close old wounds, even if the scars remain.'

'Hold on to something,' said Lam.

'What did you say?' said Anah in a stricken voice. 'What did she say?'

But Morrigan and Cadence had already pressed themselves back against the walls of the tiny room, because there was nothing else to hold on to. Hawthorne copied them, and Mahir, Arch and Thaddea quickly followed.

There was a sound like a rush of air, then a mechanical grinding and a *thud*, and suddenly it felt like the ground had dropped out from beneath them. Anah and Francis, who hadn't taken Lam's advice quickly enough, fell to the ground and had to scramble back up again, crawling towards the edges of the classroom.

The room was moving. Falling downwards in darkness at an alarming speed.

'What is *happening*?' cried Anah.

'Be quiet,' snapped Morrigan, because Elder Quinn was still speaking calmly over the noise of their movement, and she didn't want to miss a single word.

The descent stopped abruptly, and the room moved forward like a train in a tunnel, throwing them against the back wall.

'Over many Ages and with tireless, meticulous work,' Elder Quinn continued as the room rushed onwards, 'we have managed to bring several of Nevermoor's monstrous populations under our control. We have done this using a combination of sorcery, witchery, brute force, and in some cases, good old-fashioned diplomacy and negotiation. We do this in secret, to protect our city from the deadly and chaotic forces that would prey on its people.'

Thunk. They came to another sudden stop, and they were all thrown to the right-side wall as the room changed direction.

'I think I'm gonna be sick,' groaned Hawthorne.

'Don't you DARE!' Cadence shouted at him.

Elder Quinn's voice carried on, oblivious to the drama in the room. 'Some of the threats you have just witnessed are under strict Wundrous Society regulation. For example, the Vool – those shapeshifting, mimicking avian creatures you saw perched in the trees. The Vool population was once a vicious, widespread threat to the lives of Nevermoorians. It took more than fifty years, but now their numbers – and their behaviours – are manageable. The Vool are perhaps our greatest success.

'Some of the monstrosities you saw could not be described as under our control, but after Ages of careful diplomacy they have been allied to our cause and are accepted by the Society as a force for good in protecting Nevermoor and the Free State. For example, the trees of the Whinging Woods were our invited guests to your inauguration, willing and eager to participate in what we consider an important training tool for our newest members.

'And finally, some of the monsters in this demonstration have been exploited for the predictability of their behaviours. The creatures you saw outside the gates of Wunsoc are called Slinghouls. We do not negotiate with Slinghouls. Diplomacy does not work on a Slinghoul. Fortunately, they are predictable, and can be both managed and avoided. We do our best.

'Your inauguration night was a carefully manoeuvred sequence of events designed to educate and inform, and we hope it has helped you understand what we as an organisation are trying to achieve.'

During this long speech, the room changed direction once more, twice more, three times and then again – hard left, up, left again, right, and down again. It felt like they'd travelled for miles at an ever-increasing speed, but finally the room slowed to a halt. The lights came back on.

Morrigan opened her eyes. Unit 919 sat on the ground, backs pressed against the wall, trying to catch their breath. Nobody spoke.

The door opened, and Elder Quinn entered the room. She started a little when she saw them on the floor.

'Goodness me,' she said, pointing up at the safety loops dangling from the ceiling, which they had all failed to notice. She made a little hooking gesture with her finger. 'Didn't any of you bring a brolly?'

Morrigan closed her eyes again, silently willing her lunch to stay just where it was.

Slightly battered and wholly baffled, Unit 919 followed Elder Quinn out of the tiny room and down a long, brightly lit hallway.

It was wide and rather grand, lined with portraits of former Elders and gas lamps set in sconces, and it reminded Morrigan of the Hotel Deucalion.

'Containment and Distraction is like trying to plug a thousand tiny leaking holes using only ten fingers,' Elder Quinn told them as she shuffled along more quickly than Morrigan would have thought her able to. 'It is an endless, thankless, dirty, dangerous, repetitive job, but one that we are privileged to perform. And now, that privilege is also yours.'

She turned her head to either side, glancing at the scholars scurrying along behind her.

'I know what you're all wondering. Same thing they wonder every year. What does this mean for you? Have you been unwittingly drafted into an army to fight against the forces of darkness, to spend the rest of your lives battling the creatures of the night?'

That was not at all what Morrigan had been wondering, but now she was.

'Well, perhaps. If that's what you want. If that's what you're good at. Or perhaps you will never have to see any of these wretched things again. Perhaps your destiny, your lifelong role in the Wundrous Society, is to bring light to the world, in whatever form that might take – music, or art, or politics, or making a truly excellent leek and potato soup – to balance out the dark. To distract people from it. To keep Nevermoor from being consumed by it.'

Elder Quinn stopped at the end of the hallway, just outside the doors, and turned to face Unit 919. She was several inches shorter than most of them, but Morrigan felt she was being stared down by a giant.

'I do not know what role each of you scholars will play in the vital work of the Wundrous Society,' she said in a low voice. 'That is up to you.'

The doors opened behind her.

'Welcome to the Gathering Place.'

CHAPTER THREE

The Gathering Place

It was a bit like walking into the Trollosseum. Except indoors, and darker, and smaller, and the arena-style seating was filled with reasonably well-behaved Wundrous Society members, instead of rambunctious louts bellowing encouragement at trolls to spill more blood and knock each other's heads off.

'This week's gathering has already begun,' murmured Elder Quinn, directing them to a knot of empty seats towards the back of the amphitheatre. 'Usually the junior units sit closer to the centre, as you can see, but as it's your first time attending, you may sit here in the back and observe.'

She left them to get settled and headed down an aisle of stairs to the centre of the circular room, where Elder Saga had kept her a seat. Elder Wong was standing on the dais, holding court.

A few older Society members turned around to peer curiously at Unit 919, and she might have imagined it, but she thought their eyes lingered longer on her than the others.

She felt a weight on her shoulders. The words of Elder Quinn's speech were still ringing inside her mind, and she had a sudden, deeper understanding of her place here.

It was even more obvious to her now why she had felt so much quiet animosity from the older scholars since they'd learned she was a Wundersmith. It wasn't simply that everyone in Nevermoor knew Wundersmiths were dangerous. The Society knew exactly *how* dangerous they were. Exactly how chaotic and messy, exactly how their actions – even from many years ago – could leave scars and unhealed wounds on a city, hiding in plain sight. They knew because they were still cleaning up the mess.

Still, Morrigan said to herself, sitting up a little straighter and shaking off her glumness. *It wasn't me. I didn't make a load of snake thingies and vulture-people, for goodness' sake.*

She resented being lumped in with Ezra Squall and every other Wundersmith who ever lived. She wasn't a cursed child any more, hiding in the second sitting room at Crow Manor, writing apology letters for ruined jam and broken hips. She had as much right to be here as anyone else.

Morrigan lifted her chin, kept her eyes on Elder Wong, and ignored all the sly backward glances.

'. . . and once again representing the Geographical Oddities Squadron today is Adriana Salter, Unit 871,' Elder Wong was saying. 'Mrs Salter, are you the only one picking up the slack in the Odd Squad – why don't I ever see the others here? Tell Miles we'll expect him next time. From the Department of Unnimology and Naturalism, Dr Valerie Bramble . . .'

The introductions went on for some time, and Morrigan found it hard to keep track of all the different organisations mentioned. As Elder Wong called their names, representatives from the Unusual Engineering & Infrastructure Advisory Board, the Architectural Anomalies Association, and the Gobleian Library all stood up from their seats and waved, acknowledging brief applause.

'. . . from the League of Explorers,' Elder Wong continued, and Morrigan's ears perked up, 'Captain Jupiter North, Unit 895 . . .'

Jupiter was here! She'd never seen her patron visit Wunsoc unless it was for something to do with her. She sat up straight, peering down over rows of heads much taller than hers to see a dramatic crop of bright ginger hair atop a beaming face half-hidden by beard. He'd dressed with his usual sense of theatre, Morrigan noticed: smart waistcoat and trousers in brilliant bubblegum pink, sky-blue shirt with the sleeves rolled up to the elbows and a pair of sparkling, electric blue glittery brogues.

He knows how to be seen from the cheap seats, she thought, smiling for the first time that afternoon.

When Jupiter stood, turning to acknowledge a round of applause much more enthusiastic than the others had received (and even a couple of wolf whistles), his eyes scanned the circular room. Morrigan knew he was looking for her. She was too embarrassed to draw attention to herself in a room full of people, but Hawthorne had no such qualms.

'Jupiter! We're up here!' he shouted, waving both arms over his head.

Sliding down several inches in her chair, Morrigan hunched her shoulders up so high she might have been wearing her armpits as earrings. Fortunately, nobody heard Hawthorne over the raucous clapping, and so she quickly reached up to yank him down to his seat by the back of his shirt.

'. . . and finally, representing the Beastly Division, Gavin Squires of Unit 899. Now Mr Squires, I believe you wish to begin?'

'Thank you, Elder Wong,' Gavin Squires called out as he leapt up to take centre stage, wheeling a small trolley of equipment. He was a wiry, energetic man, and covered in gnarly scars. Given that he was wearing a sleeveless vest and shorts on a cold day, Morrigan suspected he was quite proud of them. 'All right, everyone. I think you all know we're coming up to a very special time of year . . .'

There were a few knowing groans in the audience, and someone actually said 'Oh NO'.

Gavin grinned shiftily, an amused little twinkle in his eyes. 'Oh yes. Oh YES, my friends, the most *wonderful* time of the year is coming on fast – that special day we all look forward to – ladies and gentlemen, you know it and you love it . . .'

He paused to fiddle with the equipment and a moment later, a huge, moving, three-dimensional image of the ugliest creature Morrigan had ever seen in her life was projected upwards into the vast space. She felt herself physically recoil from it, and she wasn't the only one.

'. . . that's right, it's the short but magical breeding season of the NEVERMOOR SCALY SEWER BEAST!'

Morrigan had heard of the Nevermoor Scaly Sewer Beast, but she'd never seen it before, and truthfully, she'd never been certain it was real. The image was of a strange, yellow-white serpentine creature with transparent eyelids covering milky red eyes. Its bulbous belly hung low to the ground and it had six lizard-like legs ending in long, sharp claws. Its scales were rough and patchy, and entirely absent in random spots, revealing raw pink skin underneath. It had a long, powerful-looking tail that snapped back and forth in a threatening fashion. Its jaws opened wide to reveal a mouth full of far too many sharp curving teeth to be reasonable, and a forked, blackish-blue tongue.

'All right, then, all right,' Gavin continued, holding up his hands for quiet. 'You know the drill, people. The Scaly Sewer Beast breeding season brings many hundreds of nasty little baby beasts with their nasty little venomous teeth into our sewer system, and if we don't control the population growth we'll find Nevermoor overrun with these gigantic mummy and daddy versions – ' (he pointed at the picture) – 'in just a few short months, 'cos they grow up quick, the precious little blighters.

'Now I know this is nobody's favourite job – plenty of us have been injured in the annual sewerfest, and the smell takes days to leave the old nostrils – but someone's got to put their hand up to help us trap, tag and relocate these wee beasties outside of the city. There are sixteen of us in the Beastly Division, and I reckon we'll need another dozen helpers. If I don't get enough volunteers, some of you might just get voluntold. So, show of hands please: who's keen to rid Nevermoor's sewers of their scaliest scourge?'

A few senior scholars reluctantly put their hands in the air, and a handful of older members, too. Thaddea's hand, though, shot into the air so fast it might have had an engine. The rest of Unit 919 turned to look at her in horror.

'Thaddea, you don't *seriously* want to crawl down into the sewers to round up a bunch of those . . . *things*?' Anah asked in an incredulous whisper.

'You don't *seriously* think I'd miss a chance to fight the Nevermoor Scaly Sewer Beast?' Thaddea whispered back at her, practically bouncing up and down in her seat to be seen by Gavin.

'Right, that's eight brave volunteers, thank you very much,' said Gavin. 'And I'll also take Mitty Hayward, Susie-Lee Walters, Phyllis Lightyear – yes, I know you did it last year, pal, that's why I want you back. Shouldn't have done such a good job the first time around, if you didn't want to get chosen again.' There was a rumble of laughter as Phyllis made a rude hand gesture at Gavin, who ignored it. 'Oh! We've got another volunteer up the back there . . . What's your name, my young friend?'

She leapt up from her seat. 'Thaddea No-Retreat of Clan Macleod.'

Morrigan looked from Hawthorne to Cadence and back again, trying not to giggle. *Thaddea* who *of Clan Macleod?*

'Proudly born and raised atop the Highlands, in the Third Pocket of the Free State,' Thaddea continued in a resounding voice. 'Daughter of Mary the Heart-Eater and Malcolm the Mellow, granddaughter of Deirdre the Deathbringer, great-granddaughter of Eileen Never-Surrender, great-great-granddaughter of Ailsa the Tetchy, great-great-great granddaughter of Betty One-Kick, great-great-great-GREAT granddaughter—'

'Well, Thaddea No-Retreat of Clan Macleod,' Gavin interrupted, holding up a hand and smiling widely, 'if you're that desperate to risk your limbs and spend days smelling like excrement, who am I to stop you? Welcome aboard.'

There was a vaguely shell-shocked round of applause for Thaddea from the older units as she took her seat, and a general sense of relief that all the spots on the mission had been filled and nobody else needed to volunteer.

'*Such* a weirdo,' muttered Cadence, giving her a half-hearted clap.

'A weirdo who gets to go into the *sewers* at *night* and hunt *monsters*,' Thaddea pointed out triumphantly, as if she'd just been granted the best treat imaginable. Cadence looked at Morrigan, and they shook their heads in bewilderment.

Gavin gave instructions for Team Scaly Sewer Beast to meet the following day and discuss their strategy, then ceded the floor to Holliday Wu from the Public Distraction Department.

Morrigan wasn't sure she'd ever had reason or inclination to use the word 'fabulous' before, but there was no other word for Ms Wu. She wore the tallest, shiniest shoes Morrigan had ever seen, fiery red lipstick and a tailored, aubergine-coloured three-piece suit. She had a high, sleek black ponytail with a shaved undercut, and a row of hefty diamond studs along the entire outer edge of her left ear. She was better dressed than even Jupiter. She was *fabulous*.

'Right, the Unusual Engineering team will be shutting down Nevermoor's entire sewage system *and* the Wunderground network while the Beastly Division hunts for these disgusting things,' she announced without preamble. 'Gavin assures me he can get the job done in two to three hours. It will begin at dusk, because that's when the Nevermoor Ugly Sewer Whatever is most active and therefore easiest to locate.

'With that in mind: we need a massive, cross-borough Distraction that will keep a city full of people occupied for three hours at peak travel time on a weeknight, during which they cannot use trains or flush the loo. Not a small ask, and the last thing we want is to create mass panic.' Holliday brought up a map of Nevermoor on the projector, marked in several places with a large red X. 'We also need to ensure the population is kept away from these thirteen locations specifically, which have been identified by the Beastly Division as high-risk areas – breeding hotspots for the Nevermoor Creepy Vomit-Thing. We will need to shepherd as many people as possible away from these locations, including those who live there. Now, as usual—'

'Why?' Morrigan called out, before she'd even realised she'd opened her mouth. The room fell silent and everyone turned to look at her.

'Why what?' asked Holliday, a line of confusion creasing her brow.

Morrigan's face burned. The question had been percolating in the back of her head ever since Elder Quinn's speech to Unit 919. But she hadn't actually meant to *ask it out loud*. Her gaze flicked over to Jupiter, and she saw he was smiling at her. He gave a small, encouraging nod. She cleared her throat and sat up straight.

'Why . . . do we have to distract people?'

There were a few sniggers from the front rows, but most people just looked perplexed. Holliday, however, narrowed her eyes in suspicion.

'Are you trying to be funny?'

'No!' Morrigan said quickly. 'I just mean . . . well. Why can't people know the truth about Nevermoor? They live here. Wouldn't it be sort of . . . easier? And maybe safer? If everyone knew, they could just stay calm and . . . I suppose . . . keep out of the way.'

She trailed off as her question was met with a rumble of laughter. Many of the older Society members were shaking their heads.

However, just as she was wishing a large bird of prey would swoop into the room, pluck her from her chair and carry her very far away, Elder Saga the bullwun took the floor and glared them all into silence. It was a formidable glare, made all the more impressive by the sight of his enormous horns, broad shaggy chest, and the intimidating way he was inclined to stamp his hooves.

'It's not an unreasonable question,' he said in his deep, rumbling voice. 'There *are* occasions when we tell people – at least some people. Those who need to know. Our own internal law enforcement regularly liaises with the Nevermoor City Police Force, for example, and authorities across all Seven Pockets of the Free State. Sometimes we even share information with the Prime Minister's office, who will pass it on to the public as they see fit. But that's a last resort, generally speaking.'

Morrigan swallowed, and couldn't help asking again: 'Why?'

'Because often, Miss Crow, telling people they are at risk creates a different, sometimes even greater risk. People are dangerous when they're frightened. Remember that.'

Elder Saga said those last few words to the room at large, fixing them with his trademark unwavering gaze, then yielded the floor to Holliday Wu – who carried on as if there had been no interruption.

'As usual, we *do* expect backlash. We can't avoid that. What we *can* avoid is people getting in our way, getting hurt, and messing things up for us.' Holliday crossed her arms and swung her ponytail back over her shoulder. 'Ideas?'

'What about what we did last breeding season?' called out one of the older scholars. 'Fireworks night? It got everyone looking up instead of down.'

She gave one short, sharp shake of her head. 'It also scared the sewer beasts deeper into hiding. Stupidest idea we've ever had, to be honest – too noisy, too expensive.' Holliday's expression was cool, but her jaw tightened very slightly. Morrigan could tell the memory of this failure still rankled. 'Anyone else?'

A round of ideas shouted from the gallery included a parade, a citywide blackout and a targeted tornado, each of which Holliday shot down in flames.

'Come on, people, you've just named all the things we did the last four years. Let's try to *innovate*.'

'We could declare war on the Second Pocket!'

Holliday shot a scathing look at the person who suggested that. To Morrigan's utter lack of surprise, it was the odious Baz Charlton, Cadence's patron.

'Idiot,' Cadence whispered next to her.

'And then what?' Holliday asked Baz in a flat voice.

He shrugged. 'And then . . . cancel it?'

She rolled her eyes and then scanned the audience again. 'Any ideas that won't incite further mass panic?'

The Gathering Place fell to quiet muttering as people seemed to run out of steam. Finally, Jupiter raised a hand, and the muttering instantly ceased. Morrigan could almost feel the room leaning forward to hear what Captain Jupiter North had to say.

'What about Golders Night?'

'Golders Night,' Holliday echoed, and her expression grew thoughtful. She tapped a finger against her mouth. 'There's a thought . . . what's it been, twelve years since the last one?'

'Fourteen, I believe,' said Jupiter. 'Spring of Seventeen in the Age of Poets. A Wunderground train had gained sentience and was holding the other trains hostage underground. It required an extraordinary distraction.'

Morrigan, Hawthorne and Cadence shared a look. It was a very *specific* look of mingled bemusement, horror, exasperation and resignation. The kind of look one reserves for special occasions, such as when you've just learned that trains can come to life and hold other trains hostage, and that you've unwittingly joined an organisation full of people who have for some reason decided to nose into this sort of business, and you don't really feel like getting involved but you're just going to have to go along with it because everybody else is. That kind of look.

'The Treasury won't let us do it very often – for the obvious reason,' added Jupiter. 'But it's always effective. Almost guarantees an eighty-five to ninety per cent participation rate.'

What was 'the obvious reason', Morrigan wondered? What even was a *Golders Night*?

'Fifteen per cent non-participants – nothing we can't manage,' said Holliday, waving a hand. 'Right, Golders Night. Sounds promising. Let's workshop this.'

They carried on for another hour, and the meeting became a freewheeling, rapid-fire session of strategic planning, with Mundane and Arcane members of all ages jumping in to give suggestions, criticisms and offers of assistance. Morrigan felt like she was finally seeing the real Wundrous Society in action.

What emerged by the end was an exhaustive, fool-proof plan to distract the entire population of Nevermoor from Operation Scaly Sewer Beast. Even Unit 919, excluding Thaddea, had a small role to play . . . something Morrigan was a little apprehensive about.

Sometimes it felt like *everything* about the Society was a test. A trial. And just when you thought you'd passed all the trials there could possibly be, another one popped up.

Be honest. Be smart. Be brave. Be loyal.

Now this.

Be *useful*.

Jupiter had warned Morrigan about this, two whole years ago, when he'd first explained to her what the Wundrous Society was offering. Respect, adventure, fame! Reserved seats on the Wunderground! *Pin privilege*, he'd called it.

But it was a privilege the Society expected you to earn not just once, not just in the entry trials, but *over and over again, for the rest of your life*.

She hadn't thought about it much at the time. But he *had* warned her.

Morrigan had hoped to speak to Jupiter after the meeting, but he appeared to be deep in discussion with Holliday Wu and Elder Saga. She dithered for a moment, but soon she and Unit 919 were caught up in the stream of people leaving the Gathering Place and it was too late.

The mood in Proudfoot House was celebratory. Cheerful, excited chatter rose up around them as groups of junior scholars discussed their plans for the Christmas holidays, but Morrigan and her friends didn't speak for a long time. It felt like someone had just thrown a hand grenade into their midst. They'd had a vague idea that the Wundrous Society was up to more than they knew – the Elders had dropped hints, after all. Nobody had ever mentioned, however, that Wundersmiths were the source of almost all their problems and the focus of their work. Jupiter certainly hadn't. She would need to speak with him about that.

Morrigan knew she had to be the first to say it, but as they pushed through the doors of Proudfoot House into the chill air of the grounds, they were met with a group of older scholars who'd evidently been waiting for them.

'Now you know why everyone hates Wundersmiths,' said a boy from Unit 917, taking the words right out of her mouth. 'Because we're always having to clean up your mess.'

'I told you she was dangerous!' A familiar girl with moss-green hair and a nasty scowl squared up to Morrigan, casually tapping a steel throwing star against the side of her leg.

Heloise Redchurch was one of Morrigan's absolute least favourite people in the world (and the world contained both Baz Charlton and Dulcinea Dearborn, so that really was saying something). The older scholar had once made her friends pin Morrigan against a tree while she lobbed throwing stars at her head, so Morrigan thought she might even have been in the number one spot.

'Maybe that's why the Elders kept your knack a secret so

long,' said the boy. 'They were worried we'd make you answer for Ezra Squall's crimes.'

Heloise grinned maliciously. 'Maybe we should.'

Morrigan felt a little tingle in her fingertips, and while she was sorely tempted to summon Wunder and give Heloise something to really be frightened of, the ironic truth was that she wasn't entirely sure what she'd do with it.

Dangerous, Morrigan thought. *Sure.*

She opened her mouth to say something but was interrupted by Cadence.

'Yeah, she is dangerous.' The mesmerist took a very deliberate step forward. 'So am I. Wanna have a go?'

Morrigan was surprised, but Heloise and the older scholars *jumped* in alarm; it was clear they hadn't noticed Cadence standing there at all (which, incidentally, was part of what made mesmerists so dangerous).

'Me too.' Thaddea stepped forward, hands on hips. Morrigan had to stop a gurgle of shocked laughter escaping her throat. 'I know six different martial arts and I can swing a sledgehammer like it's a yo-yo. Shall I demonstrate?'

'Yeah, and I know dragons,' said Hawthorne. 'Lots of 'em.'

Morrigan couldn't help giggling for real at that. She felt suddenly filled with warmth as the eight other members of her unit crowded in around her. The words of the Wundrous Society oath they'd taken at their inauguration rang in her ears: *Sisters and brothers. Loyal for life.*

'I have poisonous mushrooms at home,' added Francis ominously.

'And – and I could cut out your liver with a SCALPEL!'

This last, nervy declaration came from the most unlikely source.

'Anah!' Morrigan cried in shock.

'Well . . . I could,' Anah insisted, and there was only the tiniest tremor in her voice. 'In sterile conditions, obviously, and only if they were under a general anaesthetic.'

The rest of the unit burst into laughter, Thaddea clapped Anah on the back and Mahir shouted, 'Brava!' and just like that, all the tension of the confrontation had dissipated. Unit 919 pushed past the older scholars as one, leaving their shocked assailants behind on the marble steps.

Morrigan grinned at Anah as they marched across the grounds towards the Whinging Woods. 'Not supposed to use your knack on other students, you know.'

'Oh, shush,' was Anah's slightly shaky response.

But she looked quite pleased with herself.

Not long after Morrigan got home, there was a knock on her bedroom door.

She knew instantly who would be standing on the other side when she opened it. For a moment, she considered yelling at him to go away and that he could come back only when he'd decided to stop keeping really rather important information from her.

But she changed her mind when a slightly fretful voice from the hallway called out, 'Mog? Mog, are you there? I come bearing cake.'

Sure enough, the door swung open to reveal an enormous ginger beard, a pair of sheepish blue eyes and a smile that was at least seventy per cent wince. Jupiter was struggling to hold up a truly *enormous* rectangular cake, covered in pale yellow buttercream with words written in bright pink icing. He seemed to have sacrificed punctuation and legible print to fit the whole message, which read:

SORRY I DIDN'T TELL U ABOUT C&D BUT THE THING IS I
CAN'T ALWAYS TELL U EVERYTHING & I KNOW THAT'S
NOT IDEAL BUT IT IS WHAT IT IS SOMETIMES THERE ARE
OTHER PEOPLE I HAVE TO PROTECT & OTHER PROMISES I
HAVE TO KEEP BUT I PROMISE I WILL NEVER LIE ABOUT
ANYTHING THAT MIGHT ENDANGER U BECAUSE EVEN IF
TELLING U ALL MY SECRETS CAN'T BE MY TOP PRIORITY I
PROMISE THAT PROTECTING U ALWAYS WILL BE. KINDEST
REGARDS JUPITER
P.S. HAPPY LAST DAY OF TERM

Morrigan read the entire message, her lips forming the words silently, then read it again. Jupiter's arms were shaking with the effort of holding up the gigantic cake, but she didn't invite him to put it down and to his credit, he didn't ask.

'Kindest regards?' she said finally.

'I was going to write "lots of love" but I thought it would embarrass you.'

'Hm. What flavour is it?'

'Lemon butter raspberry ripple layer cake with crumbled meringue pieces and raspberry cream filling,' he said, looking hopeful. 'Your favourite.'

It was her favourite.

'All right.' Morrigan nodded once and stepped aside to let him in. 'I hope you brought plates.'

CHAPTER FOUR

Dangerous Levels of Cheer

'Ohhhhh, he took up his bag with the toys inside and he snapped at the reins of his magical ride and the reindeer took to the sky with pride and the elves sat right by Saint Nick's side and the flight was—'

'How many verses does this song have, exactly?' Jack muttered.

Morrigan counted on her fingers. 'I've heard . . . sixteen, so far.'

'What? No. It's easily been twenty. Remember he sang all those verses about responsible sleigh maintenance yesterday.'

'—but the chimney was narrow and Nick was wide, and the elves couldn't help him although they tried—'

'Yes, I was counting those,' she said. 'What does it look like now?'

Jack – or John Arjuna Korrapati, as he was also known – lifted his eye patch cautiously. It was the one barrier he had between seeing the world as an ordinary person would, and seeing the world as a Witness – with all its hidden threads and connective tissue, all its secrets and dangers and histories laid bare in full, moving, sometimes hideously confusing colour. It was a dubious gift he'd inherited from Jupiter.

'Very . . . shiny.' Jack winced a little and snapped the eye patch back into place. 'Potentially dangerous levels of cheer.'

Morrigan leaned her elbows on the rail of the spiral staircase, peering down into the lobby. It was her and Jack's favourite spot in the Hotel Deucalion for people-watching.

Today, though, they'd mostly been Jupiter-watching – partly for entertainment, and partly out of a genuine concern for his safety. He'd gone a bit mad on tinsel, carols and eggnog, and Jack was worried that his uncle's Christmas spirit had risen to such dizzying heights that he just might . . . burst a valve, or something.

Morrigan tilted her head to one side, watching as her patron leapt around the lobby like a ballet dancer, throwing handfuls of sparkly red and green confetti over the guests checking in, and bellowing tunefully all the while.

'Do you think he's making new bits up?'

'—all round the Realm in just one night, in his smart red suit, what a splendid sight! Susie got a truck and Millie got a kite and the elves got into a big fist fight—'

Jack snorted. 'Absolutely.'

'So much for Jupiter not being a Saint Nick supporter, then,' said Morrigan casually, casting Jack a sideways glance. He flicked his shiny black hair out of his face irritably. 'I don't think I've heard him singing any Yule Queen carols yet . . . have you?'

The dual figureheads of Nevermoor's holiday season, Saint Nicholas and the Yule Queen, were in an Ages-long war over who best embodied the spirit of the season. Nevermoorians were expected to show allegiance to one or the other by donning their colours – red for flashy, jolly Saint Nick or green for the elegant, understated Yule Queen – and people took it far more seriously than Morrigan considered strictly necessary.

Each year, the conflict culminated with the Battle of Christmas Eve, a spectacular magical combat between the two champions. If Saint Nick won, his promise was a present in every stocking and a fire in every hearth. If the Yule Queen won, she pledged a blanket of snow on Christmas morning and a blessing on every house. (Of course, it was an open secret that every single year, the pair would declare a truce so that everybody won.)

Jack scowled at her. 'It's not Uncle Jove's fault that Saint Nick has catchier songs. The old fraud's probably got a whole team of jingle composers on staff!'

Morrigan grinned. Jack was firmly pro-Yule Queen, and it was almost *too* easy to get him riled up about it. It had become her favourite holiday activity.

There was less than a week now until Christmas Day and Morrigan was feeling rather festive herself. It was her second Christmas since making her home at the Hotel Deucalion – a Wundrous, *living* building that often altered itself without warning, according to its own mysterious whims – and she thought the place had really done them proud this year.

The Smoking Parlour was particularly over-excited and kept changing its mind about what seasonal smoke to roll out from the walls. In the space of ten minutes it could change from brandy butter smoke (which Morrigan thought was lovely, if a little rich), to deep purple waves of pickled sugarplum smoke (so tangy and sweet it was almost dizzying), to the gently comforting, smoky scent of roasting chestnuts. Jupiter found it funny, until khaki-coloured waves of boiled sprout smoke began wafting from the walls, at which point he'd kindly asked the Smoking Parlour to pull itself together.

Throughout December, the lobby had changed slowly, day by day, as if wanting to savour each step of its holiday transformation. It started on the first of the month with a single sapling fir sprouting from the black-and-white chequerboard floor. The tree shot straight upwards, splitting the marble with ease, spilling broken rubble from the base of the trunk and frightening the life out of poor old Kedgeree, who'd been minding his own business at the concierge desk nearby.

By the next morning, the sapling was all grown up, nearly to the full height of the room. It stopped just beneath the sparkling black bird chandelier, which had turned silver for the occasion and looked a *bit* like an angel perched on top of a Christmas tree, if you squinted sideways at it.

A mere three weeks later, the entire lobby was a wintry evergreen forest, filled with birdsong and the earthy smell of fir trees, their branches dusted with snow.

It wasn't real snow. But that was part of what made it so magical. The thick, sparkling blanket of white on the lobby-forest floor never melted, never turned ice-slick or went to slush. Day after day it was crisp and glittery, powder-soft, dry to the touch . . . and *so* satisfyingly crunchy to stomp through in boots.

After the first few days, Dame Chanda Kali – opera singer extraordinaire and Dame Commander of the Order of Woodland Whisperers – had decided she'd quite like to see some wildlife among the trees, so she threw open the Deucalion's front doors and sang her favourite carol ('The Yuletide Hymn') until a cohort of enamoured woodland creatures gathered in the lobby, drawn irresistibly to the sound of her voice, and made themselves at home among the trees. Morrigan's favourite was a friendly red robin who greeted her each morning after breakfast and left tiny little tracks in the snow.

Kedgeree the concierge took to wearing his coat, scarf and mittens indoors, and he and Charlie the chauffeur had to dig out a few fire pits here and there so that the guests could gather round them for warmth while waiting to check in or check out. But these minor inconveniences aside, staff and guests alike were altogether delighted with the transformation. Jupiter was so full of Christmas cheer, he began studding his prodigious ginger beard with tiny bells and fairy lights every morning.

'As if he wasn't noisy enough,' grumbled Fenestra the Magnificat, the Deucalion's head of housekeeping, every time she heard him jingling down the halls.

But even cranky Fenestra, who like most cats wasn't terribly fond of cold weather – or change in general – was eventually taken by the holiday spirit.

'I actually saw Fen frolicking today,' Martha, the young housemaid, whispered one evening as Morrigan drew a bath in her talon-foot tub. '*Frolicking!* In the snow! Like a playful little kitten!'

'*What?*' Morrigan's eyes had shot up from the dresser, where she was choosing an elixir. In her shock, she managed to knock over her favourite pink rose bubble oil, splashing half the bottle into the water. The bubbles turned into floating rosebuds, and within seconds the bath was in full bloom – hundreds of flowers spilling out of the porcelain and on to the marble floor. 'Fen? Are you sure?'

Since Fenestra the Magnificat was roughly the size of an elephant and scornful of most things that brought others joy, Morrigan found this hard to picture in her mind.

'On my life, I did.' Martha held a hand to her heart, her face utterly solemn. 'She swears she was chasing a hare through the trees, but I know a frolic when I see one.'

The only person who hadn't been overly pleased about the festive decor was Frank the vampire dwarf. The Deucalion's resident party planner was rather put out that his chosen theme for the annual Hotel Deucalion Christmas Soiree had been vetoed by the hotel itself.

'I had everything planned!' Frank moaned, when it was becoming clear the forest was here to stay for the season. 'I've got the invitations all ready to go out. Now I'm going to have to do them again. I was going for dark glamour this year – all black and gold and dripping red. Tuxedos and evening gowns. Diamonds and dim lighting. It's impossible to do dark glamour with a bunch of big-eyed woodland unnimals hopping around, looking *cute*. I try to bring a touch of class to this place and look what it gives me in return. Bunnies and badgers.' He downed a full teacup of eggnog in dramatic fashion, then wiped his mouth and stared miserably at a little bluebird singing on a branch. 'My talents are *wasted* again.'

Frank was further offended (though no doubt quietly relieved) when the last-minute change of theme resulted in the Deucalion's most successful Christmas party ever. The society pages in all Nevermoor's major newspapers the next day were plastered with full-colour photos of celebrities and aristocracy throwing back candy cane cocktails and cooing over the sweet woodland unnimals (while Frank bared his fangs broodingly in the background).

It had been such a very silly season so far, and there was still nearly a week to go.

On Christmas Eve, in the sanctuary of her bedroom, Morrigan was practising. Just as she had done every night that week, and the week before that, and in all the weeks that had passed since the night she'd shut down the Ghastly Market. She had started the nightly ritual at Jupiter's suggestion, to manage the ever-growing volume of Wunder that was drawn irresistibly to her as a Wundersmith. That energy was constantly swarming around her, invisible and undetectable but nonetheless *there*, waiting impatiently for her to do something with it. But only an accomplished Wundersmith could wield it, and while Morrigan had picked up a couple of new skills in the past year, she was nowhere near accomplished.

She knew now what a dangerous position it had put her in, that great yawning chasm between her potential as a Wundersmith and her actual ability. It was this gathering of Wunder – this *critical mass*, as Ezra Squall had called it – that had allowed him to take control of her power and use it for his own purposes.

Most people in Nevermoor knew Squall as 'the last Wundersmith', and spoke about him only in hushed, fearful tones, as if he was some imaginary bogeyman. Morrigan, however, knew that he was very much a real, living threat.

Not that she was about to share that with anyone, outside of her closest friends. It was bad enough that everyone at Wunsoc now knew she was a Wundersmith too. If they knew she'd also met Nevermoor's greatest enemy several times – had even reluctantly learned from him – she'd likely be driven out of town with torches and pitchforks.

Morrigan didn't know if or when Squall would return. Though the ancient magic of the city prevented him from physically entering Nevermoor, nothing could stop him travelling there incorporeally on the Gossamer – the invisible web of energy that connected everything in the realm. If Morrigan allowed too much Wunder to gather around her unchecked, Squall could use it to 'lean' through the Gossamer and manipulate her powers, making her his puppet. Summoning Wunder and using it was the only way Morrigan could keep the city she now called home safe.

'*Morningtide's child is merry and mild,*' she sang quietly. The tingling feeling came to her fingertips with barely any coaxing. She was getting better at this. Even if her voice was still a tiny bit wobbly. '*Eventide's child is wicked and wild.*'

To her endless frustration, Morrigan still knew very little about the Wretched Arts. But the knowledge she had, she treasured.

The Wretched Art of Nocturne. The summoning of Wunder. *Singing to make it so.*

And the Wretched Art of Inferno. The creation and manipulation of fire.

Those were the two things Squall had taught her.

She raked over this meagre knowledge again and again, every night, polishing and perfecting her technique. Hoping the next steps in her journey to becoming an accomplished Wundersmith might just one day be miraculously laid out for her.

'*Morningtide's child arrives with the dawn. Eventide's child brings gale and storm.*' Morrigan smiled to herself, eyes closed. She could feel the gentle yet insistent hum of energy swimming around her, pooling contentedly in her upturned palms. '*Where are you going, o son of the morning? Up with the sun where the winds are warming.*'

She didn't really understand why *singing* should be the signal to Wunder that you were ready to put it to use . . . but then, there were lots of things she didn't understand yet about being a Wundersmith.

Most of it, really.

Almost all of it.

'*Where are you going, o daughter of night?*' Morrigan opened her eyes cautiously and saw that her bedroom was bathed in a now familiar white-gold light.

This was at least one thing she could understand: she had called Wunder, and Wunder had come. It danced all around, throwing speckled patterns across the floor and pulsating as if to say that it was happy to see her.

Morrigan grinned. She didn't even need to finish the song.

She really was getting better at this.

All down the hallway outside her bedroom, Morrigan ran from gas lamp to gas lamp, candelabra to candelabra, blowing out every light until the entire fourth floor of the east wing was bathed in darkness. Then she stood very still, eyes closed, as smoke from the extinguished wicks swirled around her. She breathed in the scent and pictured a tiny spark of fire.

A single flame, burning brightly inside her chest.

Inferno.

She focused for a moment on that fire, feeling it grow and warm her from the inside out. Then she opened her eyes and ran all the way back around again, gas lamp to gas lamp, candelabra to candelabra. At each one, she breathed a puff of perfect, precise flame, relighting them with ease, feeling utterly gleeful.

'You are *such* a show-off,' said Jack, coming out of his bedroom a few doors down from hers. He shook his head as Morrigan breathed life back into the last wick. The hallway glowed cheerfully once again. 'Is that *really* necessary? Every night?'

She took one look at him and snorted, ignoring his comment. 'Nice hat, broccoli head.'

'Nice ribbon, capitalist scum.' He tweaked the scarlet bow in her hair with one hand while adjusting his strange, utterly unstylish green hat with the other. It was the same hat he'd worn last

Christmas Eve, and it still looked like he was sprouting a bizarre growth from his skull. Morrigan could not for the life of her understand why he'd ever be caught dead in it. But then, she supposed *he* couldn't understand why she'd ever support Saint Nicholas over his beloved Yule Queen.

Truthfully, after last year's Battle of Christmas Eve – the first she'd attended – Morrigan *had* been tempted to switch her allegiance. While she enjoyed the jolly, showy man in red Jack liked to call an 'elf-enslaving home invader', there was something deeply impressive – even *moving* – about the elegant, understated Yule Queen and her devoted Snowhound.

But it would give Jack too much satisfaction to know that she agreed with him, even a little bit.

He checked the angle of his hat one last time in the hall mirror, adjusted his eye patch slightly and then nodded at his reflection, apparently liking what he saw.

'Come on,' he said to Morrigan. 'Let's get downstairs before we end up sharing a carriage with Uncle Jove. I am *not* having another singalong today.'

CHAPTER FIVE

Six Swifts, Two Cats

The atmosphere in Courage Square was heavy with expectation, ready to tip over into unbridled delight at any moment. Thousands of Nevermoorians were gathered – a sea of crimson and emerald, breathless and silent – awaiting the final moments of the annual Christmas clash.

It had been an epic, exhilarating battle once again. Morrigan could still taste the warm, buttery, perfectly spiced mince pie that had shot from one of Saint Nick's canons and floated down into her hand, wrapped in a tiny red silk parachute. That had been her second favourite moment so far, after the cloud of twinkling fireflies the Yule Queen had conducted to fly above Courage Square like a murmuration of starlings, a hypnotising dance of light. Morrigan had been certain nothing could beat last year's show, and thrilled to find she was wrong.

'Candles out,' whispered Jupiter, and Jack and Morrigan – like everyone else in the square – retrieved from inside their coat pockets the candles they'd brought with them, lifting them high in the air.

In one last spectacular effort, Saint Nicholas rubbed his hands and started to spin in a circle, around and around and around, arms extended towards the audience. One by one, the candle wicks spontaneously ignited, a spiral of light moving outwards from the centre of the square to its very edges in a long *whoosh* of flame.

The square was aglow with candlelight. Still nobody made a sound.

The silence was broken by the Yule Queen's gigantic white Snowhound who, on her command, lifted his head to bay at the moon. Answering howls rose from all corners of the city, and for one lingering moment, Nevermoor became a communion of dogs. The sound sent an agreeable chill down Morrigan's back.

This was her favourite part. She closed her eyes and turned her face to the sky. The air was perfectly still. She could smell the promise of snow.

It came slowly at first, flake by flake.

Then faster. And faster.

The flurries and eddies of snowfall drew together, swirling and transforming into something with a life and a will of its own. Before Morrigan knew it, a wintry snowstorm had filled the air all around her. It built so quickly she was suddenly blinded by the force of its whiteness.

Then there came a beautiful, terrible sound – something between the roar of fifty lions and the tinkling of a thousand silver bells – and the shapeless storm rose into the air, reborn as a long, serpentine dragon made of snow. It flew through the sky above them, tumbling over and around itself in the most extraordinary display. Snowflakes fluttered down from its outspread wings, landing gently on Morrigan, Jupiter and Jack, who held up their hands and cheered along with the rest of the Courage Square crowd.

'Oh, YES!' shouted Jupiter, eyes wide. 'Brilliant! Absolutely brilliant.'

Jack whooped loudly, casting Morrigan a rather smug look. 'Now THAT'S a finale.'

But it wasn't over yet. Saint Nicholas, not to be out-Christmassed, motioned for everyone in the audience to hold their candles high. The thousands of tiny flames grew brighter and larger, until finally they seemed to leap from the wicks and band together, forming a cloud-like bonfire in the sky above them. Morrigan closed her eyes briefly against the flash of light. She felt heat blooming on her face.

When she opened her eyes, the flames had reshaped themselves into a golden-red firebird, blindingly bright and beautiful, borne higher and higher into the sky as it beat its fiery wings.

'YES!' Jupiter shouted again in elation. 'MAGNIFICENT! BRAVO, SAINT NICK, BRAVO!'

Morrigan could hardly believe what she was seeing. She turned to Jack with a joyous laugh, and even he looked impressed. 'You were saying?'

The firebird and the snowdragon danced around each other, spiralling together to form a tower of vivid orange and dazzling white that reached high into the atmosphere . . . until at last, in one final glorious act of mutual destruction, the flames were extinguished and the snow evaporated. Dragon and bird disappeared in an instant, leaving nothing but the ghostly shape of their light blinking against the black sky, emblazoned on everyone's retinas.

A moment of stunned silence.

Then a roar of delight so loud, Morrigan had to cover her ears.

Morrigan wasn't sure she'd be able to find Hawthorne and his family amidst the sea of people surging in every direction after the battle – she realised too late they'd forgotten to plan a meeting spot. But she needn't have worried. They found her instead.

'MORRIGAN! There you are. Oi!' her friend shouted eagerly, running to where she, Jupiter and Fenestra were waiting by the fountain in the middle of the square, hoping to maximise their visibility. Jack and the others had been too cold to wait around in the snow; they'd already taken the carriages home.

Hawthorne's mum, dad, brother and sisters followed close behind him, and there was no mistaking the Swift family's allegiance to Saint Nicholas. All six of them were decked from head to toe in varying shades of red. (Although Morrigan thought she spied a flash of green socks beneath Dave's scarlet corduroy trousers.)

Morrigan beamed. 'Jolly Christmas!'

'I'm glad you managed to find us,' said Jupiter, rubbing his hands together and blowing on them for warmth. His beard was collecting snowflakes.

'Oh, it was easy, I just looked for Fen's great big head in the crowd – hello, Fen, Jolly Christmas!' Hawthorne puffed cheerfully, and Fenestra scowled at him in return. He gave a good-natured chuckle as she turned away, her tail stuck high in the air. 'Classic Fen. Helena, didn't I tell you how hilarious Fen is?'

Morrigan had already met Dave, and Hawthorne's mum, Cat, several times, as well as his older brother Homer and baby sister Davina, whom everybody called Baby Dave. But this was her first time meeting the eldest Swift sibling. Helena was completing her fifth year of study at the Gorgonhowl College of Radical Meteorology, a school situated on a tiny island off the coast of the distant Sixth Pocket in the eye of a perpetual cyclone, and it was rarely safe enough for her to travel home.

'She is *tremendous*,' Helena declared, staring at the Magnificat with open admiration. 'An absolute queen.'

At that precise moment, a young man walking past Fen accidentally stood on her tail. She yowled in pain, then shoved her enormous face right up to his and bared her great yellow fangs at him with a dangerous *hisssss*. The man fainted on the spot.

'*Queen*,' whispered Helena.

Seeing the whole Swift family together, Morrigan noticed how perfectly they were split down the middle. Hawthorne and Helena both took after Cat with their long, wild brown curls and gangly limbs. Homer and Baby Dave, on the other hand, favoured their father's side of the family – sturdy, yellow-haired Viking stock.

'We'll bring Morrigan home later,' Dave was telling Jupiter.

'Oh, don't worry about that,' said Jupiter, gesturing vaguely in Fen's direction. 'I'll send my housekeeper to collect her.'

Dave cast a nervous sideways look at Fen, who'd overheard Jupiter's magnanimous offer of her services and was glowering at them both. 'Er – are you sure about that, Captain North? We, um . . . we really don't mind.'

'No honestly, it's fine,' Jupiter assured him. 'Truth be told, Magnificats are pretty rubbish at housekeeping. But she's on the payroll, and if I don't send her on the occasional errand she'll snooze her nine lives away. Right, Fen?' he called out to her with a wink.

'Tonight you sleep with the fishes,' she growled.

'That means she's going to put sardines in his bed,' Hawthorne whispered loudly to his mum, smiling fondly at the Magnificat. 'Classic Fen.'

'How-tawn,' said Baby Dave, tugging insistently at Hawthorne's red jumper as they made their way out of Courage Square. 'How-tawn, pick me up. I tired.'

'*No*, Baby Dave.' He shook her off. 'You're a big girl now. You're almost three! Almost-three-year-olds have to walk on their own legs like everyone else.'

The toddler was not happy to hear this, and Morrigan could understand why. (After all, she thought Hawthorne might have a better chance of convincing Baby Dave she was a 'big girl now' if he and the rest of his family stopped calling her *Baby Dave*.)

Davina glared up at Hawthorne from beneath her pale blonde eyelashes. 'HOW-TAWN!' she growled in a voice that made Morrigan jump. 'PICK ME UP! I TIRED!'

'Oh, *fine*,' he said, and stopped to heave her into his arms with great effort. She sat there beaming contentedly at the crowd, like a small but statuesque Viking queen surveying her subjects, as they followed Hawthorne's dad through the turnstile at a busy Wunderground station.

Adult Dave had suggested they circumvent the post-battle crowds by avoiding Courage Square's nearest station, Caledonia Circus, and heading straight for Greenery Gate instead. He hadn't counted on most of the people at the battle having that same idea. When they reached the busiest part of the station, of course, Baby Dave got bored of being carried and insisted 'How-Tawn' let her down *immediately*.

'Hold hands! Single file!' Hawthorne's dad shouted at their group as they made their way through the maze of stairwells and down to the platform. 'Form a human chain! Don't get – pardon me, madam, I'm just trying to keep this lot togeth— Oh, well excuse you very much! All right, team, don't let's lose each other – oof!'

It was a lost cause. The crowd was a sea that had taken on a life of its own. A train arrived at the platform and a new wave of passengers spilled out of its doors. Those waiting paused just long enough for them to disembark before surging instantly forward, everyone eager to board so they wouldn't have to wait an agonising *two whole minutes* until the next train came along.

Somewhere in this mess, one hand slipped out of another and the Swift family's human chain was split in two. Morrigan watched as Cat, Dave, Helena and Homer got swallowed up by the momentum of the crowd and pulled to the open doors of one carriage, while she, Hawthorne and Baby Dave were pushed to the next.

'Where's Baby Dave?' Hawthorne's dad shouted in a panicked voice. Meanwhile, Cat was trying to elbow people out of the way to get back to them, to no avail. 'Who's got Baby Dave?'

'We do!' Morrigan called back from farther up the platform. She tightened her grip on Davina's pudgy, sweaty little right hand (the left was firmly in Hawthorne's).

Dave looked clammy and anxious, his eyes bugging out of his head as he jumped up and down in the crowd, trying to keep sight of them while he shouted instructions. 'RIGHT, STAY TOGETHER, YOU THREE! WE GET OFF AT TUCKER PARK PLACE! THAT'S TWELVE STOPS AWAY! DID YOU HEAR ME?'

'I know where we live, Dad!' Hawthorne shouted back, rolling his eyes. 'We'll be fine!'

The carriage was full of chatter and high spirits, even though they were all crammed in like pickles in a jar. Someone down one end started a rousing chorus of 'Green Is the Colour of My Cheer', and seconds later a round of 'Zoom Goes the Big Red Sleigh' started at the other end, and the two competing groups managed to merge and harmonise quite pleasantly together.

'Dad is *such* a worrywart,' said Hawthorne. Morrigan noticed, however, that his eyes narrowed as they swept over the carriage and he was still gripping Baby Dave's hand tight – they both were, in fact. It was a lot of responsibility to be separated from the others with a toddler to take care of.

Hawthorne leaned down to pick up his baby sister again. 'Oof. Yikes. What are Mum and Dad feeding you? Whole chickens? You're almost as big as I am.'

'How-tawn, put me DOWN!' demanded a wriggling Baby Dave, but this time Hawthorne refused.

'Shush, Baby Dave,' he said. 'It's too busy in here. Just— OW!' She had bitten him, hard enough to leave teeth marks. Hawthorne held up his wrist, looking half shocked, half impressed. He turned to Morrigan, laughing. 'Will you look at this? She's part shark.'

Baby Dave grinned at Morrigan, who leaned away slightly, making a silent vow never to allow those chompers anywhere near her limbs.

The crowding in the carriage eased a little at each stop as groups of passengers disembarked. After they'd passed through a handful of stations there was finally enough room for Hawthorne to put his still-complaining sister down on the floor.

'Mogran, pick me up. I tired,' moaned Baby Dave less than a minute later. She gripped Morrigan's hand, leaning dramatically backwards, and Morrigan had to use all her strength just to keep them both upright.

'Please, Baby Dave, be good,' she said coaxingly. 'It's only a few more stops.'

'PEAS, MOGRAN, PEAS PICK ME UP,' Baby Dave wailed, her enormous blue eyes filling with tears. Morrigan stared at her in horror, uncertain what to do.

Hawthorne laughed, and said in a sing-song voice, 'She's playing you.'

A group of elderly ladies sitting nearby clucked their tongues in sympathy at the display, shooting them disapproving looks.

'Heartless,' Morrigan heard one of them mutter. She felt her face turn pink.

'Aye,' said another, looking right at Morrigan and whispering just loudly enough for her to hear. 'The poor wean's obviously exhausted.'

Morrigan gave in as the train pulled up to its next stop, and heaved a delighted Baby Dave into her arms.

'*Oof,*' she grunted, shifting the toddler to one side. 'Not sure I'll be able to hold you for very long, Baby Da—'

She was cut off by a squeal at one end of the train car, followed by a roar that sounded a bit like Fenestra when she was furious. Morrigan looked around uneasily, trying to see the source of the commotion, but there were too many bodies in the way.

'What's going on?' asked Hawthorne.

An indignant voice came from the end of the carriage. 'It scratched me! That beastly creature just *scratched* me! Clarissa, look, I'm bleeding, I'm actually *bleeding.*'

Morrigan stood on tiptoes to get a better view, and nearly fell over in surprise. 'Oh! Goodness. It's a leopard – er, leopardwun.'

She said *leopardwun* rather than *leopard* only because the big cat wore a chunky string of beads around its neck and a big, expensive-looking diamond earring in the tip of one of its furry ears. And, well, because it was riding the Wunderground, which would have been highly irregular for an ordinary leopard.

At a distance, it was *sometimes* tricky to tell the difference between Wunimals (sentient, self-aware creatures who were capable of human language and fully assimilated to human society) and unnimals (normal creatures who went about their normal creature business in their normal creature societies). It was of course easier if you were looking at a Wunimal Minor – a sort of human-unnimal hybrid, usually with more humanoid features than unnimal.

With Wunimal Majors – who were physically indistinguishable from their unnimal counterparts – there was more scope for confusion . . . that is, until they opened their mouths to complain about the weather, or to ask where they might find the nearest Brolly Rail platform. That's why most Majors wore specially tailored clothes, or at least accessorised with a jaunty hat or a monocle or something, to signal their sentient Wunimal status and avoid the embarrassing assumptions of strangers.

If it wasn't for the leopardwun's jewellery, however, and the fact that it had somehow managed to board public transport on its own, this could very well have been an escaped unnimal from the Nevermoor Zoo. It seemed almost completely unnimalistic to Morrigan, sniffing the air like a big cat on the hunt, as if it had quite lost its mind.

The leopardwun snarled as it prowled through the carriage in their direction, snapping its powerful jaws at the terrified passengers, who all shrieked and tried to scramble away. Morrigan felt fear grip her throat. She tried to swallow, but her mouth had gone dry. All she could do was tighten her hold on Baby Dave. Hawthorne stood in front of Morrigan, shielding his sister.

The lights of the next station suddenly came streaming in through the windows, and Morrigan breathed a sigh of relief as the train began to slow.

'Let's get off at this stop,' said Hawthorne urgently. 'We'll catch the next train and meet everyone at Tucker Park Place. Mum and Dad will understand, and we'll only be a couple of minutes behind them.'

'Good idea,' agreed Morrigan, keeping her gaze on the bizarre behaviour of the Wunimal as they made their way to the nearest exit.

But the doors were taking too long to open, and the leopardwun was stalking towards them, still sniffing the air like it was *looking* for something. An oblivious Baby Dave laughed happily as she yanked the scarlet ribbon in Morrigan's hair.

The leopardwun grew still at the sound. Her eyes fixed on Baby Dave, who made another happy squealing sound.

It happened so quickly.

Morrigan saw the big cat's eyes flash a bright emerald green, as though somebody had turned on a light behind them. It leapt up on to the windows, then on to the ceiling, seemingly defying gravity, bounding between passengers and leaving startled screams in its wake, until suddenly it landed just in front of them, growling and baring its teeth.

Morrigan had the briefest flash of a thought that she ought to call Wunder and . . . and *do something* . . . but it all happened in a matter of frantic milliseconds, and after all, what could she possibly do with Baby Dave in her arms, even if she *knew* what to do?

The leopardwun crouched, preparing to leap straight towards them and then—

WALLOP!

The group of ladies had leapt up from their seats, swinging their heavy purses and carpet bags filled with heaven-knows-what. They lunged for the leopardwun as a single entity, fury trumping fear as they surrounded the big cat and thumped it into submission. It yowled and cowered away from them.

'How very dare—'

'A baby!'

'You ought to be ashamed—'

'A BABY!'

'Bog off, spotty!'

'A WEE LITTLE BABY, for goodness' sake!'

'This station is Scholars' Crossing,' intoned the calm, pleasant voice on the loudspeaker. 'Alight here for Nevermoor University, West Campus.'

The doors of the train finally pinged open at Scholars' Crossing station and the leopardwun had no choice but to get off, since it was being steamrollered out on to the platform by the gang of surprisingly vicious elderly ladies.

'Gwan, get orf!'

'And let this be a lesson!'

'*Why* they ever let Wunimals on trains to begin with—'

The doors closed with a *whoosh*, and the whole carriage broke into loud applause.

'Th-thank you,' said Hawthorne in a shaky voice.

'Yes,' Morrigan said breathlessly. 'Thank you.' She couldn't think what else to say. Her brain had gone numb.

'Poor little love,' said one of the women, clucking sympathetically and pinching Baby Dave's cheek. 'Got the fright of her life, didn't she, the braw wee thing.'

But braw wee Baby Dave wasn't frightened at all. In fact, she seemed utterly tickled by the whole episode. She giggled and waved goodbye to the leopardwun as the train took off, leaving the Wunimal stalking up and down the platform, snapping its jaws in an agitated state and heaving in great shuddering breaths. Morrigan noticed that Hawthorne, on the other hand, had gone a bit pale.

'Let's, er . . . let's not tell Dad about this,' he muttered as he took his little sister from Morrigan, trying unsuccessfully to bounce her up and down on his hip. 'He'll only get upset and blame himself for us being separated. I'll tell Mum later, she'll be a bit calmer about it. Tomorrow, maybe, or – no, that'll ruin Christmas. Maybe the day after.'

Morrigan nodded and allowed Baby Dave to yank violently at her scarlet ribbon for the rest of the trip.

'Oh, the *marching band*!' said Helena, snapping her fingers. 'Saint Nick's invisible marching band, all those instruments playing themselves. *That* was the best bit.'

'Did you taste one of those mince pies? Best I've ever had,' said Cat, who was sitting with Dave on the squishiest sofa. Baby Dave – tuckered out from their Wunderground misadventure – had fallen asleep between her parents with one hand stuck in a bowlful of popcorn, snoring softly. 'Morrigan, what was your favourite bit?'

Morrigan thought about it as she watched her skewered marshmallow sizzle in the flames, turning it over to blacken all the sides. (The Swift family's Christmas Eve tradition of sitting by the fire and toasting absolutely any item of food that could be pierced on the end of a stick was one she could really get on board with.)

'I liked the firebird,' she said at last.

She couldn't stop thinking about that firebird, actually. How had he *done* it? Now that she knew exactly what was involved in the act of bending fire to one's will – in making it appear seemingly from nowhere – she found this signature move of Saint Nick's even more mystifying than she had last Christmas.

His mastery of fire was just *too* precise – had he somehow learned the Wretched Art of Inferno? Was that how he could be so utterly in control of it? Or was this just some elaborate trickery?

66

An act of complicated illusion wrought by many hands, taking practice, precision and planning?

Or . . . could Saint Nick, perhaps, be a Wundersmith too?

Was that such a ridiculous idea? There *used to* always be nine, after all – that's what Elder Quinn had said. Could there be seven others out there somewhere? Could one of them be the jolly man in a red suit who brought presents at Christmastime?

Morrigan smiled a tiny, secret smile. The thought that there might have been another living Wundersmith standing in front of her gave her the strangest thrill of . . . *hope*.

But it was a crazy idea. A fantasy.

'Full credit to the Yule Queen, though,' Dave was saying when Morrigan emerged from her daydream. 'That snowdragon was brilliant. Baby Dave said she wants one as a pet, so that's her next birthday sorted. Ha!'

'I'll have a dragon one day. A real one,' said Hawthorne matter-of-factly, licking toasted marshmallow from his fingers. Helena scoffed, and Homer rolled his eyes heartily, giving a sarcastic thumbs-up. 'No, I will. I *will*, Nan said so! She said if I keep going the way I am and training hard, and if I do well in the annual tournaments in the next few years, when I graduate from junior to senior scholar she'll see about getting me a dragon youngling of my own, to raise up and train to respond only to me. My own dragon, that nobody else can ride! It's true, Homer, stop laughing.'

Morrigan looked up in surprise at the silent Homer, to find he had indeed written *Ha ha ha* on his blackboard. As a student of the Conservatory of Thought, Homer had taken a vow of silence for all but one day of the year, so the blackboard went everywhere with him. He had not, however, taken any kind of vow against mockery, sarcasm or scorn, and she liked that about him.

'Hawthorne-In-My-Side,' said Helena, as she poked a chunk of cheese on to the end of her skewer. 'Why are dragon names so stupid?'

Hawthorne screwed up his face. 'What? Shut up, they are not.'

'Yes, they are,' she insisted. 'They've all got those long, pompous names like *On a Glorious Flight to Valour and Victory*, or *Defeats His Enemies with Fire and Fury*, or whatever.'

'Oh, those are tournament names,' Hawthorne replied with a shrug. He paused to take a noisy sip of hot chocolate. 'Every dragon entered into a tournament has to have a unique name to log in the record books. It can't be too close to a name that any other dragon has had in the history of the tournament, and that goes back about four hundred years. So they've had to get creative.'

'They're not creative, they're narcissistic,' said Helena. 'Like that one who got gold in the Melee last year – *Look How Big His Talons Are?* I mean, honestly. Everyone knows that whatever name a rider gives their dragon, they're *really* talking about themselves. They should just be more honest about it, that's all. If you *do* get a dragon, Hawthorne, you should call it something true about yourself, like . . . I don't know. *Tries His Best But Is Mostly an Idiot?*' she finished with a grin.

The Swifts all laughed at that, even Hawthorne.

'Needs to be more specific,' said Cat, her eyes twinkling. 'How about . . . *Practises Posing Heroically in Front of the Mirror?*'

'Nice one, Mum,' said Hawthorne, reaching over to steal a marshmallow from the end of her skewer. 'If you had one we could call it *Doesn't Realise How Loud She Snores*.'

'HA!' Cat threw her head back in a booming laugh. She tossed a piece of popcorn at him in retaliation, but he caught it in his mouth and cheered.

'What would Dad's be, then?' Helena continued, grinning slyly at Dave. 'How about—'

'*Farts Like a Draught Horse*,' said Cat in a stage whisper. Morrigan and Hawthorne went into fits of giggles at this, while Helena groaned, 'Ugh, Mum! Gross.'

'Oi – careful, Catriona Swift, or yours'll be *Makes All Her Own Cups of Tea From Now On*,' Dave replied indignantly, though he was trying not to laugh.

Hawthorne's eyes lit up. 'What about Homer?'

There was a moment's silence. Morrigan looked from Hawthorne to Helena to Cat to Dave. She could practically see the gears in their brains turning as each tried to come up with the best zinger. But Homer was too quick – he'd already scrawled out a name on his blackboard, and he held it up for them to see.

Hopes He's Adopted.

There was an eruption of laughter as they all applauded the clear winner of the unofficial dragon-naming competition. Homer speared the last marshmallow, looking quietly pleased with himself.

It was a cheerful ending to a brilliant Christmas Eve. But when Fenestra showed up to take her home, Morrigan was surprised to realise she felt a certain amount of relief.

She adored Hawthorne's family. She really did. She loved the way that Cat and Dave teased each other. Homer made her laugh all the time, and even though she'd only just met Helena, she liked her already. She didn't even mind being tyrannised by Baby Dave. And Hawthorne, well . . . he was her best friend.

But, although she would never have let it show, being around the Swifts all together like this made Morrigan feel a tiny bit . . . what was it? Not jealous, exactly. Just . . .

Well, yes. Jealous. If she was being honest with herself.

She couldn't even articulate precisely *what* she was jealous of. It was something about their ease with one another, the natural way they all just seemed to . . . fit. They were a puzzle with no missing parts.

Morrigan's family – her father, stepmother, grandmother and twin half-brothers – lived far away in the Wintersea Republic, and they didn't have any missing parts either. They used to have an unwanted spare part, but now she lived in Nevermoor at the Hotel Deucalion.

It was just a small ache, coming from some deep and probably unimportant place inside, almost imperceptible if she didn't pay too much attention to her feelings. (And Morrigan *tried* not to make a habit of paying too much attention to her feelings.)

But it was there, and she didn't like it. The Swifts were good people. They were always kind to her, always made her feel welcome. It seemed ungrateful, somehow, to nurse this small resentment.

And yet on the way home, when Fenestra muttered, 'Very *obnoxious*, that family,' Morrigan felt a mean little laugh bubble up out of her chest before she could stop it.

Then the sting of instant regret. She dug her fingernails into her palms, leaving tiny red marks in the shape of crescent moons.

CHAPTER SIX

De Flimsé

Morrigan slept with her curtains open that night so that she would wake to the sight of a winter wonderland outside her windows, and when morning arrived she wasn't disappointed. It looked as if the snow hadn't stopped all night long, and it was impossible to see much of anything through the flurries of white still falling thick and fast.

Blinking groggily, she propped herself up in her bed. It had transformed while she was sleeping from a four-poster into something resembling an enormous replica of Saint Nick's sleigh, filled with dozens of plump velvet cushions and soft woollen blankets.

'Very nice,' Morrigan said to her bedroom, in a voice still croaky from sleep. She'd recently decided to be more complimentary when it did something she really liked. A few weeks earlier she'd made a vague noise of distaste at a very modern, abstract painting that had shown up on her wall, and she *swore* it must have hurt the room's feelings or something, because the next three nights her bed had turned into a dog kennel, then a hamster cage, then a large terracotta pot full of cactus plants. She'd been extra cautious ever since.

Saint Nicholas had once again delivered; a plump, overfilled stocking hung from the mantelpiece. Even more inviting, a pile of gifts sat on the end of the sleigh bed.

Martha had given her a wicker basket full of brightly coloured bubble baths and carved soaps. Kedgeree's gift was a small, exquisite version of the bird chandelier in the lobby, handcrafted from glittering black beads and silver wire. Frank had given her a book bound in blood-red cloth called *One Hundred Gruesome Deaths in the Age of the Nightwalkers*. There was a delicate amethyst bracelet from Dame Chanda, a pair of jodhpurs and a promise of horse-riding lessons from Charlie, and a large dead pheasant without a gift tag, which Morrigan presumed was from Fen. (*It's the thought that counts*, she reminded herself as she tried to delicately push the feathered corpse off her bed with one toe.)

But the most interesting present was hanging from the bony wrist of her skeleton coat rack: a pair of ice-skates made from crimson leather, their laces loosely knotted together. There was a small handwritten card that Morrigan couldn't read from this distance, but she knew instantly who this present must be from.

Tumbling awkwardly out of the sleigh, she crossed her bedroom floor and took the skates down from the hook. Sure enough, the card read:

Jolly Christmas, Mog.
–J.N.

Morrigan grinned, shaking her head. They were shiny and beautiful, but she had no idea how to ice-skate.

Still, she thought, holding up the skates to admire the fine red leather and stitching. *Very pretty*. As the skates spun in a circle, a glint of reflected light caught her eye. Attached to the laces was a small, old-fashioned silver key.

Ah! An excited little tornado of moths began to flutter in Morrigan's stomach. This wasn't, after all, the first time that Jupiter had given her a slightly odd gift. It wasn't the first time he had given her a *key*.

A memory came to her of a strange locked door on a quiet floor of the Hotel Deucalion. The tip of her oilskin umbrella – a birthday present from Jupiter – turning in the lock with a satisfying *click*. An enchanted lantern-lit room full of shadow monsters within.

A strange but splendid present, from her strange but splendid patron.

There was a sudden knock on Morrigan's bedroom door. She ran to open it, Jupiter's gift still clutched tight in one hand, and was greeted by a confused-looking Jack. His pyjamas were rumpled, eye patch crooked and hair an absolute mess . . . and he, too, was holding a pair of ice-skates. His were made of rich forest-green leather.

'Right,' Jack said, blinking down at Morrigan's red ones. 'Thought so. Weird, though, 'cos there isn't any—'

'—skating rink nearby?' she finished for him. 'Yeah, that's what I thought. But did you also get—'

'—a key?' He held out his other hand, where a silver key sat, catching the light. 'Yep. You?'

She held up her identical one, grinning. 'Do you think we should—'

'Definitely,' he agreed. 'And bring the skates.'

It was still early, and the Deucalion was mostly quiet but for the occasional rustle of someone in a pink-and-gold uniform hurrying down a hallway. Jack and Morrigan tried at least a dozen doors throughout the hotel (avoiding guest bedrooms and places they already knew) before at last finding their present on the ninth floor: a large oak double door with two locks. They each tried to open it separately first, to no avail.

'Ugh, I knew it,' Jack groaned as they turned both keys simultaneously and the door opened with a soft *click*. 'I knew he'd make it so we had to *cooperate*, or something. That's *so* Uncle Jove.'

The doors swung open and a gust of icy wind hit them fair in the face. Morrigan and Jack stood still, both entirely speechless for once as their brains tried to make sense of the room's vast interior.

The room was not a room, it was a lake. A proper, for-real lake, inside the Hotel Deucalion. Frozen solid and surrounded by rolling snow-covered fields. The far opposite wall, on the horizon beyond the fields, was made of floor-to-ceiling arched windows, frosted over and letting in enough wintry sunshine to light the whole gargantuan space. Morrigan would never even have guessed the hotel was big enough to contain such a thing.

And in the middle distance, twirling and spinning across the lake like he'd been doing it all his life, was Jupiter North in a pair of smart blue ice-skates.

'Took your time, didn't you?' he shouted, cupping his hands around his mouth. He swept over towards them at high speed. 'Come on, then. It's a very good lake. Get your skates on!'

Jack didn't hesitate; within moments, he'd laced up his boots, tottered out on to the ice, then glided away like a professional athlete.

Typical, Morrigan thought, making a face at the two of them as they circled each other, skating backwards and then switching direction seamlessly to go forward again.

Jack called out to her, 'Morrigan, hurry up and get out here! This is so much fun! It's a *very* good lake.'

She wasn't so sure. She'd never ice-skated before. Growing up as a registered cursed child, she'd learned to avoid any activities that had even the smallest chance of ending in catastrophe. Ice-skating had most definitely been off the list.

'Mog!' shouted Jupiter. 'What are you waiting for?'

'I don't know how to ice-skate.'

'What?'

'I DON'T KNOW HOW TO ICE-SKATE!' she shouted.

'Nor do I,' said Jack, taking off to the other side of the lake with an uncanny grace.

'No, nor do I,' echoed Jupiter.

Morrigan rolled her eyes. 'Oh yeah, I can see that. That quadruple spin thing you just did looked really *amateurish*.'

Her patron soared over to where she stood at the edge of the lake and came to a neat stop, breathing heavily but smiling all over his stupid ginger-bearded face.

So annoying, thought Morrigan.

'No, Mog, *really*,' Jupiter said. 'I've always been rubbish at ice-skating. I've got no idea what I'm doing. Just try it, all right? It really is a very good lake.'

She hesitated, looking down at the skates still in her hand.

'Do you trust me?' he asked.

She looked up. He'd asked her that once before, when there'd been much higher stakes than just an awkward fall on the ice, and her answer then had been an unequivocal yes.

It was still a yes.

Morrigan gathered her nerve, laced up her skates, lurched dubiously out on to the ice and took a few wobbly steps, certain she was going to fall flat on her face at any moment . . .

. . . then launched into a series of perfect pirouettes, followed swiftly by an arabesque spin and ending with a neat little axel jump. Jack and Jupiter burst into applause. A surprised laugh tumbled out of Morrigan's mouth and skipped across the frozen landscape.

They skated for hours, and it was the most extraordinary sensation. It felt as if the ice and her feet were connected, like they were communicating somehow without her even having to think about it. She felt cushioned and weightless. There was no risk of falling. No risk, in fact, of *anything* bad happening while she was on this lake.

It was a *very* good lake.

Lunch was held in the fancy dining room for the paying Deucalion guests as normal, but this year Jupiter had set up a long table in his private parlour for the staff (and Jack and Morrigan) to share the meal as a family. They enjoyed five delicious, meandering courses, ending with a plum pudding that Morrigan set alight with a triumphant *whoosh* of Inferno, to thunderous applause from all.

Several hours later there they still were, everyone full of food and good cheer, and nobody yet willing to call an end to the festivities. Martha and Charlie were working on a one-thousand-piece jigsaw puzzle together, sitting closer than was strictly necessary, whispering and giggling an awful lot. Frank and Kedgeree had briefly fallen out over a passionate argument about how they would rank the top five hotels in Nevermoor, but then reconciled over their shared belief that the Deucalion was *definitely* number one, and that their chief rival, the Hotel Aurianna, didn't even make the list.

Dame Chanda had a pile of newspapers and was scouring the cultural sections for reviews of her Christmas pantomime performance at the Nevermoor Opera House, reading the best bits aloud to the room. Morrigan, Jack and Jupiter were sitting by the fire playing round after round of an old game called Tax Collector, while Fenestra snored loudly on the rug beside them. (Jupiter won every round by exploiting various mysterious loopholes in the rulebook, but Jack was determined to beat him. Morrigan enjoyed the bit where you set the other players' villages on fire if they couldn't pay their taxes. She'd already melted two playing pieces and singed a hole in the middle of the board.)

At one point there was a sudden, dramatic gasp from Dame Chanda.

'Jupiter!' she cried, beckoning him over to look at her newspaper. 'Did you see this?'

Jupiter stood and crossed the room to read over Dame Chanda's shoulder. His forehead wrinkled as his eyes flitted across the page.

'Oh dear,' he murmured. 'How awful.'

'Poor, sweet Juvela.' Dame Chanda turned her mournful face up to Jupiter's and grasped his arm. 'Darling, we *must* send flowers. No – we must *take* flowers immediately. A whole carriage full of them. It's De *Flimsé*.'

'Quite right,' Jupiter agreed, nodding.

'What's De Flimsé?' Morrigan asked.

'Oh, you've heard of De Flimsé, darling,' said the opera singer with an airy wave. 'Of course you have. It's De Flimsé. You know . . . De *Flimsé*.'

Jack looked up from where he was assembling the board for

round five of Tax Collector. 'De Whosay?'

The soprano sighed. 'Darlings, De Flimsé is everything. De Flimsé is life.'

'De Flimsé is a genius,' added Frank, looking sombre as he picked up the discarded newspaper and read the news for himself.

'*This* is De Flimsé,' Dame Chanda continued, gesturing to her green embroidered silk gown. 'At least a third of my wardrobe is by De Flimsé. My favourite perfume is *Flimsé by De Flimsé*. My second favourite perfume is *Whimsé by De Flimsé*, which I am wearing as we speak, and for which I am a brand ambassador and billboard model.' She held a hand to her chest and lowered her head, taking a little bow.

'What a coincidence,' said Frank, sniffing at his wrists. 'I'm wearing *Whimsé by De Flimsé For Himsé.*'

Jack caught Morrigan's eye, and they both had to look away quickly, trying not to grin.

'Oh, I thought so, darling, you smell delicious.' Dame Chanda beamed at him, before returning her attention to Jack and Morrigan. 'Juvela De Flimsé is an icon, my dears. A giant of the Free State fashion world. She once called me her muse, you know,' she added as an aside to Frank.

'She's been to seven of my parties,' he replied, puffing himself up with pride. 'Eight, if you count the one she left in disgust because Countess von Bissing wore a gown made of summer weight fabric. In *autumn*.'

'Oh, but this is just dreadful,' said Dame Chanda, taking the paper back from Frank. 'It says here she was found early this morning, lying half-buried in the snow, eyes wide open but completely, catatonically unresponsive. Nobody knows how she got there. She's in the Royal Lightwing Wunimal Hospital in some sort of . . . waking coma? They don't know when or . . . or

78

if she'll recover. Oh, poor *Juvela*. Whatever could have happened to her?'

Voice breaking, she tossed the paper down and buried her face in her hands. Frank slid off his chair, disappeared underneath the table and emerged at Dame Chanda's side, reaching up to pat her comfortingly on the shoulder, while Jupiter, Kedgeree and the others made noises of quiet sympathy.

Morrigan leaned over to get a better view of the photograph accompanying the article, and gasped. 'Oh! Oh, I've seen her.'

Dame Chanda tutted miserably from behind her hands. 'Yes, that's just what I'm saying, darling, of *course* you've seen her, it's *De Flim—*'

'No, I – I mean I *saw* her,' Morrigan clarified, snatching up the newspaper. 'Last night. On the Wunderground.'

It was the leopardwun. Juvela De Flimsé was the leopardwun who had tried to attack Baby Dave. She looked a lot more composed in her photograph, of course. It was a very glamorous shot of her attending Nevermoor Fashion Week, draped in an oversized pink pashmina, but it was unmistakeably her. She had the same big, expensive-looking diamond earring studded in the tip of one ear. She was wearing enormous sunglasses in the photo, so Morrigan couldn't tell whether her eyes were the same startling shade of green, but even so . . . she was *certain* it was the same Wunimal.

Dame Chanda looked up, frowning. 'I don't think so, darling. Juvela doesn't take *public transport*. She has a driver.'

'I heard she has a whole roster of drivers,' said Frank. 'And a fleet of motorcars.'

'*I* heard she rides a *unicorn* everywhere she goes,' said Fenestra from her spot on the floor, in a tone of mock reverence. Everyone turned to her in surprise; they'd all thought she was asleep. 'And uses it to stab people wearing last season's shoes.'

Jack, Kedgeree, Martha and Charlie put in a heroic effort not to react to this entirely inappropriate joke.

'It has to be her,' Morrigan insisted, ignoring them. 'Look, it says she was found near the Nevermoor University West Campus. That's where she got off the train, at Scholars' Crossing! Well, it's where she was forced off the train, actually.'

Morrigan recounted for them what had happened on the Wunderground the night before.

'Oh, no,' said Dame Chanda when she'd finished. 'No, no, no. That doesn't sound like Juvela at all. Juvela wouldn't harm a fly. She's a vegetarian! Well, a weekday vegetarian, but still – she would never, *ever* try to hurt a *child*.'

'But I'm telling you, she *did* try,' Morrigan insisted. 'I watched her do it. There was a whole train carriage full of eyewitnesses! Hawthorne was there too, you can ask him if you don't believe me.'

'Of course we believe you, Mog,' said Jupiter firmly, casting a pointed look at Dame Chanda, who still looked troubled.

'Oh! Yes, darling, of course,' she said hurriedly, reaching out to give Morrigan's hand a gentle squeeze. 'Of *course* I believe that you *believe* you saw—'

'But why didn't you tell me about this last night?' Jupiter interrupted. 'It sounds terrifying. Is Hawthorne's sister all right?'

'Oh, she's fine,' Morrigan replied with a shrug. 'Baby Dave has the fortitude of an ox. I didn't tell you because I forgot. It happened so quickly and . . . well, it wasn't a big deal, honestly. Just a bit weird.'

'Very weird,' Jupiter agreed. 'And very much the sort of thing Juvela's doctors might need to know about. Perhaps it could help them understand what happened to her. But otherwise, Mog,

I think we should keep this information to ourselves, all right?'

'Why?'

Jupiter pressed his mouth into a line, and he and Dame Chanda shared a sombre look. 'When it comes to Wunimals, some people already have certain . . . opinions. The tabloids love a story about Wunimals behaving badly, and a *famous* Wunimal, well . . . we just don't want anyone forming a conclusion about what happened before we *know* what happened, that's all. It wouldn't be fair to Juvela.'

Morrigan agreed to keep it quiet, but privately thought that if this De Flimsé person was as famous as they said, the tabloids would know about it soon enough. The train car had been full of people, after all.

'Right!' Jupiter snatched up his coat. 'Come on, then, Dame Chanda. To the hospital!'

The soprano rose gracefully and headed for the parlour door, glancing back over her shoulder at him in a deeply dignified manner. 'To the florist, Jove. *Then* to the hospital. We are not *monsters*.'

CHAPTER SEVEN

Rook

It was drizzling outside Morrigan's bedroom window on the day she was to return to school. She grimaced at the sight of it, rubbing her eyes as she sat up in bed (a thin, too-firm mattress this morning and one uncomfortably lumpy pillow, as if it knew she'd need the extra push to get up). The rain didn't bode well – drizzle in Nevermoor could mean a torrential downpour inside Wunsoc. Not an ideal start to the new term.

There was a soft knock on the door, but when she crossed the room to open it, nobody was there. She looked down; on the floor sat a breakfast tray with a pot of tea, a dish covered by a silver cloche and a handwritten note.

> *First day back, Mog! Huzzah!*
> *Don't forget your brolly.*
> *–J.N.*

Jupiter must have written this note days ago, she thought, and left it with Martha before heading off-realm. As a captain in the League of Explorers, he was regularly called away to travel into one of many mysterious other realms outside of their own. Morrigan didn't know much about his work in the League, but she knew it was both very important and surprisingly dull. A lot of Jupiter's missions seemed to be tedious diplomacy trips to attend coronations and summits and ceremonies.

Scowling at both the enthusiasm and the unnecessary advice in the note, she set it aside and carried the tray over to her slab-like prison bed. Underneath the cloche was a big bowl of steaming hot porridge swirled with honey, and she ate the whole thing in silence, staring out at the rain.

Morrigan knew she ought to be excited to go back to Wunsoc, but all she felt was a mild sense of underwhelm.

She had been practising Nocturne and Inferno every single night of the holidays without fail, and every morning too. The same thing, over and over: calling Wunder, lighting candles. Calling Wunder, lighting candles.

She wanted to do *more*, wanted to learn something *new*, but in truth she was too frightened to try it on her own. The act of lighting a candle made her feel formidable and in control. She didn't want to risk going too far, creating something dangerous that she couldn't contain. The memory of what had happened the first time she'd breathed fire – the way it had roared up from her lungs and set the canopy of Proudfoot Station ablaze, injuring the awful Heloise and getting Morrigan temporarily kicked out of Wunsoc in the process – was still painfully fresh. Safe to say she was hesitant to overextend herself.

What she needed was a teacher. Someone to give her lessons in the *Wretched* Arts, not the Arcane Arts. Murgatroyd the Scholar

Mistress had promised her an education in being a Wundersmith, and Morrigan was planning to gather up her courage, march right into her office and demand that she finally fulfil that promise.

Something caught her eye – the golden circle on the black station door was pulsating with a soft golden glow, the signal that Hometrain was on its way. With a resigned sigh and a last sip of tea, she snatched up her brolly and pressed the W imprint on her index finger to the circle. It swung open to reveal the small brightly lit room she knew well.

In Morrigan's Wunsoc wardrobe her usual uniform hung on the back of the door, but alongside it was a second jumper, a heavy coat, a pair of leather boots with thicker-than-normal woollen socks, leather gloves and a scarf – all in black. Morrigan's lip curled at the sight of it; clearly, the Wunsoc weather phenomenon had something unpleasant in store.

She sighed again, wondering whether she might just get away with climbing back into bed. Unfortunately, the door was one step ahead, and had locked itself behind her.

'Rude,' Morrigan said under her breath, and reluctantly got dressed.

Miss Cheery welcomed Unit 919 back to school with a rousing cheer she'd written herself that went on for a full seven minutes. (She'd even made her own pom-poms from leftover Christmas tinsel.) She handed out their new timetables, stuffed their coat pockets full of biscuits for the walk to class and then waved them off at Proudfoot Station like a proud mother hen.

On the chilly walk through the Whinging Woods, Hawthorne wasted no time in regaling Morrigan and Cadence with dramatic holiday tales from the Swift family. Their house had been invaded by a swarm of aunts, uncles and cousins from the Highlands on Boxing Day, and Morrigan hadn't heard from him since Christmas Eve.

'I've been trapped in a hell made of toddlers,' he moaned, 'with no news of the outside world. My cousin Jordy did a wee in my left dragonriding boot! I am *so* glad school's back.'

'That makes one of you,' said Cadence with a sigh. 'I had a brilliant holiday. My gran treated Mum and me to a volcanic spa break in Moonrise Bay. Ten days steaming in a hot lagoon and watching molten lava pour down the side of a mountain. It was *lush*.' She tugged her collar up against the wind, looking highly resentful.

Morrigan recapped all that had happened at the Deucalion in the week since Christmas. 'Oh – and we lost Frank for three days!' she finished. 'Turned out Fenestra had buried him under six feet of snow in the lobby and forgotten about it. I mean, he's a vampire, so it's not like he was any more dead than usual when we dug him up, but I've never seen him so cross. He *still* isn't talking to Fen.'

They said goodbye to Cadence outside in the grounds – her first lesson was in identifying poisonous fungi in the Whinging Woods, something she could not have been less excited about.

'Does anything normal ever happen at your place?' Hawthorne asked Morrigan sincerely, as they climbed the marble steps of Proudfoot House and headed inside to the bank of brass railpods. Even at this early hour, a massive queue was already forming.

She snorted. 'No. If I had my own dragon, it'd be called *Lives With Lunatics*. Oh – I almost forgot! Remember that leopardwun from Christmas Eve?'

'I was trying to forget it, to be honest,' he said, cringing. 'Still haven't told Mum and Dad about that.'

'They'll probably hear about it anyway,' said Morrigan,

'because she's famous!'

She proceeded to tell Hawthorne all about Juvela De Flimsé (he'd never heard of her either) and about Dame Chanda's visit to the hospital with Jupiter.

'But they were turned away,' she said. 'Even with their W pins. Then the next day they tried again but she'd been taken somewhere else, and they weren't even allowed to know where. Isn't that weird?'

'Bit weird,' agreed Hawthorne, sounding only vaguely interested. He craned his neck, counting the people queueing in front of them. Railpods whooshed in and out of the platform. 'We're gonna be late.'

The large brass spheres were part of the Society's internal-external travel network and could take you anywhere inside Wunsoc (if you had permission to be there), and to most of the Wunderground stations in Nevermoor. They hung suspended from a cable in a long line, and as each pod disappeared into the narrow, tunnel-like shaft at one end of the platform, another would arrive at the other end to replace it. Like gigantic beads being threaded on a wire.

'Where's your first class, should we take a pod together?' Hawthorne asked her.

'Oh, no. I'm just going down the hall.' She glanced towards the Scholar Mistresses' office, and a feeling of dread swelled up inside her. 'Free period this morning, so I'm . . . I'm going to go see Murgatroyd.'

Morrigan swallowed, picturing the Arcane Scholar Mistress warping into her ice-cold Mundane counterpart, Ms Dearborn. The transformations were unscheduled and unpredictable – like a roll of the dice. If you sought out one, you were just as likely to get the other.

'Really?' asked Hawthorne, grimacing. 'You sure you don't want to come down to the arena and watch me train instead?'

It was tempting.

'I'm moving up a weight class today,' he went on. 'Fingers Magee wants to try me on a Low Country Luminescent – their scales glow in the dark!'

Luminescent dragons *were* beautiful to watch. Morrigan supposed she didn't *have* to see Murgatroyd first thing. She could wait until lunchtime, perhaps. Or tomorrow . . .

She opened her mouth to say so, but shrieked instead as she felt a hand grasp her white collar, yanking her backwards.

'You,' said a harsh voice. 'Come with me.'

Morrigan turned to see the Scholar Mistress herself, as if summoned there by telepathic thought. 'Mrs Murgatroyd! I was . . . I was just coming to—'

'Yes, I'm sure you were. Do shut up,' grumbled Murgatroyd. She grabbed Morrigan's arm and pulled her to the front of the queue.

Morrigan looked back at Hawthorne. He winced in sympathy but stayed very still, like a small woodland unnimal hiding in the grass while a hungry bear went on a rampage.

At the front of the queue, Murgatroyd kicked a bespectacled older gentleman out of his pod and propelled Morrigan inside, following close behind.

'I say! How *very* dare— Oh, pardon me, Mrs Murgatroyd,' he said, cringing away from the Scholar Mistress and bowing his head in capitulation. 'Please, take my pod, you're very welcome, do take it.'

'Just did, dummy,' Murgatroyd snarled, and then shut the door in his face.

She pressed her imprint to a small golden circle on the wall, then instantly began operating the chains, buttons and levers in a pattern Morrigan would never remember. The pod rocked forward at great speed, then felt suddenly as if it was freefalling from a height. Morrigan grasped at a loop hanging from the ceiling, trying to steady herself.

'Um . . . Mrs Murgatroyd . . . what are we—'

'It's time.' Murgatroyd's cracked lips retreated from her brownish teeth in a terrifying leer. 'Now you've had your first C&D gathering, it's time for you to learn what you need to learn to become a productive Society member . . . before you explode like a human volcano and take us all down with you.'

Morrigan felt a little flip of excitement somewhere in the realm of her diaphragm (although it might have been nausea; the pod was travelling in a *violently* erratic manner). This was it. She was finally going to learn the Wretched Arts. Properly. Not on her own in her bedroom, with barely a clue what she was doing.

No. She was going to learn them where she should have been all along: in a classroom. With an *actual* teacher! With books and desks and exams and definitely *no* imminent danger.

Ever since Murgatroyd had promised her a chance to learn the Wretched Arts, Morrigan had wondered who there could *possibly* be to teach her? Supposedly the only people who could use them were Wundersmiths. Ezra Squall was the only other living Wundersmith, and she would have bet her favourite boots, her beloved umbrella, and the Hotel Deucalion itself that Squall had *not* been hired as her teacher.

She'd finally worked up the courage to ask when the pod came to a sudden, aggressive halt, and the door swung open on to . . .

Nothing.

They'd arrived at a tiny platform surrounded by darkness, at the end of which was a set of stairs which led down to . . . who knew?

'Well,' said Murgatroyd, cracking her neck to the side as they stepped out on to the platform. She nodded at the stairs. 'S'down there.'

'What's down there?'

'Sub-Nine.' Murgatroyd sniffed, as if she'd just said something of no real importance. As if she hadn't just brought Morrigan to the one place in Proudfoot House that was off-limits to all scholars. 'Good luck.'

Morrigan felt her stomach lurch. 'Aren't you coming with me?'

The Scholar Mistress chuckled, then instantly winced. 'Me? Not likely.'

Morrigan heard a series of tiny little pops, then a familiar *crack-crack-CRUNCH* that made her skin crawl.

'You can't just leave me here by myself!' she insisted.

'You won't be by yourself.' *Crack-pop-pop-pop-CRRRRUNCH.*

Morrigan cringed. 'No – please, *please* don't change into Ms Dearborn now!' A wave of panic rose in her chest.

The change took mere moments, but Morrigan felt as if time had stopped. Murgatroyd's cracked and purpling lips, sunken grey eyes and stooped posture warped and reformed until the person who stood before her was no longer Murgatroyd.

Nor was it Dearborn.

The changes wrought on their shared body to create this third person were subtle, yet utterly transformative. Murgatroyd's murky, mudflat eyes had sharpened not to Dearborn's cool blue but to a deep slate, framed by thick black lashes and heavy brows.

Her spine had straightened, shoulders broadened, jaw squared. The stripped-white hair had not returned to silver, but had darkened instead to pewter, and smoothed into long, thick waves. She was younger than Murgatroyd, plainer than Dearborn, taller than both. And she peered down at Morrigan with a mingled expression of academic curiosity and wolfish delight.

'Wundersmith,' the woman greeted her. Her voice was not icy, like Dearborn's, nor was it guttural and rasping like Murgatroyd's. It wasn't a voice that needed to be any of those things to be unnerving. It didn't need to shout or snap or growl. It was low and calm. Weighted and sure of itself. The kind of perfectly pleasant voice Morrigan imagined a dragon might speak with, just before it ate you.

The dark eyes blinked placidly, surveying Morrigan from head to toe before landing at last on her pale, frightened face.

When Morrigan spoke again, it was in a voice as thin as paper.

'Who are you?'

'Rook.' Her eyes gleamed almost black in the dark. 'Rook Rosenfeld. Scholar Mistress for the School of Wundrous Arts.'

CHAPTER EIGHT

Basement Nerds

'Wundrous . . . Arts,' Morrigan repeated.

The phrase was brand new and yet somehow entirely familiar. Like the bit in all of Dame Chanda's arias when everything got louder and higher and more dramatic, and you knew it was coming but even so, it sort of took your breath away when it arrived.

She waited for Rook to elaborate, but Rook did not. Instead, she turned and began to descend the stairs into darkness. She didn't ask Morrigan to follow and, for a moment, the sensible voice in Morrigan's head told her to get back inside that railpod, go straight upstairs to the dining hall, sit herself down with a nice cup of hot chocolate and pretend this never happened.

But an odd thing about living in Nevermoor, and joining the Wundrous Society, and having Jupiter North as her patron, and being best friends with Hawthorne Swift, was that the sensible voice in Morrigan's head seemed to be getting quieter by the day. Some days she could scarcely hear it at all.

Morrigan sighed, already annoyed at herself before she'd even taken a step. Of *course* she was going to follow the scary stranger down a dark stairwell into a secret basement. Of *course*.

The stairs curved around and around in a wide spiral, and Morrigan had to go slowly and trail one hand along the cold stone wall so that she didn't trip and tumble all the way down. When they reached the bottom, she followed Rook along a chilly, narrow, pitch-black passage for what felt like an age, but was probably more like a minute.

Morrigan shivered and tried to convince herself it was because of the cold. 'Where exactly are we going?'

Rook didn't answer. She didn't need to. Morrigan flinched as somewhere up ahead of them, a letter T – tilted on its side – began to glow in bright, luminescent gold, piercing the near-perfect darkness. More letters followed, blinking into life one by one, until they formed an enormous sign carved on to a stone arch above a wooden door.

The second-to-last word had gashes and scorch marks all over. It looked as if someone had tried to violently remove it, first with a blade or chisel of some sort, then with fire, and finally they had simply crossed it out and painted over the top.

THE SCHOOL OF ~~WUNDROUS~~ WRETCHED ARTS

Rook looked at the sign and gave a small, unimpressed grunt. 'Ignore the vandalism.' She lifted her hand as if to push open the door, then paused, glancing at Morrigan with a slight incline of her head. 'Ready?'

Morrigan stared up at the golden words. A tempest had begun

to gather in her stomach. Of nerves, and excitement, and more than anything, a burning hunger to know more. She felt a tiny little smile creep around the corner of her mouth. 'Yes.'

It must have been quite a grand school once upon a time, Morrigan thought – much grander, in fact, than the floors that housed the Mundane and Arcane schools. On the other side of the wooden door, she and Rook stood at one end of a long, broad hallway made entirely of white marble from floor to ceiling. There were no other doors, only tall open archways leading to vast, uninhabited chambers left and right. It was so cold their breath clouded in the air.

Rook led her past chamber after empty chamber, their footsteps echoing. Morrigan peeked through each archway, trying to get some idea of what these spaces might once have held. Were they classrooms, laboratories, workshops? But there was no furniture anywhere, just vast, empty space.

There were words carved into the arches also, and as Morrigan and Rook passed each one, they lit up on cue, glowing golden from within the stone. But they didn't give much away. They were just words in languages Morrigan didn't understand, like *Kalani* and *Hamal* and *Zhang* and *Siskin* and . . .

Wait, she thought, pausing outside one of the rooms to stare up at the glowing sign. *I know that word.*

Siskin.

Morrigan frowned. She'd read it somewhere. It was a name.

'Juno Siskin!' she cried, and her voice bounced around the space. 'Oh – *oh*! Kiri Kalani! They're all Wundersmiths – these rooms are all named after past Wundersmiths, aren't they?'

'Not just any Wundersmiths,' Rook called from up ahead, without slowing down or waiting for her. 'The original nine.'

Morrigan ran to catch up, checking each sign that blinked into life along the way. Every name she recognised gave her a strange sort of thrill. It was like walking through history. *Her* history.

She'd read about some of these people in the awful class she'd been made to take last year, *A History of Heinous Wundrous Acts*, with Professor Onstald. She'd had to study his book – *Missteps, Blunders, Fiascos, Monstrosities and Devastations: An Abridged History of the Wundrous Act Spectrum*. Onstald's book didn't have anything good to say about Wundersmiths, but Morrigan now knew for certain that at least *some* of his book – and possibly all of it – was an absolute fiction.

Magnusson. Tyr Magnusson, according to Onstald, tried to stage a political coup. He occupied the Lightwing Palace for seventy days, taking the entire royal household hostage and starving half of them to death in the process.

Williams. That had to be Audley Williams, Morrigan thought, the Wundersmith who supposedly invented the measles by accident.

Vale. Vivienne Vale, who'd lived for several Ages as a hermit, trying to write the world's first objectively perfect song, but instead wrote one that went down in history as the most annoying earworm of all time. It sent dozens of people clinically insane and was banned throughout the realm. (The song went unnamed in Onstald's book for fear of it getting stuck in the reader's head for ever.)

Had Onstald's book been right about any of them? It was wrong about Odbuoy Jemmity, who created Jemmity Park, and about Decima Kokoro, who built Cascade Towers. Jupiter had proven that by taking her to those places and showing her how profoundly brilliant they were. There were even plaques there, left over a hundred years ago by the Committee for the Classification of Wundrous Acts. Jemmity's secret theme park had not been classified a *Fiasco*, as the book would have had her believe, but a *Spectacle*, a thing of joy for deserving children. And Cascade Towers was a *Singularity*; an original work of absolute genius.

If Tyr Magnusson, Audley Williams and Vivienne Vale were as dreadful as Onstald believed, would the Wundrous Society have celebrated them with grand marble halls in their names? Morrigan doubted it.

At the farthest end of the hall, they took a sharp right into the tenth and final chamber, the smallest she'd seen so far but, in contrast to the other mausoleum-like chambers, it was comfortable and welcoming, warmly lit by gas lamps and an enormous fireplace.

The walls were littered with photographs of odd creatures, beautiful buildings and famous Nevermoorian landmarks. There was a huge, colourful map of the Wunderground, and one entire wall was covered with gilt-framed oil paintings, mostly portraits.

There was one long farmhouse-style table in the centre of the room and – a surprise to Morrigan after the deathly silence of the other empty rooms – actual *people* sitting at it, at least a dozen, maybe more. They were hunched over papers and surrounded by enormous stacks of books and piled-up teacups, everyone still and quiet and concentrating. This was a room for study.

As they entered, Rook cleared her throat. The group looked up and then leapt to their feet, practically knocking over book piles and lamps in their haste. Morrigan wondered if this visit had been sprung on them, and if they were terrified of Rook or just excited to see her. Should *she* be terrified of Rook, she wondered? She didn't seem anywhere near as bad as Dearborn.

It took Morrigan a moment to realise that none of them were, in fact, looking at the Scholar Mistress. They were staring at *her*.

And to complete this entirely unlikely scenario, they burst into applause.

'Welcome!' cried one of them, and another shouted, 'Bravo, Morrigan!' (Bravo for what, exactly, she didn't know.)

'Mr O'Leary!' Morrigan said, suddenly noticing a familiar, smiling face. She stared at her *Opening a Dialogue with the Dead* teacher, an elderly gentleman with bright, piercingly blue eyes. He leaned on a handsome carved walking stick, and his snow-white hair was combed neatly and parted down the side.

'You might as well call me Conall, Wundersmith,' he told her, eyes twinkling with merriment. 'We don't indulge in formalities down here.'

Rook gestured vaguely at the group. 'Morrigan Crow, meet the basement nerds. Basement nerds, Morrigan Crow.'

Conall arched an eyebrow at the Scholar Mistress. 'I can only presume you meant to introduce us by what you well know is our *actual* name – the Sub-Nine Academic Group.'

'Presume away,' Rook said, staring back at him.

Morrigan found that she recognised a few of the group members, by faces if not by names. Next to Conall O'Leary stood a young man Morrigan had seen on the Arcane floors, who might have been a senior scholar, or a very recent graduate, and there were a few teachers she'd seen around Proudfoot House. Rounding out the group, a foxwun wearing a coat of burgundy velvet sat calmly on the floor in front, watching her with a polite curiosity.

'Welcome!' shouted the teenager, making his way to the front of the group to shake Morrigan's hand, a little too eagerly.

'Inside voice please, Ravi. We don't want to scare her off,' said the foxwun kindly. She looked up at Morrigan and nodded. 'Hello. I'm Sofia. Unit 897. I hope you don't mind the ambush,

Morrigan, it's just that we're so happy to be meeting you at last. It's truly an honour.'

Morrigan looked around at all the faces beaming back at her and was shocked to find that she believed that improbable statement. Nobody had ever been *honoured* to meet her before.

'Sofia, Conall,' said Rook, beckoning the pair of them, 'I think we'll take Morrigan to the Liminal Hall. The rest of you just . . . carry on nerding.'

Morrigan followed Rook, Sofia and Conall from the warmth of the study room and back to the cold marble hallway. They turned left into one of the cavernous chambers, and the word *Williams* lit up above the doorway as they entered. They didn't stay in *Williams*, however, but crossed the floor into another room called *Muhrer*, which led to another called *Treloar*.

'I can't tell you how thrilled we were to learn that the Wundrous Society would have its own Wundersmith once again,' Sofia continued as they walked. 'We wanted to speak with you – to congratulate you – as soon as you made your announcement. It truly was *so* brave of you.'

'But Elder Quinn said we had to wait until after your first *C&D* meeting,' said Conall.

Morrigan looked up at him. 'So the Elders are in charge of the School of Wundrous Arts, too?'

Conall, Sofia and Rook exchanged a look.

'Let's just say there's an *extremely* unofficial understanding between the Elders and us,' said Conall carefully. 'It suits them to ask us no questions, so we tell them no lies. We think they must understand that what we're doing in the Sub-Nine Academic Group is important, even if they don't know much about it. They let us carry on quietly, so long as we don't cause them any trouble.'

Morrigan smiled at that. She found she liked the thought of

the Elders not knowing about *everything* that happened in the Society. 'What exactly is the Sub-Nine Academic Group?'

'It *was* the School of Wundrous Arts,' said Sofia. They'd entered a fourth chamber now: *Gibbs*. Every room had so far looked the same: white marble floors and walls without windows. 'But you can't have a school without any scholars, so after the last Wundersmith was exiled from Nevermoor, this floor lay empty and abandoned for a very long time. Until a few Ages ago, when the Sub-Nine Academic Group was founded here in the name of research and the preservation of important Wundersmith history.'

'We are a co-operative of likeminded scholars and researchers,' said Conall, 'with a passionate interest in the Wundersmiths. We work largely in secret, to salvage and preserve Wundersmith history, and there's no better place to learn about them than here on Sub-Nine, where they once were educated. The School of Wundrous Arts.'

'How many of you are there?' asked Morrigan.

'About fifteen or so at Proudfoot House,' he said. 'But there are others like us, dotted all around the Seven Pockets. We share information sometimes. Not many of us are audacious enough to study the so-called Wretched Arts under the Society's own nose. Though it's all academic, of course.'

'Not for me it isn't,' said Morrigan.

'No. Not for you,' he agreed, smiling. 'How extraordinary.'

'And you three are the leaders?'

Conall and Sofia shared a look.

'Well . . . we don't really have leaders, as such,' said Sofia slowly. 'And as for Rook, well . . . she, erm—'

'Oh, I'm not with them,' Rook interjected, a little disdainfully. There was a brief, awkward silence while Sofia and Conall seemed to search for the best way to explain.

'Rook just sort of . . . showed up one day,' Sofia said finally. 'About a year ago. We knew Dearborn and Murgatroyd of course, but well . . . we'd never met Rook. We weren't sure why she was here. I'm not sure she knew herself, really—'

'I felt like it,' Rook said simply.

'But she kept showing up and one day, a couple of months ago, it all fell into place. The day after Hallowmas. The day we learned we had a Wundersmith among us, for the first time in over one hundred years.'

'We realised then that Rook had first appeared around the time of your inauguration,' Conall explained, casting the woman a brief look of baffled wonderment. 'When the School of Wundrous Arts somehow realised it would be needing a new Scholar Mistress.'

Morrigan's brain stumbled a bit on that information. She glanced at Rook. 'Where . . . um . . . sorry, but where were you . . . before then?'

'Oh, you know. Around. Keeping busy,' Rook replied vaguely. She fixed Morrigan with an owlish look. 'You can't have a school without any scholars, but you only need one.'

They entered yet another room. Morrigan was trying to keep up as they moved briskly from chamber to chamber, one leading on to the next; she'd counted six so far. Sub-Nine was like a maze.

'And you're going to teach me the Wretched – sorry, the Wundrous Arts? Even though you're not Wundersmiths yourselves?'

'In a manner of speaking,' said Conall.

'For now, Morrigan, we just wanted to bring you here to try something. But your proper lessons will begin tomorrow,' said Sofia. 'We've spent weeks with Rook devising what we think will be a rigorous and challenging curriculum, and we're excited to begin.'

'I can't be here all the time, for obvious reasons,' Rook explained. 'I'll drop in when I can, but I've appointed Conall and Sofia to supervise your daily studies. The rest of the nerds are not to bother you and you're not to bother them. Understood?'

Morrigan nodded distractedly. They'd finally stopped outside a closed wooden door; the only one she'd seen so far. The name carved above it had lit up like the others as they approached, as if it could sense their presence.

'The Liminal Hall,' she read aloud. There was a small metal circle set in the centre of the door. But nobody moved to touch it. Morrigan looked from Rook, to Sofia, to Conall. 'Are we . . . going in?'

'We can't open it,' said Rook. 'Everyone here has tried their imprint . . . and we've also tried just about everything else, short of a battering ram. No luck.'

'What's in there?' asked Morrigan.

Conall cleared his throat. 'We're not . . . entirely certain,' he admitted.

It took Morrigan a moment to realise that the three of them were watching her eagerly, expectantly. 'Oh! Should I, er . . .?' She wiggled the W imprint on her index finger.

'Try it,' urged Sofia, nodding.

Morrigan felt a nervous, excited flip in her middle. She reached out and pressed her trembling index finger to the circle, and—

Nothing.

She tried again, pressing harder.

Still nothing.

Her excitement deflated. She should have known nothing

would happen. The ring was cold and unlit, after all. The only time she could open the circular seal on the door in her bedroom was when it was warm and gently pulsating with light.

She turned reluctantly to face their disappointment. Rook pressed her mouth into a line and said nothing, but Conall patted Morrigan consolingly on the shoulder.

'Ah, well,' he said in a bracing tone. 'Never mind.'

'Maybe I could . . . try again tomorrow?' she suggested feebly.

'We thought that would probably happen, Morrigan,' Sofia added. 'It's quite all right.'

That was clearly a lie, and Morrigan knew it.

Rook said nothing.

CHAPTER NINE

The Book of Ghostly Hours

There were two notable additions to Morrigan's timetable the next morning. The most exciting change was that all her previously blank periods had been filled in with four words: *SUB-NINE ACADEMIC GROUP*.

Morrigan smiled so much at the sight of those words, it made her face hurt. She couldn't wait to begin her proper lessons. Rook had said it was okay to tell Unit 919 about the School of Wundrous Arts, because they were bound by unit loyalty to keep her secrets, and of course Morrigan's conductor and patron had to know about her new classes, for practical reasons.

'But try to keep it quiet around Proudfoot House,' the Scholar Mistress had told her. 'It probably won't stay a secret for ever, but the longer we can operate without everyone else nosing in, the better. So many *busybodies* in this place.'

The entire afternoon train trip home that day had been taken up with telling and retelling the story over and over. Miss Cheery and the rest of Unit 919 had been satisfyingly shocked and excited to learn that there was a third school at Wunsoc they hadn't known about. In fact, the Hometrain journey seemed to take three times longer than usual, and Morrigan suspected Miss Cheery had taken them on a circuitous route so they could hear every tiny detail a second and third time.

'And the classrooms are all empty?' Anah asked with a little shudder. 'Spooky.'

'Do you think they'd let us come see Sub-Nine too?' asked Mahir.

'I can't believe Dearborn and Murgatroyd had another one of them just hanging out in there this whole time!' said Hawthorne.

'If you're not a whitesleeve any more,' said Cadence, 'or a greysleeve, then . . . what are you?'

Morrigan hadn't had an answer for that, but Lam pointed silently at a poster hanging on the wall of Hometrain. It had been there since the first time they'd stepped on board a year ago, but she'd not given it a thought since that day, when Miss Cheery explained its meaning to them. It was an unevenly proportioned target sign made up of three concentric circles – the large grey outer ring represented the Mundane school (or greysleeves), she'd told them. The narrower white middle ring represented the Arcane school (whitesleeves). And in the centre was a much smaller black circle, which Miss Cheery had thought represented the Society as a whole, but . . .

'Oh!' cried the conductor as she stared at the poster. She looked lightning-struck. 'Oh, I see!'

Morrigan saw it too. They all did. The existence of the School of Wundrous Arts had been right here, staring them in the face all this time.

(Disappointingly, though, when she'd entered her wardrobe

that morning, her white Arcane shirt was waiting for her, pressed and starched. Morrigan supposed it wouldn't do for her to start wearing a black shirt around Proudfoot House when she was supposed to be keeping the School of Wundrous Arts under wraps, but even so, she couldn't help feeling a bit let down. She'd liked the idea of being a blacksleeve.)

Jupiter had also listened with rapt attention when she'd burst into his study after he arrived home the night before to declare that for once, she knew something he didn't. (It really was *so* satisfying to know something he didn't. She hoped it would happen again someday.)

Morrigan was staring at her new timetable for the hundredth time, so delighted by seeing the words *SUB-NINE ACADEMIC GROUP* that she didn't notice the second addition.

'What's that smell?' asked Hawthorne.

Morrigan's brow furrowed as she cautiously sniffed the air.

'It's Thaddea's sweaty wrestling kit,' said Anah, wrinkling her nose. 'Is that still sitting there from yesterday? *Honestly.*'

'Well, I've got wrestling again this morning, haven't I?' Thaddea fired back at her as she stuffed the kit into her satchel. 'No sense washing it twice, is there?'

Anah looked exasperated. 'There's an *awful* lot of sense in doing that, Thaddea.'

'I wasn't talking about Thaddea's stinky socks.' Hawthorne held up his timetable, pointing to a class on Thursday morning. 'Look. *What's That Smell? A Masterclass in Minor Distractions.* Anyone else got that?'

'You've all got it,' Miss Cheery called out from her driver's seat at the front of the carriage. 'Everyone does *What's That Smell?* once they've been invited into the Gathering Place. Think of it as an introduction to small-scale mayhem. Clever ways to get out of sticky situations, help others and maybe even save lives by distracting and confusing the people around you. Throwing your voice, crying on cue, that sort of thing. Useful stuff – it will really help you on Golders Night, and you've only got a few weeks to prepare for that. I still use some of the tricks I learned in – OH MY DAYS, NOBODY PANIC.' Miss Cheery leapt up from her seat, eyes wide as teacups, and everyone immediately panicked.

'What? What? What? WHAT?' said Anah, jumping up from her cushion.

'STAY STILL, FRANCIS, DO NOT MOVE. THERE IS A SPIDER ON YOUR SHOULDER. I SAID DO NOT MOVE.'

'WHERE?' Francis yelped, frantically craning his neck to see his shoulders. He ran his hands repeatedly over his close-cropped hair and shook out his cloak. 'WHERE IS IT? GET IT OFF ME!'

'Calm down, Francis,' said Arch, looking terrified but determined. 'I'll help you, just stay still and stop shou—'

'GET IT OOOOFFFFFF!'

Screams, flailing and spider-searching ensued, and it took a good fifteen seconds for Unit 919 to realise they'd been had. They turned as one to glare at Miss Cheery, who was already back in the driver's seat, grinning at them.

'My mistake,' she said, shrugging as she polished off the last chocolate biscuit.

Morrigan didn't have to wait long to begin learning the Wundrous Arts; it was her first class of the day. Mrs Murgatroyd met her on the ground floor of Proudfoot House, kicked a group of senior scholars out of their brass railpod and waved a slightly embarrassed Morrigan inside.

'Watch carefully and memorise,' said Murgatroyd as she

pushed and pulled the complex sequence of buttons and levers. 'I won't always be here.'

Murgatroyd made her transformation during the journey, while Morrigan winced and averted her eyes, trying to ignore it. She would never get used to the horrible sound of the Scholar Mistress's spine cracking and popping like tiny fireworks.

When they arrived on Sub-Nine, Rook led her once again down the deserted hallway of the School of Wundrous Arts, but left her with Conall and Sofia before making a hasty retreat.

They carried on down the darkened hall, Conall leading the way. 'Have you learned about ghostly hours yet, Wundersmith?' His cane clicked sharply on the marble floor.

'No. I mean, I've only heard the phrase.' Her old teacher, Henry Mildmay, had briefly mentioned ghostly hours once during Unit 919's *Decoding Nevermoor* class, but they'd not had the chance to study them. Mildmay had betrayed her – had betrayed the entire Wundrous Society, in fact, by conspiring with the Ghastly Market to kidnap Society members and auction them off for their knacks – and she'd tried to banish him from her mind, just as he'd been banished from Wunsoc. She preferred not to dwell. 'Aren't they some sort of . . . what do you call it? A geographical oddity? Like Tricksy Lanes? Are there actual ghosts involved, or—'

'Bah. The name is a stupidity,' Conall grumbled. 'They're only called *ghostly hours* because some idiot once got the false impression that they were a phenomenon somehow created by the dead. Now we're stuck calling them that.'

'It is misleading,' Sofia agreed. 'But usefully misleading. Ask most people in Nevermoor what a ghostly hour is and they'll say it's a thing that doesn't really exist, or otherwise they know they exist and they're afraid of them. Everyone's heard an urban myth,

106

some friend of a friend of a friend who stumbled into a moment from the distant past and witnessed it as if they were there. But mostly they're hard to find unless you know what to look for, and that protects them from scrutiny.'

They stopped outside a chamber with the name *Corcoran* carved across the arch. The room itself was vast – easily the size of the Deucalion's largest ballroom – and, like all the others, it was cold, bare, windowless and dark. Morrigan shivered as they stepped inside, even though she was wearing a second jumper.

'Even here in the Wundrous Society, it's only the oddballs from the Geographical Oddities Squadron who've given them more than a passing thought. Good for us. Shame for everyone else. They don't know what they're missing.' Conall took a few steps in one direction, then another, gazing around the room, apparently looking for something. He frowned, checking his pocket watch. 'Eight-sixteen, wasn't it, Sofia?'

'Eight-seventeen,' she told him. 'We still have time.'

'Ah.' Conall glanced from his pocket watch to the centre of the room and back again. 'Three . . . two . . . one.'

Morrigan flinched as a long, tiny sliver of light appeared exactly where Conall was looking. It was as if someone had taken a very sharp knife and sliced open the air, or perhaps pulled at a tiny Gossamer thread and unravelled reality, revealing something else on the inside. She could hear distant, muffled noises from within.

Sofia went first, nudging the incision with her snout. It opened up just enough for her to slip through it . . . and disappear. Morrigan breathed in sharply, looking up at Conall, but he was unfazed.

'Nothing to fear, Wundersmith. Off we go.' He opened the air like a curtain, confidently following the foxwun.

Morrigan reached out cautiously. Her fingers met the line of light. She felt warm air and a gentle pull, like whatever was inside had arms and they were reaching out for her, welcoming her in. She stepped forward, slipped through the gap and felt time shudder.

It was the strangest sensation.

Like she was made entirely of water, and she'd somehow . . . rippled.

Sofia and Conall were waiting for her on the other side, watching for her reaction.

'Isn't that something, Wundersmith?' asked Conall. His eyes crinkled in the corners when he smiled.

It was something, all right. They were in the same room, but everything was different. It was brighter and noisier – and warmer, too. From one corner of the room came occasional blinding bursts of orange light that made Morrigan blink, accompanied by the sound of roaring flames and a smattering of cheers and applause. Whatever the show was, a small group of people dressed in old-fashioned clothes were gathered around, obscuring it from view.

'Bravo, Stanislav, bravo!' cried an elderly man. 'Extraordinary improvement in such a short time, my boy. Who's next? Amelia! Three cheers for Amelia, gang – huzzah!'

'What is this?' Morrigan whispered.

'It's okay, they can't hear us,' Sofia replied at a normal volume.

'Can they see us?'

'No. Come closer. Let's see if – ah!' She weaved between their legs and disappeared into their midst. 'Excellent choice, Conall. It's annotated.'

Nobody seemed to have noticed the presence of the three newcomers. Morrigan was reminded of Christmas night, her first year in Nevermoor. She and Jupiter had taken the Gossamer Line train – a magical, highly dangerous and decommissioned railway line – all the way to Crow Manor, her childhood home in Jackalfax, and while she'd stood in the middle of a room full of people, the only one who'd been able to see her was her grandmother. To the rest, she didn't exist. Her father had walked right through her.

'Are we travelling on the Gossamer? I've done this before – oh!' She'd bumped right into the man who'd given three cheers for Amelia. He turned and looked right at her, and she felt her face flush with heat. 'Oh – I'm so sorry—'

But the man turned away again, as if it hadn't happened.

'Come on, through we go.' Conall took hold of her elbow and steered her amongst the group.

'Are you sure – shouldn't we be more careful?'

They were actually *jostling* people. Occasionally someone flinched or even turned to look, but almost immediately their eyes would glaze over and look away again, as if it had never happened. Nobody looked at them directly.

'Your turn, Jimmy!' cried the elderly man.

One by one the group members were called on and ran eagerly to the front, where they showed off an eclectic, extraordinary range of skills. One plucked a shadow from the wall and draped himself in it like a cape of darkness. Another made a collection of three-dimensional, glowing, brightly coloured shapes seemingly from nothing, and sent them dancing through the air in formation. A teenage girl performed a series of sly impersonations of everyone else in the room, imitating their walks and posture and voices and laughter – but it was more than just an impersonation, she was *becoming* them, her features twisting and remaking themselves into exact replicas of her fellows, to their uproarious delight.

The most curious thing, however, was the words that appeared in the air beside them while they performed, scrawled in glowing letters as if by some invisible hand, hanging there momentarily until they began to fade and float away:

Veil
Weaving
Masquerade

Something *pinged* in Morrigan's memory.

Ezra Squall. The Museum of Stolen Moments.

Nocturne. Weaving. Tempus. Veil.

'Are these the Wundrous Arts?' Morrigan whispered.

'Some of them,' said Sofia. 'The person who created this ghostly hour has annotated it, so we would know what we're looking at – the mark of a dedicated historian.'

'All right, all right,' called the elderly man in charge, 'we've had our bit of morning fun. Well done, everyone, now – can tell me – yesterday's lesson, if you – and why – for ten points – but nobody ever—'

Morrigan blinked in confusion. The man's words were cutting in and out like a static-filled radio, and the room had begun to slowly dim.

'Come on, Wundersmith,' said Conall, ushering her away. 'That's our cue.'

They found the gap again, but from this side, the sliver of light was a sliver of darkness. Morrigan reached out to gently open the way back and instead of warmth, her fingers met cool air. She stepped through the strange rippling sensation again. The fabric of the world shook itself out like clean laundry.

Conall and Sofia followed her back to the cold, familiar darkness of Sub-Nine. Morrigan watched as the cut in the air stitched itself back up and the light disappeared completely. She reached out to run her hands over the spot where it had been, and felt nothing, not even a trace of residual heat.

'What was that? Where did those people come from?' she demanded breathlessly as they made their way out of *Corcoran* and down the dark hallway, and without waiting for answers, 'Can we do it again?'

'You'll do it every day, if you wish to,' Sofia told her. 'But first, we have something important to show you.'

When they reached the cosy warmth of the study room, the foxwun leapt up on to the big wooden table, which had been cleared of yesterday's teacups and paper piles and basement nerds. Cleared of everything, in fact, except one enormous book, right in the centre. It was bound in faded blue cloth, its pages swollen and warped from use.

Sofia touched it lightly with one paw. 'This book is our most treasured possession.'

It was incredibly old, but lovingly cared for, that much was plain. The corners had been stitched up neatly in blue thread where the fabric covering had frayed. There wasn't a speck of dust on it.

Morrigan ran her fingers along the black embossed title, reading aloud. '*The Book of Ghostly Hours.*'

'More of a ledger, really,' said Conall. He opened it with great care, turning to one of the early pages, and beckoned Morrigan over to see.

Each page was divided into columns and rows, each column and row filled with tiny, meticulous handwriting. Dates and places and names. Her eyes flitted across the page, trying to make sense of what she was reading.

LOCATION	PARTICIPANTS & EVENTS	DATE & TIME
School of Wundrous Arts, Sub-Nine of Proudfoot House, *Williams*	Brilliance Amadeo, Rastaban Tarazed	Avian Age, Seventh Tuesday, Winter of Six
	A conversation between Amadeo and Tarazed concerning the theory behind possible self-projected travel on the Gossamer	13:02–13:34 Ⓐ
School of Wundrous Arts, Sub-Nine of Proudfoot House, *Shaw*	Griselda Polaris, Mathilde Lachance, Decima Kokoro	Age of the East Winds, First Friday, Autumn of Eight
	An advanced workshop in Tempus given by Polaris to Lachance and Kokoro	09:52–11:44 Ⓐ
School of Wundrous Arts, Sub-Nine of Proudfoot House, *Van Ophoven*	Brilliance Amadeo, Elodie Bauer, Owain Binks	Age of Endings, Second Wednesday, Spring of Two
	A beginner's lesson in Weaving given by Amadeo to Bauer and Binks	13:00–15:47 Ⓐ

'I don't really know what I'm looking at,' Morrigan admitted.

'We wouldn't expect you to,' said Sofia. 'Morrigan, this is a list of every ghostly hour that has ever been created – at least the ones within Wunsoc. This book has helped us conduct most of our research on Wundersmiths and the Wundrous Arts. And it's going to teach you everything you need to know.'

Conall pointed to a spot at the bottom of the page. 'See that? There you go.'

Morrigan read from the last row.

School of Wundrous Arts, Sub-Nine of Proudfoot House, *Corcoran*	Caw Molloy, Hani Nakamura, Melvin Hall, Amelia Allaway, Spencer Holland-Wright, Hathaway Savage, Griselda Polaris, Jimmy Bishop, Stanislav Radkov	Age of Poisoners, Sixth Tuesday, Winter of Six 08:17–08:34 (Ⓐ)
	Morning 'free-for-all'; a warm-up showcase of various Wundrous Arts, led by Molloy and involving all contemporaneous Wundersmiths, to promote team spirit and boost morale	

She saw the name of the room – *Corcoran* – and the names of those present, and the date and time, and it all made sense.

'We travelled to the past?' she said.

'Strictly speaking, the past came to us,' said Sofia. 'A ghostly hour is a little parcel of time that has been plucked from the annals of history, to be witnessed and observed in the present day, in the exact same place. Retrieving and saving a ghostly hour is horrendously difficult – only someone with prodigious skill can do it, but done right the hours will *relive* themselves indefinitely.'

'For example,' continued Conall, 'this one here, look: First Wednesday, Spring of Two, nine o'clock. Room Tarazed. An intermediate lesson in shadowmaking.'

'Shadowmaking!' Morrigan shouted in pure delight. 'Like the man we just saw. Am I going to learn that?'

'Shadowmaking falls under Veil, so yes, all in good time.' He pointed to the last column. 'Now, this is an annually recurring ghostly hour. You see that little circled "A"? That means that every year on the first Wednesday of Spring at nine o'clock in the morning, you can watch the events that occurred in that precise location.'

He pointed out another listing on the same page. 'But look – you'll notice some of them have this little symbol here, can you see that? That little arrow circling in on itself? That means the ghostly hour exists on a perpetual loop. You could sit and observe it for the rest of your life.'

'Though we don't suggest it,' added Sofia. 'The name is deceiving in another way, too, because you'll notice they're not always hours. Sometimes they're only minutes long. Sometimes they go all day, though that's very rare.

'Morrigan, ever since we learned there was a Wundersmith among us again, Rook and Conall and I combed through the book, looking for the most useful and interesting lessons. That's what all these ghostly hours represent – lessons in the Wundrous Arts, from the best teachers in history. You will be taught directly by your predecessors, stretching back through the Ages – hundreds and *hundreds* of years. There is so much here for you to learn.'

Morrigan flipped through the ledger, more excited than she could ever remember feeling. There must have been *thousands* of ghostly hours recorded in these pages. Thousands of opportunities to witness the Wundrous Arts in action, to learn them for herself. This book was a treasure chest and a time machine and a dream come true.

She was going to become a proper Wundersmith.

Finally.

'How is any of this possible?' she asked.

'It's possible, Morrigan, through the Wundrous Art of Tempus,' said Sofia. 'Tempus is the manipulation of time in various ways – moving through it, recording and preserving it, looping it, shrinking it, stretching it—'

'Stretching it?' Morrigan looked up in surprise. 'Like Professor Onstald? That was my teacher last year, he . . . was teaching me the history of Wundersmiths, or at least he was supposed to be. But *he* could do that, he could stretch time! Are you saying that's a Wundrous Art?' She burst out laughing. 'If Onstald had known his knack was a *Wundrous Art*, he would have—'

'He did know that,' Conall said gravely.

Morrigan frowned. 'But . . . he can't have been a Wundersmith, he *hated* Wundersmiths.'

'No, he wasn't a Wundersmith.' He shook his head. 'He was one of us.'

Sofia trotted lightly to the end of the table and stood up on her hind legs, nodding at a small drawing on a piece of paper torn from a sketchbook – a very good rendering of Professor Onstald the tortoisewun's green leathery face, tufty white hair and enormous domed shell. Morrigan hadn't noticed it before. It was stuck up on the wall at a careless angle, dwarfed by the many framed paintings and printed maps that surrounded it. Written across the bottom were the words '*Sub-Nine Academic Group Founder*'.

'His record keeping was meticulous,' said Sofia.

Morrigan looked down at the pages in front of her. The hundreds of tight, nearly microscopic rows of text in neat, precise handwriting. 'Professor Onstald did this?'

'He wrote *The Book of Ghostly Hours*, yes,' said Sofia. 'And he created a few of the ghostly hours himself. But most of them already existed here, preserved by other Wundersmiths throughout history. Ghostly hours have always been used by Wundersmiths as a teaching and learning tool. Onstald found the ones that already existed, annotated them and recorded their details.'

'This book was Onstald's life's work,' said Conall, tapping the pages. 'Part of it, anyway. The other part was learning the art of Tempus. That wasn't his knack, Morrigan, it was his lifelong mission and obsession. His knack was – lord, I don't even remember, do you, Sofia?'

'No,' she said thoughtfully. 'Something Mundane, I think. I didn't really know him.'

'The point is,' said Conall, 'anyone can learn the Wundrous Arts.'

Morrigan's eyebrows shot upwards. 'They *can*?'

'Well . . .' Sofia tilted her head from side to side as if she didn't quite agree. 'I wouldn't say anyone can learn *the* Wundrous Arts, Conall. Perhaps . . . anyone can learn a Wundrous Art. At least partially. Take Saint Nicholas, he learned Inferno—'

Morrigan gasped. 'I KNEW IT! I *knew* that stuff he does had to be Inferno!'

'Some of it is,' Conall said with a disapproving grunt. 'The rest is illusion, crafty mechanics and the talents of an underpaid elvish workforce.'

'But although he's prodigiously talented,' Sofia continued as if she hadn't been interrupted, 'Saint Nick doesn't have an exhaustive knowledge of Inferno, by any means. And Professor Onstald dedicated his entire life to learning *only* Tempus. He was very good, but he didn't master it. There's simply too much to learn, one lifetime isn't enough.'

Morrigan felt her excitement wilting slightly. 'Oh.'

Sofia wrapped her bushy red tail around her body. 'That's why Professor Onstald founded the Sub-Nine Academic Group – he was trying to preserve the Wundrous Arts in the absence of Wundersmiths, some time after Squall was exiled. There were

116

nine founding members, and each vowed to dedicate their life to mastering one of the Wundrous Arts in secret, to keep that knowledge alive.

'Onstald came the closest. Others, like Nicholas and Stelaria – you'll know her as the Yule Queen, of course—'

'The *Yule Queen* studied here too?' Morrigan asked, delighted.

'Oh yes, she's quite a good Weaver. They had some degree of success, but most of those original nine failed miserably, became disheartened, and abandoned the project altogether. They passed what they'd learned on to Conall's generation, though, and his generation passed it on to the next, and then the next . . . and on we go, trying to keep the torch of knowledge burning.'

Morrigan peered curiously at the foxwun. 'Which Wundrous Art are you learning?

'Me?' Sofia chuckled. 'Heavens, no! I'm here to witness the arts, not to use them. A few of the other academics have dabbled a little – young Ravi is determined to learn Masquerade – but in recent years the Sub-Nine Academic Group has become much more focused on preserving history than reliving it.'

'For us ordinary people,' Conall explained, 'trying to learn a Wundrous Art is like trying to learn an incredibly complex language, when you don't know anyone else who speaks it and have never heard it spoken aloud.'

'I'm not very good at learning languages,' Morrigan admitted.

Sofia came closer and sat right in front of Morrigan, looking at her intently. 'He said that's what it's like for *ordinary people* to learn a Wundrous Art. For a Wundersmith, it's more like . . . suddenly remembering you've been able to speak another language all along.'

Sofia allowed this information to sink in. For some time, there was no sound but the crackling of flames in the hearth.

Morrigan stared at the pages of *The Book of Ghostly Hours*, frowning. 'I don't understand. Professor Onstald did all this – *and* spent his life learning one of the Wundrous Arts – but all he ever taught me was how evil and stupid and dangerous the Wundersmiths were. He said it was a good thing they were all dead. Was he . . . do you think he was just . . . jealous?'

Conall and Sofia shared a look.

'We know he was like that in his later years,' said Conall. 'But *that* Hemingway Onstald bore no resemblance to the one I used to know. The Hemingway I knew – my friend – was as passionately interested in the lives of the Wundersmiths as I am. But something changed in him. Couldn't say what, exactly, because the stubborn, angry old fool left the group one day and never spoke a word to any of us ever again.'

Sofia made a soft, sad noise. 'That was long before I came to Sub-Nine. But his life is a great loss for the Wundrous Society. Greater than even the Elders could possibly understand. We think his mastery of Tempus was probably unique in the living world. Not including Ezra Squall, of course.'

Morrigan thought back to Hallowmas night. The Museum of Stolen Moments. She could still see Onstald's face, still see the slow blink of his eyes as he mouthed the word 'RUN'.

'I'm sorry you lost your friend,' she told Conall.

Sofia put her front paws on Morrigan's arm, peering up at her. 'Nobody blames you for Onstald's death. You understand that, don't you? It had nothing to do with you.'

'It had a bit to do with me,' she said. 'He died saving my life, after all.'

'And that was a very noble thing to do,' said Conall. 'But it was his choice. Nobody could have persuaded Hemingway Q.

Onstald to do something he didn't want to. Believe me.'

With that declaration, Conall picked up his walking stick.

'Enough of this maudlin chatter,' he said. 'Morrigan has Wundersmiths to meet.'

CHAPTER TEN

Golders Night

The next few weeks were unlike anything Morrigan had experienced in her time at the Wundrous Society. It felt like she was standing in a sweet shop, taking her pick of whatever she pleased. *The Book of Ghostly Hours* was a feast, when for so long she had been in famine.

Even so, Rook was strict about Morrigan sticking to the timetable she, Sofia and Conall had created for her, and warned her against dropping into any old ghostly hours she pleased. They'd selected each lesson carefully, the Scholar Mistress said, to build on the last and provide a bridge to the next. So far, they had only focused on two of the Wundrous Arts: Inferno and Weaving.

'Weaving is a good skill to pick up early – the art of making and remaking the world,' Rook had explained. 'Of taking energy and matter from one source, or many different sources, and adjusting or transforming it completely. Most Wundersmiths seemed to consider Weaving the most versatile of the Wundrous

Arts, though of course not everyone would agree with that.'

Morrigan would have spent all day, every day on Sub-Nine if they'd let her. She was having the time of her life. She'd already learned greater control over Inferno (and in one particularly memorable lesson, how to breathe fire in a whole rainbow of colours), and in her Weaving lessons she was working on moving furniture across the room without touching it.

Weaving didn't come as naturally to Morrigan as Inferno had. It was *hideously* difficult to understand and even harder to perform. Moving a chair seemed like it should have been easy, but in fact she wasn't just moving a chair. She was creating a world in which the chair had moved. Or . . . she was convincing *Wunder* to create a world in which the chair had moved.

Or something like that. She was still fuzzy on the physics of it.

Either way, when Morrigan had finally made the chair fall on its side, she and Sofia had whooped in delight.

Conall had taken Morrigan to watch some more advanced lessons, too, so she wouldn't get disheartened while learning the basics. The things the old Wundersmiths could Weave were *extraordinary*. She'd watched one grow a tree from a table leg. Another had turned his own tears into diamonds.

Morrigan knew full well that she was miles away from diamond tears territory. But with every scrap of skill gained, every fragment of wisdom gleaned from one of her predecessors, her confidence grew and – even more surprisingly – spilled over into the rest of her life at Wunsoc. She still heard the occasional savage whisper in the halls of Proudfoot House, but now they seemed to bounce off her like rubber. She still had to keep up appearances as a whitesleeve, but her bizarre timetable of Arcane classes began to interest her again, rather than annoy her.

For the first time ever, Wunsoc made sense, and Morrigan made sense in it.

One Tuesday afternoon following their workshop in *Obscure Unnimal Languages*, Morrigan and Mahir packed up some sandwiches from the dining hall and took them down to the dragonriding arena on Sub-Five.

With some extra help from Unit 919's accomplished linguist, Hawthorne's Dragontongue was slowly improving (*very* slowly, according to Mahir), and he'd recently become determined to use it. Previously uninterested in learning a single word, after a year of lessons Hawthorne had become convinced that speaking directly to the dragons he trained with was the only way to achieve his ambition of one day becoming the world's greatest dragonrider.

Morrigan and Mahir observed his attempts at small talk from up in the stands, wincing every time *Burns With the Fire of a Thousand Wood-Burning Stoves* snorted steam from his nose or twitched his enormous tail with irritation. Eventually the dragon turned his back on Hawthorne quite pointedly and closed his eyes, apparently settling down in the middle of the arena for a nap.

'Awkward,' murmured Mahir.

'The thing they don't tell you in Dragontongue class,' said Hawthorne when he'd finally joined them, still glaring at the taciturn *Burns With*, 'is that you can be as fluent as you like, but if the big stupid things don't want to talk to you, you'll never get a word out of them as long as you live.'

Morrigan shrugged, unwrapping her cheese and pickle sandwich and handing half of it to Hawthorne, who gave her half of his cress and roast beef in return. 'You've only been trying for a few weeks, though, haven't you? Some of these dragons are *hundreds* of years old, Hawthorne. You might just need to have patience.'

'I've *had* patience. I'm sick of having patience, it's boring,' Hawthorne moaned. 'They're so *rude*. I mean, I can't even get so much as a *mish kadrach f'al* to my *hal'clahar fejh alm'ok*.'

Mahir made a choking noise, and hastily swallowed a mouthful of chicken sandwich. '*Hal'clahar fejh alm'ok*? Why are you telling them you've got a meat grinder at home? Don't you think that sounds a bit . . . threatening?'

'What?' Hawthorne frowned. 'No, that means *your fire burns bright as the sun*.'

'Um, *no*,' said Mahir, sounding half amused and half exasperated. 'It really doesn't. And I don't know what you think *mish kadrach f'al* means, but I wouldn't expect a dragon to tell you *your eyes are as hungry as a foot* any time soon.'

Morrigan laughed so hard she snorted chocolate milk out of her nose.

'So how come they keep letting me ride them?' said Hawthorne, scowling as he threw a paper napkin at her.

'Maybe because your riding skills are better than your abysmal Draconian. I bet they all talk about you behind your back, though.' Mahir stood up and brushed sandwich crumbs off his uniform, grinning down at them. 'I've got to go – I promised Francis I'd translate a recipe for his gran. See you on the train.'

Morrigan was still struggling to contain her giggles after they'd waved Mahir off, and Hawthorne finally gave in and laughed too, shaking his head. 'Shut up, milk-dribbler. Where have they stationed you tonight?'

'Tenterfield,' she said. 'Outside the Wunderground station. It's a grey zone. You?'

'Solsbury Station. What's a grey zone?'

'The safest and most boring place to be, apparently.' Morrigan sighed, rolling her eyes. 'Far away from all the Scaly Sewer Beast breeding hotspots, but nowhere near the Golders Night action, either. I'm supposed to stop people entering the train station and direct them to the green zones. You know – the imaginary people who definitely won't be there, because they'll already *be* in the green zones.'

'You're in for a fun night, then,' he said, smirking.

'Hate to tell you this, meat-grinder, but Solsbury's a grey zone, too.'

'Oh, *what*?' Hawthorne slumped back in his seat, stretching his legs out in front of him. 'Why have they split us up, anyway? Shouldn't we be with our own unit?'

Morrigan finished the last bite of her sandwich before responding. 'Miss Cheery said they're partnering each of us with someone more experienced, since it's our first Distraction.'

'How much experience do you need to stand outside an empty train station for three hours?' Hawthorne slid down even further until he was practically horizontal, and let out a long, low sigh like a deflating tyre. 'I should have volunteered for the sewer mission with Thaddea. At least that won't be boring.'

'Well, cheer up,' said Morrigan, scrunching up the paper bag their lunch came in as she got to her feet. 'If you *really* want to wade through waist-deep sewage, there's always next year.'

Morrigan would have chosen waist-deep sewage over being stuck with her designated 'more experienced partner' for three hours. Five minutes in, she was wishing she'd volunteered with Thaddea, too.

'Just hurry up and do it.'

She scowled. 'Do *what*, Heloise?'

'You know what . . . *Wundersmith*.'

'Shush.' Morrigan whipped around, making sure nobody had overheard. 'Are you insane? We're in public! Nobody outside the Society is supposed to know. Do you realise how much trouble you could—'

'Oh, *please*.' Heloise rolled her eyes back in her head. She held one of her throwing stars in one hand while using it to clean the nails on her other. They were painted a vibrant, venomous green to match her badly coloured hair. 'There's nobody here. Everyone's off hunting for treasure.'

'They're not hunting for treasure.'

They weren't *exactly* hunting for treasure, but they might as well have been. Golders Night turned out to be quite a clever idea, although Morrigan didn't fully understand the whole thing. It was a massive operation. The Wundrous Society had spent weeks organising it down to the very last detail, and Holliday Wu's Public Distraction Department had been promoting it to death. Excitement levels in Nevermoor were so high even the Hotel Deucalion staff had been buzzing about it.

From what Morrigan could gather, Golders Night was some sort of scavenger hunt. There were maps and riddles individualised to every citizen in Nevermoor, with routes perfectly tailored to steer everyone to designated 'green zones' – far away from any potential Project Scaly Sewer Beast spill-over – and prizes to guarantee high rates of participation.

There were only one hundred 'treasures' to be found by almost a whole city of participants, and the way people were talking about it, some of them would just about sell their own grandmother to find one. The treasure wasn't gold or jewels or anything quite so tangible. It was something most people in Nevermoor considered even more valuable: a favour from the Wundrous Society.

'Treasure, favours, whatever. It's the same thing.' Heloise hoisted herself up on to a guardrail, crossing her legs. 'My point is, *nobody's coming*. Trust me, I've done loads of these stupid Distractions, and they never put me anywhere anything interesting happens. Just shut up and get on with it.'

'Ugh, why do you even *want* me to do it again?' Morrigan snapped. 'I *burned you* the first time. Is your memory that bad?'

'You can't do it, can you?' Heloise's face split in a malicious grin. She jumped down from the guardrail and moved closer, getting in Morrigan's face. 'You can't do anything. Obviously. If the Wundrous Society really had an *actual, proper* Wundersmith – instead of a loser like you – they'd put them somewhere more *important* than out here in the middle of—'

The moment the fire blazed up from Morrigan's chest and out of her throat, singeing a street sign above their heads, she knew she'd been played like a fiddle. Heloise gasped and seemed genuinely shocked. Then she shrieked with laughter.

'Are you *insane*? We're in *public*!' she said, echoing Morrigan's earlier objection in a high-pitched, mocking voice. 'Not supposed to do that sort of thing outside the Society, are you? Wouldn't want anyone to know YOU'RE A WUNDERSMITH.'

'*Shush*, Heloise.' Morrigan glanced around nervously.

'I'm afraid I'm going to have to tell the Elders about this,' Heloise continued, tapping the steel star against the side of her leg. '*Or* you could stand against that wall while I get a bit of throwing practice in? Promise I won't aim for your head.'

'Oh, shut up.'

The older girl turned suddenly serious. 'It should have been you, you know. You should have been the one to lose your knack. Not Alfie.'

Morrigan swallowed, head spinning at the sudden change of

gears. She'd often wondered about Heloise's boyfriend, Alfie Swann, who she'd helped to rescue from the Ghastly Market. He'd once been able to breathe underwater, but his knack was stolen from him when he was kidnapped and put up for auction – nobody at Wunsoc seemed to know exactly how. Morrigan hadn't seen him at school since. She wasn't even sure if he was still a member of the Society.

'Do you . . . still see him?' she asked haltingly. 'Is he still . . .'

Heloise's eyes were suddenly red-rimmed, but she scowled, blinking fiercely.

'Knackless?' she snapped. There was a tiny catch in her voice. 'Yeah. His mum reckons—'

But Morrigan didn't find out what Alfie Swann's mum reckoned, because Heloise was interrupted by a sudden bellowing sound from down the street, and both girls jumped about a metre.

Morrigan looked around for the source of the strange noise and, to her horror, saw a large figure ambling down the middle of the street, a few hundred metres away. Had they seen the fire and come towards it?

She bit down hard on her lip. Had they seen where it *came* from?

They watched in tense silence as the figure came close enough for them to see.

'He's from the Society!' Morrigan said, a little louder than she'd intended. 'It's . . . Brutilus Brown, Thaddea's wrestling coach.'

'Oh! The bearwun,' said Heloise. 'Great. I'll just go and tell him how the nasty Wundersmith set fire to a street sign—'

'No – Heloise, WAIT!' Morrigan grabbed the older girl's arm and yanked her back against the station wall, into the shadows.

'Ow, what are you—'

'Shush. *Look.*'

There was something very wrong with Brutilus. He was behaving like a bear.

The last time Morrigan had seen him he was calmly telling Thaddea where she'd gone wrong in her last match. He'd been standing on his hind legs. Carrying a clipboard. Wearing *lycra*, for crying out loud.

Now he was tearing through rubbish bins, throwing their contents all over the ground, snorting and grunting like a rogue grizzly at a campsite.

'Is he *drunk*?' Heloise giggled.

He did seem sort of drunk, but not, Morrigan thought, in a remotely funny way. As he came closer, she noticed the line of thick white drool all around his muzzle, and the strange way he kept sniffing the air. Every now and then he lashed out at a letterbox or thumped erratically on the bonnet of a parked motorcar.

Morrigan felt sick for thinking it, but . . . he looked like a rabid unnimal.

She thought suddenly of Christmas Eve. Of Juvela De Flimsé, the leopardwun on the Wunderground. The way she'd prowled the length of the carriage, sniffing the air just like Brutilus was now, and how she'd lunged for Baby Dave with that vacant, vicious look in her eyes.

'We have to get out of here,' she whispered. 'He's going to attack us.'

'What?' said Heloise, snorting. 'No, he's not. He might be drunk, but he's still a teacher.'

At that moment, as if to prove Morrigan's point, a stray cat crossed the bearwun's path and he batted it violently out of his way, letting out a thunderous roar. The cat zoomed off and disappeared up a tree, yowling.

Heloise gasped and covered her mouth.

Morrigan looked for a way to get out of his path, perhaps some shadows that would cloak them while they slipped down a side street, but it was no good. This was a Wunderground station, so of course the whole place was lit up like a night match in the Trollosseum. They were standing in the only shadow around.

'We need to cause a distraction,' she said.

Heloise was breathing heavily, having suddenly realised the gravity of their situation. 'And then what?'

'We just need to make him look somewhere else so we can make a run for it.'

'Easy.' Heloise aimed one of her stars at a letterbox diagonally across the road, and it hit its target with a loud *ping*. The noise distracted Brutilus long enough for them to sprint fifty or so metres away from the station, stopping to duck down behind an overflowing rubbish bin.

'What next?' Heloise whispered, having apparently decided Morrigan was in charge, despite being three years older.

'I . . . I don't know, just let me think.'

Morrigan had hoped the bearwun would move towards the sound, but he'd already spotted the still-smouldering street sign where she and Heloise had been standing moments earlier. He gazed at it, transfixed, and sniffed the air. His nose quivered. His face registered confusion, then anger, and he let loose a furious roar that filled the whole street.

The noise was so close, so loud and so sudden that it made both Morrigan and Heloise jump again. Whether one of them knocked it, or the vibrations caused it to move, the lid began to slide off the bin, clattering loudly to the ground.

Brutilus turned at the sound, a low growl reverberating from deep in his chest. Morrigan's mouth was dry. She could feel the ancient, primal fear of a hunted unnimal coiling in her stomach.

He sniffed the air again. Then he stood up on his hind legs, bellowing, and – Morrigan was *absolutely certain* – his eyes flashed a bright, glowing green.

Tossing his enormous head back and forth wildly, as if he had some creature in his jaws and was trying to snap its neck, Brutilus ran straight at Morrigan and Heloise, bounding down the street on all fours.

'RUN!' said Morrigan.

They ran, right down the centre of the empty road. Morrigan's chest burned with the effort of it and her ears filled with the clash of their boots on the cobblestones and it wasn't until she heard her name being cried out some ways back that she realised Heloise was no longer running beside her.

She turned around and her eyes landed on the green-haired girl, crumpled on the ground, while the enormous bearwun barrelled towards her. She must have fallen and hurt herself, or else she was frozen with fear.

Brutilus was almost upon her. Morrigan hummed a few notes and felt her fingers start to tingle with gathering Wunder, trying to come up with a plan, but panicking— *Get up, Heloise*, she thought desperately. *Move!*

But improbably, unbelievably, Brutilus ran straight past the girl on the ground, as if he didn't even see her. He was coming for Morrigan.

So Morrigan did the only thing she could think of. She turned and kept running, and hoped that Heloise would be all right, that maybe she would even be able to go for help.

She ran fast and as far as possible, for streets and streets, zigzagging and taking unpredictable turns, but he was bigger and he was faster and he was gaining on her. She couldn't outrun a bearwun.

She had to outsmart him.

Morrigan's brain went into overdrive, taking inventory of everything she passed, anything that might help her.

Brolly Rail cable. *No platform, and you don't have a brolly.*

Tree. *He'll climb up after you.*

Fire hydrant. *No idea.*

Tricksy Lane.

Wait.

Tricksy Lane. Red Alert.

A Red Alert Tricksy Lane meant *High-danger trickery and likelihood of damage to person on entry.* Morrigan had to make a choice: risk unknown danger down a Tricksy Lane, or the absolute *certain* danger that when her body tired out, she would be mauled by a vicious nine-foot bearwun with claws the size of pocketknives. She hadn't learned enough of the Wundrous Arts yet to protect herself – maybe Inferno, but she had no idea what to do with that. Something was wrong with Brutilus. He needed *help*, not an errant fireball.

It really wasn't much of a choice.

Without slowing down, she turned into the tiny street, ready to confront whatever it had in store. She was barely three metres past the Red Alert sign when water blasted at her from every direction, filling the alleyway and her nose and mouth and ears and tumbling her over and over like she'd just fallen from a ship in a storm. Wave after wave slammed into her, and every time she managed to get her head above the surface she was hit by another.

Morrigan had no idea if bears – or bearwuns for that matter – could swim, but she knew she had an advantage over Brutilus. She knew how Tricksy Lanes worked.

She knew that if you wanted to get through one, you had to lean into whatever horrible trick it tried to play on you. Let it happen, push farther into the lane until you could hardly stand it any longer, until you thought it might just about be the end of you . . . and only then would it let you go.

At least, that was how the Tricksy Lanes she'd come across before had worked.

She stopped trying to fight against the onslaught, stopped trying to keep her head above water. She swam *into* the tumultuous oncoming waves, not away from them, diving beneath them one after the other, feeling like she might be about to drown or be swept away. There was nothing to hold on to, nothing to keep her safe.

Morrigan felt a sudden searing pain down the side of her leg and screamed underwater.

A flash of green light, a cloud of blood.

She kicked out and her foot met something solid. Brutilus Brown. His face loomed above hers briefly, all open jaws and enormous teeth and ferociously glowing green eyes, as they tumbled over each other in the water. He swiped at her again, missed, and then another wave hit and he was gone.

Morrigan tasted blood and salt. Her chest ached.

Her lungs had nothing left in them and her limbs had stopped working and she was sinking to the bottom of the alley like a stone and – oh, this was it, it was over, this was really it, and then—

Air.

Morrigan emerged, gasping, from the water at last. She slumped in a twisted heap on the cobbled ground as the ocean departed in a sudden, deafening *whoossssshh*.

Then silence.

She'd done it. She'd pushed through the trick.

132

And all she'd had to do was drown.

Every bit of her was heavy with saltwater – her clothes, her hair, her boots. She coughed up mouthfuls of it, choking and spluttering as she tried to heave air into her lungs. Her throat was burning.

But there was no bearwun in sight.

When she'd mastered her breathing, Morrigan forced herself to sit up, wincing from the pain and effort of that simple task. Her left trouser leg was torn. Big, deep claw marks ran from above her knee to halfway down her calf. She was still bleeding, and now that the adrenaline had worn off, her entire leg ached and throbbed. She wasn't certain she'd be able to stand without help.

Even more worrying, Morrigan had no idea where she was. She couldn't go back the way she'd come, that she knew. The streets were dark and she was shivering with cold and there was nobody around to help her . . .

And . . . and she'd just been attacked by a *bearwun* and *drowned*, for goodness' sake!

Suddenly, Morrigan felt like crying. She thought she might do exactly that – just sit there on the ground, in her wet clothes, and cry. A small, sensible voice in her head told her that would be highly impractical and wouldn't get her any closer to home. But the small, sensible voice sounded very far away, and frankly Morrigan just wanted it to shut up.

She closed her eyes, leaning back against the brick wall. Her breaths came in short, shallow bursts. She was so tired.

She just wanted to sleep. Just for a minute.

Her eyes fluttered open, then closed again.

The night grew dim and silent.

CHAPTER ELEVEN

Visitors

Morrigan was at the bottom of a deep, tranquil ocean, and everything was fine. She could have stayed there for ever, and perhaps she would have, but her quiet peace was interrupted.

A voice dropped into the stillness, like a pebble breaking the surface far above.

Get up, it said. *There's nobody coming to help you.*

Was someone there, or had the voice come from inside Morrigan's own head? Either way, she wasn't interested. A dark, warm blanket of nothingness had enveloped her, and she only wanted to burrow deeper into its folds.

Get up, the voice said again. *Unless you want to die here.*

'Go away,' she whispered croakily.

Silent moments passed. Morrigan slowly became aware of the steady, rhythmic sound of her own breathing, still warm in the cocoon of half-sleep.

Suit yourself, said the voice.

The sound of footsteps faded into the distance, while Morrigan floated gently up, up, up into consciousness.

Her eyes fluttered open. She was alone.

One deep, shuddery breath, and then another. Clenching her jaw as tight as she could, Morrigan began to pull herself up the alley wall, sliding bit by bit and trying to put her weight on her good leg. She'd almost made it to a standing position when her good leg gave out beneath her and, slipping sideways, she landed heavily against the cobblestones.

Morrigan cried out at the flash of pain that radiated down her leg, and stayed statue-still for a long time until it diminished to a dull throb. She listened hard for any sound – footsteps, a distant voice – and again contemplated staying put until help magically arrived.

But the streets were still. The voice in her head was right. Nobody was coming.

'Get up,' she told herself through gritted teeth. 'GET. UP.'

It took her ten minutes, a lot of groaning and shivering and a very stern self-talking-to, but she made it to her feet and began her slow, squelching journey, keeping her eyes open for a street sign or landmark she recognised. Once she knew where she was, she was certain she could figure out a way home. That's what she was good at.

She pictured a map of Nevermoor inside her head. Usually it gave her a strange sort of comfort. She liked the way it was disorderly and chaotic, and yet it could be memorised and mastered. The monster could be tamed.

But something was wrong now. The streets in her head were jumbled, and she couldn't quite keep the map in focus.

She'd barely made it half a block from the alley when a manhole in the middle of the street flew open.

'What *now*?' she groaned, swaying on the spot. Had she wandered into a red zone, right in the middle of Scaly Sewer Beast territory? Was this yet *another* thing that wanted to kill her tonight?

But up from the sewers came half a dozen black-clothed, sweaty-faced Society members, dropping their equipment right in the middle of the street to high-five each other, chug bottles of water and drop to the ground from exhaustion.

'Morrigan?' said a familiar voice, and Thaddea's wild ginger head came into view. Her horrified expression suggested that Morrigan must look about as terrible as she felt. 'Morrigan, what's – your leg – you're bleeding! What *happened*?'

'S'just a scratch.' Morrigan had always wanted to say that about an injury that was demonstrably *not* a scratch. She felt quite pleased with herself for having sufficient wits about her when the opportunity arose. But even as she shot Thaddea a proud grin, she felt it sliding woozily off her face.

'Whoa, whoa – easy now,' said Gavin Squires, and Morrigan felt a pair of muscular arms grab her around the waist as the ground came suddenly closer. He had a strong whiff of the sewer about him.

'You smell . . . terrbel.'

'Right, she needs a hospital. Macleod, send up a flare, let's get a medic down here.'

'No,' said Morrigan, while the street tilted nauseatingly around her. 'Hotel.'

'She's delirious,' said a third voice, a woman. 'We're getting you to the hospital, dearie. The *hospital*. Don't worry—'

'HOTEL,' Morrigan shouted, and then in a slurred clarification she added, 'Doolekion. Doykelion. Durkel . . . loyne,' before the world went sideways, then black.

Morrigan did not wake up in the Hotel Durkeloyne, or in any hotel.

At first, she thought she was at home. That perhaps Room 85 was annoyed with her again and had transformed her bed into some weird, uncomfortable slab. But no. Apparently, that was what passed for a bed in the Wundrous Society Teaching Hospital.

It took several minutes to piece together the night's events, while her brain slowly stretched itself awake. She remembered a lot of water. She remembered being attacked by Brutilus Brown, and . . . had Thaddea been there? Was that how she got to the hospital?

Morrigan's left leg was neatly bandaged, and it throbbed dully in time with her pulse. She tried to bend her knee but failed, groaning loudly as the pain shot all the way down to her toes.

'Got yourself a nasty scratch there, pet,' drawled the bored-looking nurse who brought her breakfast. 'You've had a rubbish night, haven't you?'

Understatement of the Age, thought Morrigan. Slowly, gingerly, she propped herself up on her pillows to look around. Half the other beds on the ward were occupied, mostly by grown-up Society members, and one or two scholars. She'd never been in a hospital before. It was very . . . clean. And white. And it smelled a bit weird.

'Not my best,' she croaked in agreement. 'I got chased by a bearwun and then I drowned.'

'Oh aye,' said the nurse, with minimal interest. He lifted Morrigan's wrist to take her pulse, making a note on his clipboard.

'That's dreadful, that is. Mrs Rooper over there slipped getting out the bathtub. Terrible night all round.'

'Was anyone else brought here last night?' asked Morrigan. 'A girl named Heloise?'

'The green-haired drama queen? Aye. Treated her for shock.' He leaned in, rolling his eyes, and whispered, 'Draped her in a blanket and sent her on her way.'

So, then. Playing dead *had* been the smart tactic. Morrigan winced as her leg seized with sudden pain, fervently wishing she'd thought of it herself.

'Does anyone . . . um, know I'm here? My patron, or . . .'

'Ginger fella? Big flirt? Thinks he's funny?'

'That's the one.'

'Pet, I had to tell him to jog on. Never met such a hoverer!' he said indignantly. 'Said I'd send for him when you woke up, so I suppose I should go and—'

'MOG! Mog, you're awake! I'm here!' Jupiter's voice boomed through the double doors before they'd even fully opened.

'—let him know,' the nurse finished, rolling his eyes again as he moved on to his next patient.

Jupiter's hair was standing at an odd angle on one side of his head and his eyes were wide, as though he'd not slept all night. He crossed the room in three enormous strides and enveloped Morrigan in a bone-crushing hug.

'I – Jup— okay, then.' She crumpled and let herself be held tight, just for a minute.

Once they'd collected themselves, Morrigan told Jupiter the whole story from start to finish, piecing together her hazy, jagged memories as she went and watching his face grow paler and his fingernails shorter with every awful detail. When she got to the bit about drowning in the Tricksy Lane, he made a weird squeaking noise, jumped up and started pacing back and forth at the end of her bed, running his fingers agitatedly through his beard.

'But, you know.' She gave a casual shrug, hoping he would take the hint, sit down and be cool. 'It's fine. I'm fine. Everything's fine.'

Jupiter shot a pointed look at her bandaged leg, not bothering to dignify her comment with a response. Then he swept out of the hospital, pledging to find Brutilus Brown before he could harm anyone else.

Morrigan wasn't sure this was his greatest idea ever, and she said so as he ran for the door, but of course he wasn't in the right frame of mind to workshop a better plan. She waved him off with a resigned sigh, feeling quite certain that by morning he'd either have had Brutilus Brown sentenced for his crimes in a makeshift people's court or – more likely – been mauled to death.

She closed her eyes, giving in to a depth of tiredness she'd never felt before.

Jupiter returned the next day somewhat calmer, at least partly due to the influence of Dame Chanda, who'd come along too. She gathered a chorus of bluebirds to sing Morrigan a get-well-soon song, and squirrels to help fluff her pillows. Except the squirrels either didn't know how to fluff pillows or didn't care to; instead they went around stealing grapes from bedside tables and causing general mayhem, until Nurse Tim demanded that Dame Chanda either call off her menagerie or leave.

Only Wunsoc members or immediate family were allowed inside the teaching hospital, so the Deucalion staff had loaded Jupiter and Dame Chanda up with chocolates, fruit, books, flowers, cards, helium balloons and an old, half-chewed rubber toy that wheezed like a duck with bronchitis when you squeezed it (from Fen). Jack sent along a handwritten card that simultaneously managed to be quite sympathetic about Morrigan's injury, and quite insulting about her being the precise kind of idiot who was destined to get herself mauled by a bear one day and how they should have seen it coming.

'Well, it wasn't a bear actually, it was a bearwun,' Morrigan muttered as she propped the card up on her bedside table. 'Who's the idiot now, *Jack*?'

Dame Chanda regaled her and Jupiter with gossipy stories from the rehearsals for her new opera, *The Maledictions*, and promised to take Morrigan backstage at the Nevermoor Opera House as soon as her leg had healed. But Morrigan wasn't really interested in the romances and rivalries of the opera world; all she wanted to hear about was Brutilus Brown, and she changed the subject the second it was polite to do so.

'Do you think he's . . . do you think it could be like what happened with Juvela De Flimsé? That he could be lying unconscious somewhere?' she asked quietly. Dame Chanda uttered a horrified little yelp.

'I've been wondering that myself,' Jupiter admitted. 'I've spoken to the Elders, and I've spoken to the Stealth, and they assure me they're investigating . . .' He said this with an unspoken question mark at the end, and Morrigan understood that he had his doubts but didn't want to say so.

It was almost a week before Morrigan was allowed to go home, and in the meantime she had a steady stream of visitors. Sofia had stopped by one afternoon and sat for hours on the end of her bed, whispering stories of the most unbelievable things she'd witnessed in the ghostly hours on Sub-Nine. Miss Cheery brought her best chocolate biscuits and all of Unit 919. Thaddea was only too happy to re-enact Morrigan's dramatic fainting over and over; Morrigan *highly doubted* she'd told Gavin Squires he had pretty eyes as she was loaded into the ambulance.

Hawthorne and Cadence came every day after that, and on Spring's Eve – which was Morrigan's thirteenth birthday – Cadence managed to mesmerise Nurse Tim and the other patients so they didn't notice the fluffy, excitable puppy she'd smuggled in with her.

'You didn't tell me you got a dog!' Morrigan gasped, snuggling him up close under her chin. He licked her neck. 'What's his name?'

'No idea,' admitted Cadence. 'He's not mine, I saw him at the station and thought you'd like him.'

'You . . . bought me a puppy?'

'Borrowed,' she clarified, and then rolled her eyes at Morrigan's horrified look of realisation. 'I'm gonna take him *back*, geez. Happy birthday, you ingrate.'

Hawthorne gave her a silvery-white iridescent dragon scale he'd picked up in the stables on Sub-Five and polished to a shine.

'*Volcano In The Sky* is shedding like crazy at the moment. Hold on to that – *Volcano's* a featherweight champion, and it'll be worth LOADS if she wins the tournament this year.'

Hawthorne had pestered her to tell the Golders Night story again every day that week, and today was no exception. Morrigan obliged even though she was getting sick of telling it and Cadence was sick of hearing it.

'—and then his eyes lit up, all green and glowing, and he ran right for us, and I told Heloise—'

'Wait, hold up,' said Hawthorne. His feet were propped up on the end of the bed and he was sifting through a big box of birthday sweets Jupiter had left that morning. Cadence was ignoring them both and quietly reading a mystery novel. 'What's

141

that about his eyes glowing green? You never said that before.'

Morrigan paused, frowning. 'No. Well, I only just remembered. I don't know if . . .' She stopped again, as something else suddenly jolted into place in her head. 'Wait. Hawthorne, remember Juvela De Flimsé? Didn't her eyes flash green like that, too? Like . . . like someone had turned on a light inside them.'

'Dunno,' he said, shrugging. 'I didn't see any flashing green eyes.'

Cadence looked up from her book with interest. 'Who's Juvela De Flimsé?'

Morrigan told her the tale of their strange encounter with the leopardwun on the Wunderground, slightly hampered by Hawthorne jumping in to add extra drama.

'—and she pounced on to this man's shoulders—'

'Hawthorne, don't stand on the bed, this is a hospital.'

'—then she lifted her head and *howled*—'

'No, she didn't. Cats don't howl, you're thinking of—'

'*AAAROOOOOOOOOOO!*'

'Please stop howling.'

When they eventually made it to the end of the story, Cadence said exactly what Morrigan had been thinking, even before she remembered they'd *both* had green eyes.

'It's a bit weird, isn't it – two Wunimals just attacking people out of nowhere? That's not what Wunimals do.' She'd abandoned her book entirely and was leaning forward. 'Do you reckon they're connected somehow?'

Morrigan nodded thoughtfully. 'Yeah. Maybe. Jupiter told me nobody's seen Brutilus Brown since Golders Night . . . and Juvela still isn't awake yet, as far as we know. What if nobody's seen Brutilus because—'

'Because they haven't found his body yet,' Cadence finished for her.

'Yes! Well – no, not his body, that makes it sound like . . . I mean . . . Juvela isn't *dead*.' She turned to Hawthorne. 'You *really* didn't see the green eyes?'

'Well, to be fair,' he said, 'I was a bit more worried about Baby Dave getting her face chewed off by a vicious leopardwun. Had my mind on other things, didn't I?'

'Right,' said Morrigan, scratching behind the puppy's ears. 'I guess so.'

She made a mental note to tell Jupiter about it next time she saw him.

The novelty of being in hospital had well and truly worn off towards the end of the week. The food was boring, the bed was uncomfortable, and Morrigan found it almost impossible to sleep through the night.

Most annoyingly, her injury was sufficiently interesting that every student cohort from Mundane medics to Arcane healers wanted to poke their noses into it. Nurse Tim managed their comings and goings with a stoic resignation that suggested this was all merely business as usual – making sure the sorcery scholars sterilised their healing amulets, dimming the lights for the clairvoyant who came to check how Morrigan's aura was mending, and so on. He'd barely blinked when an excited group of surgery and engineering scholars came in on the third day, offering to remove the injured leg and put in a new one that could think for itself. (Jupiter kindly showed them the door.)

After nearly a week of every kind of treatment imaginable, Nurse Tim declared that the patient was fit to go home.

'I suppose they probably all helped, really, in their own ways,' Morrigan concluded as she was packing up her gifts and cards to leave the hospital. She examined the almost-healed claw mark, hoping it would leave at least a bit of a scar.

'Oh aye, maybe,' agreed Nurse Tim, rolling his eyes. 'Or maybe it were old muggins here who stitched you up, kept your wound clean and changed your bandages twice a day. I mean, who can possibly say?'

Morrigan left him all her flowers and chocolates.

CHAPTER TWELVE

Happenchance and Euphoriana

Spring of Three

On the opening night of famed composer Gustav Monastine's newest opera, *The Maledictions*, the foyer of the Nevermoor Opera House looked like the society pages come to life. Members of the aristocracy rubbed shoulders with celebrities, while darlings of the theatre scene swanned around with fashion industry icons. It was precisely the kind of guestlist Frank would drool over.

The city's thriving Wunimal communities had come out in force too, to support the lead playing opposite Dame Chanda, celebrated moosewun tenor Theobold Marek – who was, in Dame Chanda's words, *almost* as famous as she was.

'There's a handful of other Wunimal performers among us, of course,' Dame Chanda told Morrigan backstage, as she helped the soprano into her glitteringly elaborate costume. Somewhere outside the dressing room, a stagehand gave the fifteen-minute call, and the distant sounds of an orchestra warming up filtered through the closed door. 'The wolfwun Hebrides Ottendahl, you might have heard of him. We did *Lilibet's Lament* together, back in Winter of Six. Mrs Beverly Miller, the famous duckwun mezzosoprano. Now there's a talent! She's left the opera now, we lost her to a touring cabaret, of all things. Can you believe?'

Morrigan was struggling with a row of tiny, fiddly opal buttons, and not really listening. She was starting to regret her decision to volunteer as Dame Chanda's last-minute replacement dresser for the evening (the girl who usually helped her had been struck down with a dreadful cold). She'd learned upon arriving backstage at the opera house that Dame Chanda's character had *twelve costume changes* – and that was just in the first act. Her leg had improved a lot in the two weeks since she'd left hospital, but it was still a bit stiff and occasionally gave her a jolt of pain. She hoped there wouldn't be too much running around.

'But Theobold . . . he really is something,' Dame Chanda went on, picking up a pot of face powder and puffing great clouds of it all over her face. 'One would think a moosewun *might* have an impressive baritone, but for such an exquisite tenor voice to come from that big antlered – oh!' She caught sight of something in the mirror and gasped. 'Morrigan, my sweet, I think we have a loose thread on this sleeve, will you – that's it, carefully now. Don't pull too hard, it might unravel. There mustn't be a single stitch or sequin out of place. We must bring honour to . . . to Juvela's . . . to her beautiful . . .'

Dame Chanda trailed off, covering her mouth to hide a little sob as tears sprang to her eyes. Morrigan froze in a slight panic, wondering what she ought to do.

The Wunimal and arts communities had another reason for coming out in force to support *The Maledictions'* opening night. Before the fateful events of Christmas Eve, Juvela De Flimsé had singlehandedly designed every costume in the production. In the weeks after she'd been found in the snow, the newspapers still hadn't mentioned a word about her strange behaviour on the Wunderground (which made Morrigan suspect Jupiter was right about Wunsoc trying to hush things up), but they had *obsessively* covered every angle of the famous leopardwun's life prior to her mysterious coma. People from the fashion and opera worlds alike had lined up to preview the costumes before the season even began, lavishing praise on them as extravagant, intelligent works of De Flimsé's peculiar artistic genius.

Morrigan looked around the room for something that might help, her gaze finally landing on a box of tissues. She grabbed at them like a lifejacket on a sinking boat and thrust them in front of the soprano.

'Juvela . . . wouldn't want you to be upset tonight,' she said, offering a small, sympathetic smile in the mirror.

'No.' Dame Chanda sniffed. She returned Morrigan's smile, plucking a tissue from the box. 'No, you're quite right, darling. Tonight is a celebration! And as they say, the show must go on.' She rose fluidly from her seat, turning to strike a dignified pose. 'How do I look?'

Morrigan took in a sharp breath. The villainess Euphoriana stood before her, resplendent in a gown of deep purple and midnight black silk, shot through with a bright metallic sheen. The fabric seemed to float on her skin, pooling on the floor around her feet like oil. Draped across her shoulders was a cape of black roses, stitched together with fine silver thread and interspersed with intricate beadwork. Curling upwards from her head was a tall, elegant crown that resembled a pair of horns, hand-carved from solid onyx by Juvela herself.

Morrigan was so awestruck she could barely speak.

'Magnificent,' she said at last. Dame Chanda beamed.

Morrigan hadn't expected to enjoy the opera very much, truth be told. It was one of the reasons she'd been happy to volunteer as Dame Chanda's emergency backstage helper, instead of joining Jupiter, Frank, Martha and Fenestra in the box (she'd been somehow unsurprised to learn her patron had his own box at the Nevermoor Opera House – there was a little plaque on the door with his name on it and everything).

Jack had regretfully declined his opening night invitation, citing too much schoolwork, but he'd privately warned Morrigan that opera was quite boring, so she'd better practise looking interested and not falling asleep.

But when the lights went up and Euphoriana sang her first notes, Morrigan found herself utterly spellbound. As she watched from backstage, the sweeping music and emotional performances seemed to reach right inside her chest and poke her in the heart.

Between urgent moments of wardrobe madness, Morrigan pieced together the story of Queen Euphoriana, a woman feared and hated by her people. As a young spoiled princess, she once was rude to a troubadour in her court, laughing at his strange music and language. The troubadour cursed her to be misunderstood by everyone she met, for the rest of her life.

Years later, the maligned Queen Euphoriana has grown bitter and hateful, until one day she falls in love at first sight with a traveller called Happenchance, played by Theobold. But everything she does to show her love for him goes tragically wrong. All the words that come from her mouth are in a bizarre language he can't understand. A rose she offers him is covered in thorns that prick his fingers and make him bleed. She gives him the finest horse in her stables as a gift, and it immediately kicks him in the head (the horse was played by an actual horsewun actor, who Morrigan thought pulled off the stunt *very* convincingly). But somehow against all odds, he falls in love with her too.

Dame Chanda's grief and frustration as Euphoriana was palpable, and even though Morrigan couldn't understand a word that came out of the soprano's mouth, there were moments when she found herself almost moved to tears.

'*I am but a lonely traveller,*' sang Theobold as the wayfaring Happenchance. '*And my weary heart is lost. But in you I find a love that I must win at any cost.*'

'*Shludenverdis groll flambolicus, menk plim dooliandoo blub blub blub,*' responded Dame Chanda's Euphoriana. (Morrigan thought the last bit more closely resembled the sound a fish makes underwater than actual words.)

It was their final duet before intermission, and the audience was enraptured. Morrigan could hear actual *sobs* coming from the front row. The combined voices of Dame Chanda and Theobold the moosewun rose dramatically, as did the orchestra, building to the Act One finale.

Meanwhile, there was something of a kerfuffle happening behind the curtain, on the opposite side of the stage to where Morrigan was standing. She peered around the costumed players and painted scenery to see the horsewun actor whinnying madly, rearing back on to his hind legs and stomping his hooves on the ground. A good half-dozen stagehands were trying to calm him down.

'*To you I pledge my life, and to you I give my heart,*' warbled Theobold from downstage, completely oblivious to what was happening behind the curtains.

'*Floonk merk-begerk crindinglis, wimbly ploodful humben pppfffflllfflfllt,*' Dame Chanda sang in heartfelt response. (The last bit was just one long raspberry.)

The horsewun shook his head wildly and let out a piercing bray, but it was drowned by the music from the orchestra swelling to a crescendo. Morrigan felt her pulse quicken. Some of the ensemble had gathered behind her in the wings and were talking in hushed, worried voices.

'What's Victor playing at?' whispered a voice from behind her. 'Is he trying to go back on?'

'He's not meant to be in this scene!'

'That's what they get for hiring a *horsewun*,' muttered an actor dressed as one of Euphoriana's guards. 'Amateur. I could have played that part.'

The man playing the troubadour gave a derisive snort. 'You need hooves to play that part, Stephen, you pillock— Oh, I say! What the devil's got into him?!'

It happened so quickly that nobody could do anything to stop it. Morrigan watched in silent horror as the horsewun galloped furiously on to the stage, ploughed right through the painted scenery, and ran Dame Chanda down.

Queen Euphoriana's onyx crown tumbled from her head as she fell to the floor with a sickening *thud*. There seemed to be some confusion about whether this was part of the performance, until the orchestra abruptly stopped playing and Theobold shouted, 'Victor! What are you *doing*?' at his horsewun colleague now galloping madly in circles. Dame Chanda remained lifeless and still.

Morrigan felt like her heart was pounding somewhere in her throat, but she squeezed her fists together and forced herself to call Wunder. This wouldn't be like Christmas Eve on the train, when she stood frozen with Hawthorne and Baby Dave. It wouldn't be like Golders Night, when she was *again* too slow to act and ended up simply running for her life. She wouldn't stand by and do nothing this time, too shocked and too frightened to use whatever meagre skills she possessed. There was no time to worry about being seen.

'*Morningtide's child is merry and mild . . .*'

Wunder swarmed to her in an instant, the quickest it ever had. It gathered and gathered and *gatheredgatheredgathered*, as furiously fast as her own gathering panic. She took hold of the curtain, trying to steady herself somehow. It felt like she was standing in an ocean while waves of Wundrous energy crashed over her.

'Victor – please, stop!' shouted the stage manager, rushing on to the stage with her arms outstretched. Victor let out a frightening, screeching sound.

Morrigan swayed on the spot. '*Eventide's child is*— NO!'

The horsewun reared up on his hind legs, hooves towering above Dame Chanda, poised to land on her head.

Morrigan had thought to breathe a short, sharp burst of fire in Victor's direction – just enough to surprise him, maybe to buy a moment or two so that someone could get Dame Chanda out of harm's way.

But that wasn't what happened. There *was* a short, sharp burst – that much worked, at least – but it didn't stop there. With a sudden, terrifying *whoosh*, the curtain she was holding on to caught fire. It spread with alarming speed, like something alive and vengeful, and the theatre filled with screams – first from backstage, and then from the audience, who had finally realised this was *not* part of the opera.

Victor veered away from Dame Chanda at the last minute and, without missing a beat, began to run straight for the fire with a sudden fierce purpose.

The curtain came down like a wall of flame, bringing the

rigging down with it in a tremendous crash. This only made the horsewun wilder and angrier – more than angry, he was *savage*, filled with a furious, frenzied energy that he seemed unable to control. Even amid Morrigan's own panic, she could still recognise panic in another. Victor was throwing his body around like there was something inside him trying to get out. She could see the whites of his eyes; he was frightened of what was happening to him.

And then – there it was again. A dangerous flash of green light behind the horsewun's eyes. Just like Juvela. Just like Brutilus. Before she even realised what she was doing, Morrigan had run out on to the stage after him.

The horsewun leapt from the stage like a possessed show horse, and the audience – who were already streaming towards the exits, away from the fire – scrambled to move aside as he galloped at full speed up the centre aisle of the theatre. The exit doors were closed, but Victor was like a freight train and smashed straight through them, leaving screams and shards of splintered wood in his wake.

Barely a second later the audience's terror was renewed as a gigantic grey furball leapt from the box nearest the stage, jumped lightly over several rows of seats and landed in the aisle. Barely losing a second of momentum, Fenestra barrelled towards the broken doors and out of the opera house, in pursuit of the mad horsewun.

Jupiter swung himself over the balcony and jumped down on to the stage (rather less gracefully than Fenestra, but without breaking a limb, at least), making a beeline for Dame Chanda and yelling instructions to the opera house staff.

'Get that fire out, now – don't you have more extinguishers? Well, *get them*!' He pointed at the stage manager. 'You! Call for

152

an ambulance. Get all these people out of the theatre and into the lobby. But don't let anyone leave! The Stink – I mean, the police – will want eyewitness accounts. Chanda, no, don't move – stay still, everything's fine.'

The soprano stirred very slightly, mumbling and lifting a delicate hand to her head. Jupiter knelt beside her, looking up at Morrigan as he took off his velvet jacket and folded it into a pillow for Dame Chanda's head.

'You okay, Mog?' he asked.

Morrigan looked from Jupiter to Dame Chanda to the burnt-out remains of the wooden scenery on stage, covered in white extinguisher foam and still smouldering in places.

She nodded, but she most certainly was not okay. None of this was.

CHAPTER THIRTEEN

'Wunimal Shock at Nevermoor Opera Horse!'

'Extraordinary. Absolutely extraordinary.'

Dame Chanda was propped up on a daybed surrounded by cushions, blankets and open newspapers, while clouds of golden smoke whorled around her. She ought to have been in her suite – the doctor had told her she mustn't move from her bed for at least three days – but she'd grown bored by noon and insisted on being carried to the Smoking Parlour on her chaise longue like a queen in a litter. There were legions of devoted Deucalion staff who were only too happy to oblige, and the ensuing rush to be chosen for the honour nearly resulted in fisticuffs between one of the young groundskeepers and a sous chef.

'What's extraordinary?' asked Morrigan, jumping up for the fifth time to plump Dame Chanda's cushions. 'Is that one of your reviews?'

'Reviews?' huffed the soprano. Even with a broken wrist and a bandage covering half her head, she looked every bit as regal as she had the night before, dressed as the elegant Euphoriana. '*Reviews*? What reviews? There isn't a single review of *The Maledictions* anywhere. Not in the *Sentinel*, not in the *Morning Post*, not in the *Looking Glass*.' She held up the front page of Nevermoor's trashiest tabloid.

Morrigan frowned, trying to make sense of the headline. 'They misspelled—'

'Yes, they think they're being *funny*.' Dame Chanda sniffed, tossing the offensive paper aside. 'It's all about the horsewun and his . . . whatever that was. Barely a word about my performance, or Theobold's! And they didn't even *mention* the De Flimsé costumes.'

Morrigan picked up the discarded paper and began to read it, her frown deepening.

WUNIMAL SHOCK AT NEVERMOOR OPERA HORSE!

The superlative soprano Dame Chanda Kali was injured in a vicious and unprovoked attack by a rabid Wunimal on the opening night of Gustav Monastine's opera The Maledictions *yesterday. Onlookers at the scene talked of the terror they felt as the disgruntled equine cast member, Victor Oldershaw – playing the role of 'Horse' – brutally trampled the leading lady during the first act finale.*

Many have speculated as to the motivation behind the attack.

'He's very ambitious, Victor,' said ensemble actor Stephen Rollins-Huntington. 'Very driven, you know. I'm just saying, he'd do anything to get his teeth into a

bigger part. No one's quite sure how he got to play
'Horse', to be honest – plenty of people have told me
I'd have been a natural for it, and of course I've much
more experience in the theatre. What happened there,
that's what I'd like to know.'

Morrigan looked up from the paper. 'Do the police think it was a deliberate thing, then? That the horsewun – Victor – that he *meant* to attack you?'

'The police think no such thing, darling,' said Dame Chanda. 'There isn't a single word in there about what the police think. This is all about what the *Looking Glass* wants people to think. I contacted them this morning to give my version of events, but of course they weren't interested. The *Glass* has never been renowned for its quality investigative journalism, but they are *quite* well known for slandering Wunimals every chance they get. Poor old Victor.'

'Why don't they like Wunimals?' Morrigan asked as she skimmed the article for a second time. 'Jupiter said the same thing at Christmas, when I told him about De Flimsé on the Wunderground. He said, "The tabloids love a story about Wunimals behaving badly."'

Dame Chanda gave a deep sigh, then winced as she adjusted the bandage on her head. 'Darling, you know better than anyone, people hate what they are afraid of, and they are *most* afraid of what they don't understand. Wunimals are still something of an enigma, I suppose, and therefore some people see them as a threat. Especially – though of course, not exclusively – the older generations.'

'Why?'

'Well, of course for us *youth* – ' (Morrigan tried not to raise

156

her eyebrows too high at that statement; Dame Chanda was at least twenty years her senior) – 'Wunimals have always been part of the landscape. It's easy for us to forget that Wunimal rights are a fairly new thing – but it was only eight or nine Ages ago that it was legal to keep some Wunimals as pets.'

This was news to Morrigan. 'As pets. You mean, like . . . like *pets*? Like unnimals? With collars and leashes and – and cutesy nicknames?' She felt queasy even saying it.

'Mmm, and sometimes as witches' familiars.' Dame Chanda's face was grim. 'Thankfully, we live in a fairer, more enlightened Age. Though some still wish we were in the dark.' She threw a dirty look at The *Looking Glass*. 'Morrigan, my darling, I have a chill. Throw that worthless thing on the fire for me, won't you?'

Fenestra and Jupiter had both been gone when Morrigan woke up, and they still hadn't appeared when Jack arrived home from boarding school at lunchtime.

Jack wasn't due home until the following weekend, but he said he'd seen the article in the *Looking Glass* and wanted to make sure Dame Chanda was all right. The ailing soprano declared him 'the dearest, most thoughtful boy who ever lived', and gave him the honour of refilling her teapot.

'There seems to be some confusion about what happened last night,' Jack said to Morrigan later that afternoon. They were hanging around the lobby, playing card games and watching for Jupiter's arrival. Morrigan was determined to interrogate her patron the second he walked in the door. 'Some of the papers are reporting that there was a fire, and it startled the horsewun and he bolted from the theatre, knocking Dame Chanda over. Others are saying someone lit the fire deliberately. Oh, and . . . do you have a nine?'

'Go fish,' said Morrigan, chewing on the side of her mouth. Jack groaned as he added another card to his already loaded hand. 'Those things all happened. Just . . . not in that order. Do you have a queen?'

He curled his lip and tossed the card at her. 'It was you, then? The fire?'

'Yep.'

Jack looked like he wasn't sure whether to laugh. 'You just . . . you just felt like setting fire to the Nevermoor Opera House, or . . .?'

Morrigan rolled her eyes. 'Don't be stupid.'

'Well, I don't know, do I?' He leaned forward and lowered his voice. 'What happened?'

Morrigan described Victor's sudden attack and all that followed.

'I didn't know what to do,' she said, 'so I just . . . I don't know, I thought I could frighten him or something.'

'Mmm. Because you're so terrifying, yeah,' mused Jack.

'Shut up.'

He smirked. 'Seven?'

'Go fish. It was just supposed to be a little burst of fire, but . . . well, you know. Fire.'

'It spreads, yeah,' he said. 'Famous for it.'

'Shut up. Ace?'

'Go fish. Anyway, seems like it worked,' he pointed out. 'It drove him away.'

Morrigan winced, remembering how Victor had become so confused and agitated by the fire that he'd ploughed right through the theatre doors. 'I guess so.'

'It's not a coincidence, though, is it?' he said darkly, leaning back in his chair again. 'De Flimsé, Brutilus Brown, now this.

It can't be a coincidence. Something's very wrong.'

Morrigan couldn't agree more. And she had a feeling that Jupiter was out there right now, trying to discover exactly what that *something* was.

Fen returned to the Deucalion a little later, but Jupiter wasn't with her and she couldn't – or wouldn't – say where he'd gone. Morrigan and Jack pounced on the Magnificat the moment she sauntered into the lobby, and followed her all the way up the spiral staircase at a trot.

'Where have you been all day?' Jack demanded.

'Nunya Business Boulevard,' said Fenestra. 'Lovely spot, wish I was there now.'

'What happened after you left the opera house?' Morrigan asked. 'Did you catch him, or not?'

'In a manner of speaking. Where's Dame Chanda?'

'Smoking Parlour,' said Jack, popping up on her other side. 'What does that mean, "in a manner of speaking"?'

'Must you *surround* me?' Fen muttered, rolling her eyes. 'It means I didn't exactly have to catch him. I chased the menace for blocks, nearly broke a leg trying to dodge all the chaos he left behind him. Two traffic accidents, three smashed-up shopfronts. Even when I finally cornered him down a dead-end alley, he tried to smash through the brick wall.'

Morrigan winced. She saw flashes of Brutilus Brown. The mindless, violent aggravation, as if he simply wanted to destroy something. Destroy *her*.

'Hurt himself badly, too,' Fen continued as they entered the Smoking Parlour. 'Blood everywhere. Then he got up and tried again. And again.'

'*What?*' said Jack. 'Why would he—'

'That horsewun was out of his mind,' came a quiet voice from the daybed, and Frank's head popped up from a pile of cushions. Dame Chanda had fallen asleep on the chaise. 'We all saw it in the theatre, anyone could tell. Completely off his rocker.'

Fen clawed at the rug in front of the fire. 'He ran into the wall *four times*. It's like there was something inside him that just wanted to create havoc. Then he turned around and looked at me, and he just . . . gave up. Lay down on the ground.'

'If a Magnificat cornered me in a dark alley,' said Jack, 'I'd probably give up and lie down too.'

'No, it wasn't like that,' Fen said thoughtfully, curling up on the floor like a cinnamon roll. 'He wasn't afraid of me. I don't think he'd even realised I was *chasing* him until that moment. He was just on a rampage. I think he'd have had a go at me too, except . . . he couldn't. He'd used every ounce of whatever he had in him. All the life drained out of his eyes. Didn't blink. Barely breathed.'

'Like Juvela De Flimsé,' said Morrigan. 'She was found lying half-buried in the snow. What happened then, Fen?'

The Magnificat yawned widely, showing a mouthful of sharp teeth, and gave a sleepy shrug. 'Stealth showed up and took him.'

'The *Stealth*?' Morrigan yelped. 'What did they say? Where did they take him?'

'No idea,' said Fen. 'They're the *Stealth*, they didn't stop for a lovely chat.'

Morrigan and Jack exchanged a look. If the elite, highly secretive Wundrous Society Investigation Department was involved, something weird was *definitely* going on.

Morrigan furrowed her brow and took a deep breath of soothing milk-and-honey smoke. Fen's description had made her think of Golders Night, and suddenly it was like she was there.

The rampaging bearwun. The horrible, claustrophobic feeling of being smashed by waves, over and again. The sudden, searing pain in her leg. The flash of . . . the *flash of green light*.

'Fen, did you see his eyes?' she asked. 'Was there anything strange about them?'

'His eyes?' Fen looked puzzled by the question. 'Not that I noticed.'

'Really?' Morrigan pressed. 'Are you *sure*? They didn't . . . turn green, or start glowing, or—'

'Positive.' The Magnificat gave another sleepy yawn, stretched out and rolled over on the rug. 'Now if you've finished pestering me, I'd like to catch up on the seven scheduled naps I've already missed today.'

CHAPTER FOURTEEN

Hollowpox

If Jupiter returned at all that night, Morrigan never saw him. The next time she laid eyes on him was the following morning, from a distance, when everyone at Wunsoc was called to the Gathering Place first thing for a critical announcement.

It wasn't good news.

'For some weeks now,' Elder Quinn told them as she took to the dais, 'we have been quietly investigating a series of incidents in Nevermoor that we believed to be related. We're now certain they are.

'Several of these you may know about – the highly publicised mystery illness of the designer Juvela De Flimsé, for example. I know some of you are also aware of a recent attack on a junior scholar, and rumours about this have been circulating.' As she said this, Unit 919 all turned to look at Morrigan, but she kept her eyes straight ahead. 'I regret to confirm what many have suspected: the attacker in that instance was one of our own. A teacher.'

The room grew still, the gathering momentarily silenced by the shock of this dreadful announcement. Then a rising tide of whispers swelled as people shared their disapproval, their dismay – and their guesses as to the perpetrator.

'A third incident,' Elder Quinn said in a raised voice, quelling the chatter, 'occurred this past weekend. You will have seen it reported in the news. Again, a Society member was the victim of a violent attack at the Nevermoor Opera House – thankfully, in both cases, the injuries were minor and the victims have made a full recovery.'

Morrigan felt an indignant twinge in her enormous claw-mark scar.

'*Minor*, was it?' she said under her breath. 'Lovely.'

Hawthorne grinned at her. 'Got to keep your leg, didn't you?'

Elder Quinn continued. 'However, these are not the only incidents we've been investigating. There have in fact been nearly a dozen so far, and that number continues to rise. These attacks present a formidable threat to the people of Nevermoor, and we are building a task force to deal with the problem as swiftly and thoroughly as possible, overseen by Elder Alioth Saga and led by Captain Jupiter North. I've asked Captain North to bring us all up to date. Jove?'

Cadence leaned over to Morrigan. 'Did you know he'd got himself involved?'

'Not exactly,' she admitted. 'Though if you look very carefully, you'll notice my complete and utter lack of surprise.'

'Doesn't he have about four hundred jobs already?' asked Hawthorne.

She sighed. 'Yup. Just what he needed, another responsibility.'

How often would this one take him away from the Deucalion, she wondered.

Jupiter hit a switch and an enormous three-dimensional map of Nevermoor was projected upwards above the dais, so bright that it illuminated the whole room. Sprinkled across the city were glowing red dots. Morrigan noticed immediately that one of them was hovering at the far western point of Grand Boulevard, where the Nevermoor Opera House was located. There was also one just outside Tenterfield Wunderground Station – where Brutilus Brown had chased her and Heloise. She counted nine others scattered randomly over the map.

Had there *really* been so many attacks? How had they been kept secret?

'I think we're all agreed that this is deeply unusual and worrying behaviour, especially from one of our own,' said Jupiter. 'I will say, firstly, that this is not a case of coordinated attacks or copycat crimes. The Stealth ruled that out early in the investigation. Yesterday our resident unnimologist Dr Valerie Bramble, and Dr Malcolm Lutwyche from the Wunsoc Teaching Hospital, confirmed what they have suspected for some time.

'The attackers have all contracted the same unknown, highly aggressive virus. It causes normal brain function to shut down, resulting in erratic, violent – and, I would like to emphasise, *completely involuntary* – behaviour.

'As I'm sure many of you have realised by now,' he continued gravely, 'there is something else the attackers have in common. They are all Wunimals.'

'What's that got to do with Dr Bramble?' someone called out from a seat near the back. 'She's an unnimologist. Wunimals aren't unnimals. Don't know how many times we have to say it.'

There was scattered applause and a few cheers from the audience for this. Morrigan turned in her seat and saw that the speaker was himself a Wunimal Minor – some sort of lizardwun,

164

she thought, judging from the greenish tinge of his skin and his bulbous yellow eyes.

Dr Bramble stood up from her seat to address the growing upset. 'Apologies for the implied slight, Mr Graves,' she said, holding a hand to her chest. 'You're quite right of course, I'm no Wunimal expert. But there have been many illnesses that originated in unnimals before migrating to Wunimal populations, and it is possible that's what happened here. I've seen similar symptoms in diseases such as Fainting Meerkat Syndrome, for example, and the Equine Racing Flu, even the Foxpox. We can't disregard—'

'This is nothing like Fainting Meerkat Syndrome,' said a little voice from one of the middle rows. Morrigan wasn't sure who'd spoken, until a small furry gentleman in a tiny bowler hat climbed up to stand on top of his neighbour's head, muttering, 'Pardon me, you don't mind, do you – cheers, Barry.' The meerkatwun cleared his throat to address Dr Bramble and the gathering. 'My Aunt Lucille died of Fainting Meerkat Syndrome. It's a horrible disease. Every time she fainted we didn't know whether she'd wake up. Then one day . . . she didn't. I miss her very much, and I won't have you suggesting she was some kind of vicious unnimal, going around attacking folks willy-nilly!'

'Hear, hear,' said the lizardwun from the back, and there was more applause and cheering.

'Dr Bramble isn't suggesting anything of the sort,' Jupiter called out over the noise. 'Let me be clear: we don't know anything, and therefore we can't rule anything out. We're determined to get to the bottom of this, and we will use every scrap of information we can find.

'We don't know how it's passed on, but the illness is spreading,' he continued without pausing, indicating the map. '*Fast*. These are the casualties of the virus so far, at least the ones we know about. The red dots indicate where the infected were when the virus peaked, before apparently exiting the body and leaving the Wunimal in a comatose state. This is what we're calling the point of culmination. This culmination period seems to last several minutes for some Wunimals, and up to an hour for others. It's marked by acts of violent, frantic, uncontrollable aggression, sometimes against others, sometimes against public property, and sometimes against themselves. This frenzied culmination – and subsequent coma – is what makes the illness dangerous not only to the Wunimals it infects, but to everyone else around them.'

'Excuse me, Captain North,' Miss Cheery called out, sticking her hand in the air. 'You just used the word "casualties". Are you saying there have been deaths?'

'Not . . . deaths, no. "Casualties" may be the wrong word.' Jupiter rubbed his left temple, looking weary. He hesitated for a moment, looking to where the High Council of Elders were seated, as if seeking their permission to reveal something. Morrigan saw Elder Quinn nod silently. 'The infected Wunimals – the ones we know about – have been moved from the Royal Lightwing Wunimal Hospital to a locked ward of the teaching hospital here at Wunsoc, where they're being cared for and monitored in isolation. The good news is, they appear to be free of the virus. The bad news is that they've been left – there's no other word for it – hollow.'

The silence in the Gathering Place was as thick as soup. Jupiter's words hung in the air, the weight of their impact threatening to drop on everyone's heads.

'When the disease – or the *Hollowpox*, we're calling it, for want of a better name – when the Hollowpox leaves the body,' he continued, 'it seems to take almost everything with it. It wouldn't necessarily be obvious to anyone who isn't like me, who isn't a Witness. But they're not *just* comatose, they're . . . sort of . . . *empty*. No sense of self, no brain activity. Completely unresponsive. We remain hopeful that these effects may be temporary, but right now it's impossible to know for sure.'

Morrigan thought back to Fen's description of Victor the day before. *All the life drained out of his eyes*, she'd said. *Didn't blink. Barely breathed.*

There was a rumbling of whispers, and people began to look around the room. There weren't nearly as many Wunimals in the Society as humans, but those present seemed suddenly more visible than ever. Morrigan watched Elder Saga the bullwun closely. His face was inscrutable.

'I know you must have questions,' said Jupiter. A forest of hands instantly shot into the air.

'What about humans?' someone called out. 'Could we catch this disease?'

'How can we protect ourselves from catching it?' called the meerkatwun, still perched on his neighbour's head.

'How can we stop the attacks?'

'Do you need volunteers, Captain North?'

'Is there a cure?'

Jupiter held up his hands. 'One at a time, please. Firstly, no, the Hollowpox doesn't seem inclined – or perhaps isn't *able* – to invade a human host. We think it can only thrive in a Wunimal body. Although, again, we're not ruling anything out.'

'Because you don't *know* anything,' Baz Charlton jeered from a few rows behind Unit 919. 'Bunch of useless know-nothings.'

Cadence made a quiet noise of disgust. 'For goodness' sake. He *never* shuts up.'

Morrigan snorted. She was glad Cadence disliked her patron

as much as she and Jupiter did, because he *was* truly awful and deserved every bit of her scorn.

On the other hand, she felt bad for her friend. Morrigan was proud to have an excellent patron that other people admired. But Cadence was stuck with horrible Baz, who didn't care about her at all, or about any of the other ten gazillion candidates and scholars he'd collected for himself. She deserved much better than him.

'Correct,' Jupiter agreed, looking Baz dead in the eye. 'This is a brand-new threat that we are all seeing for the first time. If you think you have better information than we do, Mr Charlton, then by all means – come on up and share it with us.'

'If this is only affecting Wunimals,' Baz went on, ignoring the invitation. 'Why don't we just lock all the Wunimals up together? Dead simple. They can attack each other instead of us.'

There was a sudden *BANG*. The room went terrifyingly quiet as people looked to Elder Saga, who had stamped one of his great hooves on the dais and was glaring at Baz with a face like a thundercloud.

'What?' Baz said, trying to look innocent. 'Don't mean nothing bad by it, Elder Saga. Just meant . . . you know . . .'

He trailed off, and Elder Saga remained silent, staring at him until he sank down low in his seat.

'Elder Quinn mentioned the Hollowpox task force earlier,' Jupiter carried on. 'Alongside Inspector Rivers from the Stealth, Elder Saga and I are leading the efforts to contain these attacks, to lessen their impact and hopefully to learn enough to prevent them before they occur. Dr Bramble and Dr Lutwyche are investigating the symptoms and origin of the pox itself, and Holliday Wu is managing the public distraction efforts.'

'Not doing a very good job, though, is she?' Baz piped up again. 'Considering we all read about it in the papers this weekend.'

Jupiter opened his mouth to say something, but Holliday didn't need to be spoken for.

'And what can you tell me about all the other attacks, Baz?' she said coolly, not even bothering to stand up or turn around in her seat. 'Same as what's in your head: nothing. That's because I've hushed them up. How about this? I'll do my job, and you do yours . . . whatever it may be. Presumably something that requires you to smell bad and sound stupid.'

The Gathering Place erupted into laughter, easing some of the tension. Morrigan even spotted Elder Saga having a tiny chuckle.

'What about the infected Wunimals, Captain North?' a quiet, familiar voice called out as the laughter died down. Morrigan turned to see Sofia standing up on her seat, one paw raised. She felt a sharp pang of guilt for thinking anything about this could be funny. 'The ones you said were hollow. What's going to happen to them?'

Jupiter took a deep breath before answering.

'We don't know yet,' he admitted. 'But they're safe and in very capable hands at the teaching hospital. And I promise you, we're working hard to find a cure.'

CHAPTER FIFTEEN

The Gossamer-Spun Garden

Later that afternoon on Sub-Nine, Morrigan and Sofia flipped through *The Book of Ghostly Hours*, trying to find the lesson Rook had scheduled. It wasn't the first time Morrigan had seen the study chamber empty of academics – she supposed they must have jobs to go to and classes to take – but it was surprising how deathly silent the place was without the occasional stirring of a teaspoon in a mug or discreet clearing of a throat.

The quiet felt especially palpable because of the elephant-sized Thing They Were Quite Obviously Not Discussing. Finally, Morrigan couldn't bear it any longer.

'What's your knack?'

It was not one of the many questions she had wanted to ask. She'd wanted to ask, *Are you worried, Sofia? Are you scared of catching the Hollowpox? Do you think they'll find a cure soon?* But the foxwun hadn't mentioned the morning's *C&D* gathering, and Morrigan was too nervous to bring it up for fear of upsetting her. Anyway, what would be the point? Of course she was worried. Everyone was worried.

'Me? I bring dead things to life.' Sofia ran her paw down the page nonchalantly, as if she'd just imparted the most mundane piece of information. As if she'd said, *Me? I make cheese sandwiches*.

Morrigan blinked. 'You . . . sorry, did you just say you bring *dead things—*'

Registering the new eagerness in her voice, Sofia looked up, smiling apologetically. 'Oh – ah, no. Don't get excited. It's not as good as it sounds, trust me. It doesn't work on people or Wunimals. Or large unnimals. Or small unnimals, for that matter.'

'What does it work on?'

Sofia's face turned thoughtful. 'Erm . . . insects? Some rodents? Most plants, if they're small enough and haven't been dead for very long. Essentially, if you've a bug, rat or shrub that desperately needs resurrecting, I'm your gal.'

'Oh,' said Morrigan, trying not to sound disappointed and utterly failing. 'Oh, right. Cool.'

'Not remotely cool,' Sofia said with a quiet chuckle. 'Everyone makes that same face when they find out – yes, that's it, the politely crestfallen face. Don't worry, I'm not offended.'

Morrigan felt terrible. 'No – it is cool! Honestly. I've never been able to take care of a living plant, let alone bring a dead one back to life.'

'Thanks, that's kind of you.' She brightened a little. 'I suppose it is useful sometimes. In its own little ways.'

'What about Conall?'

'Oh, Conall's knack *is* good. He's a medium – he speaks to the dead.' She paused, glancing away for a second, then murmured, 'Well. He *can* speak to the dead. He doesn't any more.'

'Why not?'

'The rumour is that something bad happened to him when he was contacting the beyond one time.'

'Something bad?' Morrigan asked, leaning forward on her elbows. 'Like what?'

'I've never asked.' Sofia glanced back over her shoulder as if to make sure they were still alone in the study chamber, and added quietly, 'But . . . it must have spooked him, because for years he's absolutely *refused* to use his knack. I almost don't want to know what it was. Conall doesn't scare easily.' She tapped a page in *The Book of Ghostly Hours*. 'Here – this is the one. The Gossamer-Spun Garden, in Van Ophoven. You're going to love it.'

| School of Wundrous Arts, Sub-Nine of Proudfoot House, *Van Ophoven* | Brilliance Amadeo, Elodie Bauer, Owain Binks

A beginner's lesson in Weaving given by Amadeo to Bauer and Binks | Age of Endings, Second Wednesday, Spring of Two

13:00–15:47

Ⓐ |

There was a bit of a walk to get to *Van Ophoven* (named for the Wundersmith Emmeline Van Ophoven). Morrigan had spent her first few days in the School of Wundrous Arts utterly intimidated by its bizarre layout. But once she'd understood the underlying principle of the place, it was easy enough to find her way around.

There were ten grand arches lining the main hall, Rook had explained to her. The first nine led to nine enormous chambers, each named for one of the original Wundersmiths (the tenth led to the academics' study room). Each of those nine chambers contained another archway leading to a *second* chamber named for a Wundersmith in the generation that followed . . . which led to another chamber named for one from the next generation . . . and on and on like branches on a family tree.

Some of these branches went more than a dozen chambers deep; in fact, the farthest Morrigan had travelled was fourteen archways along to a room called *Jemmity*, named after the Wundersmith Odbuoy Jemmity. Inside *Jemmity*, instead of another archway there was a locked wooden door like the one she'd seen on her first visit to Sub-Nine, with the words LIMINAL HALL carved above it, glowing in the stone. It was the end of the line. (Morrigan tried her imprint on that door too – just in case – but again nothing happened.)

'Will I have a room named after me here someday, do you think?' Morrigan asked.

'My understanding is that it happens when a Wundersmith turns one hundred years old. Or . . . erm, when they die. Whichever comes first,' explained Sofia.

Morrigan tilted her head to the side. 'Fingers crossed for option number one.'

'Yes, quite,' the foxwun agreed. 'Now I'm afraid I must leave you here, Morrigan – I have a class to teach up on Sub-Six. Will you manage?'

'Of course. I've visited ghostly hours on my own before.'

Sofia looked reassured. 'Good. But *please* pace yourself. Don't try to do everything at once. All right?'

'Promise.'

When Sub-Nine had been occupied and properly cared for, *Van Ophoven* must have been one of the grandest chambers of all, Morrigan thought. In its current state, it had the spectral air of a cathedral fallen into ruin, all vast crumbling stone arches and staircases jostling with half-broken marble statues.

She found the tiny sliver of light in the air and nudged it open, slipping into the ghostly hour, and her suspicion was confirmed: the *Van Ophoven* of the past was strange and beautiful. A sprawling architectural landscape so exquisite it made Morrigan's heart ache to think it no longer existed.

The Gossamer-Spun Garden.

It wasn't so much *a* garden, as a thousand different gardens. Or a thousand different drawings of a garden, from a thousand different imaginations, rendered in three dimensions by a thousand different artists. There were trees that grew up to the ceiling, bearing fruit of silver and gold, and rainbow vines that moved like snakes. There was a meadow of wonky sunflowers that grew high above Morrigan's head, and a fairy-sized garden with funny little red toadstools.

The lesson was led by Brilliance Amadeo, a master Weaver who had already become one of Morrigan's favourite teachers. (It was probably quite strange, she realised, to have a favourite teacher you'd never met, who didn't know your name and with whom you would never speak because they'd been dead for over a hundred years . . . but she tried not to ponder that too deeply.)

'The Gossamer-Spun Garden is over seven hundred years old,' Brilliance was saying when Morrigan arrived. She led her students down a path lined with fluffy, misshapen daisies that swayed in an imaginary breeze and gathered buzzing clouds of bright pink bumblebees. Morrigan tried to keep up, but she wanted to stop and look at *everything*. 'Its plants and flowers and unnimals never die, its vines and trees never become overgrown or unmanageable. It's entirely handmade, woven from the Gossamer threads of the world around us.'

'Who made it?' asked one of the students, a boy of maybe seven or eight.

Morrigan hadn't quite got used to seeing children so young

inside these ghostly hours. Nowadays you had to have turned eleven to join the Wundrous Society. But Sofia had explained to her that in the old days, whenever a Wundersmith died, an elite Wunsoc team was sent out to scour the whole realm for the child who'd been born to take their place. Sometimes it took days, sometimes months, sometimes years. But whenever they found the child, their family would gladly hand them over to be raised at Proudfoot House and trained by the other Wundersmiths. It was seen as the highest honour.

When she'd asked Sofia, Rook and Conall which Wundersmith *she* might have replaced, and who among the original nine was her predecessor, she was disappointed to find they couldn't answer her. After Ezra's generation, Conall said, Wunsoc stopped searching for those children. They weren't keeping track any more.

Morrigan couldn't help wondering – perhaps a little bitterly – what kind of Wundersmith she'd be by now, if she'd been studying the Wundrous Arts since she was small.

'We all made it,' Brilliance told the little boy. 'Everyone who ever trained in the School of Wundrous Arts. You might think of it as a collaborative canvas, shared through the Ages. Wundersmiths have long practised the Wundrous Art of Weaving here in the glorious, cocoon-like safety of everyone else's past mistakes,' she said, her eyes twinkling. 'Look over here – see this . . . I suppose one might call it a flower?'

The students laughed, and Morrigan could see why. The 'flower' resembled the floppy, misshapen ear of an elephant, all grey and leathery and tough-looking. It was like a very young child's impression of a flower, if all they had to draw with was a grey crayon held between their toes.

'Would you believe me if I told you that this flower here is the earliest known work of Alfirk Antares?' Brilliance asked, smiling fondly at it.

Morrigan had no idea who Alfirk Antares was, but obviously these children did. They all three gasped, absolute glee written on their faces, as if they'd been told their favourite celebrity was in the room.

'He was only nine years old,' she said, nodding at the older boy. 'Same age as you are now, Owain. Not bad for his first act of Weaving, don't you agree?'

Brilliance led them farther along the winding path, reaching out now and then to touch the velvety petals of a rose, or to run her hand lightly through a pond, leaving a rippling bioluminescent trail in its wake. The children followed, open-mouthed, eyes darting in every direction. Morrigan tagged along, feeling equally overcome.

'We're going to start with the same task assigned to every Wundersmith who has ever entered this garden,' explained Brilliance. 'You will find it incredibly simple to do, yet monstrously difficult to do *well* . . . and just about impossible to do perfectly. But that's what the Gossamer-Spun Garden is for. Mistakes. Failures. Practice. So let's get started. Please begin by calling Wunder.'

Morrigan followed along with Brilliance Amadeo's instructions, and to her delight, found she could do everything the other children could. Brilliance was a wonderful teacher – patient and precise, always willing to slow down or repeat herself if needed.

'Weaving is about expanding and contracting one's imagination, weaving together thought, creativity and physical matter to manipulate and create our own reality and bring our vision to life. When we Weave, we pull threads from the Gossamer

176

and rearrange them, either to influence the world as it is . . .' (She paused for a demonstration, and sent an enormous vine swinging back and forth in the distance with a casual flick of her wrist.) '. . . or to make the world anew.'

When Morrigan narrowed her eyes, she could just make out the near-invisible, golden-white threads of Wunder working in the background, darting to and fro to obey their unspoken orders. She soon discovered that she needn't properly sing to call Wunder – it was paying closer attention to her, like a dog alert to its owner's every command. In this kind of constant communication, she only had to hum a few notes to feel it gathering to her fingertips.

Just like Ezra Squall, she thought. The realisation came with a strange mix of alarm and satisfaction.

By the end of the lesson, the students – Morrigan included – had each created their own clumsy sort of pseudo-flower, wonky and imprecise as they were. In her little patch of garden bed, Morrigan had tried to make a red rose and instead ended up with something more closely resembling a vomit-green pillbox hat on a stick.

Nevertheless, it was *her* vomit-green pillbox hat on a stick. Morrigan felt elated. *I made that*, she kept thinking while she sat on the ground, staring at it. She felt powerful and brilliant and artistic, just like Brilliance Amadeo herself.

As the ghostly hour ended, her ghostly teacher and classmates and the beautiful Gossamer-Spun Garden began to cut in and out, turning staticky, and then simply melted away. Morrigan preferred to watch the ghostly hours she visited fade, rather than step back through the curtain. It took longer, but there was something calming about remaining still whilst the world around her gently transformed.

Once Morrigan was alone again in *Van Ophoven* she noticed how tired she felt. No, *exhausted*.

She should leave. She should get up and go back to the study chamber, or . . . what time was it? Maybe she ought to be going back to Hometrain by now.

Get up, she told herself silently. But nothing happened.

She was so tired. Her body simply wouldn't do what she was telling it.

It made her think of Golders Night, when she'd sat on the ground in that alleyway, soaked to the bone and shivering, her leg bleeding and throbbing. But at least she'd known what was wrong with her then, known specifically what the obstacles were to her getting up and moving: the cold, the blood loss, the pain.

This felt different. Not as if something had happened to her body, but as if something had been removed from it. Drained out of her. Just . . . gone.

How long had she been *sitting* there, she wondered? Her muscles were aching all over, and she was so cold, and *so* hungry. Had she ever been fed in her entire life?

'Didn't pace yourself, did you?'

She very slowly turned to see Rook towering above her.

'Sofia said she warned you. Better listen next time.'

Rook didn't seem to expect a response, which was good because Morrigan was too tired to give one. Instead, the Scholar Mistress put a bowl of chicken soup in her hands, dropped a blanket clumsily around her shoulders, and sat down beside her.

They sat in reasonably comfortable silence, broken only by the scraping of spoon against bowl. Rook seemed quite content to stare around the empty room, lost in her own thoughts. It took quite some time, and almost all the soup, but eventually Morrigan had recovered enough energy to speak.

'Where do the others go?' she asked.

'Hmm?' Rook snapped out of her dreamy state, turning to Morrigan with a suddenly sharp gaze. 'Where do what others go?'

'You know,' mumbled Morrigan. It was uncomfortable, having the Scholar Mistress's full attention, without anyone else in the room to buffer it. Like standing under a spotlight. 'The others. Ms Dearborn and Mrs Murgatroyd.' She hastily shoved another spoonful of soup into her mouth, wondering if she'd overstepped a boundary.

But Rook didn't seem offended. 'Oh . . . we're all in here,' she said vaguely.

Morrigan swallowed. 'All the time?'

She nodded. 'All the time. Only . . . some of us are more here than others. I don't come out much.'

'Why not?'

'I don't have a reason to. Or at least, I haven't until recently.'

Morrigan paused before asking her next question, but finally decided if there was ever a moment to ask, this was probably it. 'How many of you are in there?'

A tiny muscle twitched at the corner of Rook's mouth. 'Nobody's ever asked us that before.'

'Are there more than three?' Morrigan pressed.

'Oh . . . I should imagine so.'

'How can you not *know*?'

Rook tilted her head to one side, then the other, looking pensive. 'Have you ever seen a set of nesting dolls, Wundersmith? You open up one, and there's another inside her, and another inside *her*, and another . . .' Rook trailed off, and Morrigan nodded. 'Could one of those dolls know how many others she carried within her? Could she know how deeply they'd nested inside her brain?'

Morrigan couldn't have explained why, but those words made her skin crawl.

'The answer is no, of course she couldn't,' continued Rook. 'Not for sure. But perhaps sometimes, if she paid close attention, she might feel them . . . rattling around in there.' She gave her head a tiny shake from side to side. 'Who knows? Maybe we go on for ever.'

Morrigan thought about that for a moment. She was picturing not dolls, but the chambers of Sub-Nine, following on one after the other like branches on a tree. If you wanted to get to the last chamber, you had to go through all the others first. There weren't any shortcuts.

'Does that mean Dearborn doesn't know about you?'

Rook frowned. 'I'm not sure. Certainly, she and I have never met. Not in transition, I mean, the way you could say I've "met" Murgatroyd. We've never had a reason to.' She glanced at Morrigan. 'I hear she's awful.'

Morrigan nearly spat out her soup. 'She's, um . . . not great.'

'Yes, that's the rumour.'

On the train ride home, all Unit 919 wanted to talk about was the Hollowpox – rumours they'd heard, theories they'd come up with. There'd been mounting speculation all over Wunsoc about exactly *who* was under quarantine in the teaching hospital, how dangerous they were, and whether any other famous Wunimals like De Flimsé might have been infected.

'I heard they've got an elephantwun in there,' said Mahir. 'Apparently, some boy from Unit 916 helped bring him down. He saved a whole platoon of the Stealth from being trampled.'

'Ugh, that's just *Will Gaudy*,' Thaddea groaned. 'There's no elephantwun, he's been trying to get people to believe that stupid story all day. *I* heard there's a giant snakewun in there that went on a killing spree and ate a family of five and they all had to be cut out of its stomach.'

'Thaddea!' said Miss Cheery. 'That's horrible, and very much *not true*.'

'It's only what I heard, miss.'

The conversation went around in circles, and Morrigan found it hard to focus. She truly *was* worried about the Hollowpox, but . . . she couldn't stop thinking about the afternoon she'd just had. About Brilliance Amadeo. About the Gossamer-Spun Garden and her tiny contribution to it.

She was really becoming a Wundersmith. It was a thought she kept having to squash down, because it was making her grin like a fool while everyone else was discussing the awful matter of the outbreak.

'What did you do today, Morrigan?' Lam asked her quietly as Hometrain pulled into Station 919.

Morrigan jumped at the sound of her name.

'Oh! Um . . . I made a flower.'

'That's nice.'

CHAPTER SIXTEEN

Extracurricular Activity

The warning signs showed up one morning later that week. Walls and bulletin boards of Proudfoot Station, normally filled with club sign-up sheets and lost property notices, were suddenly plastered with black-and-white posters. Cadence yanked one down and read it out loud to the rest of 919.

HOLLOWPOX

Are you at risk?

What is the Hollowpox?
A potentially deadly disease caused by a virus which spreads
quickly from Wunimal to Wunimal.

Could you be infected?

If you are a Wunimal and are experiencing extreme
distraction or forgetfulness, dramatically increased appetite,
an inability to sleep or sit still, or episodes of aggression
that seem out of character, <u>you may be infected</u>.

If you have experienced any of the above symptoms,
see Dr Bramble, Dr Lutwyche or a member of staff
at the Wundrous Society Teaching Hospital
<u>IMMEDIATELY</u>.

**BE MINDFUL
DON'T DELAY
ASK FOR HELP**

'Was this your patron's idea?' Mahir asked Morrigan. 'Is he
still leading that task force?'

Morrigan took the poster from Cadence. 'He is, but . . .
this doesn't really seem like his style. No colour. Not enough
exclamation marks.'

She re-read the notice in her head. *Distraction. Forgetfulness.
Increased appetite. Inability to sleep. Aggression.* Nothing about
the eyes. Had Jupiter forgotten? She made a mental note to
remind him.

Their first lesson that morning was a workshop called *What's
That On Your Face?*, a follow-up to their previous masterclass in
minor distractions – *What's That Smell?* – from weeks earlier. As
their resident sleight-of-hand master, Arch had of course achieved
top marks in *What's That Smell?*, and nobody was surprised when

Hawthorne also proved adept at creating small-scale mayhem. Mahir turned out to be good at throwing his voice like a ventriloquist, Lam was brilliant at asking for complicated directions and talking people round in circles, and even Francis had a decent go at jumping out of a birthday cake.

But the real revelation had been Anah, whose ability to cry on cue was unsurpassed (an absolute must-have skill, the teacher had told them, when enlisting the aid of kindly strangers and getting out of trouble with the Stink). She didn't even need to fake it; she was just really good at thinking of sad things that made her cry.

The rest of Unit 919 was quite looking forward to today's workshop, and the opportunity to practise the skills they'd learned so far. But Morrigan couldn't help feeling a little frustrated. It all seemed like a colossal waste of time.

Why bother learning to shout 'FIRE' in a crowded building when she could be down on Sub-Nine, making *actual* fire? Or tending to her slowly growing patch of the Gossamer-Spun Garden? And what could their Minor Distractions teacher possibly show her that would compare with learning how to Weave still water into waves from Decima Kokoro herself? Surely, building her skills as a Wundersmith was more important than anything else?

But when she'd spoken to Miss Cheery about it, the conductor told her that Mundane and Arcane skills were still useful, and it was important to be an all-rounder.

And when she'd spoken to Rook about it, the Scholar Mistress told her it was important to remember this was a marathon, and not a sprint.

And when she'd spoken to Sofia about it, the foxwun told her it was important to go gently, to pace herself, to use caution.

But inside her head, drowning all of them out, she heard the words Ezra Squall had spoken the last time they'd met.

You are not a mouse, Morrigan Crow. You are a dragon.

'Why aren't you telling people about the green eyes?' Morrigan asked Jupiter over dinner that night.

'Hmm? Oh yes, you said . . . the eyes.' He bit the end of a spear of asparagus and chewed thoughtfully. 'Mog, what exactly did you see?'

She groaned. 'I already *told* you . . .'

'Tell me again.'

'It was the same with all three of them: Juvela, Brutilus and Victor. I know it sounds weird, but it was like someone switched on a lightbulb inside their skulls and they glowed bright green.' Morrigan paused, pushing food around her plate. 'It's just that . . . you didn't mention it during the gathering and it's not on the list of symptoms on those posters you made.'

'Oh, I didn't make those. Black and white? Not really my style,' he said. 'That was Dr Bramble's idea and between you and me, I'm not sure it was a good one. That list of symptoms is more like a list of *guesses* we've cobbled together from questioning family and friends of the infected. They were all pretty vague and contradictory, nobody seemed certain of much at all. I'm not convinced there *are* any proper symptoms before culmination.'

'You did *tell* Dr Bramble about the eyes, though, didn't you?' Morrigan pushed. 'Because that's not a guess. I saw it. Three times.'

Jupiter set down his cutlery and leaned his chin in one hand, looking at her seriously from across the table. 'I did tell her and we are taking it seriously, I promise. But Mog, so far there haven't been any other witnesses who've seen it.'

'But you believe me, don't you?'

'*Yes,*' he said emphatically. 'I believe you're telling the truth.'

His careful phrasing wasn't lost on her. She scowled. 'You believe I'm telling the truth . . . but you don't believe I saw what I think I saw. Right? You think I just imagined it or something.'

'No. I think it's entirely possible you *did* see that, but I'm afraid you're the only one who has.' He chased a single pea with his fork, trying to pierce it but never quite gaining purchase. 'But that's not why it's not on the posters, Mog. I discussed it with the task force and the Elders, and we decided that it's not a good idea to talk about Wunimals having "glowing green eyes". We're worried it might send the wrong message.'

'What do you mean?'

'People are already frightened,' he said. 'They're already poised to view the infected as *attackers*, rather than victims of an illness they can't control. If we describe them as having *glowing green eyes*, you can be sure some numpty will claim they've been possessed by demons or some such nonsense.'

'Who cares what *some numpty* thinks?'

'The thing about numpties, Mog, is that they can always find plenty of other numpties to believe their numpty nonsense. You know what they say: you're never more than six feet away from a numpty.'

'I think that's spiders.'

'Either way,' he continued, 'we're keeping it under wraps for now. If it's a symptom that only shows up during the culmination period, it won't matter much anyway. We don't need glowing green eyes to tell them apart when they're tearing through town on a rampage.'

Morrigan supposed that was true enough. She stabbed a bit of roast chicken with her fork, but didn't eat it. 'What's happening with all that, anyway? The task force. Is Dr Bramble any closer to finding a cure?'

'I don't think so. And the numbers of infected keep ticking upwards.' He closed his eyes for a few seconds, still leaning his head in his hand. Morrigan almost thought he'd fallen asleep, but then he sat up suddenly and shook it off. He looked miserable and exhausted. 'The problem is, we're only finding infected Wunimals at the point of culmination, or *after* the virus has left them catatonic, so what have we got to study? If we could at least prevent some of the attacks before they happen . . . but it's *impossible* because we don't know who's infected or how they get infected. We can't have eyes on every Wunimal in the city.'

'Why don't you tell the public?' Morrigan suggested. 'Then if they see someone acting weird, you could go and investigate.'

'I think we'll have to, sooner or later,' he admitted. 'But that's going to come with a whole new set of problems. Imagine! "Hi, everyone, please look out for Wunimals who might have a disease that could cause them to violently attack you. Oh, and you won't be able to tell who it is *until* they attack you, because we don't really know what the symptoms are, we're just guessing that it might be *these* perfectly normal things that anyone could reasonably feel at any time, whether they're infected or not. Good luck!"' He gave a short, humourless laugh. 'Bet Holliday Wu can't wait to broadcast that message.'

Morrigan had never seen her patron so dejected. She didn't know what to say, so she poured a glass of water and pushed it across the table towards him. He accepted it with a grateful smile.

'Have you seen any of the infected?' she asked. 'What do they look like afterwards? To you, I mean, as a . . . you know. As a Witness.'

Jupiter took an enormous bite of chicken, and Morrigan

knew it was so that he had time to think about how to answer.

'It's hard to describe, Mog. I've never seen anything like it. I've heard stories about *hollow people* – it's sort of a dark fairy-tale among Witnesses. Someone always knows someone who has a friend who once met a stranger who was completely hollow, but . . . I've never believed it was actually possible, until now.' He shook his head, as if he still didn't quite believe it.

Morrigan frowned. 'What do you mean, "hollow people"?'

'When I look at someone,' he said, pushing his plate aside and leaning in, '– really look at them, I mean – I see a whole, complete, unique person. I spoke to Dame Chanda this afternoon, for example, and she had a song stuck in her head; it fluttered around her ears like a moth. She was cross about something; it cast a little black shadow over her face. Beyond the surface, she was cloaked in a deep, melancholy blue, like she was under the ocean. That's the sadness she feels for her friend Juvela, I think.

'Beyond that, she has this constant, steady kindness – right here around the sternum – like a candle burning in a windowless room. Some people only ever have flashes of kindness, but hers is a permanent fixture.' He stared into the middle distance for a moment. 'Beyond *that* . . . well, I don't often look beyond that. The deeper layers are harder to unravel. People lock them down, hold them as close as possible, even if they don't realise it. That's a boundary I won't cross unless invited.

'But those Wunimals in the teaching hospital . . . there's nothing there,' he said softly. 'Nothing on the surface. Nothing underneath. No past, no present.'

'Well . . . I mean, they're *asleep*, aren't they?' Morrigan reasoned. 'Maybe when people are sleeping—'

'They're not asleep. They're not anything. Someone in a coma still has all the things that make them a person. They still have dreams and physical afflictions and the imprints other people have left on them, scars and smudges from loved ones and enemies. They still have a past. But these Wunimals, they're like . . . black holes. There's *nothing there*.'

Jupiter's eyes were wide, his pupils big and black. He was frightened. Morrigan felt the hairs on her arms stand up.

'Honestly, Mog, I'd rather be dead than hollow.'

In the weeks that followed, it became clear there was no containing the Hollowpox, even if they could distract people from it.

Their *C&D* gatherings soon became Hollowpox gatherings for all intents and purposes, with all other matters temporarily shunted aside. There'd been at least one attack every week since Christmas, and the numbers kept rising until it seemed like every second or third day there was some fresh rumour, some new tale of a rhinoceroswun running riot in a grocery store or a catwun slicing someone's face like a scratching post.

Holliday Wu warned them that it wouldn't be long before the public started connecting the dots, and the truth came out.

Meanwhile, the locked ward in the teaching hospital on Sub-Three was already full, and a second ward on its way to filling up too. The meagre hospital staff worked in rotating twelve-hour shifts to the point of exhaustion, until one day Nurse Tim marched into the Gathering Place threatening to lead his fellow nurses in a strike. In response, the Elders drafted in any Society members with medical expertise who could assist, and they came from all over the Seven Pockets without hesitation.

Even some of the students were called on to help. Senior scholars with medical experience were promoted to positions of authority on the regular wards, and junior scholars like Anah had chunks of their timetable taken over by hospital duty.

It worked out well for Unit 919, because Anah became their personal hotline to information about the affected Wunimals – her quiet, unobtrusive nature made her an excellent eavesdropper.

'They won't let us assistants see them, of course – we're not allowed on the locked ward – but I heard two of the nurses talking in the tea room,' she told the unit one morning at Station 919, while they waited for Hometrain. 'They said yesterday there were *three* Wunimals brought in the night before, a family of badgerwuns. The youngest was only our age! It's just awful.'

Morrigan didn't know why this news felt so shocking; after all, why would the Hollowpox discriminate between young and old? But somehow it made it seem so much worse to think of someone their own age, lying in a hospital bed. She couldn't stop thinking of how Jupiter had described them. *Nothing on the surface. Nothing underneath. No past, no present. Like black holes.*

Hometrain 919 pulled into the station, with Miss Cheery hanging out the side waving at them as usual, and they all piled on board. The copper kettle was already boiling. Mahir dropped teabags into a mismatched assortment of mugs, Lam doled out sugar cubes according to the individual preferences they'd all memorised by now, and Francis offered around the biscuit jar.

'This is really good gingerbread, miss,' he said in a tone of approval. He snapped a piece in half. 'Good snap. Nice and spicy. And is that . . . nutmeg?'

'I've no idea, Francis,' said Miss Cheery, biting into her gingerbread bear.

His face fell a little. 'Did you not bake it yourself?'

'No, Francis, I got it from the shop like a normal person.'

'Where were you yesterday?' Hawthorne asked Morrigan as they settled into their usual spots, rucksacks abandoned on the floor. 'Were you sick?'

'What? No, I was at school.'

'But you weren't on Hometrain in the morning.'

'Or the afternoon! We didn't see you all day,' Cadence added with a slight note of accusation in her voice. 'We were wor— I mean, Hawthorne was worried. Wouldn't shut up about it. So boring.'

'Oh. No, um, I took the Brolly Rail in early yesterday morning,' said Morrigan, stifling a yawn. 'I had a ghostly hour scheduled for five o'clock. And then I had to stay late.'

'Five o'clock!' said Hawthorne. 'There's one of those in the morning, too?'

Morrigan rolled her eyes. 'Ha very ha.'

It wasn't entirely true. She *had* come in early and stayed late, but neither of those events had been mandated by the Scholar Mistress or anyone else. The day before yesterday it had occurred to Morrigan that just because Rook carefully designed her timetable each week and she still had to attend the various Arcane and Mundane classes she'd been allocated . . . *technically* there was nothing stopping her from visiting *extra* ghostly hours.

So that afternoon, when school had ended and Sub-Nine was empty of basement nerds, she'd searched through *The Book of Ghostly Hours* and spent ninety glorious, unscheduled minutes in the company of Li Zhang, one of the first Wundersmiths. He'd demonstrated an element of the art of Veil, cloaking himself in the precise colours and texture of his surroundings, like a human-chameleon hybrid. Morrigan was swept away by the magic of it, and it was nearly dinner time when she'd finally taken a railpod home.

She'd only *watched* Li Zhang, of course. She was pacing herself and exercising caution and all that, just as she'd been warned to do. Rook couldn't have complained, and Morrigan didn't think she'd be in trouble, exactly, but even so . . . she wanted to keep her extracurricular plans to herself. For now.

'And what are they teaching you in Wundersmith school?' Hawthorne continued. 'Have you learned how to kill fifty grown men with a single glare yet?'

'A hundred grown men,' Morrigan corrected him. 'And all their mates.'

'*Please* don't start this again,' groaned Anah. She was trying to sound annoyed, but in truth she looked a little scared.

'Have you made any monsters yet, Morrigan?' Thaddea piped up. 'Something with lots of teeth I hope.'

'And lethal breath,' added Cadence. 'And poisonous B.O.'

Morrigan grinned. 'All good ideas. I'll make a note.'

'And have you set a date to conquer Nevermoor?' Mahir asked her in a serious, business-like tone. 'I think a Monday would be best. Everyone'll still be tired from the weekend, so they won't be up to much fighting back.'

'Excellent point.' Morrigan shifted a bit on her floor cushion, getting comfortable. 'I'll put it in the conquering calendar.'

'Will you be conquering all of Nevermoor at once, do you think?' Arch asked, holding out an imaginary microphone to catch her answer. 'Or taking it borough by borough?'

'Borough by borough, I'd have thought,' said Morrigan. 'Seems more manageable. Pass the biscuits, please.'

'Miss Cheery, make them *stop*!' Anah whined. After several weeks of this repetitive joke (started, of course, by Hawthorne), she was still the only member of Unit 919 who didn't find it funny.

Morrigan, on the other hand, was delighted that her unit had decided to tease her about being a Wundersmith. It was much better than being afraid of her. She was holding on to the hope that one of these days, prim, panicky Anah might forget to be frightened and join in instead.

Morrigan stayed after school again that day. At the end of her final lesson she asked Hawthorne to tell Miss Cheery she'd get herself home, then raced back down to Sub-Nine, clutching a scrap of paper on which she'd copied down the details of a promising ghostly hour.

LOCATION	PARTICIPANTS & EVENTS	DATE & TIME
School of Wundrous Arts, Sub-Nine of Proudfoot House, *Kingston*	Griselda Polaris, Decima Kokoro, Rastaban Tarazed, Mathilde Lachance, Brilliance Amadeo, Owain Binks, Elodie Bauer	Age of Endings, Ninth Thursday, Spring of Nine
		15:25–16:42
		Ⓐ
	Griselda Polaris demonstrates the Wundrous Art of Ruination	

It was a glorious lesson, one of the best Morrigan had had so far, featuring a Wundrous Art she'd not yet heard of let alone witnessed and a Wundersmith – Griselda Polaris – more gifted than any of the others she'd seen.

But none of that, it turned out, was what would make this ghostly hour her most memorable yet.

Morrigan stood among the other Wundersmiths watching Griselda as she demonstrated an act of exquisite destruction. She was so ancient she could have been mistaken for Elder Quinn's great-grandmother, but she moved with surprising grace and agility.

Ruination was the opposite of Weaving and, unexpectedly, it

seemed to take nearly as much precision and care to properly Ruin something as it did to Weave it in the first place. Griselda began the lesson with the extraordinary feat of Weaving a building from scratch – a small, perfect conservatory made of hundreds of glass panels so that it resembled a little crystal palace, reflecting and refracting light all around the enormous chamber. She was much faster and more precise than Brilliance Amadeo, who until now had been Morrigan's gold standard in the Wundrous Art of Weaving.

'Anyone can throw a rock at a window,' Griselda told the group, and then she did exactly that: lobbed a fist-sized stone at one of the panes of glass, shattering it into pieces.

'But the art of Ruination is not about using external brute force. It's about unravelling a thing from the inside, separating all its constituent parts, then breaking down *those* parts, and on and on, until you have transformed the thing, made it unrecognisable to itself. The truest, purest act of Ruination is an act of transformation.'

By the end of the lesson, Griselda and her students had broken down the glass structure again and again, until it was transformed into a pile of fine white sand.

Like Brilliance, she was an excellent teacher – watchful and patient, generous with praise but quick to correct. Morrigan got so caught up in the hour that she was utterly unprepared for its sucker-punch ending, and when the teenage boy standing next to her put his hand up to ask a question, she barely even registered his words.

She was instead watching Griselda, who turned to the boy with a warm smile and said, 'Excellent question, Mr Squall.'

CHAPTER SEVENTEEN

Ezra, The Boy

He wasn't listed in any of the hours. Not one.

Morrigan felt unbelievably stupid for not thinking of it herself, for not even *imagining* that as she dived into the well of Wundersmith history on Sub-Nine, she might one day meet a past incarnation of the Wundersmith they called *the evillest man who ever lived*. The man who had tried to lead his fellow Wundersmiths in a rebellion. Who had built an army of monsters and committed a massacre in Courage Square. Who had sent his Hunt of Smoke and Shadow to kill all cursed children in the Wintersea Republic but had decided to spare Morrigan's life for his own mysterious, deranged reasons.

The man who had once looked her in the eye and said, 'I see you, Morrigan Crow. There is black ice at the heart of you.'

But his name wasn't anywhere in *The Book of Ghostly Hours*. It had been deliberately left out.

Morrigan stayed on Sub-Nine until it was so late she thought

Martha or Kedgeree might send out a search party. She skimmed as much of the ledger as she could. She looked for listings during the Ages she knew he lived in Nevermoor, just over a hundred years ago – the Age of Endings, and the Age of the East Winds. She looked for the names of Wundersmiths who must have been around at the same time as Squall, the likes of Brilliance, Owain and Decima. She flipped to the listing for her first-ever lesson in the Gossamer-Spun Garden and ran her finger down the page until she found the names in the 'Participants & Events' column: Brilliance Amadeo, Owain Binks, Elodie Bauer.

But there had been one girl and *two* boys in that lesson, Morrigan was sure of it.

How had she paid so little attention? She'd already *seen* him! Probably dozens of times by now, as a boy and perhaps a teenager. She'd skipped merrily across his history without even noticing he was there.

Morrigan took out a notebook and meticulously copied down details of ghostly hours where she was sure Squall would be. Once she'd filled half a dozen pages, Morrigan tucked it away in a hidden pocket of her rucksack.

She was going on a Squall hunt.

The next day, Morrigan skipped lunch to stay on Sub-Nine and visit the first hour on her secret list. She wasn't disappointed.

LOCATION	PARTICIPANTS & EVENTS	DATE & TIME
School of Wundrous Arts, Sub-Nine of Proudfoot House, *Williams*	Decima Kokoro, Owain Binks, Elodie Bauer	Age of Endings, Ninth Friday, Spring of Twelve
	An advanced lesson in the Wundrous Art of Weaving	12:15–12:53

The sprawling, spidering chambers of Sub-Nine echoed inside the ghostly hour with shrieks of laughter and great, crashing waves of water as Decima Kokoro Weaved a river like a ribbon, in and out of the many archways of the School of Wundrous Arts.

It was extraordinary and beautiful and terrifying. Morrigan felt a tightening in her chest as she remembered the waves in the Tricksy Lane endlessly crashing over her. But she pushed it deep down somewhere, focusing instead on the teenage boy running through the halls after Decima, laughing with his friends as they followed in her wake, trying (and it must be said, mostly failing) to imitate what she was doing.

This Ezra Squall was of senior scholar age – perhaps seventeen or so – and beginning to resemble the striking young man he would later become. The ash-brown hair was a little unrulier than it was in the picture Dame Chanda showed her the Christmas before last, and there was no scar through his eyebrow yet. But the angular features, the smooth pale skin . . . it was all familiar, yet somehow off. Seventeen-year-old Squall was carefree and boisterous, delighting both in the company of his friends and the insanity of seeing a river run through his school.

Beyond the physical resemblance, Morrigan barely recognised him.

LOCATION	PARTICIPANTS & EVENTS	DATE & TIME
Wundrous Society Campus, far-west corner of the Whinging Woods, underneath the oldest tree	Rastaban Tarazed, Owain Binks, Elodie Bauer A beginner's lesson in the Wundrous Art of Weaving	Age of Endings, Tenth Monday, Spring of Eight 07:30–08:22 Ⓐ

The oldest tree in the far-west corner of the Whinging Woods was predictably grumpy when Morrigan came stomping around in the undergrowth the following Monday morning.

'Oh, don't mind me,' it grumbled as she tripped over its outspread roots, looking for a tiny sliver of light hanging in the air. The gnarly old wood-grain face in its trunk curled into a sneer. 'Don't let my ancient roots bother you, they're only anchored deep in the ground in this fixed position. I'll just hop out of your way in a sprightly fashion, shall I? Hoppity hop hop.'

'Sorry, I'm just looking for – never mind! Found it.'

Morrigan widened the gap and slipped through time to a lesson that had taken place four years earlier than Decima's subterranean river.

Squall was there again, and he was her own age, and he was making funny faces at Elodie while Rastaban held an outstretched hand to the tree and talked very earnestly about communing with nature in order to understand and unravel its threads.

'Ezra, stop that,' hissed Owain, closing his eyes and pressing his palm against the tree trunk. 'Some of us are trying to listen to the trees.'

Morrigan was briefly distracted wondering why they needed to use the Wundrous Arts just to talk to a tree in the Whinging Woods; in her experience they were always quite eager to broadcast their complaints. But on closer inspection of the old oak she noticed there was no gnarly face in its trunk, nor in fact on any of the surrounding trees. In this ghostly hour, the Whinging Woods weren't the Whinging Woods. Not as she knew them. How curious.

'*Some of us are trying to listen to the trees,*' Ezra mouthed dramatically at Elodie behind Owain's back, and they both dissolved into giggles.

Morrigan walked right up to Ezra, frowning as she leaned in close to examine his bright, merry face. For a brief alarming moment, his eyes locked with hers, as if he knew she was there. She felt the hairs on the back of her neck stand up. Then his gaze slid away as if it had never happened.

LOCATION	PARTICIPANTS & EVENTS	DATE & TIME
School of Wundrous Arts, Sub-Nine of Proudfoot House, *Corcoran*	Brilliance Amadeo An intermediate lesson in the Wundrous Art of Veil	Age of Endings, Tenth Wednesday, Spring of Nine 14:21–14:38

This one was a long shot, since Owain and Elodie weren't named in the listing. But Morrigan had a strong feeling that Brilliance wasn't going to be alone in a room teaching *herself* the Wundrous Art of Veil. So strong, in fact, that she skipped her Wednesday afternoon *Undead Dialects* lecture to find out. (It was only one class, she told herself, and it wasn't as if her presence would be missed in the audience of a darkened lecture theatre.)

This ghostly hour was seventeen minutes long, and one of the few looping ones she'd seen. Morrigan didn't think it could be called a 'lesson' as such. Ezra laid his hand on a wooden desk and stared at it in silence, concentrating hard, until his skin transformed, chameleon-like, to almost perfectly resemble the wood grain.

He and Brilliance both remained silent until the very end, when she smiled at him and said softly, 'Well done, dear. You're making progress. I'm proud of you.'

Ezra beamed back at her, his cheeks colouring slightly, clearly thrilled to have earned the praise.

Morrigan watched from the corner, trying to figure out why this particular moment had been dredged up from the annals of history. There wasn't a lot of instructional value in watching two people sit in a quiet room for seventeen minutes. Perhaps whoever made this ghostly hour was simply as fascinated by the young Ezra Squall as she was.

How had this mild, happy, studious boy grown up into such a monster? Morrigan was certain that one day, if she watched him closely enough, his mask would slip. She'd see a shadow of the man he would become. He was in there somewhere.

And yet, she'd already begun to think of them as two different people. Ezra the boy and Squall the monster.

The looping ghostly hour would play for ever instead of dissolving around her, so Morrigan had to find the tiny gap in the air and step back out again. When she emerged on the other side, she found a small, furry face looking up at her.

'Hello, Morrigan,' said Sofia pleasantly. 'Shouldn't you be in a lecture theatre on Sub-Six?'

'I, er . . . yes.' Morrigan had thought briefly about making up some lie, but then realised it was pointless. She gathered up a bit of boldness, opened her notebook and thrust it under Sofia's nose, showing her the ghostly hours she'd copied down. 'I've been looking for Ezra Squall.'

The foxwun didn't blink or look away. 'Yes, I thought as much. Conall said you've been spending a lot of extra time down here.'

'You – oh.' Morrigan felt all her defiance melt away, apparently unneeded. 'Sorry.'

'No need to be sorry.' Sofia turned to leave *Corcoran*, motioning for Morrigan to follow her into the hallway. 'This is your school, Morrigan. The rest of us – Conall, me, the Sub-Nine Academic Group, even Rook – we're all just guests here. The School of Wundrous Arts belongs to Wundersmiths. It belongs to you, and so do the ghostly hours. They're here to educate you, after all. We just don't want you to wear yourself too thin.'

'Why didn't anyone tell me about Squall?'

'We discussed it before you came, the three of us,' Sofia admitted. 'Conall had the measure of you much better than I did – he said you could handle it. But I thought it might be too frightening or distracting, if you realised there was so much of Squall still down here.'

'So you took his name out?'

'Heavens, no!' said Sofia, scandalised. 'We'd never deface *The Book of Ghostly Hours*. Professor Onstald deliberately omitted Squall from the book to protect it from scrutiny. He didn't want the Elders to confiscate his life's work . . . or worse, to destroy it. Everything Squall's name touches turns to ashes.'

'But the Elders must realise that Squall would be in some of the ghostly hours?'

'You didn't, until you saw him,' Sofia pointed out. 'I don't think they *want* to know, really. It's like Conall said: they ask us no questions and we tell them no lies.'

They walked for a bit in companionable silence towards the Sub-Nine entrance, before Sofia asked, 'You really don't find it spooky? Being in a room with him?'

Morrigan shrugged. 'It's not *really* like being in a room with him. He's not much like the real Squall. Um, from what I've read,' she finished, catching herself in time. She hadn't told Sofia, Rook or Conall that she'd met Squall several times, and wasn't clear whether she ought to. She suspected Rook must know, since Murgatroyd did. But it was rather an awkward thing to bring up in conversation.

'You're much more stalwart than I am, Morrigan. I try to avoid the ghostly hours from his generation. It's unsettling, seeing him with the other Wundersmiths, even when he was a child.' She shook her head, speaking softly. 'They were his *friends*. His family – the only family he ever had, really, since his parents must have given him up to the Wundrous Society when he was young. It's astonishing to think he managed to hide his true nature, all that hatred, so successfully and for so long.'

'It doesn't seem like he hated them, though,' said Morrigan. 'He always looks so happy.'

They'd reached the end of the hallway and Sofia stopped, ready to leave Morrigan at the entrance and return to the study chamber.

'Yes, I suppose that's what's heartbreaking,' she mused. 'Seeing them in the same room, so happy together, knowing how it all ended.'

'How did it all end?'

Sofia gave her a quizzical look. 'Morrigan . . . have you not heard of the Courage Square Massacre?'

'Yes,' she said, reaching back into her memory. 'Winter of Nine, Age of the East Winds. Squall tried to conquer Nevermoor with his army of monsters. Some people confronted him in Courage Square, trying to stop him, and he—'

She broke off. Pieces of information were knitting together in her head, suddenly making sickening sense.

'He killed them all,' she finished quietly. 'The other Wundersmiths. He didn't lead them in a rebellion. They tried to stop him, and . . . and he murdered them.'

'Yes.' Sofia nodded.

'Even Elodie?'

'All of them.'

To her sudden shame, Morrigan realised she'd never really wondered who they were, the people who died in the Courage

Square Massacre. In her head they'd been faceless, nameless – an anonymous crowd. It had never occurred to her that Squall might have known them personally.

'If they tried to stop him,' she said slowly, 'if those *brave people* everyone talks about were Wundersmiths themselves . . . why does everyone hate Wundersmiths so much? Why do they act like Ezra Squall was the only one, just because he was the *worst* one?'

Sofia's ears twitched. 'It happened so long ago—'

'One hundred years isn't that long!'

'—and the history books were so thoroughly scoured, it's hard to know exactly how it happened. But we believe that after . . .' She paused, searching for the right words. 'After what happened in Courage Square, when there were no more Wundersmiths to protect people against Squall and his monstrous army . . . there was a brief, very dark period when it seemed he had won. That he'd conquered Nevermoor. And in that time, *Wundersmith* became synonymous with Ezra Squall, who had himself become synonymous with evil. A Wundersmith became a monstrous thing – something to be feared instead of loved and admired.

'When the ancient magic of the city rose up to protect its people, and exiled Squall for good, the Wundrous Society was the first place people went to for answers and retribution and *revenge* – the place that had raised him up in the first place and put him on a pedestal. If the Wundrous Society wanted to survive as an institution in a city that had come to hate the idea of the Wundersmith, then they had to hate it even more. They had to hate it the *most*.

'So Wunsoc gave itself a makeover, and made over history while they were at it. Locked up Sub-Nine, destroyed and discredited and buried over a thousand years of Wundrous Acts.'

Morrigan was silent for a minute while she processed this new information.

'I'm sorry,' said Sofia finally. She stood on her hind legs and gently touched her paw to Morrigan's wrist. 'I didn't know this would upset you so much. I thought you knew who they were. Who he murdered.'

Morrigan nearly laughed at that, except none of this was funny. *How* could she possibly know? The ghostly hours were perfectly fine tools for learning the Wundrous Arts, but they taught her precisely *nothing* about who these people really were.

Sofia and Conall knew their Sub-Nine history, but could they show her what Owain and Elodie's faces looked like in the moment they'd realised their friend had betrayed them? Could they tell her what kind, motherly Brilliance had said to Ezra before he murdered her, or what Griselda had done to fight him in her final moments?

And who could tell her what the High Council of Elders in that time had been *thinking*, how they'd possibly justified to themselves their decision to vilify eight innocent people and erase Wundersmith history?

'I suppose it should have been obvious,' she said finally, and felt her breath catch in her throat. An image came to her of Elodie and Ezra giggling beneath the oldest tree in the woods. 'Who would ever try to stop a Wundersmith except another Wundersmith?'

CHAPTER EIGHTEEN

Daylight Robbery

Summer of Three

Armed with Sofia's explicit permission, Morrigan continued to feast on *The Book of Ghostly Hours*, adding more and more listings to her notebook until it seemed she was spending more time in the past than the present.

Her once-treasured mornings on Hometrain drinking tea with Miss Cheery and the rest of Unit 919 were becoming almost an inconvenience, a thing she had to get through before she could rush down to Sub-Nine. Soon she was skipping Hometrain altogether, coming in early every morning and staying late every afternoon.

She supposed some might have found it strange, spending so much time with people you couldn't talk to, people who didn't even know you were there. But far from feeling lonely, Morrigan had come to relish the gentle, undemanding company of Brilliance Amadeo and Li Zhang and Griselda Polaris. Of Elodie and Owain and Odbuoy. It was as though they were becoming her . . . friends.

Even – and it made her itchy with guilt to realise it – Ezra.

That was the weirdest thing of all. Ever since she'd learned the truth about the Courage Square Massacre, about how he'd turned on his friends so viciously, she'd expected to find herself seething with hatred every time she saw him in the ghostly hours. But instead she was finding it increasingly hard to believe that Ezra the boy and Squall the murderer were even the same person.

Ezra was just so . . . normal. Every time he teased Owain or Elodie, or called the venerable Griselda Polaris 'ma'am', or laughed at one of his own jokes or made a mistake in class and got frustrated with himself, it just made him seem more normal. More human. He could have been anyone in her unit. He could have been *her*.

When she told Hawthorne and Cadence about Squall's regular presence in her school day, they reacted just as she expected them to – Hawthorne with alarm and curiosity, Cadence with a feigned indifference that didn't altogether mask her alarm and curiosity.

'What was he doing? What'd he look like? Did he see you? He can't see you in those ghostly hours, can he? He can't get out of them, can he? He can't travel through them?' Hawthorne finally stopped to breathe.

'It's not a time machine, Hawthorne, you idiot.' Cadence rolled her eyes. 'It's just, like, an historical record or something, right? Morrigan? That's right, isn't it?'

She looked from Hawthorne's wide eyes to Cadence's furrowed brow, and instantly felt bad for telling them. Perhaps now wasn't the time to be troubling her friends with the idea of Ezra Squall's presence in Nevermoor, historical record or not. Between Unit 919's inclusion in *C&D* and the ongoing Hollowpox problem there was already so much to worry about.

The virus had begun to infect every part of their lives.

Hawthorne's mum had had to pull Baby Dave out of nursery after her teacher, a usually very lovely llamawun, attacked a group of parents at pick-up time. Cadence's next-door neighbour, a frogwun minor, had disappeared for three days and been found floating, comatose but thankfully still alive, in the duck pond of their local park. Llamawun and frogwun were now both in the Wunsoc Teaching Hospital.

'That's right,' Morrigan agreed, smiling at her friends in what she hoped was a reassuring way. 'It's not the *real* Squall. Just an historical record.'

'Like watching a film?' Hawthorne asked optimistically.

Morrigan wanted to tell him how very *unlike* watching a film it had been that morning, when she'd seen seven-year-old Ezra cry because he couldn't breathe fire as well as Owain. He was so upset she'd almost wanted to reach out and hug him.

'Yeah,' she said instead. 'Something like that.'

Unit 919's next workshop in distraction, *What's That Behind You?*, was a practical lesson out in the city. Their teacher split them into groups of three and left them on Grand Boulevard with simple instructions:

1. Cause a distraction.
2. Steal something.
3. Don't get caught.

Anah – who'd been raised by an order of nuns called the Sisters of Serenity – immediately panicked and started asking forgiveness from the Divine Thing in advance. As the teams peeled off in opposite directions, Morrigan heard Cadence say, 'We'll give it back later, Anah. Stop your moaning.'

Morrigan was in a group with Thaddea and Francis, and Thaddea immediately took charge.

'Right.' She beckoned them closer, speaking in a low voice. 'We need to steal something impressive, because we're already at a disadvantage over the other two groups.'

'How do you figure that?' said Francis.

Thaddea looked at him and gave a huge, theatrical shrug. 'Let's think. One of them's got a mesmerist and one's got Arch, whose knack is *literally* theft.'

Morrigan scrunched her nose. 'Thaddea, I don't think this is meant to be a comp—'

'EVERYTHING IS A COMPETITION.'

Francis and Morrigan glanced at each other in a silent understanding that it was probably best to let Thaddea have this one.

They were supposed to stay within a one-block perimeter, regroup when their heists were complete and report back to Wunsoc as a unit. Thaddea chose their mark carefully: a big, sprawling pawn shop called Secondhand City.

'How *impressive* does this thing have to be, then?' Morrigan asked as they made their way up and down the cluttered aisles, eyeing the teetering stacks of furniture, antiques and oddities.

Francis shrugged. 'What about a bicycle? Or a suit of armour. Ooh – what about this gramophone? I've always wanted a gramophone.'

Morrigan frowned. 'You do know we don't get to keep it afterwards?'

He cast a longing look at the antique music player. 'Oh. Right.'

'You two are thinking about this the wrong way,' said Thaddea. She pulled her long tangle of red hair into a messy ponytail and rolled up her sleeves. 'We're not here to do the bare minimum. We've got to go big or go home.'

'Oh, good! I vote we go home,' said Morrigan, and Francis laughed.

They wasted ten minutes running up and down the aisles, making dozens of suggestions that Thaddea turned down.

'What about that?' Francis pointed out a mannequin. 'We could dress it up in clothes and pretend it's one of us. Just walk right out of here.'

Thaddea rolled her eyes. 'That's the stupidest idea I've ever—'

'Shhh,' said Morrigan, holding an arm out to stop them as they came to the end of an aisle. There were voices coming from the next aisle over. They peeked around the corner and saw two men standing next to a large, spherical, mechanical-looking thing made of metal and rusting in places. It was almost as tall as they were.

'. . . had five offers come in already and it's only been here a week. Real collector's item, this is.'

The customer looked sceptical. 'What is it?'

'A railpod, innit,' replied the other man, who must have been the shop owner.

'Doesn't look like a railpod to me,' said the customer.

The owner lowered his voice. 'That's 'cos it's not a *local* design, is it? This is rare, genuine, bona fide property of the Wintersea Party—'

'Oh, pull the other one! It's just some rusty old piece of junk. I'll give you thirty kred for the scrap metal.'

'Thirty? You're having a laugh, squire. I won't sell it for less than a thousand.'

'*One thousand kred?* You're out of your *mind*!' The potential buyer shook his head and sauntered away, chuckling.

They watched the shop owner chase him all the way down the aisle until they were out of sight, then Francis ran eagerly to the machine. 'It *looks* a bit like a railpod but it's too small for that. And look – it's got a propeller and a motor. This is a vessel made for the water.'

Morrigan walked around it, trailing her hand on the metal sidings. 'You think it's a boat?'

'Weird-looking boat,' said Thaddea, jiggling a rusty handle.

The door fell open, revealing a small space inside with a single seat and controls for a navigator. They gathered around, peering inside.

Thaddea and Morrigan withdrew immediately, covering their noses.

'Ugh, it *stinks*,' said Thaddea. 'It smells like seaweed and dead fish.'

Morrigan nodded in agreement, trying not to retch. It wasn't *just* seaweed and dead fish. There was something else familiar but hard to define – a sort of muddy, decaying smell. She didn't dare take her hand away from her nose and mouth, and instead said in a muffled voice, 'Shut the door, Francis, it's disgusting.'

'It's not a boat, it's a *submarine*.' Francis was apparently too excited to notice the smell. 'Look, that's a periscope! And that stuff there is sonar equipment, I'm sure of it. It's a personal vessel, made to transport one passenger. I think . . . I think it's for *spies*!'

'How do you know all this?' asked Morrigan.

'My Great-Aunt Iyawa was an officer in the Sea Force before she retired – Admiral Iyawa Akinfenwa, you can look her up, she was really famous in her day. She has a whole library of books about seafaring vessels.' In his enthusiasm, he reached out to open the door wider, but Thaddea slammed it shut.

It was the Juro, Morrigan realised. The River Juro that snaked through the middle of Nevermoor, dark and deep and meandering – *that* was the familiar smell.

'Sometimes people travel from the Highlands all the way to Nevermoor via the river,' Thaddea told them. 'Doesn't mean they're spies.' She walked around the vessel in a circle, knocking on random parts of the outer shell.

But Francis was convinced. 'All that technology – it's much too expensive to be for ordinary people. Anyway, nobody else would be desperate enough to travel underwater in the Juro when there are venomous river serpents and Great Spiny Demonfish and Bonesmen and Waterwolves and all sorts.'

Thaddea stood between Francis and Morrigan, placing a hand on each of their shoulders. Her eyes were suddenly shining. 'Guys, this is it. This is what we're stealing.'

Morrigan stared at her. 'Thaddea . . . you cannot be serious. That thing is huge. How are we going to carry it out of here?'

'There are three of us! And I've easily got the strength of three people, so technically there are five of us.'

'Technically still three,' Francis disagreed.

Thaddea's face had turned bright pink with excitement. 'Come on, can you *imagine* everyone's faces when we show up back at Wunsoc with this thing?'

'Back at *Wunsoc*?' Morrigan gave a short, incredulous laugh. 'You think we're going to get that thing all the way back to Wunsoc? Thaddea, *how*? That'll take us all day, and I've got to be back on Sub-Nine by—'

'Ugh, not Sub-Nine again,' Thaddea groaned.

'What?'

'Shut up about Sub-Nine, will you? It's all you ever *talk about* lately.' She kicked at an old table-leg in frustration. 'Sub-Nine this, Wundrous Arts that. Whiny Binky this—'

'It's Owain Binks actually—'

'I'm sick of hearing about it!' said Thaddea, her eyes flashing.

'How you'd rather be down in your secret school on your private floor while *we're* all trying to get better at this stuff – you know, the stuff that the Wundrous Society actually *exists for*? It's like you don't even *care*.'

Morrigan gave an indignant sputter and looked around at Francis for support, but he had suddenly become very interested in the floor. 'I'm *so sorry* that crawling around in the sewers isn't my idea of a good time. We can't all be Thaddea No-Retreat of Clan Macleod.'

'It's not supposed to be about having a good time, though, is it? We have a job to do. We're supposed to be working hard and making ourselves useful and doing some *good* in the realm!'

'We're THIRTEEN.'

'I asked Gavin Squires if I could join the Beastly Division and you know what he told me?' Thaddea barrelled on. 'He said we had to start proving ourselves if we want to join the big kids. All of us. *We* have to prove ourselves as a *unit*.'

'I don't care what Gavin Squires said!'

'Well, maybe you should,' she spat. 'Since out of all of us, *you're* the one who's got the most to prove. *Wundersmith*.'

She said the word with so much venom that Morrigan flinched.

Francis looked nervously from her to Thaddea and back again. 'Maybe . . . maybe we should go back and find that mannequin—'

'Oi! You three – get out here, quick!' Hawthorne stood at the entrance of the shop, face red and chest heaving from running, and waved them urgently out into the street. 'Come *on*, hurry. You've got to hear this.'

The rest of Unit 919 was already waiting for them in the sunshine on Grand Boulevard, a little knot of black cloaks gathered at the outer edge of a crowd.

'What's going on?' Morrigan asked a glowering Cadence as they approached.

Cadence shook her head. 'Listen to this fool.'

The fool in question was a smartly dressed man standing on a crate and shouting into a megaphone at the assembled audience. It was an angry, booming, unpleasant sound, and the things he was saying were even more unpleasant.

'This is simply a matter of nature righting itself! These so-called Wunimals are UNNATURAL. They are an AFFRONT TO HUMANITY. They were never meant to walk among humans as our equals!'

Morrigan scowled. It seemed to her that the crowd's response to this was an even split of cheering and booing, but everything was so loud it was hard to tell.

'This was inevitable!' he bellowed. 'We have strayed too far from the natural order with our tolerance of these abominations, and now the true nature of the beast is exposing itself. We must protect ourselves and our families, and we must have the RIGHT TO DO SO. But those in power would DENY US that right!'

The man slammed his fist repeatedly in the air with every sentence, as if striking an imaginary gavel. His face was such a deep shade of red it was nearly purple. If he wasn't so obnoxious, Morrigan might have been *mildly* concerned he was about to keel over.

'Mark my words, there is a cover-up afoot! You read the newspapers, you've seen the violent outbursts and mysterious attacks. And that's just the ones we know about! I believe the Wundrous Society is concealing important information that the public has a RIGHT TO KNOW. I have it on good authority that right now inside the lavish, private, taxpayer-funded and *unscrutinised* Wundrous Society campus, they are sheltering not just one or two, but scores of KNOWN WUNIMAL ATTACKERS!'

Morrigan shared a nervous glance with Cadence and Hawthorne. Their W badges gleamed golden in the sunlight. She resisted a sudden urge to reach over and tuck their collars inside their shirts.

Could there be a leak at Wunsoc? All it would take was someone with a big mouth, and the Society didn't exactly have a shortage of those. Or perhaps someone outside Wunsoc had simply figured it out. She supposed the truth was bound to come to light sooner or later.

Morrigan felt someone grab her upper arm so hard it was sure to leave a bruise.

'OW! What are you – Lam?'

'Let's go.' Lam's face was stricken. She began to round up the others, ushering them away from the crowd. 'All of you, let's go. Brollies out.'

Morrigan and the rest of Unit 919 followed Lam around the corner at a pace. Nobody questioned her, and nobody was surprised when they made it to the nearest Brolly Rail platform with perfect timing. They hooked their umbrellas on to nine empty loops in a row, just as the rail came whizzing past.

On their return journey to Wunsoc, they soared above the crowd gathered in Grand Boulevard to find the rally had devolved into an all-out street brawl and the Stink were arriving to break it up. Lam the oracle had – of course – got them out of there just in time.

Things were still tense between Morrigan and Thaddea when they got to Hometrain later that afternoon. Morrigan couldn't forget the way Thaddea had hissed *Wundersmith* at her, and Thaddea was positively *seething* over the other teams' successful

214

thefts. (Cadence's group had swiped a diamond necklace from a heavily guarded jewellery shop, and Arch's group came back with their pockets full of pilfered items and a long list of where to return them.)

But if the others picked up on the friction, they didn't say anything. All their chatter since jumping off the Brolly Rail had been about the man with the megaphone and the spontaneous riot. Arch thought he'd spotted a lynxwun in the crowd, and Hawthorne swore up and down that he'd seen a furious-looking goatwun head-butting someone.

'Do you think they were infected?' he said. 'Or just—'

'Angry?' Morrigan finished. 'Don't know.'

'I'd be angry if someone called me an abomination,' said Mahir. 'Very shoddy.'

Miss Cheery arrived then, bang on time as always, and leapt breathlessly from the carriage.

'Did you hear?' she asked them. 'Tomorrow's lessons are cancelled! The Elders have called a senior summit and announced that junior scholars get the last day of term off as a treat, to do something fun with their units.'

'What's a senior summit?' asked Cadence.

'Oh, just a slightly more urgent *C&D* meeting. About all this Hollowpox business, you know,' Miss Cheery said, in what sounded to Morrigan like a practised breezy tone, with a carefully careless wave of her hand. Morrigan glanced at Cadence, who raised an eyebrow back at her. She knew they were both wondering if this had something to do with the rally on Grand Boulevard. 'Society members will be returning from all over the Seven Pockets, and the Gathering Place won't be big enough to fit all those extra people, so it's a day off for us. We can go anywhere we like!'

The announcement was met with cheers from most of

Unit 919, but Morrigan was less than excited. She dropped into a beanbag and peeked inside her notebook of ghostly hours; there was a promising one tomorrow that she was dying to see – a lesson in the art of Masquerade. The last thing she wanted was the day off school, when she was about to go a whole summer without any ghostly hours.

Thaddea gasped as if she'd just had the most important revelation of her life. 'Miss! This is destiny. There's a fight on at the Trollosseum tomorrow between Grimsgorgenblarg the Mighty and Fladnak the Fit. Can we go, miss? *Please?*'

'Nah, let's go to the pool!' said Hawthorne. 'It's meant to be scorching tomorrow.'

'The *pool?*' Thaddea looked as if he'd just suggested setting fire to an orphanage.

'Oh!' Mahir sat up ramrod straight. 'Can we go to the Gobleian Library? Apparently they have the only existing copy of *Fitherendian's Compendium.*' He looked around for a reaction but was met with blank stares. '*Fitherendian's Compendium?* The illustrated collection of all seventy-seven syllabaries and alphabets of the known elvish languages? Handwritten three thousand years ago by a silent order of monks—'

'CAN WE GO TO THE POOL, PLEASE, MISS?!' Hawthorne interrupted loudly.

But Miss Cheery was looking thoughtful. 'Actually, the Gobleian's not a bad idea at all, Mahir. An old girlfriend of mine works at the Gob. She just got promoted from bookfighter to librarian.'

'Really, miss, a *library?*' said Cadence, making a face. 'I thought this was supposed to be a treat, not the opening ceremony of the Boring Festival of Things That Are Boring.'

Mahir frowned. 'The Gobleian's not boring, Cadence.'

'Said the Boring Master of Ceremonies.'

'Master of *Boremonies*,' Hawthorne amended.

Cadence reluctantly granted Hawthorne a high-five.

'It was founded by the Wundrous Society itself,' Mahir went on, undaunted, 'and there's a whole private section dedicated to the history of Wunsoc. Members only,' he finished, holding up his index finger and wiggling the tiny gold *W* tattoo.

Morrigan perked up. If there was a section about Wundrous Society history, surely that included Wundersmith history? Maybe even *real* Wundersmith history, instead of the propaganda they were peddling at Proudfoot House.

She put her hand up. 'I vote for the Gobleian.'

Cadence and Hawthorne looked at her as if she'd gone mad. Thaddea scowled.

'Hmm.' The conductor had a coy, slightly dreamy expression when they pulled into Station 919. 'Be great to see Roshni again. I bet she'd give us a tour if I asked nicely.'

'Miss, I don't think you understand,' said Thaddea as they all disembarked. 'Grimsgorgenblarg and Fladnak—'

She was interrupted by the short, sharp shriek of the Hometrain whistle and a *whoosh* of white steam.

'See you bright and early!' Miss Cheery called over the noise, waving them off as Hometrain disappeared into the tunnel.

Thaddea gave Mahir a swift, hard punch in the arm.

CHAPTER NINETEEN
The Gobleian Library

'Miss, *please*,' whinged Hawthorne, for the fifth time that morning. He'd been dragging his heels the whole walk from Wunsoc, in the North Quarter of Old Town, to the Gobleian Library in the West Quarter. 'Can't we go to the pool instead? Unit 918 went to the pool. It's *scorching*.'

'But *we're* going somewhere better than the pool, Hawthorne,' Miss Cheery called back to him, also for the fifth time, from her spot at the front of the group. '*We're* going to the Gob. Come on, keep up.'

'She can give it a cool name all she wants,' Hawthorne muttered to Morrigan. 'Doesn't make it any less of a *library*.'

The walk through Old Town (Miss Cheery *insisted* on walking) was long and sweaty. On the way, they saw several ice-cream wagons swamped with customers, a group of nursery-aged children squealing and running under a fountain, and packs of picnickers in the Garden Belt, looking cool and content as they

218

sipped lemonade beneath the shade of enormous fig trees. With every scene of summertime bliss they passed, Hawthorne let out a doleful whimper, and Morrigan had to haul him along by his arm to keep him moving. Thaddea was even worse, walking at a snail's pace in silent protest. (She still hadn't spoken to Mahir or Morrigan. 'Macleods Don't Forgive,' apparently.)

At last, they arrived at an imposing sandstone building on Mayhew Street that Morrigan had passed many times but never visited. They went in groups of three through the enormous revolving door. She entered last with Hawthorne and Mahir, pushing through together and filing out the other side into . . . Mayhew Street.

At first Morrigan thought they'd done a full circle and come back out the way they'd gone in, but . . . no, that wasn't it. They *were* outside again, they were standing in front of the Gobleian Library façade on Mayhew Street . . . but it was different this time.

The Mayhew Street they'd left just seconds earlier had been bright and sunny, and swelteringly hot, full of people enjoying the summer day. This Mayhew Street was as cool and crisp as an autumn evening, twilight-dim, and empty of life. There was no traffic. No sound at all.

'Did I just . . . black out, or something?' Morrigan asked Hawthorne and Mahir. But they were as confused as she was.

'Come on,' called Miss Cheery. She was already halfway back down the steps they'd just come up, heading for the street. A little dazed, but still determined to find something interesting, Morrigan ran to catch up with her conductor.

In the middle of Mayhew Street, where she knew there ought to have been a row of cherry trees, there was instead a large wooden desk with a sign across the front that said 'LOANS'. A primly dressed, bespectacled young woman with a gold W pin on her collar stood behind it, watching the group as they approached. She didn't look very pleased to see them.

'There she is!' shouted Miss Cheery, running over and enveloping her in a big, enthusiastic hug. 'My friend, Roshni Singh: youngest librarian in Gobleian history. You did it, girl. I'm proud of you.'

As they embraced, the librarian stared in dismay over Miss Cheery's shoulder at Unit 919. 'Um, Maz . . . you never said you were bringing an entourage,' she said. 'What are all these kids doing here?'

Miss Cheery looked back at Morrigan and the unit. 'Who, this lot? They've come to worship at the altar of knowledge.'

'Marina,' said the librarian seriously. '*None* of them is old enough to have a library card here.'

'But I've got one,' said Miss Cheery. She beamed and held up the thin metal card hanging around her neck on a chain.

'*Marina*,' Roshni said again, folding her arms and looking sternly over her spectacles. 'The Gobleian Library is no place for children.'

Morrigan heard Hawthorne whisper a jubilant 'Yesssss', and even Thaddea perked up a little.

But Miss Cheery clicked her tongue and gave an unruffled shrug. 'Okay, but see . . . your scary librarian face doesn't scare me, Rosh, 'cos I've seen you practise it in the mirror about a thousand times. Listen, they'll be good, I promise. Right, 919?' She looked at them pointedly, and they all nodded (with wildly varying levels of enthusiasm).

Roshni shook her head despairingly, the ends of her shiny black bob brushing against her shoulders. She lowered her voice. 'Maz, you're gonna get me in trouble. It's only my first week as a full librarian and you're asking me to break the most important rule there is.'

'No! Not break,' said Miss Cheery. 'Just . . . bend? Slightly?'

'*No*. I won't do it.'

'Oh, go *on*,' Miss Cheery cajoled, turning on the full wattage of her winning smile. 'You used to let me in all the time when you were a bookfighter, even when I didn't have a library card. After closing time and all.' She raised an eyebrow.

'*Shhhh*.' Roshni blinked repeatedly, looking scandalised as she glanced around to see if anyone had heard, but the street was empty. She grabbed Miss Cheery's arm and pulled her away from the loans desk, speaking in a harsh whisper. Morrigan strained to hear, whilst trying not to look as if she was straining to hear. 'Marina, I'm not just a bookfighter now. I'm a *librarian*. I've got my own beat. I can't keep bending the rules for you, Maz. We're not kids any more.' She pulled at her sleeve. 'I wear a *cardigan*, for goodness' sake.'

Miss Cheery tugged at the bright yellow sleeve too. 'Suits you, that cardigan,' she said in a low voice. 'The glasses, too. They're well academic.'

Roshni tried not to smile, but she was clearly pleased. 'I had to wear contacts when I was a bookfighter or else they'd get stolen by a monkey or blown off by a tornado or something.'

Morrigan, still trying to look as if she wasn't eavesdropping, was torn between amusement and alarm at this comment. *Blown off by a tornado . . .?*

Miss Cheery nudged Roshni's arm, and the librarian finally smiled. 'Come on, Rosh. One hour. The kids'll *love it*. I've been bragging about you. They just want to see where you work, that's all.'

Roshni peered around Miss Cheery at Unit 919, who were

standing still and silent as instructed, and trying to look like obedient, well-behaved children.

The librarian sighed. 'Fine. ONE hour.'

Miss Cheery punched the air. 'Yes! I knew you'd come through, Roshni Singh, that's why you're my best girl in all the Seven Pockets.'

'All right, listen up,' said the young librarian, hiding a smile as she turned back to Morrigan and the others. She pushed up the sleeves of her yellow cardigan, adjusted her spectacles and placed her hands on her hips. 'Welcome to the Gobleian Library, yeah? I cannot stress this enough: it is *extremely* dangerous in here. You must be vigilant *at all times*. You must stay with the group *at all times*. You must pay attention, and listen to my instructions, and the instructions of my bookfighters. If we tell you to run, you run. If we tell you to drop to the ground, you drop to the ground. If we tell you not to pat the bunny in the waistcoat, then *trust me* – you do NOT want to pat the bunny in the waistcoat.' She paused, looking around at them impressively, her eyes owlishly large behind the thick glass of her specs. 'Because he has rabies.'

Miss Cheery cleared her throat. 'Rosh,' she said quietly.

'Okay, fine. He doesn't have rabies,' Roshni admitted. 'But he *could* have rabies. Or he could have a truncheon. You wouldn't know. So do as I say, understand?'

'Yes,' mumbled Unit 919.

'I SAID,' she shouted, 'DO YOU UNDERSTAND?'

'YES!' they shouted in return.

Roshni stepped behind the loans desk and took out a heavy-duty utility belt bearing some surprising items – a pair of handcuffs, a large knife, a silver whistle, a radio, a roll of masking tape, several chocolate bars, a leather whip and a ring full of keys. She fastened it around her hips.

'Right. Leave any brollies and bags here. Let's go get some wheels.'

The Gobleian Library wasn't just a library.

The Gobleian Library was another realm.

'A pocket realm, technically. Attached to the side of our own, like a weird growth,' whispered Miss Cheery, beckoning Unit 919 to lean in closer. They were gliding silently through the library's version of Old Town in the back of a coach enclosed entirely by thick, pale green riverglass. Roshni had told them it was mined from the bed of the River Juro, and that it was the strongest and most durable material readily available in Nevermoor. Morrigan thought it was rather like being inside the waterfall skyscraper of Cascade Towers, or at the bottom of the sea. Everything outside the coach was bathed in an ethereal green glow. Miss Cheery continued in a low murmur, 'An accidental duplicate of Nevermoor. Exactly the same, but . . . well, a bit different. It popped into existence around thirteen Ages ago. Nobody really knows why or how. The League of Explorers thought one of their people had messed around with the gateways and made it by mistake, but nobody ever put their hand up to take responsibility. Eventually City Hall took control and these really rich people called Lord and Lady Gobbleface bought it—'

'You *know* their surname is Gob-le-Fasse,' Roshni protested wearily from the driver's seat.

'—and the Gobblefaces turned it into . . . this,' Miss Cheery finished with a vague wave around them.

'This' was perhaps the most extraordinary thing Morrigan had ever seen. And that was saying something, because in her two-and-a-bit years since coming to Nevermoor, she'd seen some extraordinary things.

This was Nevermoor, but not. The streets were just the same. Courage Square was there, with its golden fish-statue fountain in the middle. All the buildings were the same, and the street signs and gaslights and benches. Even the post boxes were plotted out exactly as they were in the normal Nevermoor.

But the square was empty of people. The streets and buildings were eerily silent. The fountain had no water in it. The trees had no birdsong, no leaves moving gently in the breeze. There was no breeze. The air was still and cool. The sky still hadn't changed from that dusky grey-blue.

And instead of people, birds and breeze . . . the library-city was filled with books.

Well, naturally. Morrigan had expected it to be filled with books. What she *hadn't* expected was to find the streets populated by endless rows and rows and rows of shelves reaching almost as high as some of the buildings, stacked with millions – maybe *billions* – of books, as far as the eye could see.

'It's always nearly night,' explained Roshni. 'And it's always a bit nippy. We're not sure why; probably that's what the real Nevermoor was like in the moment when this duplicate popped up. It's not a real realm, you see – it's just a very good reproduction of the city. Lucky for us about the weather, though, and the time of day – if it was sunny, the book covers would fade. Never rains, either. And the cool temperature goes a long way to helping control the inhabitants.' She shrugged. 'Most of them, anyway.'

Morrigan put her hand up. 'Excuse me, but . . . what do you mean, *inhabitants*?' She peered through the green glass. They'd travelled blocks and blocks but hadn't passed a single living soul.

'The inhabitants of the books,' Roshni said simply, as she brought the coach to a halt. 'Sometimes they get out. But don't worry, that's what bookfighters are for. To round up the rogues and – ah, here we are. The Nevermoorian History section, part of my beat: Reference, General Non-Fiction and Special Collections.'

Miss Cheery followed Roshni out of the coach, but the scholars of Unit 919 didn't move. Morrigan wondered if she looked as horrified as the others. She certainly felt it.

Arch was the first to speak. 'Sorry, did she just say—'

'*Sometimes they get out?*' finished Anah, her bottom lip quivering.

'What did she mean by "the inhabitants of the books"?' asked Cadence.

'She was joking, wasn't she?' said Hawthorne. He looked directly at Morrigan, who didn't have an answer for him.

'Come on, you lot!' came Miss Cheery's voice, and they all clambered reluctantly out of the coach.

Morrigan could almost forget they were outside. The rows of tall shelving made everything feel closed in, as quiet and serious as the Jackalfax Public Library, which she had visited once or twice back in the Republic.

But this was so much vaster than the library in Jackalfax. Morrigan looked left and right along shelves that seemed to go on forever in both directions, lining every street and alley and dotted with enormous wheeled ladders. Every fifteen metres or so, a gas lamp made of riverglass was hung on a hook protruding from the shelves, providing a small amount of greenish illumination. She wasn't sure if she was imagining it, but occasionally Morrigan thought she saw something dart through one of the puddles of light, or flit from one ladder to the next.

'You can go have a look around,' Roshni instructed Unit 919, who had instinctively gathered in a tight knot, intimidated by their surroundings, 'but don't stray too far from the coach. Be mindful if you open any books. Don't crack the spines, don't dog-ear the pages, don't hold them open to one page for too long, *always* shut them and shelve them in their proper spot when you're finished, and shout my name if anything jumps out at you. If something really dangerous shows up, I want you all back here and into the coach *immediately*. Riverglass will protect you from most inhabitants.'

'Is it true the Gobleian Library has the only known copy of *Fitherendian's Compendium*?' The question burst out of Mahir as if it couldn't wait a second longer.

Roshni eyed him appraisingly. 'Elvish culture buff?'

'Linguist.'

'Ah! Well, it is true, but I'm afraid you won't be seeing it today; rare books are over in Swordsworth. Plenty here in Old Town to interest a linguist, though! On Cordelia Street you'll find all eighty-seven volumes of *The Odyssey of Goyathlay the Wakeful*, printed in the original Old Draconian.'

Mahir clutched his chest, making a very high-pitched sound of what Morrigan assumed was happiness.

'Go on now, have a wander,' said Roshni. 'Listen for my whistle, that's your signal to meet back here.'

The scholars peeled off in groups of two or three, but Morrigan stayed hovering around Roshni and Miss Cheery. She needed to talk to the librarian.

'What about a visit to Lilith Gate?' Miss Cheery was asking her friend.

Roshni gave her a look of exasperation. 'Lilith Gate? Are you *mad*? You want me to take a bunch of children into *Lilith Gate*?'

'Well . . . it is the children's section.'

'Which makes it the most dangerous part of the library, Maz, you *know* that. It's riddled with dinosaurs and evil sorcerers.'

Morrigan's eyes widened.

'And puppies,' protested Miss Cheery. 'And picnics! Remember that lovely picnic we had with Little Miss Muffet?'

'Yeah, I also remember the spider who came to sit down beside her. It was the size of a dog, Marina.'

Morrigan cleared her throat timidly. 'Excuse me, er . . . Miss Singh. Is it true that there are sections of the library just for members of the Wundrous Society?'

The librarian turned to her in surprise. 'Oh! Still here? There are a few private Wunsoc collections in the Gob, so it depends which one you're after. If you want the School of Arcane Arts collection I'm afraid it's down in Eldritch, but the Mundane is only a block from here.'

Morrigan felt her heart skip. 'There are . . . private Mundane and Arcane Arts collections?'

'Of course. Although they shouldn't be, if you ask me,' she added. 'Private, I mean. We're a library, not a country club – our collections should be available to all, Wuns and Unwuns alike. But what do I know? I just work here.'

Morrigan strongly agreed. Even the words 'Wun' (for a member of the Wundrous Society) and 'Unwun' (a non-Society member, i.e. everyone else) sounded stupid to her, and not particularly friendly.

'Is there something specific you're looking for?' Roshni asked her.

What she *wanted* to ask, of course, was if there was also a Wundrous Arts collection . . . but of course she couldn't.

'Oh, just . . . something about . . . um, the history of Wunsoc,' she mumbled. It was a feeble lie, but Roshni perked up a little, looking pleased.

'A fellow historian! I think there are a few volumes that might interest you on the corner of Fitzgerald and Phelps – come

227

on, I'll take you there. Marina, keep an eye on your scholars, will you? That curly-headed boy looks like a right little shelf-climber.'

Morrigan followed Roshni through several rows of towering shelves, from one pool of green light to the next.

'You know, I think we might have the new edition of *Inside Proudfoot*—'

The librarian was interrupted by a buzzing, crackling sound from the small silver radio mounted on her belt, followed by a static-drowned voice.

'Librarian Singh, this is Librarian Feathers. Do you copy?'

Roshni picked up the mouthpiece and pressed a little button on the side. 'Copy, Colin. What's up?'

Crackle, crackle, buzz. 'Mate, we've had a situation here in Lilith Gate.' It sounded like he was trying to catch his breath. 'That infestation from last week came back. We've driven them off but I'm afraid now it looks like they're headed south. They might be coming your way. Just a heads-up.'

Roshni groaned. 'Copy that, Colin. Contact Dispatch and see if they can spare a crew to send into Old Town. My lot are busy in the Military History section – *The Battle of Buckthorn Glen* busted out of its cover yesterday, they're still cleaning up. I'm here in the Nevermoorian History section with . . . some guests.'

Buzz, crackle. 'Copy, Rosh. I'll let them know.'

'Infestation?' asked Morrigan. Just the word *infestation* made her feel itchy. Infestation of *what?*

'Nothing to worry about.' Roshni touched each of the items on her belt in turn, as if checking they were still there.

Morrigan frowned. 'Maybe we should go back?'

'It's really nothing,' Roshni assured her with a smile. 'Look, here we are – Wundrous Society History. Listen, will you be okay to find what you're looking for? I should just go back to the coach and . . . check on things,' she finished vaguely.

Morrigan nodded and made her way down the shelf, trailing a finger along the spines of such books as *Inside Proudfoot House* and *From Aaron Ashby to Zola Zimmerman: A History of Great Wundrous Society Elders and Their Achievements*.

Now that she was alone the library was eerily quiet, but every now and then she thought she heard something. A rustling of pages. The creaking of a spine, the soft dull thud of a book cover closing. And other things, sounds she couldn't quite explain, like the cry of distant whale song, or snatches of old-fashioned music and clinking glasses.

As Morrigan neared the end of a row, something caught her eye at the narrow mouth of a side street. A small sign fixed to the brick wall read:

DEVILISH COURT
BEWARE!
BY ORDER OF THE GEOGRAPHICAL
ODDITIES SQUADRON
AND THE NEVERMOOR COUNCIL,
THIS STREET HAS BEEN DECLARED A
RED ALERT TRICKSY LANE
(HIGH-DANGER TRICKERY AND LIKELIHOOD
OF DAMAGE TO PERSON ON ENTRY)
ENTER AT OWN RISK

With a tiny jolt, Morrigan suddenly realised which part of Old Town she was in. *Devilish Court*. This was the Tricksy Lane she'd discovered by accident last year! The one that turned out to be hiding the Ghastly Market.

But there was something different here, something that hadn't been there in the real Devilish Court . . . or at least, she hadn't noticed it. Inlaid on the brickwork beneath the sign was a tiny golden circle. Morrigan stepped closer and it began to glow, pulsing in time with her quickening heartbeat. The imprint on her finger tingled.

Had the circle started glowing for *her*? Like it sensed she had permission to enter and was inviting her inside?

If one was going to hide a private collection of books on the Wundrous Arts, she thought, a Red Alert Tricksy Lane seemed like the perfect place. Seized by a sudden sense of ownership, Morrigan took a quick look over her shoulder to make sure nobody was watching, and went in.

It was just as awful as she remembered, the feeling of air being sucked from her lungs. But she knew what to do. It was like ripping off a plaster – the quicker the better. Closing her eyes, she took the darkened Devilish Court at a run, battling the urge to turn back, ignoring the burning in her chest and the pressure in her head. Seconds later she emerged, gasping for breath . . . and found herself in the square where she and Cadence had seen the Ghastly Market last summer. But instead of a bustling market filled with contraband horrors and nefarious customers, here in the pocket realm there were simply more shelves of old books.

It felt almost . . . *cosy*. A little wilder, a little more overgrown than the rest of the library, with more trees shading the books and more vines strangling the shelves. Perhaps, if this *was* the Wundrous Arts collection, it was only accessible to Wundersmiths? It may have been over a hundred years since anyone had stood on this spot. What a thought.

Morrigan knew she didn't have long. She marched up and down the rows of shelves, peering down at the titles. She didn't really know what she was looking for, exactly, but as she rounded a corner into the next aisle, a familiar word jumped out at her from the spine of a large leather-bound book.

-SINGULARITIES-

She pulled the heavy tome from the shelves with great difficulty and read its full title in a whisper. '*Curiosities, Marvels, Spectacles, Singularities and Phenomena: Volume One of an Unabridged History of the Wundrous Act Spectrum* . . . by Lillian Pugh.'

The book Onstald had written had a slightly different name. It was called *Missteps, Blunders, Fiascos, Monstrosities and Devastations: An Abridged History of the Wundrous Act Spectrum* and was an abridged account of all the supposedly terrible things Wundersmiths had ever done. Had he re-written Lillian Pugh's book to push his own warped agenda?

The book in Onstald's classroom had disappeared before he'd been killed. But it had been enormous, much bigger than this one. Morrigan was confused. Shouldn't the *unabridged* version be bigger than the *abridged* version?

Then she reread the title: *Volume One.*

And right next to it: *Volume Two.*

On and on down the row of bookshelves, it seemed there were dozens – no, *hundreds* – of near-identical successive volumes. She replaced *Volume One* on the shelf and pulled down *Volume Two*. It was also by Lillian Pugh, as were *Volume Three* and *Volume Four*. But Five and Six were by Daniel Middling-Blythe, and the next six volumes after that were by Ruby Chang.

Morrigan was smiling so much she thought her face might break. This was the same feeling she had when she'd first seen *The*

Book of Ghostly Hours, only magnified a hundredfold. The whole of Wundersmith history – every glorious achievement, every *Spectacle* and *Singularity* and *Phenomenon* – was laid out before her, each book a lit beacon guiding her into the past.

She ran all the way down the aisle to the final book (*Volume Three Hundred and Seven* by Sudbury Smithereens), pulled it from the shelf and sat down to open it in her lap, flipping through the pages.

The names were all familiar. Griselda Polaris. Rastaban Tarazed. Decima Kokoro. Mathilde Lachance. Brilliance Amadeo. Owain Binks. Ezra Squall. Elodie Bauer. Odbuoy Jemmity. The Wundersmiths of Squall's generation. The Wundersmiths he murdered in Courage Square.

Suddenly, the short, sharp sound of a whistle came from somewhere in the distance – that was Roshni's signal. With a sigh, Morrigan began to put the book back in its spot on the shelf, then faltered. She slid it in, then out again, biting the side of her mouth.

Could she come back and read it another day? Maybe Jupiter would bring her, or Sofia or Rook . . . but *when*?

The whistle blasted again and, in a split-second decision, she heaved the book into her arms and ran with it towards the mouth of Devilish Court.

Moments later she emerged from the suffocating Tricksy Lane, desperately gasping air into her lungs, and made her way back to the corner of Phelps and Fitzgerald, still holding the leather-bound volume tight.

'There you are!' came a voice out of nowhere, making her jump and turn around. Cadence was leaning against an unlit gaslight with a bored, lazy grin, but she perked up as soon as she saw Morrigan trying to hide the book behind her back. 'Whatcha got?'

'Nothing.'

'Don't lie, you're lousy at it.'

'It's . . . it's a book about Wundersmiths,' Morrigan admitted. It was too late to put the thing back now.

'And what are you planning to do with it, exactly?' Cadence pushed away from the gaslight and crossed to where Morrigan stood. 'You don't have a library card.'

'Miss Cheery will let me use hers.'

'Not for that book. That book's got a black tag.' Cadence pointed at the spine. 'See? You need a Wunsoc library card, written permission from the High Council of Elders and a level eight security clearance to borrow books with a black tag. Miss Cheery's only got a six.'

'What?' This was all news to Morrigan. Her heart sank. 'How do you know all that?'

'My gran comes to the Gob all the time. She's got an Unwun library card so she can only borrow books with a blue tag, but she only likes murder mysteries and books about heavy machinery anyway. Why don't you just get something else?'

Morrigan held the book tighter. She pressed her fingers against it until they turned white. 'I'm taking *this* book.'

'That would be stealing.'

'It's not stealing! It's just – borrowing.'

'No. It's only borrowing if you've got a *library card*.'

'Says the girl who "borrowed" a puppy from a stranger!'

Cadence shrugged. 'That's different.'

'How is it different?'

'It's *different* because I'm actually good at this stuff and you're actually rubbish,' she said. 'I know how to smooth things over so nobody misses anything. And it's different because . . . because this is a library, for goodness' sake! My gran would *kill me* if I stole a book from a library.'

233

Roshni's whistle sounded again, three short, urgent blasts. She called from the next aisle over, 'Girls? It's time to go, where are you?'

'Are you going to tell?' Morrigan whispered.

Cadence stayed silent as Morrigan clumsily tried to hide *Volume Three Hundred and Seven* of *An Unabridged History of the Wundrous Act Spectrum* underneath her summer cloak.

'There you are! Time to go, your hour's almost – what are you doing?' Roshni stopped abruptly as she rounded the corner and spotted Morrigan covering the book with the folds of her cloak. 'Do you understand how serious it is to steal a book from the Gob? Do you have any idea how much trouble you could get in? Give me the book,' she demanded, her voice high-pitched and incredulous.

Morrigan felt her face burning. She scrambled in her brain for an excuse, for a decent lie, but came up with nothing. All she knew was that she wasn't leaving without this book, or giving it back until she'd read every single page within its covers.

She turned to look desperately at Cadence, a silent plea for her help. Cadence stared belligerently back.

'*Please*, Cadence,' she whispered.

'Why should I?' her friend hissed at her. 'You're so *weird* lately. Are you really so obsessed with your ghostly Wundersmith mates that you want me to help you *steal*?'

'What? I'm not *obsessed*.' She tightened her grip on the book, wondering whether Cadence was really going to hang her out to dry. But at last, with her trademark eye-roll, the mesmerist gave in.

'She hasn't stolen anything,' she told Roshni in a bored, reluctant voice. 'We've just been having a nice conversation.'

'What?' snapped Roshni. 'She's stolen a book, I *saw* her!'

'No,' said Cadence simply. 'She hasn't.'

'Yes, she *has*,' the librarian insisted. 'She's stolen . . . she took a . . . a book. I saw . . .' Morrigan heard the note of confusion creeping in, and held her breath.

'You didn't see anything,' said Cadence, her voice a pleasant hum. 'We've been having a lovely chat about . . . history or whatever. You think Miss Cheery's scholars are just delightful. So well behaved. You'd love us all to come again.'

Roshni shook her head, trying to clear the fog. 'I'd love you all to . . .'

Miss Cheery approached them, carrying a large stack of books she could barely see over.

Roshni stared fixedly at Morrigan for a fraction of a second, a frown creasing her forehead, and then an agreeable sort of blankness broke across her face. 'Your scholars are just delightful, Maz,' she said.

Miss Cheery snorted. 'Delightful? Wouldn't go that far. They're all right. Give me a hand with these, will you, Rosh?'

Morrigan watched as the librarian and the conductor split the pile of books and carried them back down the street towards the riverglass coach. She breathed an enormous sigh of relief.

'Thank you,' she told Cadence. 'Seriously, *thank you*. I owe you one.'

'You owe me more than one, you filthy book-stealer,' muttered Cadence. 'Don't worry, I'm keeping a tally.'

The rest of the unit was already heading for the riverglass coach as Morrigan and Cadence caught up. Morrigan made sure to walk slightly behind Cadence, trying to hide the large book-shaped lump beneath her cloak.

Hawthorne was bargaining with Miss Cheery about how many dragon books he could borrow on her library card. Thaddea and Anah were poring over a medical journal and arguing about the best way to splint a broken leg.

Suddenly, a klaxon sounded. The lanterns hanging off the shelves changed from murky green to a fiery, glowing red. Everyone stopped talking.

Morrigan felt her arms seize up, still wrapped tight around her waist, pressing the large book against her stomach.

'They know I've got it,' she whispered to Cadence. 'I'm going to be arrested!'

'Shush,' hissed Cadence, but she looked worried too.

The sirens were growing louder . . . and there was another sound. A strange, high-pitched, whining metallic sound a bit like a buzz saw, then a noise like two pieces of sandpaper being rubbed together.

Keeeeeehhh . . . chchchch.

Keeee-keeeeehhh . . . chchchchchch.

'What is that?' asked Francis, putting his fingers in his ears.

Keeeeeehhhh-keeh-keeeh . . . chchchch.

They all looked to Roshni, who was staring up at the shelves high above them, eyes wide as dinner plates.

'Everyone get to the coach!' she shouted. 'NOW!'

They turned to run, but it was too late. The riverglass coach was two rows away. Before they made it even halfway there, Morrigan's whole unit, Roshni and Miss Cheery all pulled up abruptly, their escape thwarted by a sight that made the skin all over Morrigan's body crawl as if she'd instantly broken out in hives.

They were surrounded. The infestation had arrived.

CHAPTER TWENTY
Book Bugs

They came from everywhere. Swarming out from the gaps between books, crawling up from storm drains and pouring from shelves in a monstrous, chittering tidal wave of wings and eyes and legs . . . *so many legs*. It was an infestation of many-legged, multi-coloured, chihuahua-sized—

'BUGS!' squealed Francis. 'GIANT BUGS!'

'Brilliant observation, Francis, cheers for that!' Cadence shouted angrily. Beneath her usual ferocity, there was a note of terror that reflected how Morrigan felt – how they *all* felt. They had formed a tight circle and were facing outwards, eyes boggled at the encroaching plague.

'Rosh, how dangerous are these things, exactly?' asked Miss Cheery. She had dropped her pile of books and was holding her arms out, trying to protect Mahir and Thaddea, who were nearest to her.

'To the books? I'd say . . . slightly dangerous?'

237

'No, Rosh, to *us!*'

Roshni cringed. 'Oh! Then I'd say . . . quite dangerous? Jagdish got a nasty bite on his ear during an outbreak last month and Elise lost half a pinky.'

'Oh, terrific,' said Miss Cheery. 'So how do we fight them off?'

Morrigan could think of one way. She took a deep breath, hummed a few notes, then knelt on the ground and breathed a low, even line of fire towards the horde of insects. The rest of 919 threw their arms up to shield from the heat. In that moment it was hard to tell if the fear on their faces was because of the bugs or her, and she almost regretted acting on impulse . . . except that it had worked.

Just as she'd hoped, the bugs skittered backwards. However, they also seemed to become even more agitated, the *keeeeeh-keeh-keeh* noises suddenly louder and more urgent.

'Marina, what is she *doing*?' shrieked the librarian, stomping out the fire with her boots. 'Is she *mad*?! Make her stop!'

Morrigan swallowed, and felt the flames die in her throat. 'I just thought – I'm sorry, I just wanted to—'

'Well, *don't*. Get back!'

Miss Cheery grabbed Morrigan around the shoulders and pulled her back from the fire while Roshni extinguished it. 'She was trying to help, Roshni.'

'Yes, because starting a fire is a *famously* helpful thing to do IN A LIBRARY!'

'Then what *can* we do?' said Miss Cheery. 'How do you stop these things?'

'We have mechanical swatters,' said Roshni, moving in a slow circle and keeping her eyes on the advancing bugs. 'And tanks of foam laced with a pesticide that won't hurt the books. But they're all on the trucks.' She pressed the button on her radio again. 'Calling all brigades. Bookfighters, can you hear me?' Nothing. 'Librarians, are you there? Colin? Jagdish? Come ON!' There was no sound but static. She groaned in frustration. 'Right, all of you kids listen carefully. I need you to—'

She was interrupted by a piercing scream from Anah. An iridescent green insect the size of a shoebox had broken apart from the pack and was crawling up her leg, up her side, along her shoulder . . . the screaming intensified as it latched on to her hair, and Anah squeezed her eyes shut, waving her hands helplessly. 'GET IT OFF ME GET IT OFF ME GET IT OOOFFFFFF!'

THWACK.

Archan seemed to have acted without thinking. He swung a huge book through the air, using its momentum to brush the bug away from Anah, only *just* missing her head. The bug went sailing away in a bright green arc and then landed hard – *SQUISH!* – against a high shelf of books. They watched the carcass slide all the way down to the ground, down the rows of coloured spines, leaving a thick, unctuous, foul-smelling trail of greenish-yellow guts that looked rather like a festering wound.

Eyes wide with horror, Arch dropped the book. Francis, meanwhile, leaned over with his hands on his knees and vomited right there in the street.

Roshni was horrified too, but for a completely different reason. She pointed a shaking finger at Arch. 'Y-you – you just – that's a *book*! That's – that's *vandalism!*'

'Is that the priority right now, Rosh?' shouted Miss Cheery. She started gathering up her dropped books and handing them out to the scholars. 'Right, new plan. We've got no swatters. No tanks. No bookfighters. So, we're going to use what we DO have.' She ducked to avoid a gigantic pink-spotted bug as it swooped low over her head, then took aim at it with a large book called *Famous Nevermoorian Impressionists and Their Muses*. *THWACK!* The bug exploded on impact, sending a shower of slime over the whole group, to their great revulsion. 'Come on, you lot – get swinging.'

Roshni stared at her friend, open-mouthed. 'Maz. You're not serious!'

'Rosh, it's either this or get eaten by a swarm of bugs.' She handed her friend *An Encyclopaedia of Modern Witchery*. 'Which would you prefer?'

The librarian whimpered. She looked like she was being asked to spit on her grandmother's grave. She clutched the book to her chest, closed her eyes tight and whispered, 'Forgive me, Lady Goble-Fasse, for what I am about to do.'

And with one perfectly aimed swing, Roshni knocked a black-and-blue striped bug straight out of the air, a rainbow of slime radiating outwards in its wake. Without pausing for breath, the librarian began swinging left and right, a ceaseless barrage that sent dozens of bugs to their deaths within moments. Morrigan could see why she'd been promoted. Roshni was a bug-murdering machine, fierce and unrelenting.

'Move towards –' *THWACK* – 'the coach!' she shouted between swings.

And they did – slowly, painstakingly, fighting their way through the creepy-crawling onslaught, the unit made their way together in the direction of the riverglass coach, leaving a trail of dead bugs and slime puddles behind them.

Morrigan pulled *Volume Three Hundred and Seven* out from under her cloak and took aim at a monstrous purple thing hovering around Cadence's head, wings humming and pincers snapping. It landed with a satisfying *SPLAT* on the other side of the road, and she immediately hit another three in quick succession –

SPLAT. SPLAT. SPLAT. It was the weirdest and most disgusting thrill she'd ever experienced.

Thaddea and Hawthorne seemed to be enjoying themselves too, though Morrigan couldn't say the same for the others. Cadence was covered in slime, and Anah couldn't stop screaming. Francis looked like he was barely in control of his stomach. Lam stood in the centre of the group, hands over her head, while Arch and Mahir hovered around her, doing their best to deflect any bugs that came her way.

'Roshni!' Miss Cheery shouted. 'Look!'

The riverglass coach was gone. Or not gone exactly – it was still there, just buried beneath the enormous heap of insects that had decided to swarm it, so that it now resembled a small, buzzing mountain of glittering iridescence.

They were done for. There was no way they'd be able to fight their way through that lot.

Roshni looked horror-struck, but picked up her radio again, still swinging her encyclopaedia one-handed. 'CALLING ALL BOOKFIGHTER BRIGADES. DOES ANYONE COPY? COME ON, YOU SLACKERS! ASSISTANCE REQUIRED AT OLD—'

She was drowned out by the sudden blare of sirens, the roar of an engine. Morrigan turned in the direction of the sound, and felt her heart bounce up and down in her chest like an ecstatic frog.

A truck made of green rippled riverglass was reversing down the road towards them at top speed, scattering the swarm, splattering some and sending the rest flying for the shelves. The back doors flew open and a crew of a dozen people jumped out wearing full-body jumpsuits, heavy black boots and great metal tanks on their backs, with spraying attachments they wielded like weapons, one in each hand. One of them carried a second tank out of the truck and tossed it lightly to Roshni.

Incredibly, the brigade of bookfighters was led by an enormous ostrichwun in a tweed vest, twice as tall as the rest of them, with great big feathery wings. He had the longest legs Morrigan had ever seen, ending in clawed feet that looked like three-pronged daggers.

'About time, Colin!' Roshni shouted, but she was grinning as she turned back to Miss Cheery and the scholars. Colin didn't answer her but made straight for the mess instead, wings flapping wildly. 'Right, you lot – we'll take it from here. Into the truck and STAY INSIDE. Jagdish will come back and drive you to the loans desk once we've got a handle on this.'

She turned back to join the bookfighters and other librarians and they ran into the oncoming swarm, spraying thick rivers of bright pink foam and bellowing like warriors.

Unit 919 scrambled up into the riverglass truck and Miss Cheery shut the thick glass doors, sliding a huge metal bolt into place.

Everyone looked miserable and exhausted, but relieved to be out of the chaos . . . except for Thaddea, who gazed out through the rippled glass, watching Roshni and the bookfighters in awe. Yellow-green guts went flying as the brigade of bookfighters danced around each other, battling the infestation in what could almost pass as choreography. Morrigan thought the scene had a sort of . . . nauseating beauty about it.

Though she was *very* glad to be on this side of the riverglass.

'I'm going to be a librarian,' Thaddea declared rapturously, as a trail of putrid pus-coloured slime dripped down the side of her head.

'Is . . . everyone . . . okay?' Miss Cheery panted, pressing one hand to her chest.

Francis had his hand over his mouth, looking green and grim, and Mahir was slumped on the floor, having slipped over on a slime-puddle and not bothered to pull himself up. Arch was trying to wipe bug guts off his clothes, but so far had only managed to spread them farther. Cadence was shaking her head in disbelief – whether at the general situation or specifically at Miss Cheery's question, it wasn't clear.

'Didn't see that one coming, then?' she asked Lam pointedly.

Lam gave a small, apologetic shrug. 'I don't see *everything*.'

She was the only one who had managed to escape any degree of sliming, thanks to Arch and Mahir. She pressed herself against the wall to avoid contact with the rest of them.

'What *are* those things?' asked Anah in a trembling voice from the corner of the truck.

'Book bugs,' said Miss Cheery, still catching her breath. 'From the entomology section. There was this book – *The Big Book of Bad Bugs*. It was all about the world's biggest and gnarliest insects, and it got checked out by loads of people because it had such good pictures. It was opened and shut constantly, which is bad news around here. People got a bit careless, and about a year ago some of the bugs got out. They started breeding before the bookfighters could round them all up. The bookfighters keep fumigating, but Rosh says they get another outbreak every couple of months. They don't even try to get them back in the book any more, that's how bad it is. They just kill them.'

Hawthorne came over to Morrigan and pressed his face against the door, peering miserably out at the action and shivering. 'Wish we c-could go back out there and h-help.'

Morrigan glanced at her friend and noticed his clothes were drenched through. She cupped her hands, exhaled a little puff of fire and let it dance warmly, hovering just above her palms; a trick she'd learned last week from Rastaban Tarazed.

'Thanks.' Hawthorne rubbed his hands together over the flames and then looked up, nodding at the bookfighters with a little grunt of laughter. 'What's he playing at?'

He meant Colin. The ostrichwun was the only one who didn't have a weapon, but he didn't need one. Those clawed feet of his were weapons, and he used them to great effect. His legs bent the opposite way to human legs, and as he flapped his immense black-and-white wings, he kicked up and outwards with a terrifying ferocity.

But . . . he wasn't very *precise* in his attacks. Not carefully targeting the bugs like Roshni and the others, but rather going a bit . . . berserk. His eyes were wild and frightened. He was out of control.

It was hard to tell through the green riverglass, but Morrigan was certain that if she could have seen them properly, his eyes would have been glowing emerald.

'Miss Cheery?' she called back to their conductor, who was in the corner helping Francis. 'I think you should come and see—'

'PUT THAT OUT,' cried Lam, looking at Morrigan's hands in panic.

But the warning came too late.

Three things happened in extremely quick succession.

First, outside the truck, Roshni screamed as Colin viciously lashed out at her chest with his clawed foot.

'ROSH!' cried Miss Cheery.

Morrigan felt a sudden jolt of terror. The tiny flame cupped in her hand roared in response to her fear, growing brighter and bigger. It singed Hawthorne's eyebrows and engulfed Morrigan's hands up to the wrists so that it looked like she was wearing gloves of fire. She gasped, shaking them out to extinguish them.

And lastly – the sudden flash of fire having caught his

attention – Colin halted and turned to face the truck, lifting his beak into the air and sniffing like a wolf scenting its prey. He locked eyes on Unit 919 and, in an instant, was running towards the truck faster than Morrigan would have imagined possible.

The riverglass door lived up to Roshni's promises; it was strong enough to withstand the sudden fierce assault. Colin leapt into the air with great flying kicks and threw his head against it repeatedly, hard enough to do some damage to himself if not the glass. But it didn't stop him. He *couldn't* stop. He had descended into madness.

'Get back from the doors!' Miss Cheery shouted at Unit 919, rushing to stand between her scholars and the glass.

The bookfighters were clearly well trained to respond in an emergency. After a moment's confusion they divided themselves into three groups: one still fighting the bugs, one trying to control Colin, and one helping Roshni, who had collapsed on the ground. The half a dozen who swarmed the ostrichwun managed to pull him away from the truck, pinning him to the ground. It took the strength of all six to hold him down, and Colin fought them even still.

'Everyone get down on the floor,' ordered Miss Cheery. She ran towards the front cabin and climbed through a little latched door into the driver's seat. 'I'm getting you out of here.'

'But what about Roshni and the others?' asked Morrigan. 'We can't just leave them!'

Thaddea reached out to slide back the metal bolt. 'We have to get out there and help!'

'Do not touch that door, Thaddea Macleod!' shouted Miss Cheery as the engine roared into life. 'Everyone get down NOW.'

Those who didn't were instantly thrown to the floor as the truck lurched away from the scene. Miss Cheery careened down the aisle the way they'd come, swerving dangerously close to the towering bookshelves and almost crashing several times on their short journey back to the loans desk. Unit 919 was silent; they heard the crackle of the truck radio and, for the first time, a slight note of fear in the conductor's voice as she called for an ambulance. In her head Morrigan could still see poor Roshni lying on the ground wounded, confused by her friend's attack. She hoped the librarian would be okay.

'Right. Everyone out,' ordered Miss Cheery as they pulled up near the Mayhew Street entrance. 'And I don't just mean out of the truck, I mean out of the library. I'm going back for Roshni.'

Half the unit ran obediently to open the doors and clamber out, while the other half shouted in protest.

'Miss, we're not leaving you!'

'You can't go back alone!'

'We have to help—'

'QUIET.' They fell silent immediately. Morrigan had never heard her speak so fiercely. 'You are to walk through that revolving door, and you are not to come back inside. I need you to stand guard outside the library. Don't let anyone in. Wait for me on Mayhew Street, but *do not come back inside*, understood?'

'But—' began Hawthorne.

'UNDERSTOOD?'

Mumbling their reluctant agreement, Unit 919 turned to head for the exit as instructed.

'Morrigan, wait.'

She felt Miss Cheery's hand grip her arm and turned back.

'Take the Brolly Rail home, quick as you can, and tell Captain North what's happened. Tell him about Colin. Tell him to . . .' she paused, swallowing and breathing through her nose as if to steel herself. 'Tell him to bring the Stealth.'

CHAPTER TWENTY-ONE

Concerned Citizens of Nevermoor

The fallout from their Gobleian Library escapade was swifter and further-reaching than Morrigan could have anticipated. She didn't see Miss Cheery again before the summer holidays began the following day, but she heard from Jupiter that the Elders and the Scholar Mistresses had hauled their conductor over the coals for taking them on such a dangerous excursion.

'It's not her fault,' Morrigan told him on Saturday morning, stabbing at her toast with the butter knife. It was early, and she and Jupiter were the only ones in the staff dining room. The table was laid with all their favourites – crumpets and toast and waffles and sausages and eggs and blueberry syrup – but neither of them had eaten a bite. 'Miss Cheery shouldn't be in trouble, it was Mahir and me who wanted to go to the Gobleian Library. Hawthorne was right, we should have gone to the pool.'

And I didn't even get to steal the book, she thought glumly.

Somewhere in the fight against the book bugs and the scramble to get into the truck, she had dropped *Volume Three Hundred and Seven* of *An Unabridged History of the Wundrous Act Spectrum*. It had probably been destroyed by bug guts and pesticide foam. All that history had been at her fingertips, and now it was gone, maybe for ever.

'Miss Cheery has taken full responsibility, quite rightly,' said Jupiter. 'She's the grown-up, Mog, she should have known better than to take a bunch of thirteen-year-olds into a pocket realm. Bad things can happen in liminal spaces.'

Morrigan looked up from her badly butchered toast. 'What's a liminal space?'

'A sort of . . . inbetween. A threshold between one place and another. Tricksy Lanes are a good example – they can be unstable, unpredictable places where normal rules of the universe don't seem to apply.'

She told him about the locked doors at the end of every branch of chambers on Sub-Nine, each labelled *The Liminal Hall*. 'What do you think they could be?'

He frowned, considering it. 'I honestly don't know, but I strongly suggest you stay away. Like I said – liminal spaces can be dangerous. And the Gob is one of the most dangerous I've ever come across. I wasn't planning to take you anywhere near the place until you're at least fifteen. You certainly won't be going back any time soon. Not least because it's been closed to the public until further notice, by order of the Nevermoor Council.'

Morrigan deflated even further. She'd been hoping he might take her back there once all of this blew over. Even if *Volume Three Hundred and Seven* had been destroyed, there were still three hundred and six other volumes tucked away behind Devilish Court.

'Is Roshni all right?' She'd been feeling awfully guilty about deceiving her, even more so since she'd watched the poor woman get attacked by a raging ostrichwun.

'The librarian?' Jupiter winced a little. 'It . . . wasn't a pretty injury, but she's in the teaching hospital and Miss Cheery hasn't left her side. She's going to be all right. Not sure I can say the same for her ostrichwun friend. He seems to have hurt himself more than anyone else. He's in the teaching hospital too, of course.'

He stared broodingly into his cup of coffee, which had long gone cold. 'Another attack we could have prevented and Wunimal we could have helped, if only we'd known he was infected, if we'd had the slightest clue, some warning, just a *scrap* of information.'

Morrigan studied her patron's exhausted face. He'd been up all night for the opening of the Nevermoor Bazaar.

The Stealth had been out in force at the summer market festival, on the lookout for any strange Wunimal behaviour. Jupiter patrolled with them all night, scouring the crowds for any 'black holes' as he'd started calling them – the area surrounding those Wunimals who were nearly depleted of Wundrous energy, having had it all eaten up by the Hollowpox. In the past few weeks he'd managed to thwart three separate attacks this way. The Stealth had taken the infected Wunimals into protective custody so they'd be safely isolated when the pox reached culmination, preventing them from hurting anyone – including themselves – and finally Dr Bramble and Dr Lutwyche were able to study the virus in its host before culmination. They'd taken blood samples and talked to the three infected Wunimals about where they'd been, who they'd come in contact with, what other symptoms they'd been experiencing.

But it seemed the more data they collected, the more baffled they were as to how the Hollowpox was spreading so quickly. One of the three, a roosterwun, had just returned from a silent meditation retreat and hadn't been in contact with anyone at all – let alone any other Wunimals – for a whole month. How, then, had he caught it?

Sofia had joined the Hollowpox task force as a Wunimal community liaison, and had been reaching out to Wunimals outside the Society to help them be safe and avoid catching the pox. Her main suggestion was to stay home until the task force knew more . . . but what good would that do, if isolation didn't keep the Hollowpox at bay?

The best tool in their kit, truly, was Jupiter's sight as a Witness. But he couldn't be everywhere all at once, he couldn't possibly stop every attack before it happened, and he seemed to consider each one he missed a deep personal failing. For the three attacks he'd prevented, there were nearly a dozen he hadn't. Morrigan could see it was taking its toll.

'Well, I suppose we'll have plenty of information now,' he said with an uncharacteristic sneer. 'We'll be swamped with it. Real information, false information, who cares? Not the *Concerned Citizens of Nevermoor*.'

Morrigan glanced down at the poster Jupiter had ripped off a lamppost in Courage Square and brought home to show her. She'd read it a dozen times at least, and each time it chilled her to the bone.

BEWARE!

YOU ARE IN DANGER from the
HOLLOWPOX

The Wundrous Society doesn't want you to know that RIGHT NOW in Nevermoor, potentially THOUSANDS of RABID WUNIMALS are infected

with this dangerous virus, putting YOU and YOUR FAMILY at risk of SAVAGE ATTACKS!

The Wundrous Society has admitted that early symptoms of the Hollowpox are almost IMPOSSIBLE TO SPOT!

Could somebody YOU KNOW be
SECRETLY INFECTED?

Watch out for FORGETFULNESS, INCREASED APPETITE, FIDGETING and AGGRESSION.

If you suspect a friend, neighbour, colleague or family member may be infected, you have a DUTY to report them IMMEDIATELY to the Nevermoor City Police Force.

BE ALERT
WATCH YOUR NEIGHBOURS
DON'T HESITATE
ACT ON YOUR SUSPICIONS

Paid for by Laurent St James of the
Concerned Citizens of Nevermoor Party

The symptoms listed on the poster were the same as on the Wundrous Society's posters, but not really. They'd been *edited, abbreviated, shortened* to make them even more ridiculously broad.

Forgetfulness, increased appetite, fidgeting, aggression? That described half of Unit 919 on a good day. How many Wunimals would be wrongly accused of having the pox, Morrigan wondered, when *these* were the symptoms people were watching for?

It was that last bit of the poster that really spooked her. *Watch Your Neighbours. Don't Hesitate. Act On Your Suspicions.* It was like these 'Concerned Citizens' were just trying to turn everyone against Wunimals.

Any Wunimals. All of them.

'Who is this Laurent St James?' asked Morrigan.

'Some rich idiot,' muttered Jupiter. 'One of the landed gentry, a Lord or a Viscount or something. Now he's formed his own political party, the *Concerned Citizens of Nevermoor*. They mostly seem to be concerned with nosing into business that doesn't concern them. Here, eat something, will you.' He nudged the plate of crumpets towards her, and she nudged it back.

'*You* eat something. How does he know so much about the Hollowpox? I thought the Public Distraction Department was keeping it under wraps.'

'There's no keeping anything under wraps now, Mog. Not after what happened at the Gobleian.' He sighed and took a bite of dry toast, made a face and swallowed it reluctantly. 'It was already out there, anyway, really. Bits and pieces have been leaking for weeks now, it was only a matter of time.'

Morrigan suddenly remembered something. 'We saw a man with a megaphone shouting about it on Grand Boulevard on Thursday! He called Wunimals abominations. He said they were . . . what was it? An "affront to humanity". What a pig.'

Jupiter scowled. 'Posh bloke in a fancy suit?'

'Yes.'

'That'll be him. Laurent St James. Loves nothing more than getting up on his soapbox. He's trying to stir trouble.'

One of the kitchen staff came to clear their plates, and Jupiter sent away all of the untouched food with a sigh.

The rest of the summer flew by in a frightening whirl. Every day more posters appeared on the streets, every day the Concerned Citizens held another rally and broadcast their message on the radio, encouraging people to turn on their Wunimal friends and neighbours. The government, afraid of instigating mass panic, had yet to directly address the growing whispers about the Hollowpox, instead asking the Wundrous Society to continue trying to contain it. But in many ways the lack of official information made it worse. Rumours and inaccuracies spread like wildfire, until nobody knew what to believe.

Jupiter was constantly out helping the Stealth identify infected Wunimals, and he spent every Friday night patrolling the Nevermoor Bazaar. If there was an attack in a crowd of thousands of people, the knock-on effects could be dire. It could cause a stampede. He'd even enlisted Jack's help; his nephew's ability as a Witness was coming along in leaps and bounds, and Jupiter said he was a great asset to the Hollowpox task force.

Every Saturday morning at dawn, Morrigan would be waiting in the Smoking Parlour to make Jack and Jupiter sit and inhale waves of rosemary smoke, eat a proper breakfast and drink some tea.

To her great disgust, Jupiter had forbidden Morrigan to attend the Nevermoor Bazaar at all that summer, and to the great disgust of everyone in Unit 919, he had contacted their patrons and parents to suggest the same. It was simply too risky, he'd said. There were fewer Wunimals at the bazaar than ever before – most having apparently taken on the message to stay home – but plenty were still out and about. Some were just trying to make a living, some either didn't understand or didn't care. And some were there as a counterprotest to the Concerned Citizens of Nevermoor.

'Why don't they just cancel the bazaar this summer, if it's so dangerous?' Jack had asked him at the time.

'If you can convince the Nevermoor Chamber of Commerce to shut down their mammoth mid-year economy boost, by all means do,' Jupiter replied. 'Believe me, we've tried. The best we can do is get out there and try to head off any trouble before it arises.' He'd squeezed Jack's shoulder then, looking him dead in the eye. 'You've no idea what a help you are, Jackie. I'm proud of you.'

Jupiter had also managed to bring in another two Witnesses to help, people he knew from outside Nevermoor. So far they'd identified sixteen infected Wunimals at the bazaar. Morrigan could tell Jack was glad to be involved, even if it was draining work.

The worst things they'd reported to Morrigan weren't any attacks committed by Wunimals themselves, but attacks *against* them. At a Sweet Street stall that sold hand-stretched caramel by the metre, Jupiter had stepped in to physically remove a man yelling at a ten-year-old rabbitwun to go home. A pigwun glassblower was heartbroken when his stall in the South Quarter got destroyed by vandals, and all his delicate creations smashed to pieces.

The Concerned Citizens had set themselves up in the same spot on Grand Boulevard every Friday night to shout their hateful words for a public audience, and every Friday night their audience had grown. Jupiter and the Stealth had tried to have them moved on, but the Stink had stepped in, insisting that what they were doing was perfectly legal. Jupiter grew more furious about it with every week that passed, and on the seventh Saturday of summer he returned to the Deucalion at dawn positively incandescent with rage.

'—ill-bred halfwit with a bad haircut and an undersized heart!' he was shouting as he and Jack entered the Smoking Parlour.

'Yeah, I know.' Jack shot a wide-eyed look at Morrigan, rubbing his temples, and gratefully accepted the cup of chamomile tea she'd poured. 'You said that.'

'I'd like to shove his megaphone right up his—'

'You said that too. A few times.'

'—nose!' Jupiter paced the parlour floor, hands on hips, chest heaving. 'And I'll tell you what else, he's making it more dangerous for himself and everyone else at the bazaar, only he's too stupid to know it. Every week, more Wunimals join in the counter-protest at Grand Boulevard. Any one of them could be infected, any one of them could attack him and, frankly, who would blame them?'

'The Concerned Citizens of Nevermoor would probably love it if one of them got injured.' Jack sighed. 'Think of the publicity.'

'Can I come next week?' asked Morrigan, 'I want to help.' (She also wanted to see the bazaar at least *once* before summer ended.)

'Absolutely not. Even Jack's not coming next week.'

Jack cracked open his one visible eye. 'I'm not?'

'He's not?'

'He's not,' said Jupiter, then turned to Jack. 'You're not.'

'But we stopped two attacks last night!' Jack sputtered indignantly, sitting up and glaring at his uncle. 'You wouldn't even have *seen* that second one if it wasn't for me!'

'You were brilliant,' Jupiter admitted, 'and I couldn't have done without your help this summer. But I've got a bad feeling about next Friday night. It's the last night of the bazaar and the Concerned Citizens of Nevermoor Party are stirring the place up like a hornet's nest. Dr Bramble's been hearing rumours that some of the Wunimal rights activists are organising some kind of response. If there's going to be a clash, I don't want you anywhere near it.'

'But I can *help*!' Jack insisted, pressing a hand to his chest. 'You need me.'

'I need you to be *safe*, is what I need.' He looked from Jack to Morrigan with an apologetic smile. 'Besides, I've ill-advisedly told Frank he can throw a *very small* end-of-summer dinner party in my absence, since his events schedule has taken such a hit this summer . . . so *actually* what I need is for you two to be here and supervise so he doesn't completely wreck the place.'

Jack opened his mouth to protest one more time, closed it again and shook his head. Both he and Morrigan both knew it was pointless arguing with Jupiter when he'd set his mind to a course of action. Jack got up and made for the door. 'Fine. I'm going to bed.'

'Jack—'

'I said it's fine.'

The door slammed shut behind him. Morrigan and Jupiter sat in an awkward silence, sipping their tea, until finally he lay down on the chaise longue, heaved a deep, weary sigh and closed his eyes.

'I'm not trying to be boring, Mog. Just . . . responsible.'

She thought about it for a moment. 'Same thing.'

That, at least, made him laugh.

That night, Morrigan was woken by a soft *tap-tap-tap* on the black door in her bedroom. A glance at the clock told her it was eleven-thirty.

Tap-tap-tap.

Throwing off the bedclothes, she crossed the floor and pressed her imprint to the glowing circle in the middle of the black door. She tiptoed through the unlit wardrobe and opened the station door, yawning.

At first, she thought there was nobody there. Then a quiet, calm voice came from somewhere down near her feet, and she nearly jumped out of her skin.

'Good evening, Morrigan. Having a nice summer?'

'Sofia!' She rubbed her eyes, trying to wake up. This was the last person she'd been expecting. She hadn't *really* been expecting anyone at all, on a Saturday night during the school holidays. 'Er, yes, very nice thanks. I . . . is everything okay?'

'Quite okay, yes,' Sofia assured her. Morrigan thought she detected a tremulous note of excitement in her words. 'But there's something I think you'll want to see.' The foxwun ran to a little brass railpod waiting at the platform, looking back over her shoulder at Morrigan.

'We'll have to hurry. Come on!'

LOCATION	PARTICIPANTS & EVENTS	DATE & TIME
School of Wundrous Arts, rooftop of Proudfoot House, southern end	Gracious Goldberry, Avis Ku, Henrik Reiner	Age of Industry, Seventh Saturday, Summer of Four
	An advanced lesson in the Wundrous Art of Inferno, given by Goldberry to Ku and Reiner	23:42–01:15

On the cold, dark rooftop of Proudfoot House, Morrigan and Sofia stepped through an incision in the air and felt time shudder around them.

The night was on fire.

Two young Wundersmiths stood back, watching a third wield Inferno in a way Morrigan had never seen before. The woman was tall and statuesque and cut an impressively frightening figure, with long waves of red hair that whipped around her in the wind.

'Gracious Goldberry,' Sofia told her. 'And the students are Avis Ku and Henrik Reiner.'

Morrigan looked down at her, dragging her eyes away from the spectacle. 'Wasn't Gracious Goldberry sort of . . . horrible? Didn't she—'

'Call for the imprisonment of all Wunimals?' Sofia finished for her. 'Yes. She was a nasty piece of work. Very good at Inferno, though. Maybe the best I've ever seen.'

Gracious sent a tiny spark of flame dancing on the wind. It curled around Avis and Henrik, coming dangerously close to their hair and clothes and skin without burning a single bit of them. The small flame was followed by another, and another, and dozens more, one after the other. They were as tiny and delicate as dandelion puffs blowing on the wind, and yet they weren't at the mercy of the wind at all. They were being directed, every single one of them at every single moment, by Gracious Goldberry, whose focus never wavered.

Flames danced between her fingertips. They grew and reshaped and swam in perfect patterns through the air, like a school of fish underwater.

'Wow,' Morrigan whispered.

'I told you you'd want to see it,' murmured Sofia. The firelight reflected in her eyes. 'I come here every year on this night. I've seen it seven times now. It never stops taking my breath away.'

This feat of Gracious Goldberry's, while perhaps not quite so visually spectacular as a golden firebird flying high into the sky, was breathtakingly good. Only someone with an intimate knowledge of how Inferno works would know how incredibly difficult it was to do something this precarious, this *precisely*. Gracious never lost control for even a moment. Morrigan relished the display of skill, while simultaneously feeling slightly heart-sunk.

'I could never do this,' she whispered. 'Not even if I lived for a hundred years.'

'If you live for a hundred years, Morrigan, you will do a great many things you wouldn't believe.' Sofia paused. 'And as a Wundersmith, you may live a great deal longer than that. Griselda Polaris lived to nearly three hundred. Wundrous energy is a great preserver.'

Morrigan's eyes widened. She knew that Ezra Squall had lived an awfully long time, even though he still looked like the young man he had been when he was thrown out of Nevermoor a hundred years ago. But *three hundred*? Would that be her one day, she wondered? Three hundred years old, still hanging around Wunsoc, all her friends long gone? She didn't like to think about it.

The display went on, and Gracious talked through her actions, encouraging her Wundersmith students to imitate her. They tried (rather clumsily and with mixed success) and so did Morrigan (rather clumsily and with mixed success).

Unlike most of the other instructors Morrigan had seen, though, Gracious had no patience. She never slowed down, never repeated herself, never paused to allow Avis and Henrik a moment to think or catch up. She was a relentless, unyielding teacher.

Morrigan moved closer, trying not to get distracted by the show itself, but peering *through* the flames to observe the woman conducting them. She noticed tiny things she'd never seen any other Wundersmith do before.

Gracious held her head at a peculiar angle as she breathed out; Morrigan tried it, and her airways felt instantly clearer, unimpeded.

Gracious, at times, seemed to be inhaling through her nose and exhaling through her mouth at the *same time*. Morrigan couldn't believe such a thing was possible.

'Sofia, can you *see what she's doing?*' She beckoned the foxwun closer. 'She's inhaling air and breathing fire *simultaneously*. How is she *doing* that?'

Sofia gasped. 'How extraordinary. It's called "circular breathing"; notoriously difficult, but very much a learnable skill – certain musicians can do it, and opera singers. I can't believe I'd never noticed before. Excellent, *excellent* observation, Morrigan.'

Finally, the ghostly hour began to darken and fade, signalling its end. In seconds, Gracious Goldberry and her two students had disappeared from the rooftop, as had the warmth from their Inferno.

'Doesn't it bother you?' Morrigan asked Sofia, shivering as the last spark died and a cool summer breeze blew past. 'About Gracious Goldberry? What she tried to do to Wunimals, I mean.'

Sofia twitched her bushy tail closer around her and seemed to think about the question for a moment. 'When I first spotted this hour in the book, seven years ago, I came up here because I wanted to see what she looked like. I was convinced she'd be some awful crone with black eyes and—' Sofia cut herself off, looking up guiltily at Morrigan. 'Oh – I'm sorry, I didn't mean—'

Morrigan snorted. 'No offence taken. Go on.'

'Sorry,' she said again. 'Well, anyway, I came up here filled with hatred and spite, ready to scorn this awful person, and what did I find? Quite possibly the greatest wielder of Inferno who ever lived.'

'That must have been annoying.'

'Very annoying,' Sofia agreed. 'I was incredibly angry at the time. I spent the next year being outraged that someone so awful should have been blessed with such a singular gift. But the following year I went back anyway, and I decided that this extraordinary talent could not be wasted on this wretch of a woman. I wouldn't allow it to be. I would render it useful somehow. Someday.' She fixed her gaze on Morrigan. 'And then you came along. So, tell me, Morrigan Crow. Did you get something useful out of that lesson?'

'Yes,' Morrigan said truthfully, making a mental note to ask Dame Chanda about circular breathing. 'I did.'

'Good.' Sofia nodded, and turned back to where the ghost of Gracious Goldberry had stood moments earlier. 'Take that, you nasty old fool.'

Morrigan grinned.

CHAPTER TWENTY-TWO

The Sunset Gala

As the event planner for Nevermoor's most glamorous hotel, Frank was the city's undisputed Lord of the Party, but his mood had taken a dark turn this summer. As the Hollowpox took hold of Nevermoor, event after event had been scaled back or postponed or, in most cases, altogether cancelled. Jupiter didn't want to put any of the guests or staff at risk, nor could he bear to hurt his Wunimal friends by singling them out and asking them to stay away. It had been a very quiet summer at the Deucalion indeed . . . except for Frank's constant, very loud complaining about the injustice of it all.

After weeks of wailing, Jupiter *finally* relented and said Frank could throw a little themed supper for guests staying at the hotel.

Then, while Jupiter was distracted by his all-consuming work on the Hollowpox task force, Frank added a few valued regulars and longtime friends of the Deucalion to the guestlist.

At some point in the week, Morrigan noticed he'd stopped

referring to it as a supper – now it was a 'little soiree'. Then a 'dance'. By the time Jupiter left for the bazaar on Friday evening and the guests began to arrive, Frank was welcoming people to the 'Hotel Deucalion end-of-summer Sunset Gala'.

'*Gala?*' Kedgeree said heatedly. 'Frank, this was supposed to be a *dinner*. Do you know what the difference is between a dinner and a gala? About *two hundred people*, that's what.'

'Goodness, I know. Isn't it *dreadful?*' Frank was utterly unable to hide his glee as a cavalcade of motorcars pulled up noisily in the forecourt. 'I suppose word got out that I was throwing a little *do*, and people just couldn't stay away. Bless them.'

Kedgeree rounded up Fen and the rest of the staff, and they decided the only thing to do was to keep things under control and shut it down at the first sign of trouble. It wouldn't do to bother Jupiter now – it was the last night of the bazaar, after all, and he had much bigger fish to fry.

Morrigan realised Jupiter would be furious, but she couldn't help feeling a *little* excited about the party, even if she knew it was somewhat ill-advised. The summer had been so long, tense and boring, punctuated by disappointments and terrible news . . . truly, she'd been *yearning* for a bit of fun.

Frank had chosen his 'Sunset Gala' theme to celebrate the end of summer and usher in the autumn chill. The lobby had transformed from floor to ceiling into the most beautiful sunset Morrigan had ever seen. The chequerboard tiles had turned all black, and the walls looked like they'd been dip-dyed in shades of peach, pink and yellow. The black bird chandelier had given itself a temporary makeover, becoming an enormous ball of shimmering gold, high up near the ceiling. As the night wore on, it deepened to orange and then to a brilliant red, sinking lower and lower like a sun slowly setting. Guests had been asked to wear all black, and the effect was breathtaking: they were silhouettes against a fiery horizon.

Trees had grown up from the lobby floor again, reminding Morrigan of the Christmas forest – but these were the leafy, deciduous kind. They swayed in a breeze that seemed to come from nowhere. Early in the evening it smelled of jasmine, citrus and the ocean, then later as the sun set and the leaves began to curl and change colour, it smelled of rain and apples and rich, dark soil. By midnight, the leaves were a thousand shades of orange and red, the temperature in the lobby had subtly dropped, a fire was roaring in the hearth and the scent of wood smoke filled the air.

All the guests agreed that the Sunset Gala was a sensory triumph and the hottest ticket in town that night. Hundreds of hopeful gatecrashers were turned away at the door . . . but the later it got, the bigger the party seemed to grow.

Morrigan had invited Hawthorne and Cadence, and also managed to lure Jack from his room, where he'd spent most of the past week sulking. He even obligingly pulled his eye patch aside to play Morrigan's favourite party game. The four of them were stationed behind the concierge desk for maximum visibility of the guests (and proximity to the door from which the party food was emerging – Hawthorne's stipulation).

'He's having a fight with his mum,' said Jack, pointing to a young man scoffing canapés with abandon. 'She thinks he's not applying himself to his studies and he thinks she's overbearing. The woman at the top of the staircase is cheating on her wife. Those two sitting by the fire are secretly in love, but each one believes it's unrequited because they both think the other is too good for them.'

'Ooh!' said Hawthorne, clasping his hands delightedly. 'Should we go and say something?'

'Definitely not.' Jack swiped a canapé from a passing waiter (Hawthorne took three). 'They'll either figure it out or they won't, but Uncle Jove says nosing into people's love lives is never helpful. He must have learned from experience, because we all know how much he loves nosing into things.'

A rather noisy group of guests arrived just then, and among them was a giraffewun, a Wunimal Minor. She was long of neck with a spotted pattern covering her skin, languid brown eyes and large ears a bit like a deer, but otherwise quite humanoid.

Morrigan glanced at Jack, who was watching the giraffewun carefully, but after a moment he shook his head. He'd been examining every Wunimal that came through the doors and monitoring them throughout the party, but so far none posed a threat. Frank had had the decency to look sheepish when the first Wunimals arrived (unexpectedly), but the rest of the staff agreed they couldn't ask anyone to leave. It wouldn't feel fair and would risk the Deucalion's reputation being tarnished, even if it was for safety's sake . . . but it had certainly put the staff on edge.

She knew Jack was trying to keep track of every Wunimal guest, because she was doing the same thing. The owlwun major perched on the railing of the staircase. The wolfwun minor howling with laughter at his own joke. The iguanawun major playing on the bandstand. The fact that some of the human guests were giving the Wunimals a wide berth certainly made them easier to spot in a crowd.

'She must be a celebrity among Wunimals,' Jack whispered to Morrigan and the others. He gave a subtle nod towards an elegant dogwun with flowing silvery-white fur, wearing a black velvet bow above each ear and a string of black pearls around her neck.

'How do you know?' asked Morrigan.

'Little synchronised flashes of light,' Jack explained. 'Like lightbulbs switching on above every other Wunimal's head as they saw her come through the door.'

Morrigan was thrilled by the drama of this and was just wondering how she could get close enough to find out who the dogwun was, when another little flash of light went off nearby, and they all flinched at the sudden brightness. Hawthorne gasped.

'I just – I saw the light!' he cried. 'Jack, does that mean I'm a Witness now, or—?'

'That was a camera flash, genius,' said Jack.

He was glaring at its source: a man carrying an enormous camera and following close behind the dogwun. He had a bag full of photography equipment slung over his shoulder, and Morrigan saw with alarm that the logo embroidered on it said the *Looking Glass*.

Jack had spotted it, too.

'We should tell Kedgeree,' he murmured, with a meaningful look at Morrigan. 'If Dame Chanda finds out a photographer from the *Looking Glass* was allowed in here after that "opera horse" article, she'll never forgive Frank.'

A woman standing near the concierge desk made a noise of disgust. She carried a sunset-coloured cocktail in one hand and a beaded clutch in the other.

'Utterly disgraceful.' The woman wrinkled her nose as she watched the elegant dogwun and her pursuing photographer disappear into the crowd. Leaning in towards the man who was with her, she said in a loud whisper, 'The Deucalion really is going to the dogs, if *that's* the sort of riff-raff they're letting in.'

The man nodded in agreement. 'Hmm. Someone should call the pound and have that pooch taken away.' The pair of them shared a smug little giggle.

'She's not a dog,' Hawthorne said loudly. 'She's a dogwun.'

They turned as one to look down their noses at him. The man scoffed. '*Dogwun*. Rubbish. If it's got four legs, a wet nose and a tail – it's a dog. In my day, we called things by their real names and none of this horsewun, rabbitwun, lizardwun nonsense. I'm sick of having to be so *respectful* all the time. *Dogwun*,' he finished, shaking his head and downing his cocktail in one. 'Someone fetch me another drink,' he added, snapping his fingers in the air.

Morrigan turned to her friends, nonplussed. 'What's wrong with being respectful?'

'Obviously takes more than two brain cells,' Jack muttered.

'Yeah, and they've only got one between them,' added Cadence with a snort of laughter.

'What did you just say?' said the woman. She swayed over to the desk, leaned in uncomfortably close to Cadence and repeated her question in a waspish voice. '*What* did you just say?'

Unfortunately for her, it was hard to intimidate Cadence, who squared up to the woman without hesitating. 'I *said*, you've only got one brain cell between you. Would you like me to sing it?'

'Why, you *beastly* little—'

'Is there a problem here?' Fenestra had arrived just in time. She planted herself at the end of the desk, stationed between each side like a referee at a tennis match.

The woman twitched with revulsion. 'Another talking unnimal! Who in the Seven Pockets wrote this guestlist? They ought to be arrested for crimes against decency.'

Morrigan, Jack, Hawthorne and Cadence all looked up at Fenestra, holding their collective breath and waiting for an explosion.

But Fen surprised them by responding in what was, for her, a reasonably polite tone. 'Not an unnimal. Not a guest. I work here. How can I help?'

'A *cat*, working at a five-star hotel?' said the man with a disbelieving little giggle. 'Glad we're not staying the night, darling, we might get fleas.'

Once again, Morrigan and the others hunched their shoulders and braced for impact. But again, Fenestra managed to restrain herself.

'It's a nine-star hotel,' she told him calmly. 'I don't have fleas. And I'm not a cat.'

The man rolled his eyes. 'Sorry. *Catwun*.'

'Not a catwun either.' Fen's lip curled to reveal the tip of one gleaming yellowish fang. 'I'm a Magnificat, it's a whole other thing. Read a book, for goodness' sake.'

The woman flinched. 'You're very rude.'

Fenestra stood up to her full height. 'YOU'RE very rude. And your dress is ugly.'

There she is, thought Morrigan, torn between nervousness and glee.

The woman gasped. 'EXCUSE me—'

'No, I won't excuse you, or your behaviour,' Fen interrupted in a bored, impatient voice. 'You're a bully and a bigot and frankly I've no idea how either of you made it on to the guestlist. I can only assume you're gatecrashing.'

'Fen,' said Jack, gently tugging at the Magnificat's fur. An audience had begun to gather around the concierge desk, and they too looked nervous. 'Maybe we should just ignore—'

'We don't ignore bigotry, Jack,' said Fenestra. 'That's how cowardly bigots turn into brave bigots.'

'How dare you!' spluttered the man, clutching indignantly at his lapels. 'We shan't return to the Hotel Deucalion if this is the sort of treatment—'

'You *shan't return* to the Hotel Deucalion because from now on there'll be a great big sign behind the check-in desk with your faces on it, saying NO ADMISSION.'

The man was struck momentarily speechless, but swiftly recovered his bluster. 'I demand to speak with management. WHO is in charge here?'

Fen took two slow, deliberate steps towards him and pushed her face close to his, her enormous amber eyes dangerously narrowed. Her wet pink nose was almost the size of his head, and when she spoke, her voice rumbled like an idling engine. Morrigan could feel it reverberating through the floor.

'*I'm* in charge here.' Fen leapt up on to the desk, bared her teeth at the couple and hissed.

'She's infected!' the woman shrieked. 'The cat has the Hollowpox!'

'She's not infected!' Morrigan shouted, running around the desk to stand between them, arms thrown wide. 'She can't be infected, she's not even a *Wunimal*, she just told you that!'

'CALL THE STINK!' the man shouted.

'IT HAS THE HOLLOWPOX!' cried another guest, picking up a chair and shoving it violently in their direction. 'Get back, beast!'

Everywhere Morrigan looked, people were picking up items to use as makeshift weapons against Fen, who was – naturally – firing up in response, hissing and yowling, batting away any weapon that came too close.

Jack climbed up on to the concierge desk beside her, shouting to be heard. 'Please, everyone, calm down. This is just a misunderstanding.'

Morrigan frantically scanned the lobby and saw Charlie and Martha trying to push through the party towards them, shouting Fen's name, and Kedgeree coming from the opposite direction, and Dame Chanda from the main doors and Frank from the spiral staircase, but they were all struggling to make a path through the swollen crowd.

It was remarkable, Morrigan thought, how quickly the situation had deteriorated. She felt as if every pair of eyes in the lobby – hundreds of them – were suddenly fixed on Fenestra, either in terror or hatred. Fen wasn't helping matters either, with her fangs and claws bared and her back arched defensively.

Even worse, the photographer from the *Looking Glass* was hastily changing the roll of film in his camera, eager to get a shot that would no doubt be used to make people even more frightened of Wunimals.

Morrigan felt sick. She just wanted them all to *stop looking* at the Magnificat, to turn away and leave before something terrible happened, either to Fen or somebody else.

She began to sing softly under her breath. It had become a kind of nervous habit, something she'd taken to doing in moments of tension. She couldn't pinpoint exactly when it had begun, but she supposed somewhere between being chased and mauled by a bearwun, watching a horsewun rampage through the opera house, and being swarmed by giant bugs in a public library, she'd unconsciously decided it was best to be prepared for anything.

'*Morningtide's child is merry and mild.*' She felt her fingertips tingle and warm as Wunder instantly gathered. '*Eventide's child is wicked and wild.*'

In an instant, she decided to try something she never had before, something she'd watched over and over in the ghostly hours, but Rook said she wasn't ready to try yet: shadowmaking – a skill that required both the Wundrous Art of Weaving and the Wundrous Art of Veil.

Morrigan took a deep breath to clear her head.

She observed the room as if she was observing a painting: examining the shapes and colours of things, places the light touched, and the recesses where shadows formed – the very materials she needed.

All the while, she felt Wunder sensing her intentions and taking them as commands. And she felt herself – her *self*, that amorphous inner thing that was *her* – ballooning, growing bigger than her body, reaching out into the room with its monstrous, Wundrous arms and gathering what she needed, plucking bits of shadow here and there – tiny bits, not enough to be missed but enough to build a new shadow of her own making.

She and Wunder were perfectly, exhilaratingly in sync.

Soon the lobby was swarmed by starry darkness, a shadow that kept growing until everything was black.

Morrigan hadn't meant to make her shadow quite so all-consuming – she'd only wanted to obscure Fenestra from view – but nonetheless, the effect was the same. They couldn't see her any more, and so they couldn't attack her, and the photographer couldn't get a shot of her looking threatening. Morrigan felt a rush of relief.

The room was noisy with confusion and shouted demands for the lights to be turned back on, and later she would remember a moment in all of this when a question formed in her mind, clear as a bell: *What now?*

She'd made a whole room full of shadow.

Could she sustain it long enough for Fen to calm down? Could she hold her concentration *and* somehow communicate to Jack and Hawthorne and Cadence that they needed to spirit Fenestra away in the darkness, to hide her until everyone had gone? Could they resolve this safely and happily and let the party end as it always should have: with a mess in the lobby and a rave review in the society pages?

What now?

But Morrigan didn't have to answer that question, because it was answered for her.

Out of the darkness came a single source of light. Somewhere way across the room, a dim green glow. Morrigan felt her heart race. The hazy green light was growing closer. She saw that it wasn't one light but two; two pinpricks of glowing green moving towards her in the darkness.

Eyes. Watching her.

Before she could think straight another set of glowing green eyes appeared on her left, blinking on and off as if they were weaving in and out of shadow, low to the ground. And a third pair, gliding through the air above Morrigan's head, moving fast, growing bigger and clearer . . . and then the piercing screech of a bird, squeals and shouts of surprise from the crowd, and a scream torn from Morrigan's throat as she felt talons and beating wings upon her head and heard a snarling, snapping growl from somewhere to her left and felt a human hand grab at her face in the darkness—

And then they stopped, and Morrigan heard three distinct *thumps*. Whoever had attacked her had fallen to the ground. The panic in the room grew.

'What was that?' someone shouted.

'Darling, where are you—'

'I can't see a thing!'

The glowing green lights left the three bodies behind and came together in one strange, nebulous shape in the darkness. It swarmed Morrigan, swimming across her skin, dancing around her as if trying to find a way in. Wherever the light touched her, she felt cold.

Finally, it seemed to give up and simply floated in mid-air.

'Jack,' she whispered, her voice trembling. 'Can you see it?'

'Yes,' he said, in a soft voice full of confusion and wonder.

It felt like the light was . . . *watching* her. Assessing her. Like maybe the strange green *something* was just as baffled by her as she was by it.

And it was, she knew now with one hundred per cent certainty, *something*.

The Hollowpox was a *living thing*.

Morrigan felt her energy ebbing away; all the Wunder she'd gathered had been depleted. The shadows disappeared as suddenly as they'd arrived, like the flick of a switch, and the lobby was once again flooded with light.

In a flash, the Hollowpox was gone – split not into three, but *dozens* of tiny green specks of light that flew away in all directions. Some seemed to disperse among the crowds in the lobby, and some left the building entirely, but they all disappeared.

Morrigan felt her knees weaken. It was taking all of her energy just to remain standing. She gazed down at the floor, where the three bodies lay still, their eyes wide open.

The owlwun. The giraffewun. And the dogwun.

'They're dead!' someone screamed. 'They've been murdered!'

'No, you fool,' shouted another, 'it's the *pox* – the Hollowpox has taken them.'

'It was the CAT!'

The lobby was once again a cacophony of noise and confusion as people tried to get away from the lifeless Wunimals, as if their misfortune might be contagious. Morrigan, Jack, Hawthorne, Cadence and Fen moved quickly to form a barrier around the three bodies, protecting them from being crushed by the hundreds of people now rushing for the doors in a great stampede.

The cool autumnal breeze turned to a gale, whistling through the crimson trees. As the last guests fled into the night, the leaves turned brown, fell from the branches, and chased them out the door in one big *whoosh*.

CHAPTER TWENTY-THREE

Rescue Rings

Morrigan's bedroom was a soothing summer oasis that night, yet she didn't sleep a wink. Three hammocks strung between palm trees swayed in a light, balmy breeze. Gentle waves lapped at the sandy island floor beneath her, and above her the ceiling was a clear starry night.

Her brain and body were so exhausted from her first effort at shadowmaking she might have gone ten rounds in the Trollosseum with Grimsgorgenblarg the Mighty. But sleep wouldn't come.

It might have been Hawthorne's soft, persistent snoring on one side, or Cadence's occasional sleep-muttering on the other. Or more likely, it was the fact that Morrigan had been counting down each tick of the clock until dawn, ever since Fenestra had insisted they all go to bed.

After the ambulance had come to take away the three stricken Wunimals, Morrigan had grabbed her brolly and tried to leave for the Nevermoor Bazaar right away, to find Jupiter and tell him what had happened. But Fen scuppered those plans in a heartbeat.

'That is *exactly* the kind of distraction Jove doesn't need on the last night of the bazaar,' she'd said, marching Morrigan, Hawthorne and Cadence upstairs to bed.

Just before dawn, when the starlit black sky began to lighten ever-so-slightly, Morrigan crept out of her room. She'd thought to sneak in early to the Smoking Parlour and put the tea on, ready to tell Jupiter everything about the gala and hear everything about the bazaar in return. But Jack was already there, lingering outside in the hallway.

He held a finger to his mouth then pointed to the parlour door, which was slightly ajar. Raised voices – and a faint, sunshine-yellow trail of lemon smoke – came from within.

'—little more than speculation at this point, of course.'

'What are you going to tell the public?' The second voice was Fenestra, and she was pacing. Morrigan could tell because of the rhythmic, agitated thumping of her tail hitting the wall. 'You *are* going to tell the pub—'

'Fen, I've told you, it's not up to me. Elder Quinn believes it would only cause more panic. Inspector Rivers thinks that if it makes no material difference to public safety, we should keep a lid on it. If it *did* come from—'

'Typical Wunsoc,' Fen growled. 'Always thinking they know what's— Oi!'

Morrigan and Jack jumped in surprise as the door flew open and Fenestra pounced in front of them. She gave a low growl. 'Don't you know it's rude to eavesdrop?'

'Fenestra, just let them in,' came Jupiter's weary voice from inside the room. 'They're going to hear about it anyway.'

Fen gave a resentful, snuffling grunt and herded the pair of them into the parlour, pushing them forward with her great fluffy head.

'Ow – careful, Fen!' Morrigan protested as she stumbled into an armchair.

'Are you two all right? Fen's told me all about the gala.' Jupiter sighed, and added in a dispirited mutter, 'Shame, I could have had a lovely surprise when I read about it in the papers later.'

'We're fine,' said Jack. 'What are we going to hear about? What's going on?'

Perched on the edge of the windowsill, Jupiter rubbed his face with both hands.

'I spoke with Inspector Rivers last night. She has sources in the Wintersea Republic who believe that's where the Hollowpox originated. A couple of years ago they had an epidemic that only affected Wunimals. They called it something different of course, but their eyewitness accounts are identical: agitation and loss of language followed by a reversion to unnimalistic behaviours, leading to violence and finally ending with the Wunimal in a comatose state. Or worse.' Jupiter paused, taking a deep breath.

'If it happened two years ago, why's the Stealth only finding out about it now?' asked Jack. 'Don't they keep an eye on everything that happens in the Republic?'

'Do they?' asked Morrigan. That was news to her.

'They knew about the dwindling Wunimal populations,' said Jupiter. 'But they attributed it to other factors; Wunimals have been under attack across the border for a long time, and nobody had heard anything about a disease. And Wunimal groups in the Republic are small and scattered; they don't really talk to each other.'

'I don't understand,' said Morrigan. 'There *are* no Wunimals in the Wintersea Republic.'

Fenestra gave a derisive groan. 'Of course there are! Just because *you* never saw them, doesn't mean—'

'Easy, Fen.' Jupiter pressed the spot between his eyebrows, dropping a couple of headache tablets into a glass of water. It fizzed and bubbled and turned a cool, calming shade of lilac. 'Yes, Mog, there are Wunimals in the Republic. Lots of them. But they don't live the way Wunimals in the Free State live. They have their own communities, mostly in secret.' He downed the glass of lilac water in one.

'Why do they want to live in secret?' Morrigan asked.

'They don't want to,' said Fen. 'They *have* to.'

'The Wintersea Party doesn't officially acknowledge their existence,' Jupiter continued. 'It makes life dangerous for them. There are some Wunimals living in the Free State who came here to escape the Republic. It's possible one of them brought the Hollowpox with them.'

'But the borders are closed,' said Morrigan.

'Yes, the borders between the Republic and the Free State are, officially, closed,' said Jupiter, 'but there are ways in and out if you know what you're doing. They're risky, but if somebody is in serious need of help, there are people in the Free State who are willing to take the necessary risks. And many Wunimals in the Republic *are* in serious need of help. Fen is part of a group that specialises in bringing them to safety.'

'She's . . . part of a smuggling ring?' Morrigan said, just as Jack blurted out, 'Fen, you're a *smuggler*?'

Morrigan didn't know why she was surprised. She knew the Magnificat well enough by now to realise she was capable of pretty much anything.

Fen casually clawed at the rug. 'We prefer the term "rescue ring".'

'Hang on,' said Jack. 'Uncle Jove, are you saying the Hollowpox came from one of—?'

'AS I have been telling Jupiter, it absolutely did NOT come from one of ours,' Fen said fiercely. 'Impossible. Every Wunimal we smuggle across the border stays in a safe house for a *month* before we find them somewhere permanent in the Seven Pockets. Any sign of sickness in that time and they go straight into quarantine and *stay there* until they've been treated. There is no way – absolutely *no way* – that Hollowpox Patient Zero came into Nevermoor through me.'

'Fen, it wasn't an accusation, it was a warning. Your safe houses better be airtight, because there'll be raids before long. And tell your lot to be extra careful. The borders are being watched more closely than ever.'

'I thought the Free State was supposed to be impenetrable?' asked Morrigan.

Jupiter made a face. 'I wouldn't say *impenetrable*.'

'But Ezra Squall can't get in.'

'No, he can't,' said Jupiter. 'Because our borders *specifically* keep Squall out. They're impenetrable to him, but not necessarily to ordinary people in the Republic. It's just that most ordinary people in the Republic have no idea the Free State exists, and if they do, they don't know where it is or how to get here. But, as I say, there *are* ways inside.'

'Such as through a clockface in a giant mechanical spider piloted by a madman,' said Morrigan, recalling her own strange journey to Nevermoor, two and a half years ago. Jack laughed at that as he dropped into an armchair next to hers, swinging his legs over the side.

'Well, quite,' Jupiter said with a small, quick smile. 'If you're fortunate enough to know a handsome and enterprising redhead with friends in border control, that's one way. If not, there are various other . . . *informal* passages into the Free State.' He cast a fleeting look at Fen, who yawned widely. 'Or for those trying to go it alone, there's a long and dangerous trek through the Highlands. They'd have to get up over the cliffs first, though, and before that they'd have to sail from the east coast of Prosper across the Harrow Strait, which is very treacherous water.'

'And they'd have to do it in a small enough boat to go unnoticed by the Coast Patrol,' Fen pointed out. 'But it takes days to cross the Harrow. Someone infected with the Hollowpox would probably never make it that far.'

'And if they did, there would still be wild dragons to contend with, and the cave-dwelling clans of the Black Cliffs,' said Jupiter. 'And if they survived all that, it would take *weeks* to come down through the Highlands, and then—'

'I'm telling you, Jove, that's *not* the way they came,' Fen interrupted. 'Without inside help, the *only* viable way to make it from the Republic into Nevermoor within a matter of days would be via the River Juro, flowing in directly from the Harrow Strait. And the Coast Patrol monitors the water traffic and checks all boats in and out, every single one.'

'What if they swam?' Jack suggested.

Fenestra scoffed. 'Good luck to them.'

Morrigan remembered what Francis had said about the venomous river serpents, Great Spiny Demonfish, waterwolves and Bonesmen lurking in the Juro. No one could swim through all that. The whole thing seemed impossible without . . . a vessel.

Morrigan felt an idea gathering in her mind. She sat up very straight. 'Fen, what if they weren't in a boat *above* the water? Then they wouldn't be seen by the Coast Patrol, right?'

Jupiter's brow furrowed. 'Mog, what are you getting at?'

She told them about the vessel she, Francis and Thaddea had found in the pawn shop on Grand Boulevard, and what Francis had told her about submarines and spies.

'And the shopkeeper said something about – oh, what was it? He said it wasn't a *local* design,' she said. 'That it was *bona fide property of the Wintersea Party.*'

Jupiter narrowed his eyes. 'I'll have Inspector Rivers look into it. Good intel, Mog.'

Morrigan inched forward to the edge of her seat, suddenly remembering what she'd most wanted to tell him. 'Jack saw the green eyes! In the three Wunimals last night.'

Jupiter looked from one to the other in surprise. 'He – you did?'

Jack nodded. 'It was really weird. Bright, glowing green, and . . . sort of . . .'

He trailed off, and Morrigan took over, telling Jupiter all about the three Wunimals and how the light had flown out of their bodies just as the Hollowpox peaked, as if the light *was* the Hollowpox itself.

As he listened to the story, Jupiter's jaw clenched and unclenched repeatedly, the way it did when there was something he'd been holding back. 'Jack . . . one thing I don't understand about what happened last night. If there were infected Wunimals at the party, why didn't you say something to Fen or Kedgeree? Couldn't you *see* they were—?'

'They *weren't* infected,' Jack said emphatically. 'It wasn't like what we've seen at the bazaar, Uncle Jove, I swear. They weren't, you know, *hollow*. Then, when everything went dark –' (Jupiter glanced at Morrigan; Fen had evidently told him about the shadowmaking too) '– it was like the culminations we've seen at the bazaar, but . . . faster. Like the Hollowpox was on fast-forward.'

Morrigan described what it was like when the green lights left the infected Wunimals' bodies, how they'd swarmed around her and then split apart. 'And I've been thinking. Jupiter, what if it's not really a disease?' she finished in a breathless rush.

Jupiter's forehead wrinkled. 'What do you mean?'

'Remember when I asked you about the posters, and why you didn't tell people about the green eyes? You said if we described the infected as having glowing green eyes, people would claim they'd been possessed by demons. But Jupiter, that's exactly what it acted like! Like something *living* inside them, squatting inside them like a toad, like a . . . what do you call it, a living thing that takes over another body—'

'A parasite?' suggested Jupiter.

'Yes!' Morrigan snapped her fingers. 'Or a – a monster. It acted like one. I think it wanted to take *me* over, but it couldn't because I'm not a Wunimal.'

'A living parasite that acts like a disease,' Jupiter said thoughtfully. 'It would explain the strange pattern of infection, why the Hollowpox seems to spread so haphazardly. If it can think for itself, it can seek out the most hospitable host.' He fell silent for a moment, and Morrigan could almost hear his brain whirring.

But she wasn't finished speculating. 'And Jupiter, what if . . . what if it was *Squall* who made it and sent it into Nevermoor? That's what he does, he makes monsters! He can't come in himself, but maybe—'

'It's possible,' he agreed. 'I'll need to discuss this with the task force, but in the meantime, this conversation does not leave this room. Understood?'

Fen peered at him closely. 'Jove. Don't you think the Wunimal community deserves to know—'

'It's them I'm thinking of.' He stared miserably into the dregs of lilac water in the bottom of his glass. 'Fen, last night those guests thought you were an infected Wunimal. Why? Just because you were angry. They could have hurt you, they could have *attacked* you—'

'Pfft, don't worry about me—'

'I *do* worry about you, Fenestra! And I worry about our friends and guests and every Wunimal in this city!' He looked from Fen to Morrigan to Jack, wide-eyed, trying to make them understand. 'Because if that's how people act when they think it's a disease, imagine what will happen if we tell them it might be a monster, or that Squall might be involved! It would be as good as telling them that *Wunimals* are monsters. We'd be declaring open season on the whole lot of them.

'Just – *please* – promise me you'll keep this quiet for now.'

They promised. Even Fen.

CHAPTER TWENTY-FOUR

From Bad To Worse

Autumn of Three

'You can't do this, Jove. I won't stand for it. I'm not coming down until you take it back!'

Frank was swinging from the chandelier, and Morrigan wasn't entirely surprised. He'd been threatening drastic action all day.

'You're being ridiculous, Frank,' Jupiter called in a tense, weary voice from where he lay on top of the concierge desk, ankles crossed and fingers intertwined across his stomach. He added under his breath, 'As standard.'

'Come down, Frank, there's a good chap,' said Kedgeree coaxingly. He, Martha and Charlie were running back and forth beneath the chandelier, holding the four corners of a bedsheet up as high as they could, hoping to catch Frank when he inevitably fell. 'Come on, now, we've got you.'

'NEVER!' Frank roared. His black cape billowed in the slipstream as he swung wildly, casting light and shadows across the lobby.

Morrigan and Jack sat at the bottom of the spiral staircase, watching the spectacle unfold. Between the flickering light from the chandelier and the whole dramatic cape situation, the scene *should* have had the soothing sort of mad-ghost-haunting-an-abandoned-theatre aesthetic that Morrigan enjoyed. But the past twenty-four hours had given her a growing sense of unease.

As Jupiter had predicted, within hours of the gala's abrupt ending, the newspapers were already ablaze with news of the famous Hotel Deucalion. Its famously mad ginger proprietor, a mysterious incident AND Wunimals behaving badly all added up to excellent tabloid fodder. It didn't seem to matter that Jupiter wasn't even *there*.

The Concerned Citizens of Nevermoor were louder than ever. Their spluttering, fist-slamming founder went head-to-head with prominent Wunimal rights activist Senator Guiscard Silverback – himself a gorillawun – in a fierce debate about the dangers of allowing Wunimals in public spaces 'in these troubled times'.

The mood in Nevermoor was tense; it felt like everyone was simply waiting for the next attack. Jupiter made the decision to close the Deucalion's doors until the Hollowpox was under control. Frank had, predictably, been wailing ever since.

'Jove, *do* something,' Dame Chanda urged, pushing Jupiter's feet off the desk and forcing him to sit up with a groan. 'Make him stop this foolishness!'

Jupiter scoffed. '*Really?* If I had the ability to make Frank stop *any* sort of foolishness, do you think I'd still have a monthly bill for cocktail umbrellas that runs into the *thousands*? I told him he could have a dinner party and he *threw a whole stinking gala*, so I don't know what kind of mystical powers you think I have over him!'

Dame Chanda fixed him with her sternest look and he groaned again, sliding reluctantly off the desk.

'*Fine.*' He glared up at the swinging vampire. 'Frank, please come down. Let's talk about this.'

'NO! I SHAN'T COME DOWN, JOVE, NOT UNTIL – ARRRGHH!'

Frank lost his grip on the chandelier, came plummeting downwards, and was caught at the last second in the bedsheet and lowered gently to the ground. He scrambled to his feet and scowled at them one by one, furious at the indignity of it all.

Jupiter stuck his hands in his pockets and sighed. 'The Federation of Nevermoorian Hoteliers has given their recommendation to temporarily close, Frank, I can't just—'

'The Aurianna is still open,' Frank protested. 'They're ignoring the recommendation. They're positively *gleeful* that we've closed, Jove! Do you realise they're throwing a party every night this—'

'The Aurianna has *banned Wunimals*,' Jupiter snapped, running a hand over his face. 'Do you realise *that*? *That* is how the Aurianna is staying open.'

Frank turned away. Martha covered her mouth with her hands, while Morrigan and Jack exchanged a look of dismay. Nobody spoke.

Jupiter pushed on through the uncomfortable silence. 'Is that what you'd like me to do? Turn away some of our friends while welcoming others?'

Frank huffed and adjusted his cape a little irritably. 'I'm sure they'd – well, it is only *temporary*, after all!'

'We don't know that, Frank,' said Kedgeree. 'We can't possibly know how long this will go on.'

'What about all our other guests, then?' Frank continued,

looking to Charlie and Martha for support. 'Don't we owe *them—*'

'I think,' Martha began in a halting voice, 'that we owe all of our guests the same consideration. What they're doing at the Aurianna . . . Well. It's not right.' She pursed her lips, making it clear that was all she had to say on the matter.

'It's bang out of order,' agreed Charlie, and Kedgeree gave a sober nod.

Jupiter spoke quietly. 'You know, I'm surprised at you, Frank. For goodness' sake, there are still establishments in Nevermoor that refuse to welcome *you* because you're—'

'A vampire, yes!' Frank's eyebrows shot upwards. 'Exactly. And do you hear me complaining? Honestly, I don't blame them. I'm a liability! I bit a man at the supermarket last week!'

Dame Chanda gasped. 'Frank!'

'Oh, it was just a nibble,' he said, with a wave of his hand. 'I sent flowers. My point is—'

'This isn't up for discussion.' Jupiter hadn't raised his voice, but the muscles in his jaw were clenched tight. 'This is my hotel. I decide what it stands for, and the Deucalion does *not* stand for that.'

'*Jove—*'

'That's my final decision. We're closed to the public until this is over.'

Jupiter swept past Morrigan and stormed up the spiral staircase before anyone could say another word. Before anyone could ask the question they were all thinking, but nobody could answer.

When would it be over?

The summer had come to a crashing, miserable halt. Morrigan might almost have been pleased to return to school, except things weren't much better there. Or anywhere else in Nevermoor.

When Hometrain 919 arrived at Proudfoot Station on Monday morning, Morrigan half expected to find herself the subject of whispers and stares after all the news coverage of what had happened at the Deucalion.

But the dreadful, ever-turning news cycle had saved her. There'd already been three more attacks since Friday night's Sunset Gala: a boarwun had trampled a woman in the street, an elderly poodlewun had attacked her neighbour's grandson, and a crocodilewun had dragged a man into the Courage Square fountain and nearly drowned him in a death roll. All three attackers now lay comatose, while their victims recovered elsewhere from injuries and shock.

'I heard the crocodile was Senator Silverback's personal assistant,' Morrigan heard a girl from the unit above whispering to her friend on the platform. 'Not a good look for him, is it?'

'Crocodilewun,' Morrigan corrected her automatically.

The girl turned to her in shock. 'Are you actually defending him? He could have *drowned* someone!'

'I'm not *defending*—'

'Whatever.' The girl scowled and turned back to her friend, hissing '*Wundersmith*' under her breath. Morrigan wished they'd come up with a new insult.

As the autumn chill settled into Wunsoc, there were daily Hollowpox meetings and Jupiter and Inspector Rivers were constantly on call, leaping into action whenever strange Wunimal behaviour was reported somewhere in the city.

The task force had tripled in size and was increasingly comprised of Wunimal volunteers like Sofia reaching out to the friends and family of infected Wunimals, to collect data and help where they could. Dr Bramble and Dr Lutwyche were working round the clock trying to care for the infected and unravel the origins of the Hollowpox, desperate to find a cure, or a vaccine.

(Jupiter said that Dr Bramble, in particular, remained unconvinced of Morrigan's monster theory. 'A monster that looks like a disease and acts like a disease in the body must, for all intents and purposes, be treated like a disease – and therefore can be cured like one,' she'd reportedly said. Morrigan had sniffed at that, and asked Jupiter to relay the fact that she remained unconvinced of *Dr Bramble's* theory, if it could be called that.)

In the absence of any good news, the meetings usually devolved into an argument – typically over who the *real* victims of the Hollowpox were – when talk turned to the continued use of the Teaching Hospital's staff and resources to care for the growing number of infected.

After all, people reasoned, were the 'real victims' those Wunimals lying in hospital beds, hollowed out and unresponsive? Or were they the people those Wunimals had *attacked*?

'I propose that all Wunimals be exiled from Society grounds until we have a better understanding of what's happening,' Dulcinea Dearborn declared in that day's meeting.

Morrigan might have imagined it, but she *thought* she saw Dearborn cast a disdainful look in Sofia's direction. She clutched her book bag tightly to her chest to keep from throwing it at the Scholar Mistress's head.

'Hear, hear!' shouted Baz Charlton from the third row.

'I quite agree with Ms Dearborn.' Francis's Aunt Hester stood up from her seat to speak, and Francis sunk down low in his. 'I know that many of our adult Society members tend to forget this small fact, but we are trying to operate a *school* inside Proudfoot House. There are *children* here. Are we just supposed to wait around and hope that none of our teachers turn into raging, rabid unnimals? I for one am unwilling to take that risk any longer.'

'Unnimals?' roared Elder Saga, so loudly that Morrigan and the rest of Unit 919 all jumped at least an inch from their seats. He stamped his hooves on the ground and lowered his great horned head as if ready to charge. Nervous whispers broke out. 'Did you just call us *unnimals*, Hester Fitzwilliam? The *insolence*!'

The atmosphere was unbearably tense; the entire gathering seemed poised to flee.

'Elder Saga, compose yourself,' said Elder Wong. He put out his hands in a calming gesture but Morrigan thought she could see him shaking a little. 'I'm certain she didn't mean to—'

'To use a highly provocative slur against her fellow Society members, against her *brothers and sisters*?' Elder Saga was practically shooting steam from his nostrils. Morrigan gripped the arms of her chair. 'That is precisely what she meant to do.'

Hester was shaken by the sight of the enormous bullwun so enraged, but she recovered quickly, drawing herself up to her full height. 'What I meant was that they are losing their speech, their intelligence, they are losing everything that *makes* them Wunimals. They are, in short, *becoming unnimals*, Elder Saga, whether you have the courage to admit that or not.'

'The *courage*—' began Elder Saga, but he was interrupted by a loud *CRASH* as the doors were flung open. Holliday Wu from the Public Distraction Department ran into the room and straight to Elder Quinn, whispering something in her ear and pressing a note into her hand.

The gathering fell silent. They seemed to hold their collective breath as Holliday rushed from the room, barely pausing after delivering her news. Elder Quinn stayed still and quiet for some time after she read the piece of paper, her expression unchanged. Finally, she spoke in a grave voice.

'The Hollowpox has taken a life.'

CHAPTER TWENTY-FIVE

We're All on The Same Side, Really

Elder Quinn's words echoed in the Gathering Place.

'Last night,' she read from the paper aloud, 'at the docks. Dozens of people witnessed the culmination of the Hollowpox in a baboonwun fisherman, who attacked a group of four young men disembarking from a boat. Three of them are being treated for serious injuries. One is in a critical condition.'

Elder Quinn cleared her throat, steeling herself to deliver the final blow.

'The baboonwun lost control as the Hollowpox culminated and threw himself from the boat. Witnesses say he was comatose before his body hit the water, where it sank below the waves and didn't resurface. Some of the crew attempted to save him, but . . .' She pressed her lips tightly together. She didn't need to say any more.

There was silence. Then a slow swell of whispers.

By the end of the day, the Hollowpox death count had risen to two. One of the young men had sadly died from his injuries.

Inside Wunsoc, the mood was grim.

Outside Wunsoc, fear and rage spread like fire through dry leaves.

The Prime Minister, Gideon Steed, took the extraordinary measure of declaring a state of emergency in Nevermoor, and ordered that a sunset curfew be put in place for all Wunimals in the city.

'Those who break curfew will be arrested, charged and prosecuted to the extent of the law,' was his ominous promise.

Guiscard Silverback came thundering on to the airwaves that afternoon, blazing with righteous anger. Unit 919 huddled around Miss Cheery's old wireless radio to listen on the train trip home.

'Most of us in the Wunimal community have already taken it upon ourselves to isolate, and *still* we are treated like criminals!' Silverback roared across the airwaves. 'We don't wish to catch this virus! We don't wish to hurt our fellow Nevermoorians! Need I remind the prime minister there have been TWO deaths? One human, one Wunimal. Yet Steed does *nothing* to protect his Wunimal citizens. Instead he continues to defer all moral responsibility for the care of these Hollowpox victims – yes, they too are *victims* – to the Wundrous Society! Wunsoc can only carry this burden so far. The government must step in.'

'He's right,' Anah told them in a weary voice. She was spending a lot of her spare time assisting at the teaching hospital these days, even pitching in over the summer holidays. Morrigan had noticed the dark circles under her eyes, and the way her usually immaculate ringlets were now perpetually knotted in a messy, dirty bun. 'The locked ward has become an entire locked *wing*, and it's nearly full now, too.'

'How many are there, Anah?' asked Cadence.

'Must be a hundred. More. I've lost count, they just keep coming,' she finished, yawning widely. Arch got up without a word and began making Anah a cup of tea in her favourite mug.

Prime Minister Steed responded to Senator Silverback's denunciation by claiming that the curfew was for the safety of Wunimals as well as humans.

'If Nevermoor's Wunimals don't wish to be caught in the firing line of infection, they ought to stay home and stay safe,' he said.

Morrigan shook her head. The Hollowpox wasn't going to stop because of a curfew. Whatever it was – demon, parasite, *monster* – it wasn't going to give up just because Wunimals stayed home at night. It wasn't floating around like germs, infecting only those who came into contact with it.

It was hunting, and Wunimals were its prey.

It would find them no matter where they were.

When they arrived at Station 919, Morrigan lingered as the others waved goodbye.

'Miss,' she said. 'How's your friend?'

'Roshni?' Miss Cheery took a deep breath. 'She's still in hospital. Her injuries were pretty serious.'

Morrigan felt a stab of guilt. She wished they'd never gone to the Gobleian.

'Will she be all right?'

'Course she will. Off you go now. See you bright and early.'

She thought she saw Miss Cheery's eyes go glassy with tears – but only for a second, before the conductor gathered herself up and turned away.

'THIRTY-EIGHT WUNIMAL ARRESTS!' Conall was bellowing when Morrigan arrived on Sub-Nine the next day. His voice came from the study chamber, but she could hear it from halfway down the long marble hall. 'In one night! Senator Silverback won't stand for this. He'll put a stop to it. He *must*.'

'I'm not sure he'll be able to,' Sofia replied, calm as ever. 'The Stink are working well within their authority, Conall, and Steed has plenty of public support for his curfew. Guiscard Silverback can't be seen to be too *forceful*—'

'If Silverback can't force Steed to do what's right, we'll take it to the Wunimal Rights Commission,' Conall snapped. 'Hell, we'll storm parliament if we must!'

Morrigan reached the door and paused to peek inside. Conall paced back and forth as quickly and furiously as his walking stick would allow, clutching a newspaper in his free hand, while Sofia sat perfectly still on top of the long table.

She sighed. Her bushy red tail twitched. 'Calm down, Conall.'

'*Calm down?*' He stopped in his tracks. 'Sofia, do you not see your rights being eroded? I won't just stand by—'

'I can assure you I am aware of the precise condition of my rights, every single day. You may safely assume most Wunimals are.' There was a new edge to her voice, though its volume hadn't increased in the slightest. Conall opened his mouth to retort, then seemed to think the better of it. 'And I don't want to just *stand by*, either, but there's a proper way to address the curfew problem, and storming parliament isn't— Morrigan?' Her tail twitched again as she glanced back over her shoulder. 'Is that you?'

Morrigan jumped at the sound of her name and entered the room a little shamefaced.

'Sorry,' she said, feeling her cheeks grow warm. 'I was just . . .'

She trailed off, unsure of what to say. It was plainly obvious she'd overheard their conversation.

'What do you think about this curfew business?' Sofia asked her.

'She's a *child*,' snapped Conall.

'She's a Wundersmith.'

'She's still a child!'

'I agree with Conall,' Morrigan said quietly.

Conall looked up, blinking his bright blue eyes at her. 'She's a highly intelligent child, I've always said that.'

Sofia's ears twitched. 'How so, Morrigan?'

'It's dreadful of Steed to arrest people for something that shouldn't be a crime. It's only going to make people more frightened.' She took a seat at the table, unbuttoning her coat. 'And how is the Hollowpox mission going to keep trying to find the infected before they attack? A third of the task force is made up of Wunimals, and now you can't go out past sunset! Couldn't the Elders at *least* get special permission for you and the rest of the task force to ignore the curfew?'

Sofia shook her head. 'It doesn't work like that, Morrigan. The Elders can't petition the government for personal favours.'

'And it's not about getting special permission for *some* Wunimals,' Conall added. 'It's about fairness to *all* Wunimals.'

'Then . . . maybe you're right, Conall. Maybe we *should* storm parliament!' Morrigan insisted. 'All of us. The whole Wundrous Society. If we all came together to challenge Gideon Steed – just imagine that! All these Wuns, with all these knacks. Would *you* want to say no? Maybe it would frighten him enough to . . .'

Morrigan trailed off again at the look of disappointment on Sofia's face.

'We don't use our knacks to tyrannise people, Morrigan. It's not what the Wundrous Society is about.'

Morrigan blinked. She felt a sudden welling of some unpleasant, familiar feeling in her stomach. She felt ashamed. Tyrannising people . . . that's what Ezra Squall did.

'I know!' she said quickly, and even she could hear the defensive tone in her voice. 'I know that. I didn't really mean we should *do* anything. I just . . . never mind.'

There was a moment of awkward silence in which nobody quite knew what to say next, then Conall cleared his throat and opened his fob watch. 'Five minutes, Wundersmith.' He held it up for her to see.

Morrigan shook her head, trying to clear it. 'Sorry – five minutes?'

'Your lesson. It begins in five minutes.' He pointed upwards. 'Rooftop.'

'Oh, right. Bye.' She got up and bolted for the door, glad for a reason to leave. She dashed down the marble hall of Sub-Nine, eager to outrun her discomfort.

'Morrigan, wait!'

She stopped and turned back, feeling guilt wash over her again as Sofia emerged from the study chamber behind her. She opened her mouth to say something, but Sofia held up a paw. 'It's all right. You were trying to show you're on my side. I know that. I just want you to remember that there are no *sides* to this. Wunimals, humans . . . we all just want this to be over. Even Prime Minister Steed and the Stink. We're all on the same side, really.'

Morrigan nodded but truthfully, she wasn't sure she agreed with that sentiment any more.

LOCATION	PARTICIPANTS & EVENTS	DATE & TIME
School of Wundrous Arts, rooftop of Proudfoot House, southern end	Gracious Goldberry, Maurice Bledworth	Age of Industry, Third Monday, Autumn of Eight
	Goldberry and Bledworth practise the Wundrous Art of Inferno	09:13–10:32 Ⓐ

Morrigan made it to the rooftop just in time. Squinting against the sun, she found the tiny gap in the air (it was harder to spot outside during the day) and reached inside, feeling a cool breeze brush her fingertips. Then a familiar, gentle pull. The air around her shivered as she slipped into the past.

It was a stormy, black-skied morning in the ghostly hour, and the autumn wind had a bite to it. But within moments she was surrounded by the fierce warmth of bright orange flames. She hadn't had time to check the listing in *The Book of Ghostly Hours* and was surprised to see Gracious Goldberry again, wielding fire as if she'd invented it.

There was only one student this time – a Wundersmith older than Goldberry, Morrigan noticed, but still her inferior when it came to Inferno. Against a backdrop of thunderclouds and an occasional flash of lightning, the two Wundersmiths curled flames into flowers and shot jets of fire into the sky.

At one point Goldberry pressed her palms into the ground and sent flames spiralling outwards until, with one final pulse of light, the entire rooftop was set briefly, brightly ablaze. It reminded Morrigan of Saint Nicholas's candle trick on Christmas Eve, but Goldberry's work was even more precise and powerful – so powerful it momentarily lifted her and Bledworth several inches off the ground.

This was way past beginner level, she thought. They were

practising skills she'd never seen before. That meant Rook had either made a mistake in her schedule, or she believed Morrigan was ready for a more advanced lesson.

Part of her felt bolstered by that thought. She *had* been making progress, and it was gratifying to know it hadn't gone unnoticed by the Scholar Mistress.

On the other hand, Gracious Goldberry was the absolute last Wundersmith she wanted to see this morning. She felt furious and frightened and sick. She was worried for Sofia, and angry about Steed's curfew and the thirty-eight arrests, and furious at the memory of Dearborn and Hester's outburst at the last meeting . . . and *now* she had to spend a morning with an infamous opponent of Wunimal rights. Morrigan was tempted to leave and skip the lesson altogether.

But good *grief*, was Goldberry brilliant.

Morrigan remembered what Sofia had said about her the last time they'd stood on this rooftop: *I decided that this extraordinary talent could not be wasted on this wretch of a woman . . . I would render it useful somehow.*

And so, heart weighed down with spite and veins humming with righteous anger, Morrigan spent a long morning trying to render Goldberry's talent useful. She imagined herself a thief, stealing every bit of information she could from the way Goldberry breathed, the way she carried herself lightly, the way she planted her feet, even the way she sometimes held her tongue against her teeth. In Goldberry's hands, the fire shrank and grew and smouldered and roared. It danced like beads of water in a fountain. It burned all the way down to embers and then bloomed back into life like a mushroom cloud. She made patterns and shapes – a hand, a lion, a face – painting pictures in the air that reminded Morrigan of Saint Nicholas's firebird.

Morrigan copied her every move – not flawlessly, by any means, but with greater success than she'd ever had before. She even breathed her own firebird into life – a crow with long, trailing wings of fire – and let loose a shout of triumph as she sent it flying into the sky, imperfect but *hers*. The lesson became a meditation, and time flew. Her connection to Inferno felt smoother, somehow. Faster. *Almost* seamless.

She even had a go at circular breathing (Dame Chanda had obligingly explained the concept to her), though not very successfully. The problem with ghostly hours was that she couldn't simply put up her hand and ask a question. She had to rely on whoever had been present in the original lesson to ask, so unless they were much younger or much less experienced than she was, most of her questions went unanswered. Even if she remembered to ask Sofia or Conall or Rook afterwards, they could rarely help her with practical matters. They just weren't Wundersmiths.

Goldberry spoke only once during the lesson. The older Wundersmith, Maurice Bledworth, had stopped to watch her, overawed and unable to keep up any longer.

'How do you do that?' he asked, gesturing to her hands. 'I can't seem to see where it's coming from.'

'Where what is coming from?' asked Goldberry, looking annoyed at the interruption.

'The flame,' said Bledworth. 'Even when it's completely died, you seem to bring it back so quickly, so easily.'

The older Wundersmith – and Morrigan – watched closely as Goldberry made her entire forearm a torch, and then let it sizzle all the way down to the tips of her fingers until it was entirely extinguished.

Or . . . not entirely.

Goldberry held out one finger and, leaning in close, Morrigan could see the tiniest, most minute, almost *invisible* spark of fire, hovering at the very edge of her skin.

'Not dead. See?' said Goldberry.

She crouched low and ran the length of the rooftop, brushing her fingertips across the ground and then upwards in a wide arc towards the sky, leaving a perfect trail of flames blazing in her wake.

'Only need a spark,' she said with a shrug. 'Small sparks make big fires.'

Morrigan stared mutely as the fire, the Wundersmiths, and the whole ghostly hour faded before her eyes, leaving her alone on the rooftop again.

Small sparks make big fires.

The words bounced around her head as she watched the flames in her fingertips burn down to almost nothing. A tiny, minute, almost invisible spark.

Taking a long, deep breath, Morrigan grinned. She felt energised and buoyant and – for the first time in a long time – somehow *certain* that there was a way out of this mess Nevermoor was in.

She felt hopeful. And she couldn't really say why, because nothing had changed.

Though that wasn't altogether true. Something was changing. *She* was changing. She felt more like a *real* Wundersmith than ever before, and that knowledge made anything seem possible. It cleared her worried head just a little, and gently nudged her shoulders straight. For the first time in days, she felt . . . calm.

Then a sound from behind her brought on a rush of adrenaline.

Her heart drummed a warning before her brain even registered what it was.

Morrigan turned around slowly, while Ezra Squall hummed a song that felt like spiders crawling beneath her skin.

CHAPTER TWENTY-SIX

Squall, the Monster

The bright day darkened. A pungent smell of wood smoke filled the air.

'Is this the best they can do for you?' A tiny smile curled one corner of Squall's mouth. 'Dead, irrelevant wisdom from dead, irrelevant Wundersmiths?'

Morrigan said nothing. She rubbed the tips of her fingers together and felt a tiny shock of heat. The spark was still there.

He looked just the same as ever, she noticed. Neat, contained, deliberate; like a portrait of a man frozen in time. The perfect parting of his feathery brown hair, with a hint of silver at the temples. The pallid, porcelain complexion like a death mask, marred only by the thin scar that split his left eyebrow. The eyes so dark they were nearly black.

Yet – if she narrowed her eyes until they were nearly closed – the faint, reassuring shimmer of the Gossamer surrounding him that told her it was his mind, not his body, that was in Nevermoor.

He shook his head. 'Tell me, have you learned a single thing since last we met?'

Crouching low, Morrigan pressed her fingertips to the ground and ran the width of the rooftop, leaving a fiery trail behind her. With a triumphant shout, she swung her arm up into the air just as Goldberry had done, creating an arc of flames that burned out and left a lingering circle of smoke against the blue sky.

She turned back to Squall, lungs heaving and eyes blazing.

'I've learned plenty, thanks.'

There was a low, rumbling growl, and Morrigan felt her throat grow dry as a pack of hounds emerged from the shadows. Of course. Wherever Squall went, the Hunt of Smoke and Shadow was sure to follow. They began to circle, fur black as pitch and eyes like embers. The smell of wood smoke filled Morrigan's nostrils and made her eyes water.

He stared right back at her, unimpressed. 'You are light years away from where you ought to be. It might *feel like* the Wundrous Society is allowing you to fly, Miss Crow . . . but I'm afraid all I see is a sad little bird with clipped wings who cannot even comprehend the cage she's in.'

'Interesting,' she replied. 'All I see is a pathetic, lonely killer whose only friends are a bunch of smoky dogs. I'm not afraid of you, Squall.'

He smiled. 'What a comforting affirmation that must be.'

The strangest thing was, Morrigan found it was true. Sort of. Mostly.

Squall's presence on the rooftop had taken her by surprise, and she didn't like surprises. But she wasn't feeling the gut-deep terror she'd felt on the other occasions they'd met. Perhaps it was because she'd seen him as a child now, spent time with him in the ghostly hours.

Or perhaps she was simply getting used to him.

What a bizarre thought.

'I've told you before. There is nobody at the Wundrous Society who can teach you what you need to know. Not even the great Griselda Polaris. I am the best and only chance you have, Miss Crow.' He gently inclined his head. 'Time to stop playing. I've come to formalise the arrangement.'

Morrigan narrowed her eyes. 'What do you mean?'

'Be my apprentice,' he continued. 'Agree to learn from me everything that I am able to teach you. Work hard, pay attention, and finally become the Wundersmith you were meant to be.'

'Oh, I see,' she said, with a slightly bewildered laugh. 'And – sorry – what *exactly* am I supposed to get out of this arrangement?'

Squall raised an eyebrow. 'Aside from an incomparable depth of knowledge and the opportunity to become the most powerful person in the Free State? Aside from veering away from this path you're on to become a second-rate version of a ghostly re-enactment of a long-dead also-ran?'

'Right, aside from all that,' said Morrigan. 'The truth is you can't give me anything, because there's nothing I want from you. I have everything I need right here at Wunsoc.'

'Except . . . a cure.'

The words hung in the air. Morrigan and Squall watched each other for several silent seconds.

'A cure for what?' she said finally, her pulse quickening.

He didn't respond to that. He didn't need to.

Morrigan shook her head in disbelief. 'You'd just *give me* the cure?'

She saw a tiny flicker of amusement cross his face. 'Certainly not. But become my apprentice, and I won't just *cure* the so-called Hollowpox, I will destroy it. We will destroy it together. For good.'

'How do I know you're not lying?' she demanded. 'How do I know it can even *be* destroyed?'

'Do you think I would make something I couldn't unmake?'

Morrigan felt her blood rise. She opened her mouth, then closed it. She felt vindicated and furious all at once.

'I *knew* it was you. I *told* them!' She began to pace back and forth, agitating the spark of fire between her fingertips. 'It's not a disease at all, is it? It's one of your monsters! I'm right, aren't I?'

But Squall said nothing, gave nothing away.

'*Why*? Just because you like killing things, because you like hurting people? Or is this another one of your sick *tests*, like the Ghastly Market? Did you cause all this havoc and pain just so that I would . . .' Morrigan trailed off. Her mind had been racing ahead, but it came to a crashing halt as she connected the final dot. Her mouth twisted into an expression of disgust. 'So that I would agree to become your apprentice.'

Squall's face was impassive.

'I'm *right*,' she said again, her voice low and angry, 'aren't I? You can only get what you want by *blackmail*—'

'You're being dramatic.' It felt somehow like an insult – the contrast of his soft, disinterested voice against the anger she felt buzzing inside her like a beehive. She wanted to throw something at him. She wanted to shake him. 'Not to mention terribly presumptuous – you know, the entire world does not *revolve* around you. And if my sole aim was to swindle you into an apprenticeship, I could think of far more efficient ways.'

'I don't believe you.'

'You rarely do.'

'Why, then?' she demanded again. 'Why create the Hollowpox at all? Just your warped idea of fun?'

He gave a tiny, irritated sigh, little more than a puff of air.

'I didn't say I would give you an explanation, Miss Crow. I have never felt the need to explain myself to anyone and I don't intend to begin now. I said I'd give you a *cure*. That is my offer.'

'Maybe we don't need you.' She tilted her chin slightly upwards, clenching her hands into fists. 'Dr Bramble thinks she's close to finding a cure.'

His only response to that claim was a pitying smile that made the skin on the back of her neck grow cold.

'Come now. It's not so difficult a choice, is it? Become my apprentice and save all of Wunimalkind! Be the hero of Nevermoor! Hip, hip, hooray! Who knows, they might even give you a medal.'

Squall gave a low whistle, and the shadow hounds swarmed obediently to his side. 'I'll give you a few days to consider my offer, but don't take too long. Things are ever so much worse than you know. You'll find that out for yourself soon enough, and when you do, you will come looking for me.'

Morrigan's lip curled. 'I will *not* come looking—'

'You will,' he repeated in the same calm, conversational tone. 'On the Gossamer Line.'

'The Gossamer Line station is closed,' she said belligerently.

Squall closed his eyes, a line creasing the space between them, and shook his head as if she had said something ridiculous. 'One day, Miss Crow, you may begin to understand how much of Nevermoor lies dormant or dead, waiting patiently for you to nudge it back to life. One day, you may realise how formidably you could run this city, if only you'd put in a little *effort*.'

Squall and his hounds made to walk away, looking for all the world as if they might just saunter straight off the rooftop.

'Oh – one other thing.' He stopped abruptly, spinning back to face her. 'I should warn you. They're going to flip the script.'

Morrigan frowned. 'What?'

'The Wundrous Society,' he clarified. 'Any day now, they're going to flip the script about Wundersmiths. About you. The official Wunsoc line has long been *Wundersmiths are monsters. Wundersmiths are the cause of all our woes.* But watch. Someday soon it will change to *This Wundersmith will slay our monsters. This Wundersmith will solve all our problems.*'

'Oh no.' Morrigan glared at him from beneath half-closed eyelids. 'What an awful thought, that I might be asked to *help* people. How truly terrible.'

'You have no idea.'

He'd already turned once again to leave, cloaked in shadow, when Morrigan finally shouted at his back the thing she really wanted to say. The thing she'd been wondering for months.

'Why did you kill them?'

It had taken all of her courage to say it, and she could feel herself trembling, shocked by her own audacity. Squall halted, but he didn't face her. The hounds growled a warning. 'Why did you murder the other Wundersmiths? Your friends?'

Squall remained perfectly still.

'They *trusted* you.'

She didn't even see him move, but in a fraction of a second he was *right there*, looming above her. The pale, expressionless mask had slipped to reveal the beast inside, black eyes and blackened mouth and sharp, bared teeth. The shadow hounds whined. Even they were afraid of him.

Morrigan felt terror grip her throat. Her overwhelming instinct was to shrink away, to run, to close her eyes, but she wouldn't let herself. She held her breath, staring at the monster Squall. Committing him to memory.

'Another thing you will one day understand,' he snarled, 'is that *Wundersmiths don't have friends.*'

Morrigan recoiled from his words as if they might burn her.

And then the mask was back. So still and pale and cold, it might have been carved from marble. So ordinary, she might almost have believed she'd imagined that other, hidden face. His true face.

And then he was gone, leaving only a curl of black smoke.

CHAPTER TWENTY-SEVEN

Spark

Morrigan stayed on the rooftop for some time after Squall and his hounds disappeared into the Gossamer. She took deep, steadying breaths, and pressed her hands together to stop them shaking.

Eventually she wandered in a daze back to the stairwell, still replaying the conversation with Squall over and over in her mind, while trying to shake out the image of his monstrous face.

Things are ever so much worse than you know.

What could be worse than a hospital overflowing with comatose Wunimals? Worse than people scared to leave their homes for fear of being attacked, and Wunimals unable to break curfew under threat of being arrested? Worse than the Deucalion being closed down indefinitely? Worse than people dying? Worse than a disease without a cure – or more accurately, a monster that couldn't be destroyed?

As she descended the last steps into the buzzing Proudfoot House entrance hall, Morrigan felt a hand grab her elbow.

'Morrigan!'

'Ow! Cadence, what—'

'Where have you *been*?' Cadence began steering her through the throng of scholars and towards the front door. 'You missed our organic witchery workshop.'

'I was on the rooftop. Wait, I have to—'

'Doesn't matter now. Just come outside. You've got to see this.'

'Cadence, *wait*,' Morrigan said again, trying to yank her arm back, but her friend held on tight. 'I have to tell you something.'

'Tell me later. This is important.' Cadence let go of her arm when they'd reached the top of the marble steps. A dozen or so scholars were standing there, looking nervous.

A huge, noisy crowd had gathered at the end of the long drive, outside Wunsoc's tall iron gates. Hundreds of people carried placards and shouted at Elder Quinn, Elder Wong and Elder Saga, who stood just inside the grounds. The placards were too far away for Morrigan to read, but judging from the angry yelling, she doubted they had anything friendly written on them.

Cadence and Morrigan joined Lam on the bottom step. She had a basket of funny-looking herbs and plants from their witchery workshop and was clutching it tight to her chest, looking uneasy.

'It's them again,' she said, nodding down the drive.

A tinny, mechanical squeal made everyone wince and cover their ears, followed by a familiar strident voice ringing out across the campus.

'WE DEMAND ANSWERS,' boomed Laurent St James, and the protestors roared their agreement. It seemed the Concerned Citizens of Nevermoor Party had gained a few more members since Morrigan last saw them. 'WE DEMAND THE TRUTH. WE DEMAND THAT THE WUNDROUS SOCIETY STOP

PROTECTING MURDERERS AND VIOLENT ATTACKERS!'

The crowd cheered so loudly for this that the megaphone squealed again.

'What "murderers" are we protecting?' huffed a senior scholar leaning against a pillar. 'The baboonwun drowned in the Juro! What exactly are we protecting him from?'

'THESE PEOPLE, THE SOCIETY'S SO-CALLED HIGH COUNCIL OF ELDERS, REFUSE TO PROTECT NORMAL, HARD-WORKING CITIZENS.'

Word had evidently spread through Proudfoot House; more scholars began to trickle out into the grounds. Thaddea and Anah had snaked through the gathering crowd to join them.

'Why isn't anyone defending the High Council?' asked Thaddea. She rolled up her sleeves as if preparing for a fight. 'We should all be down there.'

'Yeah, we should,' Morrigan agreed. She hated seeing the three Elders standing alone against an enormous, angry crowd, even if there was a locked gate between them. Ordinarily she'd be most worried for tiny, ancient Elder Quinn . . . but in this particular situation, she had her eye on Elder Saga. What would happen to him if the Concerned Citizens breached the gates? She remembered how quickly the guests at the Sunset Gala had turned on Fenestra.

'We *were* down there,' said Cadence. 'A few of us. Lam and I were coming out of the Whinging Woods when it all kicked off.'

'Couldn't you have just . . . y'know. Mesmerised the lot of 'em?' asked Thaddea. 'Done your funny voice thing, told everyone to pack it in and go home?'

Cadence rolled her eyes. 'My "funny voice thing" doesn't really scale up, Thaddea. I can't just tell a whole *crowd* of people what to do, it doesn't work like that. Anyway, Elder Quinn ordered everyone back up here to Proudfoot House.'

'They don't want it to turn into a stand-off,' Lam explained in a slightly muffled voice, because she was chewing fretfully on her bottom lip. Her fingers had turned white where they were clutching the basket. 'They're trying to calm things down.'

'Not doing a very good job, though, are they?' said Thaddea. 'Listen to them, they're getting worse.'

'THE MURDEROUS JACKALWUN MUST BE BROUGHT TO JUSTICE!' bellowed St James, to resounding cheers. 'WE DEMAND SHE BE QUESTIONED BY THE POLICE AT ONCE.'

'Good luck getting her to talk,' said Anah quietly. The others looked at her. She was still in her hospital uniform and her eyes were red-rimmed as if she'd been crying, or was just about to. 'Good luck getting any of them to say a word, ever again.'

'What jackalwun?' asked Morrigan.

Anah sniffled. 'It happened this morning. A jackalwun attacked an old man at a doctor's office. He died at the scene, and she . . . she's here, of course. In the hospital.' She wiped her nose on her sleeve. Thaddea put an arm around her shoulders.

'One of ours, two of theirs,' said someone nearby, and Morrigan peeked over her shoulder to see a boy from Unit 918 – a catwun minor, almost entirely human but for his fine whiskers and little pink nose.

'What do you mean?' his friend asked him.

'The death toll,' the catwun clarified gloomily. 'It's uneven now. One Wunimal, two humans. Now they think they have the moral high ground, don't they?'

Morrigan heard Sofia's voice in her head. *We're all on the same side.*

Those words sounded even more hollow than they had before.

'We know you are frightened!' shouted Elder Quinn. Her

voice was brittle, but it carried. 'We know you want answers. But it is not useful or kind to think of the affected Wunimals as villains, as *murderers*. They are *ill*. They are the victims of a dreadful disease—'

'We know who the real victims are!' cried a woman clutching the iron bars of the gate. She was being propped up by people on either side. 'My Robbie was only twenty-five years old! Had his whole life ahead of him.' She shook the gate angrily. 'Where's the justice for my boy?'

Morrigan felt her heart sink. *Robbie*. That must have been the young man who'd been killed at the docks.

'We are deeply sorry for your loss,' said Elder Quinn. 'We share your distress, and extend our condolences to you and your family—'

'THEY EXTEND THEIR *CONDOLENCES*,' shouted St James, to jeers from the protestors. 'THEY'RE *OH* SO VERY SORRY. BUT NOT SORRY ENOUGH TO STOP PROTECTING MURDERERS.'

'He came prepared, didn't he?' muttered a voice in Morrigan's ear. She turned to see Hawthorne arriving with Mahir. 'D'you reckon he carries that megaphone around with him everywhere, just in case he gets the chance to loudly bore someone?'

The noise from St James was joined by the clanging of the iron gates as the crowd took hold and shook them back and forth. Elder Quinn tried again to address them, holding her hands up in an appeasing gesture, but her words were drowned out.

'They're going nuts!' said Mahir. 'Look at them, they're trying to break down the gates!'

He was right. The protest had become a mob – an actual, proper *mob*. The kind Morrigan had only ever read about in storybooks about long-lost villages with a witch living in the woods.

'Did you just see that bloke with a *pitchfork*?' Hawthorne's voice had jumped up half an octave, his eyes grown wide. 'Who even *owns* a pitchfork? I don't even know what a pitchfork is *for*!'

'That's it,' said Thaddea. 'I'm going down there to help. The Elders won't stand a chance holding that lot back on their own.'

Morrigan thought again of what Sofia had said to her that morning. *We don't use our knacks to tyrannise people. It's not what the Wundrous Society is about.* Was this different, though? This wasn't storming parliament, after all, it was defending Wunsoc from being stormed.

'Is it for . . . pitching or forking—'

'Shut *up*, Swift. Who's with me?' Thaddea glared.

'No.' Lam dropped her basket, spilling its contents down the steps, and grasped Thaddea's forearm with both hands. '*No*, Thaddea. Bad idea.'

'Are you saying that as an oracle, or a scaredy-cat?'

Lam thought about it for half a second. 'Both.'

But even the Elders seemed to have noticed the dangerous shift in mood. They'd finally given up their misguided mission of peace, left the mob behind at the gate, and were making their way quickly up the driveway towards Proudfoot House.

The crowd of scholars suddenly split down the middle as a group of teachers and conductors streamed out of Proudfoot House. They encircled the scholars and began pushing them backwards.

'All of you inside, this instant!' snapped Dearborn. 'This is not a traffic accident for you to gawk at. Conductors, marshal your units!'

'Oh no,' whispered Lam, watching the Elders intently. 'They're moving too slowly.' She cupped her hands around her mouth and shouted to the Elders in a voice louder than any of them had ever heard her use. 'Hurry up! *Faster*.'

Morrigan shivered; she was feeling a very particular kind of chill, one that she only seemed to get when Lam was having one of her *moments*. She looked at Cadence, and without needing to discuss it, both girls joined Lam in shouting at the Elders.

'FASTER! *RUN*, HURRY UP!'

'Girls! That's quite enough of that,' said Miss Cheery, gathering them all together. 'Right, Unit 919, let's go. Inside the house. Now.'

'But miss, look—'

'I said *now*, Thaddea.'

'No, Miss Cheery, LOOK!'

People were climbing over the walls. Somebody repeatedly smashed something against the lock on the gates – a stone or a brick or something – and there was a great deafening *CLANG* as they breached it. They poured into the grounds, shouting furiously as they began to march towards Proudfoot House. The Elders stopped halfway up the drive and turned back to face them, Elder Wong holding up his hands as if he might miraculously command them to stop.

Dearborn had given up herding the scholars inside. Everyone standing on the marble steps, young and old, gaped in horror at what was unfolding. More Society members emerged from Proudfoot House and from other corners of the campus, seeming to appear out of nowhere, as if some silent emergency alarm had gone off. They surged forward, marching down the drive to defend the Elders and the campus, even while the conductors still tried to hold back their junior scholars.

With a sickening pop-pop-pop-*crrrunch*, Dearborn warped into a snarling Murgatroyd, her face and hands frosting over, ready for a fight. Thaddea cracked her knuckles and made to duck under Miss Cheery's arm, eager to join the adults.

In that moment, Morrigan's uncertainty evaporated and she realised exactly where she stood. She agreed with Sofia. She trusted Lam.

'Thaddea, stop,' she said, grabbing hold of her cloak. 'You're only going to make it worse. This isn't what the Society's for.'

'What? This is *exactly* what we're—'

'No,' Morrigan insisted. 'It's not. Don't you remember what you said? When we had that argument before the summer holidays? You were the one who was all about learning how to *distract* people. *You're* the one who said how important it was. Containment and Distraction, *that's* what the Society's for. We're meant to be helping people, not fighting them.'

Thaddea looked at her as if she was mad. 'Oh, well, I'm sorry I never learned how to *distract an angry mob*. What do you want me to do, JUMP OUT OF A BIRTHDAY CAKE?'

She yanked her cloak out of Morrigan's hand and ran to join the Society members swarming down the drive.

'Thaddea, come back!' cried Anah.

Morrigan felt she was watching the scene in slow motion. The mob reached the Elders and, just as she'd feared, a tight, angry circle immediately formed around Elder Saga. She squeezed her hands into fists.

'Look at yourselves!' he shouted at them. 'This is extraordinary behaviour, how dare you?'

The Concerned Citizens responded by swinging their wooden placards at him, acting as if he was a violent unnimal they were keeping at bay. Unfortunately, the bullwun lived up to their expectations by stamping his hooves furiously in defence, throwing his great horned head from side to side and bellowing loudly.

The Wunsoc crowd roared as they ran to protect Elder Saga, the two groups about to clash with no real sense of what came next, and suddenly it was all happening so fast and Morrigan found herself thinking of that tiny spark on the end of her fingertip, and the way it had grown from something so small into a roaring, uncontrollable fire.

A small hand grasped Morrigan's wrist.

Lam.

'Yes.' She nodded fervently. 'Do it. Now.'

Morrigan blinked. 'What?'

'Small sparks . . . big fires.' Lam turned her gaze towards the drive, looking directly at one of the dead fireblossom trees, its black branches stretching up into the sky, splayed like great spindly fingers.

Morrigan had a sudden, vivid memory of her second visit to Wunsoc, on the day of her first trial. Instantly, she understood. She slipped out of Lam's grasp, sidestepped a distracted Miss Cheery, and ran straight for the tree.

It wasn't like being in class. It felt more like the first time she'd ever breathed fire. She could taste ash at the back of her throat.

Except this time it wasn't fuelled by fear, rage or panic.

All Morrigan felt in this moment was calm and certain.

And needed.

And without knowing exactly how, she knew what to do.

Morrigan pictured a flame burning steadily inside her rib cage. She exhaled steadily, watching the tiny sparks be carried away on her breath, and caught one in her hand.

She reached out and pressed her palm to the petrified fireblossom tree. Warmth spread from her chest, all the way down her arm, coursing inside her veins and out through the centre of her hand, bleeding life into the cold, black wood.

She closed her eyes. She felt dizzy and glorious. The whole world had shrunk to the size of her palm, to that feeling of her skin against the smooth bark of the tree. That rushing sensation of fiery energy meeting cold decay and pushing it back, forcing it into the abyss. Shucking it off like a snake sheds its skin; a violent awakening of what was so deeply asleep it might as well have been dead. A rebirth.

Squall's voice spoke softly in her head.

One day, Miss Crow, you may begin to understand how much of Nevermoor lies dormant or dead, waiting patiently for you to nudge it back to life.

Morrigan opened her eyes and looked up into the outspread branches above her. Cool green fire flickered like leaves. Here and there, a lick of orange flame, a slight turning to yellow, a dapple of deeper brown. An early autumn explosion of bright burning light that mimicked the colours of the Whinging Woods.

One by one, down both sides of the drive from Proudfoot House to the gates of Wunsoc, dozens of long-dead trees roared into life. The flames arched overhead to form a canopy above the two clashing groups, who stilled and fell silent at the spectacle.

After more than one hundred years of extinction, the fireblossoms had returned.

CHAPTER TWENTY-EIGHT

A New Threat To Nevermoor

'They're giving *tours*,' said Jupiter, swanning into the lobby the morning after the riot. It was only eight o'clock on a Saturday and he'd spent the whole night patrolling the city for infected Wunimals. But somehow, he'd already picked up a copy of every newspaper in Nevermoor, attended a Hollowpox task force meeting, spoken with the Elders *and* brought coffee, pastries and fresh orange juice back to the Deucalion. Morrigan hadn't seen him this energised in weeks. 'Free tours, all weekend! Can you believe it?'

'Who?' asked Jack. 'Tours of what?'

'The Public Distraction Department. Tours of Wunsoc.' Jupiter tossed him a brown paper bag with a delicious-smelling cinnamon roll inside, and another each to Morrigan and Kedgeree.

The three of them were hovering at the concierge desk, Jack and Morrigan still in pyjamas and Kedgeree in his usual pink tartan uniform with the gold-embroidered pocket square, despite the Deucalion having been closed for nearly a week. Jupiter had offered paid time off during the closure to anyone who wanted it, but some of the staff said they preferred to stay and keep busy, and others – like Kedgeree and Frank – lived at the Deucalion anyway, and had nowhere else to go. Kedgeree still had plenty of work to fill his days, though it was mostly taking messages for Jupiter and fielding complaints about the closure.

'What, they're letting people *inside* Proudfoot House?' said Morrigan. She could immediately think of at least twelve reasons why that was a terrible idea. 'Are they mad? There are dragons in there! And explosions. And . . . Hawthorne, sometimes.'

'Goodness no, not inside the house. Just the grounds. Well, just the front drive, really. Can't let people near the Whinging Woods – they'd be bored to death. But even so –' (he paused for a mouthful of much-too-hot coffee, spat it into a potted plant, and stuck out his scalded tongue to frantically wave cool air over it) '– outfiderv in Wunfoc? Unhearb of! And looh ah thif!'

He pulled out a stack of newspapers from under his arm and triumphantly slapped them down, one by one, on to the desk. The headlines all said things like, *FIREBLOSSOMS RETURN!* and *ARBOREAL MIRACLE OR ARSON MYSTERY?* and *BACK FROM THE DEAD: THE NATURAL WUNDERS WE THOUGHT WE'D LOST FOR GOOD.*

'Howwiday Wu if a – 'ang on.' He paused to drink a cooling mouthful of orange juice. '*Whew*. Holliday Wu is a GENIUS. If anyone noticed your involvement, Mog – or should I say, your *spectacular* achievement – if any witnesses mentioned you to the papers, none of them are printing it. No mention of you *or* the Stealth in any of these, and I've read them all. Twice.'

Morrigan wasn't *totally* surprised she'd managed to fly under the radar – after all, in the chaos, who among the protestors would

321

have noticed a single scholar standing with her hand pressed to a tree, and who could have guessed at what she'd done?

But the *Stealth?* Even in those moments of shocked silence, no one could have failed to see the entire *brigade* of Stealth officers that materialised seemingly out of nowhere, swooping in to take control. They'd arrived just in time to take full advantage of the shift in energy, calmly rounding up the bewildered protestors and escorting them off the premises with minimum fuss.

Morrigan thought there was something unsettling about the Stealth. As the Wundrous Society's own private law enforcement, they had a particular kind of mystery and *presence.* A slightly menacing aura that followed wherever they went. They gave Morrigan goose-bumps, and she couldn't understand why they hadn't rated a mention in even *one* eyewitness account.

'Even better,' Jupiter went on, 'have you noticed what else is missing from these front pages?'

Jack sorted through the stack. 'No mention of the Hollowpox.'

'No Hollowpox,' his uncle echoed. 'No Wunimals. The fireblossoms are all anyone wants to talk about. Nobody's seen one burning in over a hundred years, not in all the Seven Pockets, and now – boom! All that noise from the so-called Concerned Citizens has been completely smothered by the tree mystery. The protest isn't mentioned anywhere! Mog, you've *no* idea how glad the Elders are to have a bit of a reprieve. I think they're secretly pleased your Wundrous Arts lessons have paid off in such a timely fashion.'

'Secretly p-pleased?' spluttered Jack, coughing as he swallowed a mouthful of pastry. 'That's big of them. Maybe next time someone saves them from being trampled by a dangerous mob, they'll stretch to *mildly tickled.*'

Morrigan secretly felt a little bit pleased herself, at Jack's indignation on her behalf. She picked up the *Nevermoor Sentinel*, whose front-page headline, above a full-colour picture of the fireblossoms, read: *GREATEST ECOLOGICAL COMEBACK OF ALL TIME*.

'You think Holliday fixed it so that the protest— *ow!*' She winced as she felt a little itching prickle in one of the fingers on her left hand, like an insect bite. It'd been annoying her all morning. 'So the protest got forgotten?'

'That woman has the ear of every desk editor in Nevermoor,' said Jupiter. 'She spent hours last night talking to each of them personally, and I don't know how those conversations went, but whatever stories they'd been *planning* to publish, in the end they all went with Holliday's version. You should see Wunsoc this morning – people are *lining up* to see the trees!' He shook his head, laughing in disbelief. 'I bow to the Queen of Spin. Any messages while I was out, Kedge?'

Morrigan grinned at Jack, who raised a discreet eyebrow back at her. This was quite a change from the gloomy, fatigued Jupiter who'd been haunting the Deucalion recently. She knew which one she preferred.

'Several.' Kedgeree straightened up, flipping through a stack of handwritten notes. 'Your accountant has asked for the *third* time this week how long you intend to keep paying a full staff while three-quarters of them are off on a jolly—'

'They're not on a *jolly*,' said Jupiter.

'Her words, not mine.'

'For goodness' sake, it's barely been a week! And it's not my employees' fault the Deucalion's closed. What am I going to do, let them starve?'

'That's what I told her you'd say,' Kedgeree said calmly. 'And she asked me to remind you that the Hotel Deucalion is not a charity, nor is it currently making money, and to gently suggest that a grand re-opening might—'

'Not until we've contained the Hollowpox,' Jupiter cut him off. 'Or cured it.'

Morrigan sat up straight. She'd been waiting all night to tell Jupiter about Squall's offer, but it wasn't a conversation she wanted to have with an audience. Jupiter shot her a quizzical look, but she shook her head and mouthed, *Later*.

He turned back to Kedgeree. 'Now, do we have a status update on the Grand Sulk?'

The *Grand Sulk* was what he had taken to calling the Deucalion's current, rather strange state. Ever since they'd closed the place down, things in the hotel had started going a bit *weird*. Just little things at first; rooms you'd expect to find in one place would show up somewhere else entirely. Or some ornate wallpaper replaced with bare brick walls.

Then slowly, on the empty upper floors where the fanciest and most expensive suites lay empty, things started to sort of . . . go to sleep. The lights went out and wouldn't come back. The heating turned off, the hearths were all extinguished and it became so cold you could see your breath clouding the air. Eventually the suite doors locked themselves and wouldn't open for anyone, not even Jupiter.

Kedgeree, Frank and the rest of the staff were worried. They'd tried everything to coax the sleeping parts of the hotel awake again, even going so far as to stage a fake party one night, but the Deucalion was having none of it. It had continued slowly shutting down, room by room, floor by floor.

Jupiter, meanwhile, refused to engage, insisting it was just being childish and ought to grow up, and reminding everyone that *he* was in charge, and *he* would decide when they reopened, and he wouldn't have his hand forced by a *building*.

But Morrigan didn't think the Deucalion was being childish. She thought perhaps its feelings were hurt. Maybe it felt at a bit of a loss now that its halls were so empty, and the quiet had thrown it off its game a little. She'd been extra nice to her bedroom since the closure, just in case, complimenting its every transformation – no matter how odd. The recent addition of a terrarium full of large black spiders had been the ultimate test of her generosity, but upon its arrival she'd merely nodded and said in what she hoped was a cheering voice: 'Very skittery. Lots of legs.'

'The eleventh, twelfth and thirteenth floors are now in full hibernation,' said Kedgeree. 'The conservatory on the fourth floor has frosted over and the Smoking Parlour is showing definite signs of weariness. The second biggest ballroom was, last I checked, a mosquito-infested swampland.'

'Oh yes,' said Dame Chanda as she and Martha descended the staircase into the lobby. 'I was hoping to use it as a rehearsal space yesterday, since the music salon has shrunk to the size of a closet. But the *smell*! The *humidity*! Simply dreadful.'

Martha wrung her hands. 'Oh dear. And the lights in the Golden Lantern cocktail bar have been flickering for days. It'll be the next to go.'

'What in the Seven Pockets is happening to this place?' asked Dame Chanda. 'Jove, I fear the Deucalion is angry with us.'

'It's not angry,' said Morrigan. 'It's upset. And maybe a bit confused.'

'It's BEING A BABY.' Jupiter threw his head back and let his voice echo around the empty lobby. They all looked up, flinching as the black bird chandelier gave an ominous flicker and ruffled its light-filled wings.

It was nice, having one day when the Hollowpox wasn't all the media was talking about. But by the time the Saturday evening papers came out, it was back to being front-page news, with two new attacks having occurred just that day. Jupiter left in the afternoon and was gone all night.

She'd finally told him about Squall's offer that morning after breakfast, and was relieved by his response.

'Squall is a *liar*,' he'd told her vehemently. 'You know that. He's playing mind games again, trying to use your fears against you.'

'Then . . . you don't believe he created the Hollowpox?'

He raised an eyebrow. 'Oh, I believe he created it. It's precisely something he would do. But I don't believe he'll be the one to cure it. Even if he *did* have a cure – which I very much doubt, because when has he bothered to clean up *any* of the mess he's made in Nevermoor? – none of this is your responsibility, Mog. We're not trading you in, no matter what he's promising.'

'But what if—'

'Listen to me.' He looked her straight in the eye. 'We can't stop him from entering Nevermoor on the Gossamer, but we *must* stop him from getting into your head. I don't want you to give this a second thought, understand?'

Morrigan nodded and took a deep, steadying breath through her nose. 'Jupiter, tell me the truth . . . do you *really* think Dr Bramble is going to find a cure?'

'She's getting closer every day,' he'd said, and he was so convincing she'd almost believed him.

That evening, something very odd happened. Something that would change everything, although Morrigan didn't fully understand it at first.

Jack had gone back to school for an orchestra rehearsal, but Morrigan, Martha and Charlie were sitting around the big fireplace in the empty lobby having a supper of fish and chips and mushy peas (the staff dining room had lost its heating just that day), when Dame Chanda returned from her weekly dinner date with the man they all called Suitor von Saturday.

'My darlings, have you seen Kedgeree?'

'I think he's in the Smoking Parlour,' said Charlie, 'trying to fix the smoke flow. It has a bad cough.'

Morrigan peered over the soprano's shoulder at a scruffy young man with a knapsack slung over one shoulder, gazing up in awe at the black bird chandelier.

'Is *that* Suitor von Saturday?' she asked in a gleeful whisper. 'He's so . . . um . . .' She wasn't sure how to describe him. Dishevelled? Unshaven? Inappropriately dressed to be having dinner with Nevermoor's foremost soprano? 'So . . . not what I was expecting?'

Martha giggled, but Dame Chanda looked perplexed.

'Suitor von – who? No, darling, that's not the Count of Sundara. I just met this gentleman outside on the forecourt. He says he's here to service our gas stoves.'

'Gas stoves? Our kitchens are fully Wundrous.' Charlie looked up from splashing vinegar on to his supper, frowning, and called out, 'What company are you from, mate?'

The man trotted over to join them, digging into his knapsack, but ignored Charlie's question, instead asking, 'You Morrigan?'

Morrigan licked a bit of green gloop off her finger. 'Um, yes? Who are—'

CLICK.

The camera flash blinded them just long enough for the man to run out the front door while they sat blinking in confusion.

'OI! Come back here!' Charlie shook off his shock, jumped up and chased the man, but returned minutes later, empty-handed and bewildered.

It had been a strange, inexplicable thing at the time, but they couldn't do much about it except agree to tell Jupiter as soon as he got home (whenever that might be). It wasn't until the next morning that Morrigan understood.

WUNDERSMITH!

That was the headline. In big, bold letters right across the front page of the *Sunday Post*. It sat above perhaps the very worst photo of Morrigan that had ever been taken.

'I have mushy peas on my face,' she said miserably for the umpteenth time, still staring at the newspaper twenty minutes after it had swung into her life like a wrecking ball. 'Why did they have to print the photo in colour?'

'Is that really the most pressing issue?' Jupiter asked in a mild voice.

'*I have mushy peas on my face!*'

He shrugged. 'Makes you look less dangerous than the headline suggests. That's something?'

'It makes me look like I've got a bogey!' she said, glaring up at him.

Morrigan was *mortified* by the photo, but in truth it wasn't nearly as bad as the accompanying article on page two.

MORRIGAN CROW: A NEW THREAT
TO NEVERMOOR?

Friday's terrifying fireblossom mystery has been solved today with the shock revelation that the Wundrous Society has been secretly educating a Wundersmith for almost two years. Morrigan Crow, aged thirteen, is believed to be responsible for setting the rare arboreal species ablaze using an unknown and uncanny ability that even senior members of the Society don't understand.

According to an anonymous source inside Wunsoc, Crow is in fact a citizen of the Wintersea Republic who was brought to the Free State illegally to participate in trials for the Wundrous Society. Her membership provides immunity from deportation.

The source claims the High Council of Elders had no choice but to admit Crow, lest she put the public at risk.

'Who knows what she'd get up to outside our walls? She's what we at Wunsoc call a "dangerous entity". Nobody knows exactly what she's capable of, but she's already seriously injured another student.'

The news has come as a shock to many who believed there were no more Wundersmiths after the last living Wundersmith, mass murderer Ezra Squall, was driven from the Free State over one hundred years ago and never seen again. It is not known whether Crow could be descended from the late Squall, or if these abilities have emerged spontaneously. Neither is it known precisely what the nature of Crow's sinister powers might be, or what they might become.

What is known is that the Wundrous Society has been harbouring a dangerous, potentially lethal weapon for nearly two years, and this publication believes that

329

citizens of Nevermoor have a right to know and respond.

Crow's patron, the renowned Captain Jupiter North, owner and proprietor of the Hotel Deucalion and an officer in the League of Explorers, could not be reached for comment at the time of print.

'*Couldn't be reached for comment!* I can always be reached for comment, I'm extremely reachable,' Jupiter growled. Morrigan raised an eyebrow at him. 'All right *fine*, I'm not *always* reachable. But the fact is they didn't *try* to reach me because they knew the Elders would kill the story. Oh, and it's interesting how the fireblossom mystery's suddenly "terrifying". Yesterday it was a miracle! You know, I should—'

In a sudden fit of temper, Morrigan rolled up the paper and tossed it into the fireplace, where it blackened and curled satisfyingly. The hearth in her bedroom had been growing bigger and bigger while Morrigan paced the floor, reading furiously. It now took up half the wall, its fire burning brighter and crackling louder, practically *begging* her to hurl the offending item into its blazing maw.

'Quite right,' said Jupiter with a nod, clearing his throat. 'Good show.'

'Thank you. Do you have another copy?'

'Dozens. Bought every one I could find before anyone else did.' He glanced sideways at her. 'We can burn those too, if you like.'

'Maybe later.' Morrigan collapsed into her octopus armchair. Its tentacles twitched and rearranged themselves around her, offering silent support. 'I don't understand. How do they know? I thought nobody saw me! Who's this *inside source* they're talking about?'

'An absolute fool with no regard for anyone but himself and his own gain.'

'You think it was Baz,' Morrigan said simply.

'I absolutely know it was Baz.'

'How?'

Jupiter's expression was dark. 'I know Baz.'

Morrigan pressed a hand to her stomach. She felt sick.

There was a horrible, creeping familiarity about all of it. This was what she'd grown up with, after all. This was the life of a child on the Cursed Children's Register in the Wintersea Republic: always the dangerous one, always the untrusted one. Always the one to blame when bad things happened. Was this her fate in Nevermoor too, then? For ever fearing what she might be accused of next?

'Mog, listen,' Jupiter perched on the end of the bed, ducking his head to look her in the eye. 'It's going to be all right. I promise. This was bound to happen sooner or later. It's quite a bit earlier than you or I or the Elders would have preferred, but it's nothing we can't deal with. A few newspaper headlines, a bit of unwanted attention for a couple of days, and then everything will die down. You'll see.'

Morrigan had never known her patron to be so wildly mistaken.

By the end of the day everyone in Nevermoor must have known the name Morrigan Crow, because it was all over the evening papers. A handful of reporters showed up at the Hotel Deucalion, lingering in the forecourt and trying to catch a glimpse of the dangerous Wundersmith, shouting Morrigan's name, trying to draw her out. The precious anonymity Holliday had so kindly preserved for her had been ripped away with a single camera flash. Just like that.

Morrigan's racing, circular thoughts made it hard to fall asleep on Sunday night, so she woke late on Monday morning and almost missed Hometrain. It didn't help that her bedroom's usual wake-up cues – her lamps slowly brightening like the sunrise, and the gentle sound of birdsong – were entirely absent. It was dark and silent.

'Why didn't you *wake* me?' she asked Room 85 irritably, then caught herself and gave the wall a little pat. 'Not your fault. I like those new curtains! Are they, er, seaweed? Smells . . . lovely.'

Hometrain was already at the platform when Morrigan arrived. As she ran on board every face of Unit 919 shot up, looking guilty (except for Anah, who was snoozing on a beanbag). Francis reached out to turn the volume on the wireless radio all the way down.

So, they'd heard.

'Morning, Morrigan. All right?' Miss Cheery called from the front of the carriage, radiating warmth as always without having to say much at all. Morrigan nodded, tight-lipped, and the engine rumbled into life. 'Good. Let's get moving, then.'

'Morning, Snotface,' said Hawthorne merrily.

She scowled, taking a seat on the sofa next to Lam. 'It was mushy peas.'

'I'd stick with that story, too, if I were you.' He gave an exaggerated wink, and even though Morrigan was still furious about the photograph, she *almost* laughed. Almost.

'Shut up.' She threw a cushion at his head, then nodded at the wireless. 'Well? What are we listening to? Is it about me?'

With an apologetic grimace, Francis turned up the volume.

'—but no, of *course* the High Council isn't going to comment, Alby, because it's all lies!' said a deep, posh voice over the airwaves.

'Who is this Morrigan Crow? Where has she come from? And if she is what this *inside source* claims she is, where's the proof? Come on, Alby. The Wundersmith was exiled from Nevermoor over one hundred years ago! And now, what, we're supposed to believe he's some *little girl?*'

'That's not what they're saying, though, is it, Mr St James? They're saying—'

'St James?' said Morrigan. 'Is this—'

'Yeah, from the Concerned Idiots of Nevermoor,' said Cadence. 'Shhh, listen.'

'If you ask me,' St James barrelled over the top of the host, 'this is a deliberate intimidation tactic from the Society. The Concerned Citizens of Nevermoor protested at Wunsoc on Friday, and by Saturday night there's a "*leaked story*" from an "*anonymous source*". This is the Society trying to send a message: keep in line, don't challenge us, because look what happens when you do. We'll set our imaginary *Wundersmith* on you!'

'Then you believe the whole thing is a fabrication?'

'I *believe*,' he said with an impatient little huff, 'that I want to hear it from the Wundrous Society themselves. No – I want to *see* it. Let's see this so-called Wundersmith in action. If it's not true, then are the Society simply telling lies to threaten and silence their critics? If it *is* true, then . . . well. That is a serious problem, and it needs to be dealt with.'

At that declaration, Morrigan felt the hair on the back of her neck stand up.

Was that what she was? A problem that needed to be dealt with?

The host cleared his throat. 'If you're just tuning in now to *Good Morning Nevermoor* with Alby Higgins, we're discussing the issue on everyone's radar this morning. Is there really a new

Wundersmith, or is it all a hoax? Let's take some calls from our listeners—'

Cadence reached out and turned Alby Higgins off. 'I bet it was Baz who leaked it.'

'That's what Jupiter says.'

'I'll get it out of him. He always forgets what my knack is. He's at Proudfoot House today for the meeting. I'll make him tell me after that.'

'I'll pretend I didn't hear you plotting to mesmerise your own patron, shall I, Cadence?' Miss Cheery called back from the driver's seat.

'Cheers, miss.'

'*Cadence*.'

When they arrived at Wunsoc, Miss Cheery walked them through the Whinging Woods and all the way up to Proudfoot House. There were people at the main gates again, and she seemed to be trying to shield Morrigan from view.

'They must be here for the fireblossom tours,' said Morrigan.

She couldn't help feeling proud, despite the trouble those trees had brought her. The view from the top of the drive had completely changed. Gone were the spidery, bare black branches, like witch's hands reaching up to the sky. In their place, a fiery overstorey in what must have been a thousand different greens, glowing warmly on this cool morning, with patches turning to orange, bronze and gold here and there. Morrigan thought they made Wunsoc more beautiful than ever.

'They've had to cancel the fireblossom tours,' said Miss Cheery. 'Journalists kept signing up for them and trying to sneak into Proudfoot House, or to ask nosy questions about—' Miss Cheery cut herself off, with a glance at Morrigan.

Morrigan peered down at the gates again and saw what she

hadn't before: a sea of cameras and microphones. 'About me.'

'Ignore, ignore, ignore,' Miss Cheery told her. 'Do not go anywhere near those gates, Morrigan. This will all blow over in a day or two. Don't you worry.'

Cadence didn't get a chance to mesmerise Baz and make him confess, because their usual Monday morning Containment and Distraction meeting was cancelled.

'Any idea why it was called off?' she asked Morrigan as the pair made their way to a lecture theatre on Sub-Three for their mid-morning lesson. A famous Wundrous Society philosopher was visiting to give a talk called *Why Are We Here? Questions of Existence, Mortality and Morality* (which they both agreed was a bit much for a Monday).

'No,' Morrigan said glumly. 'Probably another attack.'

They heard a sniffle and stopped in the middle of the corridor. A round little figure in a medical uniform was huddled, shoulders shaking, behind a statue of the late Elder Atherton Lusk, founder of the Teaching Hospital.

'Anah?'

Anah jumped as if someone had shouted and peeked out from behind the stone Elder. Her face was blotchy and red, her nose running. 'Oh – it's you two. I was just . . .'

'Anah, what's wrong?' asked Morrigan, as she and Cadence hurried over. 'Has something happened?'

Anah looked surprised – not just to see them, but specifically at Morrigan's question.

She sniffled. 'I . . . Nothing, never mind. Shouldn't you be down on Sub-Nine with your Wundersmith friends?'

'Morrigan flinched at the slight coolness in her voice. 'Sub-Nine can wait. Why are you crying?'

Anah's face crumpled. She shook her head, her eyes filling up with more tears. 'I'm not supposed to tell anybody,' she whispered.

'You can tell us,' Morrigan said gently.

Cadence nodded. 'Course you can. We're your sisters. Loyal for life, remember?'

That only seemed to make things worse. Anah looked up at Cadence with a mixture of shock and gratitude, her tears now flowing freely, and choked out a sob. 'That's . . . th-that's the nicest thing you've ever said to me.'

Cadence folded her arms. 'Yeah. I'm nice. Shut up.'

'Breathe, Anah, and tell us what's wrong,' said Morrigan.

Anah took a deep, shuddering breath, and whispered, 'They're waking up.'

'Who's waking – wait, the *Wunimals*?'

'Shhh!' said Anah, glancing up and down the hall. 'Most of the majors. None of the minors. Yet.'

'But that's brilliant news! Isn't it?' Morrigan finished uncertainly, while Anah squeezed her eyes shut and shook her head.

'They're not . . . *Wunimals* any more.'

'What do you mean?' asked Cadence.

'They're just . . .' She took a jagged breath. 'Unnimals. They've turned into unnimals.'

Morrigan stared at her. 'But that's not possible.'

'It started with the leopardwun . . . the *leopard*, now, I suppose. She woke up on Saturday and at first everyone was really happy, but . . . she had no idea who she was, or where or *what* she was. She couldn't speak. She wouldn't eat anything but raw meat. Didn't understand a word we said, she was just angry and scared. Pacing and growling like a caged unnimal. And now . . .' Anah bit back a sob. 'Now that's exactly what she is. They gave

336

her a needle and sent her to sleep and when she woke up . . . they'd locked her in a cage.'

So Juvela De Flimsé was awake. Since *Saturday*.

Morrigan thought of Dame Chanda and her deep blue melancholy. This would break her heart. What would she do, if she knew?

'They've put them all in c-cages,' Anah hiccupped. 'All the most dangerous ones – the leopard and Brutilus Brown and the jackal and . . . I don't know, about three dozen more. They're sedated most of the time but when they're awake . . . oh, it's so *awful*.'

'What about the minors?' said Cadence. 'Will they be the same when they wake up? Surely if they're more . . . you know. *Human* . . .' She looked at Morrigan, unsure how to finish that thought.

'We don't know yet.' Anah sniffed and wiped her nose on her sleeve. 'But Dr Lutwyche said he wants to start moving the majors next week.'

'Moving them where?' said Cadence. She dug around in her bag and produced a rumpled but clean tissue, rolling her eyes when Anah's face dissolved at this newest small act of kindness.

'Who knows? I heard him and Dr Bramble arguing about it. Dr Lutwyche says the hospital isn't a *zoo*. But that's how they're treating them! Like unnimals in a—'

'Kahlo!' came a sharp voice from down the corridor. 'Kahlo, where are you? We need an extra pair of hands in here.'

'Coming, Dr Lutwyche.'

Anah hastily wiped her face, straightened her uniform and rushed away without another word to Morrigan and Cadence, looking almost as if nothing was wrong.

Morrigan spent the rest of the afternoon on Sub-Nine in a water-weaving class alongside eleven-year-old Elodie and Ezra, utterly unable to concentrate. When she wasn't thinking about what Anah had said, she was staring – distracted and *furious* – at the young Ezra building a whirlpool inside a glass with maddening ease.

It was a long, difficult lesson, but by the end of the day Morrigan could make a puddle of water splash without anybody jumping in it. She wasn't as quick or precise as the younger students, and she was utterly exhausted afterwards. But still, it was progress. She only wished she was as accomplished with water as she was with fire.

Two strange and upsetting things happened on the way home that afternoon: first, during their walk through the Whinging Woods to the station, someone parachuted down on to the path in front of Morrigan and shoved a camera right in her face.

'What are they teaching you here at the Wundrous Society, Morrigan Crow?' the woman demanded breathlessly. Morrigan was so shocked she said nothing, did nothing, and the woman gained a little courage. 'Are you *really* a Wundersmith? Why don't you show the public what you can do? We all know it's a lie, just a publicity—'

'Oh, go climb a tree,' snarled Cadence, and the parachutist dropped her camera and obeyed without hesitating, much to the chagrin of the nearest oak tree.

'Git orf me!' it grumbled. 'Ow, that's my nose you're standing on, you wretch!'

They left the stranger to be swatted by tree branches and swarmed by a group of senior scholars (who seemed outraged more by the campus breach, Morrigan thought, than her surprise interrogation).

The second strange and upsetting thing came just a few minutes later when Mahir turned on Miss Cheery's wireless radio.

'—from the Department of Agriculture,' a cool, calm female voice was saying, 'who reports bubbleberry farmers in the Fifth Pocket are bouncing back after last year's lacklustre harvest. More on that story to come.

'But first, the news from the capital. Laurent St James, Silver District tycoon and leader of the newly formed Concerned Citizens of Nevermoor Party, has today offered a fifty-thousand-kred reward to anyone who can provide, quote, "indisputable visual proof" of the claim made in the *Sunday Post* this weekend, that the Wundrous Society is harbouring and training a genuine Wundersmith, thirteen-year-old scholar Morrigan Crow.'

CHAPTER TWENTY-NINE

The Hunt for Morrigan Crow

The announcement was met with horror from 919 and a furious sigh from Miss Cheery, who immediately stomped over to turn off the radio.

'That scumbag,' said Hawthorne, punching a beanbag to vent his feelings. 'That foul *rat*!'

'Fifty thousand!' muttered Thaddea. 'Imagine having that much money and spending it all just to see Morrigan be a bit rubbish.'

Miss Cheery sighed again. '*Thaddea.*'

'What? She is, though. No offence, Morrigan.'

Cadence clicked her fingers. 'Oh! The woman in the parachute – that's what she wanted! She was trying to goad you into using the Wundrous Arts so she could get it on film and claim the reward. What a *cow*.'

'Good thing you didn't give it to her,' said Arch.

'Yes,' Miss Cheery agreed. 'Excellent restraint.'

Morrigan didn't say anything. Restraint had nothing to do

with it. It was just lucky she'd been so depleted from her afternoon lesson, or she might have unwittingly obliged.

While the others raged around her, dreaming up appropriate punishments for Scumbag St James (as they were now calling him), Morrigan prodded her feelings a little, trying to find the tender spot, searching for her own rage. Surprisingly, she found she was so tired and so worried by what Anah had told her about the Wunimals waking, there wasn't any room left inside her to care very much about this new development. She made all the right noises, joining in the hypothetical revenge scenarios. But – not for the first time – she felt she was down at the bottom of a cool, dark lake, while they all splashed about on the surface.

By the time she got home to the Deucalion, heavy-footed and aching all over, Morrigan could only think of hot food and a hot bath, in exactly that order, and she hoped desperately that the Grand Sulk hadn't spread to the kitchens yet. She'd just opened her bedroom door to go and find out when Jupiter strode through it – red-faced, arms and brolly swinging wildly – and flung his hat on the floor to stomp on it.

'Holliday Wu is a FIEND!'

Morrigan stared at him, nonplussed. 'You've changed your tune.'

'It wasn't. Baz. At. All,' he said, emphasising each word with another stomp on his now irreversibly damaged hat, before kicking it so hard it slid all the way across the hardwood floor and crashed with a *floomp* against the far wall. 'It was *her*. Or rather it was *them*.'

'Them who?'

'The Elders! They cooked up the whole thing with Holliday and the Public Distraction Department.' He ran a hand through his waves of ginger hair and began a feverish pacing back and forth, tapping his brolly against the side of his leg. '*Of course.* Because that's what they do, isn't it? They distract people from whatever they want to hide, using whatever – *whoever* – is most convenient. Throwing anyone they have to under a bus. In this case, Mog, that happens to be YOU.'

'What are you talking about?'

'That "anonymous source within the society" who went to the papers? It was Holliday, acting with the permission – no, under the *instruction* of the High Council of Elders.'

'What? No. Elder Quinn wouldn't—'

'Oh, Elder Quinn *did*,' said Jupiter, coming to a decisive halt. 'She did exactly what the Elders always do: she put the Society first. It's perfect, don't you see? Things were going so well for them after you resurrected the fireblossoms, nobody was talking about the Hollowpox any more or questioning our way of dealing with it. It was Holliday's idea to capitalise on it by leaking the truth about you to the *Sunday Post*, but believe me, the Elders enthusiastically signed off on the plan. Do you know,' he said, suddenly thoughtful, 'I don't believe I've ever been *quite* so angry in all my life. I think I could bottle this rage and sell it to – I don't know, competitive heavyweight boxers or something.'

Morrigan felt something dark and disquieting settle on her heart, heard Squall's words echo in her head.

They're going to flip the script.

Had he really been so prescient? Was this just the betrayal he'd meant?

'But *they're* the ones who wanted it kept a secret – I mean Elder Quinn *herself* said everyone had to uphold their oath and protect the secret and . . . *sisters and brothers*, and all that. *Loyal for life*. Those hypocrites!'

'Hmph,' Jupiter grunted. 'The thing is, Mog, it wasn't going to remain a secret for ever. It had to come out some time – these things always do – but I assumed we'd have some *warning*, some way to prepare. I'm sorry it's happened this way, I truly am.'

If Morrigan had been exhausted before, now she felt as though her skeleton might crumble to dust inside her body. It was the most unfortunate moment to notice that her bed had become a table.

She sighed, leaning against the wall and sliding all the way down to the floor. *This'll do*, she thought wearily.

'I don't get it,' she said. 'Isn't this *worse* for the Society? People are terrified of Wundersmiths, and now they know the Elders have been hiding one. That's worse than the Hollowpox! It's like covering up the fact that you have a box of spiders by telling everyone you also have a box of . . . acid-spouting land dolphins. Or something. And now that man from the Concerned Citizens is offering—'

'Oh, you heard about that,' said Jupiter darkly. He crossed the room to pick up his hat and tried (unsuccessfully) to punch it back into shape.

'It just seems like they've made themselves a bigger problem,' she said, yawning. 'I really don't think the Elders thought this through.'

'Nor do I. I suspect the decision was made in a blind panic, because . . .' He glanced at her and paused, as if uncertain he should go on. 'Because something happened on Saturday that made them realise they were sitting on a much worse story, one that could widen the rift between humans and Wunimals for good, and they needed everyone's attention elsewhere while they quietly decided what to do. Mog, what I'm about to tell you cannot leave this room. It's *extremely* sensitive information—'

'The Wunimals started waking up,' Morrigan said quietly.

'And they've become unnimals.'

His eyes widened.

'Anah told me. But don't tell Dr Lutwyche, will you? Cadence and I made her tell.'

'I won't,' he agreed. 'If you promise not to tell Dame Chanda about Juvela De Flimsé. I think it would break her heart.'

'Yes, that's exactly what I thought. Better to wait until Dr Bramble's found the cure.' She looked slantwise at him. 'She must be close now.'

'Hmm. We're getting closer every—'

'Closer every day, yeah, you keep saying that.' Morrigan raised an eyebrow. 'Jupiter, what if the only person who can cure it . . .'

'No,' he said firmly. 'I know what you're thinking, and I demand you stop thinking it this instant.'

She scowled. 'You're not the thought police of me.'

'I told you, Squall is a liar. And even if he's telling the truth, there is *nothing* he can offer that's worth what he wants in return. It's not an option. Dr Bramble is brilliant, Morrigan, *truly* – and she's on the verge of a breakthrough. I know she is.'

Was Squall altogether a liar, though, Morrigan wondered? He hadn't been lying about the Wundrous Society flipping the script.

Jupiter clapped his hands once and smiled. 'You must be famished! I'll have a meal sent up to you, shall I? Ribeye steak, I think – you could do with the extra iron. And plenty of greens. And corn on the cob, you love corn on the cob. Soup to start, of course, you must have some soup – and a great big bowl of mulberry ice cream for afters, how about that? Lovely.' Already out the door, he called back from the hallway, 'You have a nice hot bath and supper will be outside your door when you're ready.

Ooh – and chocolate sprinkles! For the ice cream, not the soup. *Although . . .'*

Morrigan knew he was running away before she could question him any more about Dr Bramble's supposed verge-of-a-breakthrough, but she was too tired to be annoyed. She closed her eyes.

Must remember to be annoyed tomorrow, she thought, before slipping fast into sleep.

Morrigan woke next morning in the exact same spot, in the same slumped, half-sitting position, feeling as cosy and comfortable as she could ever remember feeling. The table across the room where her bed once stood was gone. A new bed had grown around her in the night, soft and warm like a cocoon of wool blankets and feather pillows, propping her up where needed, holding her so gently it felt like she was floating.

She smiled, enjoying the bright, warm sunlight streaming in on her face, thinking she might just drift right back to sleep . . . then sat bolt upright with a gasp.

Sunshine! What time was it? She ought to be at school by now.

Jumping up – with some difficulty – from her pillowy cocoon, Morrigan ran for the station door and pressed her imprint to the circular lock . . . but nothing happened. It was cold and unlit.

'What? Come on, you stupid thing.'

She tried again and *again*, pressing harder each time. Still nothing.

Ugh. Was this what happened when you slept in late and missed Hometrain, she wondered?

Looking down at the wrinkled uniform she'd fallen asleep in, Morrigan shrugged. It would have to do. She grabbed her oilskin umbrella and bolted out the door – straight past a trolley holding last night's dinner of now-cold steak and melted ice cream – and all the way downstairs, to find the lobby in an uproar.

'Why not just call the police, darling, for goodness' sake?'

'I *did* call them, Chanda – they've been here twice this morning already,' said Kedgeree, in the closest thing to a raised voice Morrigan had ever heard him use. 'Every time they move people on, more keep coming!'

Dame Chanda paced fretfully across the chequerboard floor, her blue silk dressing gown sweeping behind her, while Charlie and Martha took turns peeking through the curtains. Fenestra sat by the door, glowering. She was still as a statue but for the ominous flicking of her tail back and forth, batting the floor like a drumbeat.

There was an awful lot of noise coming from outside, so loud it penetrated the thick double doors, and what Morrigan could understand of it made her feel queasy.

'COME OUT AND FACE US, WUNDERSMITH!'

'GET OUT HERE! SHOW US WHAT YOU CAN DO!'

Morrigan paused halfway down the stairs, clutching the bannister tight, her pulse suddenly thumping in her neck.

Fenestra growled. 'I'm telling you, Kedgeree, just let me at 'em. I'll have the whole greedy lot sorted in less than a minute.'

'For the millionth time, Fen, *no*,' said Kedgeree. 'None of us is to confront these vultures, *especially* not you. Captain North was very clear about that.'

Fen hissed at him. She seemed to be gathering a counter argument but was interrupted by a sudden *SPLASH!* from the forecourt, followed by a scream.

Martha laughed, then clapped a hand to her mouth a little guiltily. 'Oh dear. Looks like he's started filling them with . . . good lord, what's that, Charlie – blood?'

'Blackcurrant juice, I think.'

'And whose *brilliant* idea was it to give Frank water balloons on a day like— Oh! Good morning, Morrigan, darling,' said Dame Chanda, affecting an unconvincing breezy air as she spotted her. She smiled widely, but Morrigan thought she could see a vein pulsing in her forehead. 'Did you sleep well, my sweet? Everything's nice and normal down here, as you can see. Shall we go up to the Smoking Parlour? My, don't you look pretty in your uniform, black really *is* your—'

'I know about the reward,' Morrigan said, taking pity on Dame Chanda, who instantly collapsed on to the nearest sofa, fanning herself.

'Oh, thank *goodness*, darling, I couldn't bear the charade a second longer.' She lifted her head and gave Morrigan a searching, worried look. 'You must be ever so frightened.'

'No,' she lied. Her stomach gave an unpleasant squeeze. 'I'm fine.'

It had been one thing, hearing about it on the radio. Even the parachutist incident could almost have been amusing, if it was just one lone oddball, out *there*. But this was different. This was her home, these people were right on her doorstep. Of course she was frightened.

'That's the spirit,' said Dame Chanda, though it was clear she didn't believe the act. 'Chin up and tally ho.'

'Where's Jupiter?'

'He was summoned by the High Council of Elders early this morning, lass,' said Kedgeree. 'Wasn't sure when he'd be back.'

Morrigan sighed and ran a hand through her messy morning hair. She felt a prickling, staticky itch on her middle fingertip, but shook it out. 'I can't get into Station 919, which means I can't get to Wunsoc. I was going to take the Brolly Rail, but . . .'

There was another loud *SPLASH!* from outside, then a squeal of disgust, and Kedgeree glanced uneasily towards the entrance. 'Not advisable, I think. Perhaps a cheeky day off school is in order?'

'THAT is a brilliant idea,' said Charlie, pointing at him. 'You know, you don't skive off school anywhere near enough, Morrigan, I'm always saying – *oof*, what?' Martha had whacked him in the side, and he laughed. 'It's true, she doesn't.'

Dame Chanda clapped her hands. 'Oh! I know. Let's have a lovely girls' day, shall we? Martha, come along, darling – you too, Fenestra!'

'Pass.'

'We'll do each other's hair and share our fondest ambitions and *most* scandalous secrets and—' She cut herself off, noticing Morrigan's look of dismay, and gave her shoulder a squeeze. 'Don't you worry, my dear. I'm sure Jove is sorting all of this out right now.'

Morrigan hoped so. Most of all, she hoped he managed it before Dame Chanda did anything permanent to her hair.

One cheeky day off school turned into two, then three.

Jupiter had returned home at lunchtime the first day, bursting through the service entrance in a flustered, irascible state and refusing to tell Morrigan or anyone else what the Elders had wanted. All he would say was that the station door locking itself had not been an accident.

'Our *esteemed* High Council,' he said through clenched teeth, 'has decided it's unsafe for you to be at Wunsoc until the ridiculous mess *they so carelessly made* has been sorted out.'

(Morrigan very much doubted they'd used those exact words.)

Every day, Jupiter was summoned by the Elders, and every

day he returned more frustrated than the day before, refusing to say what they'd discussed. Every day, he brought back a pile of homework Miss Cheery had gathered from some of Morrigan's teachers, and every day Morrigan ignored it in favour of trawling through the very worst headlines. Nevermoor's major newspapers couldn't seem to decide if they were more interested in the Hollowpox, or Morrigan.

REWARD OFFERED! WUNDERSMITH SPOTTERS HOPE TO CASH IN

'WE CAN'T COPE!' SAYS HOSPITAL CHIEF
ROYAL LIGHTWING'S RECORD NIGHT OF WUNIMAL-INFLICTED INJURIES

SQUALL AND CROW: PARTNERS OR RIVALS?

ESCALATION OF WUNIMAL ATTACKS PROMPTS BIGGER POLICE PRESENCE

MYSTERIOUS MORRIGAN:
WHERE DID SHE COME FROM AND WHAT DOES SHE WANT?
THE CONCERNED CITIZENS OF NEVERMOOR NEED TO KNOW

'She wants to be left alone,' Morrigan muttered as she tossed the broadsheet into the fireplace.

Meanwhile, life inside the Deucalion was becoming claustrophobic. People just kept arriving, swarming to the hotel like bees around a hive. They camped out all day and overnight in the grand forecourt. It felt like being under siege. Thankfully the shabby service entrance on maze-like Caddisfly Alley was still in operation, or they'd *really* have been marooned. (Kedgeree was clever enough to take the small, faded HOTEL DEUCALION sign off its hinges.)

Morrigan was forbidden to go outside anyway. She stayed away from the lobby as much as possible, spending most of Tuesday and Wednesday in her bedroom. She told everyone she had schoolwork to do, but actually she was just tired of hearing strangers shout at her. Her fourth-floor windows looked down on to the forecourt, but she drew the heavy curtains closed. Room 85 seemed to take the hint and muffled all remaining sound from outside.

She finally emerged from hibernation on Wednesday afternoon, hoping Jupiter would return triumphant from Wunsoc having convinced the Elders to unlock her station door. Instead it was Fenestra who was triumphant, trotting down the spiral staircase carrying a man in her teeth by the scruff of his neck like a large, ugly kitten. Martha and Kedgeree jumped up immediately to shield Morrigan from his view.

'Let go of me!' he bawled. 'I'll have you arrested. You ripped my shirt! This is assault!'

Fenestra tossed him on to the chequerboard floor with a look of disgust. 'Found this maggot creeping around on the seventh floor; says he paraglided in through the window. I'm making a citizen's arrest. Kedgeree, fetch the handcuffs! Clap this brigand in irons!'

Kedgeree gave a weary sigh. 'I told you already, Fen, we've not got any handcuffs.'

'What, *still*? What kind of lousy concierge doesn't have – oi, don't let him *go!*'

But Kedgeree was already creaking open the front doors and shoving the terrified trespasser out. With Martha and Charlie's help he quickly slammed and locked the doors again, but not before Morrigan caught a glimpse of the crowd outside . . . and she thought one or two of them might have caught a glimpse of her, too, because the noise seemed to suddenly swell.

'WUNDERSMIIIIIIITH!'

'MORRIGAN CROW IS A FRAUD!'

'THAT'S HER! I SAW HER!'

'IF YOU'RE REALLY A WUNDERSMITH, WHY DON'T YOU PROVE IT?'

Morrigan took a deep breath, resisting the urge to press her hands to her ears.

'What was that, then?' asked Charlie. 'Number five?'

'Six!' said Martha. 'Let's see, there was the fake plumber, and the fake mailman, and the one who claimed to be Jupiter's long-lost cousin—'

'—and the one who claimed to be Morrigan's long-lost aunt,' added Charlie.

'Oh, and the one yesterday who claimed he was here for a job interview!'

'Martha offered him a position on a trial basis,' Charlie said, grinning proudly. 'Made him iron three hundred cloth napkins, then kicked him out.'

Martha looked pleased with herself. 'He was a big help, Jerry was.'

Morrigan tried to smile. She knew they were making a joke of it for her sake, so she wouldn't be scared. She just couldn't bring herself to find the idea of intruders in their home very funny.

At least these 'chancers' were trying to be clever about it, she supposed. That was more than she could say for all the people camped out on the doorstep, hoping she would suddenly appear in a flurry of . . . of what, she wondered? Did they want her to come out in a long cape with a shrieking, maniacal laugh and set an army of monsters on them, like the legend they'd constructed of Ezra Squall? What *exactly* were they hoping for?

The simple answer was, of course, fifty thousand kred.

But if they believed the money really was on the table, they must believe Morrigan truly *could* be a Wundersmith, and everyone knew Wundersmiths were dangerous . . . which made her wonder why they dared come anywhere near her.

'Folks'll do more for money like that,' Kedgeree said when she'd asked him about it. 'Greed trumps fear.'

The power of greed was underlined on Thursday morning, when Morrigan heard on the radio in the Smoking Parlour that Scumbag St James had doubled his reward.

'*One hundred thousand kred?*' Jack shrieked.

Morrigan raised her eyebrows. 'He must be getting desperate.'

'Desperate for more attention, yeah. The *Concerned Citizens* have been in the headlines every day this week. I bet that's worth more to someone like him than a hundred thousand kred.' He paused to think. 'Morrigan, how about I film you doing something Wundrous and we split the reward money, sixty-forty?'

'Am I sixty or forty?'

'Forty. Obviously.'

She pretended to consider it. 'Seventy-thirty. I'm seventy.'

'Hmm. How about ninety-ten? I'm ninety.'

'How about I get back to you never?'

He held out a hand, and they shook on it. 'Pleasure not doing business with you.'

Jack had arrived home unexpectedly the night before with an

impassioned speech for Jupiter about how he ought to take the rest of the week off school 'in solidarity with Morrigan'. (Morrigan happened to know he had a physics exam on Thursday afternoon that he hadn't studied for, but she didn't rat him out.) After two full days away from Sub-Nine and her friends, she was *so* bored, and already his company was making her exile from Wunsoc slightly more bearable. They were having such a pleasant morning, she could almost ignore the distant sounds of the crowd in the forecourt shouting her name.

By afternoon, however, news of the doubled reward *quadrupled* the crowd outside the Deucalion, making them much harder to ignore. They'd given up asking questions. They'd even stopped shouting Morrigan's name.

Now they were simply chanting one word over and over, like a magic spell that might make her appear.

WUNDERSMITH.
WUNDERSMITH.
WUNDERSMITH.

There was another surprise visitor later that day. *Not* a pleasant surprise.

Morrigan, Martha, Jack and Charlie had spent the afternoon playing boardgames in a peaceful, pinky-orange haze in the Smoking Parlour (peach smoke: to evoke sweet memories of summer), but they were drawn to the lobby by the sound of raised voices.

'There's no need to fuss, Chanda, I just want to *speak* with her.'

'It's *Dame* Chanda to you. And Jupiter has already told you, repeatedly, the answer is *no*—'

'I'd like to hear that from Morrigan herself, if you don't mind.'

'But that's just it, we *do* mind!'

In an emerald green three-piece suit and gold leather boots, with her shiny black hair piled high on her head, Holliday Wu looked like the pages of a fashion magazine brought to life. She was surrounded by half a dozen others, all dressed in black and hauling various kit – including a lighting rig, an enormous camera, and an entire rack of clothing in Morrigan's size. They were facing off against Dame Chanda, Kedgeree, Frank and Fenestra, who stood at the bottom of the spiral staircase like a team of bouncers, blocking the way.

'Where *is* Jupiter?' demanded Dame Chanda. 'Does he know you're here?'

Holliday gave a casual shrug, examining her fingernails. 'I believe he had an important meeting with the Hollowpox task force.'

'How convenient.' The soprano narrowed her eyes. 'I might remind you that you're *also* on the Hollowpox task force, Holliday. Why aren't you there?'

'Because *I* have an important meeting with— ah! There you are. Time we sorted this mess out, don't you think?' said Holliday, her eyes on Morrigan descending the stairs.

Dame Chanda whipped around. 'Morrigan! You do not *have* to do this.'

'Do what?'

'Okay, you lot start setting up, I want everything in place before we open those doors.' Holliday clapped her hands twice and her crew jumped into action, setting up what looked like a small film set, right in front of the Deucalion's closed double doors. 'Lizzie, I've changed my mind about the red dress. Too aggressive. Let's go for a nice baby blue – play up the harmless-little-girl thing. Hair out, please, Carlos, but pin the front back, we want them to see her face. Maxine, let's powder out that shiny forehead and get a touch of blush on those cheeks, she's far too pale.'

There was a sudden flurry of movement around Morrigan as dresses were held up against her, a gigantic powder puff dusted all over her face until she sneezed, and a brush yanked through her messy hair. Morrigan was so shocked she didn't even bat them away.

'All right, so. What's in your repertoire?' Holliday asked her. 'The fireblossoms were fab, but we need something fresh. Bold. But not *dangerous*, we don't want anyone out there feeling threatened. Or maybe we do, a bit – like they're on a roller coaster, yeah? *Exhilarated*, that's the word.'

'You want me to go out there and . . . and use the Wundrous Arts?' said Morrigan, frowning. 'In front of all those people?

'She's not a performing monkey!' said Dame Chanda.

But Holliday only had eyes and ears for Morrigan. 'Laurent St James is out there talking about you all day, every day, and if we don't respond, we are letting him control the narrative. You don't know how this works. Nor does Captain North. But I do. The more you hide from these people, the more they want to hunt you.

'According to St James, you're either a myth or an attack dog. A made-up threat the Society is dangling over Nevermoor, or a real danger that needs to be dealt with. We need to *change* that conversation. We need to show people that having a Wundersmith in Nevermoor again can be a good thing. And we need to start by proving you really *are* a Wundersmith. Laurent St James has put a target on your back, Morrigan. I'm here to help you take it off.'

Morrigan shook her head. '*You* put a target on my back. The anonymous source in the *Sunday Post* was *you*, Jupiter already told me the truth.'

Holliday didn't look even slightly embarrassed or sorry. She brought her face level with Morrigan's, and spoke in a soft, calm voice. 'Fine. You like truth? Here's some truth for you.'

'Madam, I think it's time for you to leave,' Kedgeree said firmly. Fenestra was flexing her claws and gazing at the rack of dresses as though she longed to shred them, and Frank was running interference on the woman with the lighting rig, blocking her every time she tried to set it down.

Holliday ignored them all. 'You are a liability. Do you know what the Society had to do to contain that disaster at the Museum of Stolen Moments last Hallowmas?' she asked. 'Do you know the lies we've had to tell, the money and resources we've had to spend, the favours we've had to cash in, all to shield you from the consequences of that night?'

'I . . .' Morrigan blinked back the tears that were suddenly pricking her eyes. She clenched her jaw once, twice. 'No. I didn't know.'

'Holliday, *leave*!' Dame Chanda shouted. 'Morrigan, darling, don't *listen*—'

'No. You didn't know,' Holliday said over the top of her. 'As good as your intentions might have been, as brave and noble and *whatever* . . . you still swooped in where you didn't belong, where you *weren't asked to be*, and made a giant mess. It takes a lot to clean up a mess that big. Guess who got to do it?'

Morrigan eyes flicked over to the door and back again. 'You.'

Holliday nodded. 'And I did it gladly, because that's my job and I'm good at it. Now you have a job. The Wundrous Society needs you. Hold your nose, put on a smile, and give us a show.'

She nodded at her assistants, and instantly one of them was

there, fitting a microphone to Morrigan's collar.

'I – I can't, I don't know what to do—'

'You're a Wundersmith. You're *the* Wundersmith.' She placed her hands on Morrigan's shoulders, spun her around, and gave her a little shove. 'You'll figure it out.'

And somehow, without having agreed to it, without even taking a moment to consider, Morrigan was walking towards the Deucalion entrance, and the enormous double doors were being opened. She paused, unable to make herself walk through them.

After their third morning of shouting for her to come out, the waiting crowd had settled into a quieter afternoon slump . . . but as soon as the doors were open, they perked up like a pack of hunting dogs on the scent of a rabbit.

'THERE SHE IS!'

'MORRIGAN, WHY HAVE YOU BEEN HIDING?'

'*WUNDERSMITH. WUNDERSMITH. WUNDERSMITH.*'

Morrigan flinched as the big lights came on, nearly blinding her.

The chant grew louder and more urgent, and the eyes and camera lenses in the crowd felt like hundreds of tiny spotlights, shining with greed.

Holliday's camera operator held up three fingers . . . two fingers . . . one . . . and pointed at Morrigan, mouthing the word, 'Go.'

'*WUNDERSMITH. WUNDERSMITH. WUNDERSMITH.*'

Panic rose from her chest up into her throat, grasping at her windpipe with cold, clammy hands. What was she supposed to do? Summon Wunder? Nobody but her and Jack would even see it. Weave a wonky flower? Not bold. Not *exhilarating*.

Could she really breathe fire in front of all these strangers? *Should* she?

What would Jupiter want her to do – and why wasn't he *here*?
WUNDERSMITH.
WUNDERSMITH.
WUNDERSMITH.

Morrigan swallowed. She began to sing in a cracked voice that was barely more than a whisper. '*Morningtide's child is merry and—*'

Faster than she thought physically possible, the enormous double doors swung closed in front of her, knocking the cameraman over and sending his equipment flying across the lobby floor. Morrigan stumbled backwards as the crowd disappeared behind the solid oak doors.

Then there came a sound like a dozen thunderclaps, one after the other. It started in the lobby and quickly spread to all ends of the hotel as heavy black shutters descended on every window, blocking out every bit of noise until the building was completely, oppressively silent.

Was this part of the Grand Sulk, she wondered? Or was it the Hotel Deucalion coming to her rescue? Room 85 was always so good at anticipating her needs, adjusting to her moods . . . but this was different. This wasn't just her bedroom, it was the entire building, and it was . . . what? *Defending* her?

'Thanks,' she whispered, just in case.

In the absence of all ambient noise, the Deucalion felt like a mausoleum. Like a giant holding its breath.

A cold voice broke the silence.

'I believe you have your answer, Holliday.' Everyone turned to see Jupiter, who had just emerged from the service entrance, the glossy black door still swinging behind him. He looked up at the shutters in astonishment; evidently the Deucalion could still surprise even its proprietor.

He snatched the swinging door just in time, holding it open for their unwelcome guests. 'Kindly leave.'

Morrigan woke the next morning with a start, her heart racing. She'd been dreaming of something strange and awful – broken glass and plumes of black smoke and a distant cry in the dark. Two button-black eyes shining at her from the shadows. A snatch of song she couldn't quite remember. A feeling of something precious, slipping through her fingers.

But that wasn't what woke her up.

She felt the new imprint before she'd even opened her eyes. Although she hadn't been expecting it, she somehow knew it was there, on the tip of her left middle finger. She knew it in the same way that she knew she *had* a finger at all.

It had been irritating her for days, but so much else was happening, it had only been a vague background bother.

Now, though, it had her full attention.

Like the W imprint on her right index finger, it was small and tattoo-like, but not a tattoo. It hadn't been inflicted; it had *emerged*. Pressed itself from the inside to the outside of her skin, like treasure floating up to the surface of a lake.

It was very early; the sun wasn't up yet, but the dark blue sky outside Morrigan's window was just beginning to lighten. She reached out, fumbling to turn on the bedside lamp, and held her finger up to examine the new addition.

It was a small flame, bright orange and red with a tiny spark of blue in the centre.

'Where'd you come from?' she croaked sleepily, peering closely at it.

Would Hawthorne and Cadence and the other members of Unit 919 have one of these too, Morrigan wondered, or just her?

They'd all received *W* imprints the morning after their inauguration into the Wundrous Society. What might they have done to earn—

Oh.

'Inferno,' she whispered. She sat up in bed, tingling with excitement. Was this because of the fireblossoms? Was this what happened when you finally got the hang of a Wundrous Art? And if it was only Morrigan who had the imprint . . . what did it do? What might it *open*?

The realisation hit her like a lightning bolt. She shot out of bed and ran to get dressed.

CHAPTER THIRTY

The Kindling in The Hearth

Morrigan half expected to find the service entrance shut down like the rest of the hotel, but she met no obstructions except an enormous, furry, snoring boulder guarding the door. Holding her breath, she tiptoed past Fenestra and down the shabby service hallway, burst through to Caddisfly Alley and pelted along the twisting backstreet all the way to the Brolly Rail station at the end of Humdinger Avenue.

Flying across a darkened Nevermoor skyline in freezing, near-horizontal rain, her teeth chattering violently, Morrigan felt rebellious and invincible.

All the way to Wunsoc, up the long drive beneath the crackling fireblossoms, into Proudfoot House and down all nine subterranean floors, through thirteen cold, dim chambers named for dead Wundersmiths long forgotten, Morrigan felt her new imprint tingling. As if perhaps it felt as excited and nervous as she did.

When at last she made it to the door of the Liminal Hall –

lungs aching, breathless with anticipation – she saw just what she'd hoped for. The circular lock on the door glowed a bright, fiery orange-gold, casting its own pool of light in the dark.

'I *knew* it,' she whispered, grinning wildly.

She pressed her finger to the lock, and the door opened – for what must have been the first time in a hundred years – on to a room so peculiar, she was struck by the urge to turn around and leave right away.

The Liminal Hall was large and bright; Morrigan had to hold up a hand to shield her eyes. It felt like a cathedral whose every window let in glaring sunshine, if the sun had been directly above them and on all other sides and close, much too close.

She'd thought the Deucalion was quiet after the shutters went down, but it was a rock concert compared to this place. If Morrigan hadn't known she was breathing, if she hadn't felt the gentle rhythm of her lungs filling and emptying, filling and emptying, she wouldn't have believed there was any oxygen in the room. There were no dust motes floating in the air, glittering in the streaming sunlight. There was no sound. Even her footsteps were silent.

The hall was empty but for a large pile of branches, twigs and dried bracken in the far corner, stacked and twisted around itself like a bonfire waiting to be lit.

Was this a test, she wondered? Was she supposed to breathe fire and light it up?

Or was that the *opposite* of what she ought to do? Perhaps she was supposed to show restraint.

'Written instructions might be nice.' Her words felt small in the enormous space.

Maybe she ought to wait for Rook or Sofia or Conall. She'd been so eager to get here and confirm her suspicions, she hadn't even stopped to think about the basement nerds. They'd love to see this – they'd waited *years* to see it. And perhaps they might have an idea of how it worked.

But before Morrigan could turn to go, something caught her eye.

Deep amid the knotted woodpile, at the tip of a spindly branch, a tiny circular lock pulsed with orange-gold light. Without thinking, she reached in to press her new imprint to it . . . and felt a spark.

The bonfire roared into life. Morrigan snatched her hand away, stumbling back and shielding her face from its heat. The Liminal Hall began to narrow and darken. Then it was gone – the bright, cathedral-like space replaced with tall stone walls closing around her on all sides, leading up to a ceiling that was either so dark, or so far away, she couldn't see it. The door, she noticed (with no small amount of alarm), had disappeared altogether.

Her nostrils filled with smoke. Tiny snowflakes of grey ash danced in the air and settled on her cloak. Sparks from the fire drifted up, up, up, but illuminated nothing. They flew so high they simply disappeared into darkness.

The fire was bigger than any she'd seen before, with flames taller than a house. She pressed her back against the warm stone wall, her heartbeat drumming in her neck, and then—

Morrigan gasped.

The firewood had moved.

Not in the normal way that logs suddenly shift and collapse as they burn down, but in a precise, deliberate way.

Perhaps it had been a trick of the light.

But the fire moved again; no mistake. The pile of black burning branches gathered themselves up, rearranging, reforming into a vast, towering shape that made the skin on Morrigan's neck turn to gooseflesh, even in this heat. There were two arms, two legs, and a large, curious face sitting in the fire, turning themselves towards her. Slowly, reluctantly.

Not a tumble of kindling, but an unfurling of limbs.

A person (or a *thing*, for Morrigan didn't think its face was very human) waking from slumber and *looking* at her. Its huge eyes peered out from the flames, glowing a deep rich red like burning coal. They reminded her of the Hunt of Smoke and Shadow.

The ember eyes blinked – once, twice – and watched her expectantly.

'Hi,' she said softly.

The great dark eyes blinked again. 'Have you come to the Hearth with no offering?'

The voice was tremendous – slow and heavy and ancient. Large enough to fill the space and make Morrigan's hands shake a little. It hissed and crackled around the edges, like the sound of flames. But more extraordinary than all of that, it sounded . . . hurt. Disappointed.

Morrigan faltered. 'Oh, I . . . I didn't know I was meant to bring anything. Um.' She thought for a moment. There was nothing in her pockets. She'd dropped her brolly outside the door to the Liminal Hall (not that she'd have given *that* away). 'I can go away and come back, if you like. What sort of offering would you, er—'

'The Kindling.'

'I'm . . . sorry, what?'

'You will please call the Kindling by its name.' The flames grew higher, and the red eyes grew brighter, and Morrigan took these things to mean that it was displeased.

She nodded, suddenly understanding.

The Kindling. The Hearth. *Inferno.*

Could this be one of the Wundrous Divinities Elder Quinn had talked about, all those months ago when Unit 919 had first entered the Gathering Place? She'd said the Wundersmiths were gifted above all others, *chosen by the Wundrous Divinities themselves, the ancient deities who watched over our realm.* Morrigan had thought about these deities, but hadn't ever imagined they were real people. It *certainly* hadn't occurred to her that one of them might be a large talking bonfire.

'Sorry,' she said, and gave an awkward sort of half-bow. 'What sort of offering would the Kindling—'

'You have the mark?' it asked.

Morrigan nodded and held up her left hand to show the imprint on her fingertip.

The Kindling reached out with its own spindly hand, fully aflame. Before Morrigan could flinch away from the heat, its burning fingers brushed against hers, the Hearth instantly disappeared, and she was outside Proudfoot House.

Familiar images and sounds and feelings came to her in a blur, loud and unwelcome. Gracious Goldberry on the rooftop. Miss Cheery crying out in pain. A wave of fury, a taste of ash in her throat. Fire bursting from her lungs.

Candles. Hallowmas. The Angel Israfel, frozen high up in the air.

More candles, *so many candles*.

The Proudfoot House rooftop on a sunny autumn day.

Small sparks make big fires. The protest. Elder Saga. Lam. *Do it. Now.* Her hand pressed to the tree and that feeling, that feeling, that *feeling*.

That's where the Kindling slowed down. Morrigan felt like it was flicking through her like the pages of a book, and had finally seen something of interest.

A glorious green canopy of ancient fire. Resurrection. Life. Power.

Morrigan opened her eyes – she hadn't even noticed she'd closed them – and was surprised to find herself still standing in the Hearth. Those two huge ember eyes were watching her again, glowing bright and steady.

'The Kindling accepts your offering.'

Their fingertips parted. Morrigan pulled her hand from the flame: pale, unburnt.

Her wonder turned to astonishment when she saw the imprint; it was *moving*. The tiny tattoo-like flame danced on her skin, flickering gently like a real, live fire. And she could feel it. Not the way she'd felt it when it first arrived, but in a much more insistent way that said *I am here, and I won't let you forget me*. There was a pleasantly fierce warmth to it. It was part of her.

Elder Quinn was right. The Divinities had gifted the Wundersmiths above all others. This was a gift.

'Thank you,' she breathed. 'Are you . . . you're one of the Divinities, aren't you?'

The Kindling looked surprised. 'Is this your first visit to the Liminal Hall?'

'Yes.'

'I'm honoured. Inferno is rarely a Wundersmith's first acquired art. But why are you so old?'

Morrigan felt a little put out by that. 'I'm thirteen.'

'Yes,' it said. 'Why have you taken so long?'

'How old should I be?'

The Kindling appeared to consider the question. 'Most Wundersmiths have made their third pilgrimage by your age. Perhaps fourth. Are you very inept? Do your teachers find you a slow learner?'

Morrigan thought of what Squall had said to her on the rooftop. *You are light years away from where you ought to be.* Perhaps he hadn't been lying about that after all. The realisation stung.

'No,' she said, and then added pointedly, 'They're happy I brought the fireblossoms back from one hundred years of extinction.'

'Hmm.'

'Who are the others?' she asked. 'The other Wundrous Divinities, like you? How will I get to see them, what should I do?'

The Kindling's eyes turned dark as coal and it fell quiet. Morrigan listened for a moment to the steady crackling of flames, wondering if it was ignoring her question or gathering its thoughts. 'What is your name, Wundersmith?'

'Morrigan Crow.'

'Tell me, then, Morrigan Crow. Why have I been abandoned?'

She noticed then, for the first time, how miserable it looked. With a sudden pang of sorrow, she understood that hers must be the first face it had seen in over a hundred years. It was lonely.

'Nobody comes to see me any more,' it said with a sigh. 'Where are Brilliance and Griselda? And Ezra and Odbuoy? They all just . . . went away. My brightest flames.'

Morrigan didn't know what to say. How could she tell it what had happened? She barely understood it herself.

'I don't know,' she lied. 'I'm sorry.'

'Do they still . . . visit the others?' There was a petulant note of jealousy in its voice.

She shook her head. 'No. They don't visit anyone at all. I promise.'

There was silence for a while as the Kindling processed this information.

'But you . . . you will come back?'

Morrigan nodded. Of course she'd be back. She had to show the others.

'Goodbye until then.' The Kindling stretched out a twig-like finger, and Morrigan mirrored the gesture without thinking. When their fingertips touched, the fire began to die. The darkness receded, the stone walls withdrew, and the Liminal Hall brightened once again. Folding in on itself, the Kindling cast her one last blazing look.

'Burn brightly, Morrigan Crow.'

Morrigan ran back through the Liminal Hall on muffled footsteps, all the way through the echoing chambers of Sub-Nine, and was shouting for the Scholar Mistress and the basement nerds even before she reached the firelit study chamber at the end of the marble hallway.

'Rook! Sofia! Conall, where are you?' The room was empty. She dashed back into the hall, calling even louder – perhaps they were in one of the other endless chamber branches and would hear her voice bouncing around the empty hallway. 'SOFIA! CONALL! Come out here, I have something to tell you – Sofia! There you are.' She came to a breathless halt, lungs heaving, and bent forward to rest her hands on her knees. There was a dim outline of the foxwun at the far end of the hallway, by the Sub-Nine entrance. 'You'll *never* guess what I just – Sofia, is that you?'

She breathed a tiny puff of a spark into her fingertips, and in that fraction of a second, two things happened. First, Sofia crouched low, lifted her head and sniffed the air. Second, Morrigan got a sick, swooping feeling in her stomach and the tiny hairs on her arms all stood up, alert to danger. Her body knew before she did. But too late.

Snap.

It was like flipping a switch. With one click, orange flames danced in the palm of Morrigan's hand . . . and Sofia's eyes lit up brilliant green, like a furnace had been turned on inside her. Teeth bared, ears and tail erect, the foxwun hurtled down the hall in a blur of red fur and emerald light. Morrigan held her hands out in a futile attempt to stop what she knew was coming, but suddenly Sofia was *there*, launching powerfully from the ground, straight for her throat. She shrieked, feeling the sting of sharp teeth grazing her skin. A burst of terror and adrenaline shot through her and she wrenched Sofia away, flinging her to the ground where she landed with a yelp and a sickening thud.

'Sofia!' Morrigan cried. She felt an urge to run to her side but knew that would be extraordinarily stupid. Ignoring the instinct, she instead snapped her fingers again, crouched down and drew a line of fire across the marble floor from one wall to the other, building a barrier between them. The foxwun ignored it, picking herself up and leaping for Morrigan once more . . . only to rear back at the last moment, yelping again in pain.

Morrigan took shallow, panicked breaths, feeling like her heart might explode. Sweat beaded on her face. The flames climbed almost to the ceiling, fencing her in with no escape. *Brilliant*, she thought. *Well done, idiot.*

'Sofia? Sofia, I know you're still in there. Wake *UP*.'

But if Sofia *was* in there somewhere, she wasn't listening. She scurried frantically back and forth, snapping her jaws, trying to find a way through the flames then rearing back again, barking in fierce frustration.

The line of fire was already dying – in the cold, empty marble hallway, there was no fuel to burn. Morrigan could feel her energy seeping away with it. What happened when there was no barrier between her and Sofia? Would Sofia fight to kill? Would Morrigan have to hurt her friend in order to stop her?

And *then what*? The Hollowpox would take everything with it, emptying Sofia out until there was nothing left of her. Morrigan would never forget the haunted look on Jupiter's face when he'd said, *I'd rather be dead than hollow*.

What would Sofia be when she wasn't Sofia any more?

As if in response to this unasked question, the foxwun let loose an unnimalistic scream, trying one last time to leap through the flames . . . and succeeded at last, landing on Morrigan's chest – paws outstretched, jaws ready to close on her white throat – just as the light in her eyes extinguished and the Hollowpox left her.

With a soft *oof*, Morrigan caught the small, limp body in her arms.

The fire died, and the curious green light swarmed around the pair of them for just a moment, before it dispersed and disappeared altogether, scattering like dandelion seeds on the wind.

The ends of Sofia's fur were singed and smoking. The sight of it was too much to bear. Morrigan knelt down, took off her cloak, and gently wrapped it around the feather-light foxwun, hands shaking. She felt a slightly hysterical sob bubble up in her chest, and pressed her lips tightly together so it wouldn't escape.

There was a choice to be made, Morrigan thought. She could sit here in the cold, dark hallway on Sub-Nine and sob. She could wait for Rook or Conall to arrive. They would take care of Sofia and send Morrigan home and tell her everything was going to be all right. Jupiter would promise her that any day now this nightmare would be over and Sofia would be okay and she would *never*, *ever* turn into an unnimal . . . and Morrigan could pretend his gentle, well-meaning optimism was rooted in truth.

It would have been so easy. It would have felt so good to let herself be comforted, to indulge in the lazy hope that someone else would fix everything, to feel it envelop her like a warm bath.

But Morrigan didn't have that luxury. Because she knew it was a lie. And because Sofia was her *friend*. How could she leave her friend to a fate worse than death, when she knew there was another option? She had to make the other choice instead. The hard choice.

As Morrigan bundled Sofia up and fled Sub-Nine with her, heading for the teaching hospital, she heard a quiet voice inside her head saying the same words, over and over.

Things are ever so much worse than you know.

You'll find that out for yourself soon enough, and when you do, you will come looking for me.

CHAPTER THIRTY-ONE

Call Me Mog

Not half an hour later, Morrigan stepped from a single brass railpod on to the platform for the forbidden Gossamer Line, clutching her umbrella tight with both hands to stop them shaking.

She hadn't been certain it would work. The bank of railpods in Proudfoot House could take her to most stations, but she'd hardly dared to hope that one of them would agree to take her to a locked, abandoned platform somewhere deep in the labyrinth of Nevermoor's Wunderground network. Not when she couldn't even remember where it was, or how she'd managed to get there with Jupiter the first time she'd (illegally) travelled on it. Yet, here she was. All she'd had to do was ask.

Morrigan thought, perhaps, it was her two secret weapons that had sealed the deal: the new fiery-warm imprint tingling on her fingertip, and the words of Ezra Squall ringing in her head.

'*One day, you may realise how formidably you could run this city, if only you'd put in a little effort.*'

The abandoned station was just as she remembered it. It had been shut down years ago, when the Gossamer Line was declared unfit for public use. The posters on the walls were faded and old-fashioned, advertising products that probably didn't exist any more, but other than that the place was immaculate. The green tiles looked shiny and new. The wooden benches had barely been used.

She remembered what Jupiter had said on her first Christmas night in Nevermoor, when they'd travelled together on the Gossamer Line to visit Crow Manor. *If anyone can ride the Gossamer Line, it's you.* He'd said it was because she was with him, but he'd lied. That was before Morrigan knew she was a Wundersmith.

That's why she ought to be able to ride the Gossamer Line without trouble. It was a Wundrous Act, and *she* was a Wundersmith. It didn't matter that she had no idea what she was doing. Wunder knew what it was doing.

So why wouldn't her hands stop shaking?

I should have told someone, Morrigan thought, suddenly gripped by fear. *I should have told Hawthorne where I was going, or Cadence. I should have told Jupiter!*

But it was a hollow thought. She knew she never would have told them. They would only have tried to stop her.

Taking a deep breath, she hung her oilskin umbrella on the platform railing. It would be her anchor – a precious personal object left purposefully behind with her body, ready to tug her back into the physical realm when she was ready.

Before her last nerve could abandon her, Morrigan closed her eyes, stepped up to the yellow line, and waited for the whistle of the Gossamer train.

The first time she'd travelled this way, Jupiter had made her close her eyes, and she could understand why. It felt like travelling through a dream, while standing on a cloud made solid. But the cloud was bright as diamonds, golden-white as Wunder. And the dream was an entire universe, wild and confusing, whizzing by at high speed. It was a rush of blood to the head, so blindingly brilliant it was hard to think. And Morrigan *needed* to think. She covered her eyes.

The problem was . . . she didn't know where to go. Where was Ezra Squall? She knew the name of his company – Squall Industries – but where in the Wintersea Republic *was* it? Would he even be there if she found it?

As it turned out, none of that mattered. The Gossamer Line didn't need a map. It didn't need to be coerced or convinced to go anywhere. The Wundrous golden-white train seemed to read her thoughts the instant she had them, and within *moments* it had arrived at its destination.

Morrigan stepped down from the train carriage and found herself inside a large wood-panelled room. It reminded her of some place she'd been before. The furnishings were grander and darker, the décor much statelier, and altogether it was *much* less of a pigsty . . . but it made her think of the Angel Israfel's dressing room at the Old Delphian Music Hall. There was a large wardrobe, and an elegant sofa, and a dressing table laid out with all sorts of things. Brushes and bottles of greasepaint and little glass trinket trays.

There was a double door made of dark wood, with an unusual set of silver handles that interlocked to form a large, ornate W.

Was she back at Wunsoc?

She mustn't have done it right.

Morrigan sighed – and had just closed her eyes to picture her brolly and call the train back – when the double doors opened and a woman entered the room, stopped, and looked at her.

It was strange. The first time Morrigan had travelled on the Gossamer, she'd been invisible to everyone at Crow Manor. Everyone except her grandmother because, as Jupiter had explained, she'd *wanted* Ornella Crow to see her.

Surely, then, the woman standing in front of her wearing a grand white wig and black robes should *not* be able to see Morrigan, because in this moment Morrigan most assuredly did not want to be seen.

And yet . . . the woman was definitely *looking* at her.

Morrigan breathed in sharply.

She knew precisely who this was. Her brain rushed to make connections, one after the other, *click-click-click* . . . and suddenly she also knew *where* she was. She'd never seen the place in person before, but she'd heard about it her whole life.

The W on the door didn't stand for Wundrous.

It stood for Wintersea.

She was inside the Chancery, in the heart of Ylvastad, the capital city of the Wintersea Republic.

The Gossamer Line must have misread her intention. Or maybe – *ugh*, she could have smacked herself in the forehead – maybe when she'd wondered 'where in the Wintersea Republic' Squall was, it had simply responded in the most efficient way possible by taking her to the *heart* of the Republic.

Morrigan felt a little of her courage seep away. She wasn't prepared for this.

The woman was still watching her expectantly, and she absolutely could *not* think what the proper thing was to do . . . so she bobbed an awkward half-curtsy, held up her hand in a sort-of wave and mumbled, 'Hello . . . er, ma'am.'

President Wintersea blinked back at her.

She looked nothing like her official portrait, which hung in homes and schools and government buildings all over the Republic. The painting made her look stern and powerful and forbidding, but in person she had quick eyes and a pleasant, curious face – despite its thick coat of stark white makeup. She watched Morrigan as one might watch a pigeon that had flown in through the open window and made itself at home.

'Who are you?' she asked simply.

'Mor— uh, Mog.' Morrigan had been about to say *Morrigan Crow*, but then she realised that in the Wintersea Republic, Morrigan Crow was a girl on the Cursed Children's Register who had died right on schedule, two and a half years ago. President Wintersea might remember, given Morrigan's father was the State Chancellor of Great Wolfacre.

The president narrowed her eyes. 'Moramog? Strange name.'

'Just . . . just Mog. Sorry.'

'*Mmmog*,' she echoed, with considered and deliberate enunciation. 'Still strange.'

Morrigan didn't really know what to say, though she quite agreed. 'Um. Yes, it is. Sorry.'

'Why do you keep apologising?' asked President Wintersea. 'Dreadful habit for girls to get into, you must break it at once.'

'Oh. Sor— I mean. Nothing. Sorry.' Morrigan squeezed her eyes shut, shaking her head. *Why* was she making such a fool of herself?

But when the president spoke again, she sounded amused. 'Oh, I'm afraid there's no hope for you. You'll be apologising for things you didn't do all your life. At least you're good at it. Mog – it really is an appalling name, but if you insist – Mog, what are you doing in my private chambers? This is highly unorthodox. Have you come to assassinate me?'

'Wh-what?' Morrigan just about choked in her haste to deny the accusation. 'No! I wouldn't even know h—' But she stopped, seeing President Wintersea's eyes twinkling. 'You were joking.'

'Of course I was joking. If I really thought you were here to kill me, don't you think I'd have called for security by now?' She tilted her head. 'Why *are* you here?'

Morrigan tried to think fast. 'I . . . came to talk to you.'

Wintersea raised her eyebrows. 'People normally just send their angry letters to my office, you know. But fine. You may speak for as long as it takes me to deal with all of . . . this.' She gestured vaguely at her wig, black robes, dramatic face paint and the heavy gold chain she wore around her neck – the ceremonial garb of the Chancery. Crossing the room to sit at the dresser, she kept an eye on Morrigan in the mirror. 'Come on, then. What's got your goat?'

This was not at all what Morrigan imagined the president of the Wintersea Republic would be like. The informality of it all had completely thrown her . . . not to mention the fact that she *shouldn't be there*. It was Squall she needed to speak to.

'I wanted to ask you some questions. About . . . about, um, Squall Industries,' she finished, plucking a topic from the air.

'Right,' said Wintersea, deftly removing hairpins. 'Fascinating. Squall Industries. How old are you, Mog?'

'Thirteen.'

'Why in the world would a thirteen-year-old care about the machinations of the energy industry?' As she removed the pins, she dropped them on to a ceramic tray, where one by one they landed with a clatter. Her eyes briefly met Morrigan's in the mirror. 'Shouldn't you be . . . I don't know. Skiving off school and setting things on fire?'

Morrigan felt a lurch in her stomach. She *was* skiving off

school, sort of. She *had* been setting things on fire – quite recently, and quite publicly. Could Wintersea possibly know—

'Unless – oh dear, you're not one of those teenagers who *cares about the state of the world*? How dreadful. Help me with this, won't you?'

Morrigan rushed forward to help her remove the heavy Chancery wig, but as she reached for the powdered white monstrosity, her hands went straight through it. She gasped. The Gossamer. How could she have *forgotten*? She looked up at the president, her black eyes widening in the mirror.

Wintersea's gaze, however, was flatly unsurprised. Even expectant.

She'd laid the trap, and Morrigan had walked into it.

'I am the President of the Wintersea Republic,' she said, unsmilingly. 'Don't you think I know who you are, Morrigan Crow?'

Morrigan said nothing. She knew nothing could happen to her while she was here on the Gossamer, but still she couldn't fight her rising panic.

She should just leave, she thought. She should think of her oilskin brolly, call for the Gossamer train and get out of there. But something in Wintersea's steady, unflappable expression had her pinned to the floor.

'Maud,' the president said finally.

'I . . . sorry, what?'

'My name,' she clarified. 'Maud Lowry.'

'I thought your surname was Wintersea.'

Maud laughed through her nose, just a little – short and sharp. 'When I took the role, I inherited the title. *I* am Maud Lowry. My *job* is President Wintersea, leader of the Wintersea Party. Though the distinction rarely matters these days.' She paused. 'You might find the same thing happens to you, as you grow up. You are Morrigan Crow, but your title is *Wundersmith*. People will begin to confuse the two. You may even begin to confuse them yourself.'

Morrigan, frozen somewhere between fear and curiosity, didn't respond. She wondered whether the woman was subtly prodding for confirmation that she was, indeed, a Wundersmith.

Maud finished removing the wig with a sigh of relief and placed it on the dressing table. She closed her eyes, massaging her scalp and ruffling her hair a little. It was maybe a couple of inches long, and a deep, rich auburn colour, messy and matted with sweat, plastered in uneven tufts against her skull. She took a handful of translucent powder from a small glass dish, sprinkled it over her head and rubbed it in vigorously, drying and smoothing her hair until it looked, if not immaculate, at least presentable.

The transformation was instant and profound. Without her white wig, she was almost ordinary. She looked like somebody's mum. She looked like a *Maud*.

She began divesting herself of the President Wintersea costume, carefully, piece by piece – removing the golden chain from around her neck and locking it away in a wooden box, arranging the Chancery robes over a wooden mannequin in the corner. Beneath the endless folds of black fabric, she wore a pair of grey trousers and a pale blue jumper, soft and expensive looking. As she rolled up the sleeves, Morrigan spotted a tiny hole in one of them.

'How do you know my name?'

'I'm the *president*,' Maud said again, sounding mildly exasperated. She returned to the dressing table and scooped up a blob of white face cream from a small glass jar. She began to massage it roughly into her skin, speaking to Morrigan through the mirror while smearing away black eye makeup. 'I have an entire government department dedicated to finding out interesting things. I know who you are and that you escaped to the Free State. I know you're here on the Gossamer Line. I know you're a member of the Wundrous Society. A *Wundersmith*. I know you brought the fireblossoms back to life and, frankly, I suspect I know precisely why you're here.'

Morrigan swallowed. Could she possibly know about Squall's offer?

'The Hollowpox,' said Maud, wiping away the face cream with a flannel until her skin was pink and clean, every trace of makeup gone. 'You've come to ask for my help.'

'I – no,' Morrigan began haltingly, and Maud's face snapped upwards. She spun around on the chair to look at her directly, eyes narrowed again with suspicion.

'No? Then why are you here?'

'No, I meant . . . yes. That's why I'm here.' What else could she say? 'I've come to ask for your help. Er, please.'

'Awful business,' Maud said quietly. A line creased her forehead. 'We didn't call it the Hollowpox, of course. We didn't really call it anything at all. The Wunimals have always just got on with things, you see. Kept themselves to themselves. When they finally reached out, well . . .' She pursed her lips, looking away. 'I'll only say that if they'd involved us sooner, we could have done more. The cure came too late for too many.'

'Cure?' Morrigan felt her heart leap into her throat. 'You have a *cure*?'

'Of course. We're the Wintersea Party. We have the greatest scientists and innovators and thinkers in the realm at our disposal.' Maud threw the flannel into a laundry basket.

A cure. The Wintersea Party had an *actual* cure for the

380

Hollowpox, and it came without any of Squall's strings attached. Had the Gossamer Line known that, somehow? Was *that* why it had brought her here instead, and allowed Maud to see her? Morrigan felt she could burst into song.

'*Thank you*, President Wintersea,' she effused, unable to keep the relief from showing on her face. 'I can't tell you how this is—'

'Morrigan—'

'Honestly, I don't know how to thank you. This means—'

'Morrigan, stop. Stop. STOP.' Maud stood, holding her palms up to stem the flow of gratitude. 'This *means* nothing. I can't just . . . give it to you. I'm sorry, it doesn't work like that.' She sounded genuinely regretful. 'I know it took courage to come here. It was a noble thing to do, but—'

'I don't understand.' Morrigan said quietly. 'You said you have a cure.'

Maud nodded. 'We do.'

'But you don't want to share it.'

'It's not a question of what I want.'

'*Why*, then?' She felt anger and confusion bubbling up inside her. 'Why can't you help us? Just because the Wintersea Republic and the Free State are supposed to be enemies? That's not real life, that's not even real people, it's just *governments*.'

'It's not that simple.'

'It *is* that simple!' Morrigan insisted. 'Wunimals are turning into unnimals. People are *dying*. It's always simple when people are dying, you either save them or you don't!'

'Am I suddenly the prime minister of the Free State? I don't wish to sound callous but, politically speaking, your epidemic isn't our problem.'

'Politically speaking, it *is* your problem! It came from *your* Republic, didn't it?'

Maud leaned back in her chair and surveyed her with cool surprise.

'Why would you believe such a thing?' she asked in a level voice. 'All borders between the Republic and the Free State are closed. How could this disease have entered one from the other?'

Morrigan stared at her. Was it possible that President Wintersea didn't realise how porous her own borders were? That people were smuggling Wunimals and humans across them on a regular basis?

She *couldn't* be that uninformed.

'I just meant . . . nobody's ever heard of this disease in the Free State,' Morrigan mumbled, tiptoeing herself backwards out of what felt like a trap, 'but you said you've had it here in the Republic before. I thought maybe that meant . . . it could have come from here. I guess that was stupid, sorry.'

The 'sorry' was deliberate this time. Morrigan chose her words carefully, making herself small and unthreatening, a mouse before a lioness.

Maud steepled her fingers together and held them to her lips, looking thoughtful. 'I'm not unsympathetic, Morrigan. It's a terrible and dangerous disease, but a decision like this – to offer aid to a state that considers itself our enemy – must be made by my entire government, and I'm afraid the Wintersea Party is something of a dragon. A big, weighty old beast that can be difficult to reason with and impossible to steer. They'll never agree to help the Free State without some sort of quid pro quo. A deal,' she clarified, noting Morrigan's look of confusion.

'But they're *your* party,' Morrigan pointed out. 'Aren't you the one with the power?'

Maud stiffened slightly and cast her a wary, calculating look. Morrigan rushed on, worried she'd said something rude.

'I just mean . . . well, you're the president, after all. Shouldn't they do what you say?'

'You'd think so, wouldn't you?' said Maud, and the wary look melted away with a perplexed chuckle. 'But no, I'm afraid the political world doesn't quite work that way. Not here or anywhere else – the Wintersea Party might be stuck in its ways, but I can assure you, your own government isn't much better.

'For more than one hundred years the Republic and the Free State have been at an impasse, with little communication and no cooperation in either direction. Even if I could persuade *my* party to do the right thing – and I'm not saying I won't try – there's no guarantee Steed and *his* government would come to the table. Once upon a time, when I was a young idealist . . .' She paused to raise one sardonic eyebrow in Morrigan's direction. '. . . I hoped to change things. I've been trying for years to seek an audience with Steed. Even so-called enemy nations should have an open dialogue, but he's been utterly unwilling to engage. I'm afraid I can't imagine the Hollowpox has changed his attitude.'

Morrigan felt a tiny glimmer of hope.

'What if I could persuade him to talk to you?'

'Morrigan.' Maud gave her a kindly, sympathetic look, as if she'd just said something incredibly silly. 'You are an impressive girl. It was brave and clever and humble of you to travel all this way on the Gossamer Line, to stand alone before the leader of an enemy nation and *ask her for help*. But even all of that – even being a *Wundersmith* – doesn't mean you have the power to change a stubborn man's mind. Believe me.'

'I don't mean me personally,' Morrigan clarified. She was thinking of the Elders, and of Jupiter, and of Holliday and the entire force of the Wundrous Society – surely *someone* among them had access to the prime minister. She had the utmost faith in

Jupiter to change anyone's mind if he got the chance. 'If somebody could get Steed to talk to you, if we could create a – what did you call it, an open dialogue – would you help us then?'

Maud seemed to teeter for a moment between amusement and bewilderment, but finally made a sort of sweeping gesture, yielding to Morrigan's persistence.

'All right,' she said. 'All *right*. I will ask Steed one more time to meet with me, leader to leader. If you can somehow persuade him to accept my invitation, I'll put our Hollowpox cure on the negotiating table. You have my word.'

Standing aboard the golden-white Gossamer train just minutes later, feeling the rhythmic *chug-chug-chug* of the invisible tracks disappearing beneath her, Morrigan felt a gentle tug on some corner of her consciousness.

She ought to go straight home, she knew that. She had what she'd come for, after all, even if it *was* from an unexpected source. She had hope, of a sort. She just had to convince the most powerful man in Nevermoor to do as he was asked. Easy.

She should go straight back to the Deucalion to make a plan with Jupiter.

But there was this little thought in the corner of her mind, a quiet nudge of her curiosity. She *should* go home, yes, but . . . since she was already riding the Gossamer, perhaps she should visit Crow Manor. Just a *quick* visit. Just to see if anything had changed since she'd seen it last. Surely it wouldn't hurt just to—

And suddenly she was there, as quick as thought. Standing in the grounds of her childhood home, its hulking black façade looming above her against the grey sky.

No need to knock. She walked straight through the closed front door, incorporeal and – she hoped – invisible, just in time to see the swish of Ornella Crow's trademark grey dress disappear around the corner at the top of the stairs.

'Impossible,' whispered a voice from the dining room down the hall. Morrigan jumped, wondering how she would explain herself, but the voice went on, 'That wretched old vulture is *impossible*.'

'Shhh, she'll hear you.'

'So what if she does? I'm sick of this place. I'm going to tell the agency that Madam Crow is the worst mistress I've ever—'

'*You* may not want to keep your job, Hetty, but I do. Now help me clear this table before the old vulture comes back and pecks your eyes out.'

Morrigan rolled her eyes. Ornella hadn't changed, then.

She scurried silently up the stairs and followed her grandmother down the long corridor, stopping when she saw her take a sharp left into the Portrait Hall. Grandmother's favourite room in Crow Manor. Her favourite obsession, really. When she was young, Morrigan used to hover near the doorway, too frightened to step inside, watching Ornella stare at the oil portraits of her ancestors and deceased family members.

She was older now, and she wanted to follow her grandmother inside. But she *couldn't*. The idea of it suddenly made her feel ill, and flashes of memory from her last visit choked her thoughts.

Her grandmother's terrified face on Christmas night. *You shouldn't be here.*

Corvus Crow, her father, walking straight through her as if she didn't exist. *We swore we'd never speak that name again. That name is dead.*

Through her haze of dread, Morrigan was struck by a sudden wave of nausea. She swivelled on the spot, turning to hurry back down the corridor in the opposite direction, away from the

385

Portrait Hall where her scowling eleven-year-old self was now immortalised alongside the other dead Crows.

Stupid. What was she *thinking*, coming here of all places?

Morrigan paused near the top of the stairs, one hand pressed to her diaphragm, willing the nausea to subside. She needed to leave.

She was going to walk out the front door. She was going to call the Gossamer train and go home to Nevermoor and never, ever return to this house. She was going to—

She was going to vomit. She was going to vomit, right here, through the Gossamer, she was suddenly sure of it. (*How exactly would that work?* she somehow had the presence of mind to wonder.)

A noise from behind made her turn to see her grandmother leaving the Portrait Hall, firmly shutting and locking the door behind her with a large iron key.

Don't see me, Morrigan thought desperately. *Don't let her see me.*

She lurched sideways into the nearest room and found a darkened corner to slide down on to the floor, where she sat trying to catch her breath.

Across the room, something else was breathing. Two something elses. Two small lumps in two little wooden cot beds, rising and falling beneath the bedclothes. In the very moment when Morrigan realised whose room she'd entered, the door opened quietly. A familiar young, pretty blonde woman tiptoed inside with a rustle of her blue dress. She was humming something sweet.

Morrigan felt somehow certain that, unlike her grandmother, her stepmother wouldn't be able to see her. But even so, she stayed hidden in shadow while Ivy checked on her sons and then left the room.

Pausing for a moment at the door, the young mother cast a quick look back at her snowy-haired boys, light from the hall illuminating her face. Morrigan had never seen Ivy look like that – all softness and maternal affection and quiet, contented joy. She felt a strange little curl of something, right in her centre, and it made her flinch to realise the something was envy.

Not just envy. Longing.

But that couldn't be right. She didn't long for Ivy. She didn't even *like* Ivy!

It was something else Morrigan longed for, some piece of her that was missing. She couldn't say exactly what it was. But in the darkest, most secret part of her – the part she would never share with anyone – Morrigan knew that whatever that missing thing was, she'd never had any of it at all. And little Wolfram and Guntram Crow had somehow taken her share without asking.

She felt a shadow fall across her heart.

You have a wonderful life, Morrigan reminded herself sternly. *You have everything you need.*

She really did. She had things in Nevermoor that these boys would never have, things they could never even *imagine*! She had rides across rooftops on the Brolly Rail, and trips to the opera, and spectacular battles on Christmas Eve. She had an actual *magical* bedroom that transformed itself according to her wants and needs, for goodness' sake.

More importantly, she had Jupiter and Jack and Fenestra and all her friends at the Hotel Deucalion. She had Hawthorne and Cadence and Miss Cheery and Hometrain and Sub-Nine. She was a member of an elite society of Wundrous people with remarkable talents, and she had *eight* loyal sisters and brothers of her own! What more could she possibly want? How greedy could one person be?

But they're not your real sisters, are they? said a small, annoying voice inside her mind. *Not your real brothers.*

Morrigan angled her head to the side. She stood up, stepped gingerly out of the darkness and crossed the floor to peer into the two wooden cribs, side by side. Each had a name carved across the top. Tiny, rosy-cheeked Wolfram slumbered peacefully. Little Guntram seemed to have a cold; he snuffled in his sleep.

These, she supposed, were her *real* brothers. Her half-brothers.

Morrigan knelt in the narrow space between the cribs.

'Hello,' she whispered. 'I'm your sister.' The words felt strange, but nevertheless, she persisted. 'Your big sister. I bet you wouldn't believe that. I bet nobody's told you about me. But it's true. My name's Morrigan.' She paused, considering for a moment. 'You probably won't be able to say that, because you're too little. Just . . . call me Mog.'

Guntram stirred a little, one eye cracking open to peer up at her sleepily. For a breathless moment Morrigan thought he might wake up and scream the house down, but she whispered a soft, '*Shhh,*' and he nestled back into his blankets.

That was close, she thought. It was definitely time to go.

As Morrigan crept out of the room, however, something caught her eye – another chubby little lump, slumped over on the windowsill behind the gauzy curtain.

She gasped. 'Emmett!'

He was just as she remembered him. Her battered stuffed rabbit with his missing tail and black glass eyes . . . only now he was covered in a thick layer of dust, as if he'd been left there for a long time and forgotten. She reached out to grab him but her hands, of course, fell straight through.

Morrigan felt her throat tighten uncomfortably, and she blinked against the sudden stinging in her eyes. Emmett was the one thing in Crow Manor she missed. She imagined holding him tight, as she used to. She would never have left him slumped on the windowsill like that, all on his own. He might catch a cold, or . . . or get a crick in his neck!

As Morrigan looked around the room in dismay, she filled up with a mingled anger and sadness that her body felt too small to contain.

Look at all these things, she suddenly wanted to shout. All these piles of toys and books and blocks, and yet the *one* thing that had been hers, the one piece of her left in Crow Manor, had just been handed over to these ungrateful little beasts like he was *nothing*. Just another toy for them to neglect and forget. And now he was all alone.

Morrigan wanted to reach right through the Gossamer and grasp Emmett tight and take him home with her, where he belonged.

But that was impossible.

She squeezed her eyes and fists tight and pictured her oilskin umbrella. The Gossamer train whistled in the distance.

CHAPTER THIRTY-TWO

Squid Crow Po

A red haze of anger accompanied Morrigan all the way home on the Gossamer train. It was with her when she snatched up her brolly from the platform handrail, and by the time she got to the Deucalion her anger was so unwieldy it had swung all the way back around to grief.

She ran up the spiral staircase from the lobby without stopping or even noticing where she was going. She *thought* she was headed for her bedroom, and was most surprised when she arrived in Jupiter's study.

It was only when Jupiter looked up from his desk, a confused smile sliding off his face, that Morrigan realised what a sight she must be to him.

'Mog?' he said, suddenly stricken with worry. 'What is it?'

What could he *see*, she wondered? How much of what had happened today was still hovering around her? Grey clouds and dark smudges and goodness knew what else – a visual history of the world's longest morning. (Was it still only morning? Was it not *next year* yet?)

'It's . . . it's Emmett!'

Morrigan felt herself spill over, face crumpling like an empty milk carton. Trying to herd her sadness back towards anger (an infinitely more manageable feeling), she stalked across the little room, picked up a cushion from one of the leather armchairs and threw it so hard it knocked a picture frame off the wall. Jupiter watched in bewilderment.

'They d-don't even *need* him, and he's *mine*, he's been mine since I was a *baby*, and Ivy always said he was so *filthy*, why would she give Emmett to *them*?'

'Them who?'

'Wolfram and Guntram! My . . . *brothers*.' She paced before the fireplace, hands curling into fists, tears stinging in her eyes.

'Okay . . . but who's Emmett?' Jupiter looked quite at sea trying to make sense of her monologue through the jagged crying.

'My rabbit!' she sobbed. 'My toy rabbit. My *friend*.' *My only friend*, she thought. 'I left him b-behind. He was my friend and I just . . . left him behind.'

She was thinking of Eventide night, two and a half years ago. The night she'd been cursed to die. The night Jupiter had arrived without warning and rescued her, brought her to Nevermoor and given her an unimaginable new life.

She remembered how the Hunt of Smoke and Shadow had arrived at Crow Manor close behind him, and together she and Jupiter had run from her certain death without looking back. In all that excitement and danger, she hadn't given a single thought to small, grubby Emmett, tucked amongst the pillows on her bed. Waiting faithfully for her to return.

Morrigan flopped heavily into an armchair. She knew it was

irrational; she was old enough to know that her stuffed toy didn't have a mind of his own, didn't have any feelings to hurt. But that didn't matter. She'd poured so much of her heart into that little rabbit, told him so many of her fears and hopes and secret wounds over eleven years. He carried them all inside him. Her one friend in a cursed, lonely childhood.

Jupiter clicked his tongue sympathetically. 'Oh, Mog. You didn't leave him behind. You were running for your life. If it's anyone's fault, it's mine. I'm the one who swept in and spirited you away without any warning.'

'I want to go back,' she said, jumping up to pace the floor again. She felt skittery and electric, full of nervous energy. 'Not on the Gossamer. For real. I want to rescue him—'

She stopped when she saw the alarm on Jupiter's face.

'We can't do that. You know we can't,' he said in a careful voice. 'I'm so sorry your brothers haven't cared for Emmett as they should have. As you did. But, listen – I bet they love him more than you think. And if they don't now, they will. When they get older and smarter, they'll know who he belonged to, even if they don't *know* they know. That's how it works with friends like Emmett, who have been so dearly loved. They wear that love like an invisible coat. It never comes off, it's always there, and in the quiet moments, you can feel it. Wolfram and Guntram will feel it one day.'

Morrigan wanted to find reassurance in his words, she really did, but she knew they were just that – words. He was trying to make her feel better. She didn't believe a bit of it.

Jupiter frowned. 'What in heaven's name were you doing there, anyway? You shouldn't be using the Gossamer Line on your own, Mog – I told you, it's *dangerous*!'

'Oh. Right. Um . . .' She shook her head as if trying to dislodge water from her ears, feeling ridiculous all of a sudden. *Why* was she talking about her toy rabbit? The visit to Crow Manor had thrown her so completely, the real news had fallen out of her brain. 'I . . . I went to find a cure. Squall said—'

'*Squall* said—?'

'Yes, on the rooftop that day, remember? I told you, he said he had a cure for the Hollowpox and he'd hand it over if—'

'If you agreed to become his apprentice, yes I do remember that conversation, believe it or not.' Jupiter had his hands over his face now and was watching her through the gaps in his fingers. 'Mog, please, *please* tell me you didn't—'

'No!' she said quickly. 'I mean . . . I was going to find him –' (Jupiter uttered a faint moan) '– but the Gossamer Line got confused and took me to the wrong place and I met – Jupiter, will you stop pulling at your hair like that and *listen* – I met President Wintersea!'

He stopped pulling at his hair. He listened.

'Right.' He stared at her. 'Okay.'

'Yeah.' Morrigan shrugged. 'I think . . . I was thinking of the wrong thing and the Gossamer Line misread my intentions and – anyway, it doesn't matter. I met her, and she knows who I am, and that I'm a Wundersmith, and she knows about the Hollowpox and everything.'

She told him all that had happened in the Chancery, and Jupiter listened intently with his mouth slightly agape.

'—and then Maud said the Wintersea Party was like a big old dragon, impossible to steer—'

'Wait – you're on a first-name basis,' he interrupted her, 'with the President of the Wintersea Republic?'

'Yes, *shush*. Maud said the Wintersea Party *might* help if there was a squid crow po.'

'Quid pro quo?'

'Right, one of those. She said they won't do something for nothing, but if we could convince Prime Minister Steed to meet with her, just to have a conversation, then she would try to convince her party to share their cure. So, can you? Or can the Elders? One of you must know Steed, surely.'

'I do know him, as it happens, and I can't say I'm overly fond of the man, but Morrigan . . .' Jupiter paused, shaking his head. He looked horrified. 'President Wintersea is the leader of our enemy nation. Making a deal with her on behalf of the Free State government without their knowledge or permission is technically, well . . . *treason*. We can't tell *anyone* about this.'

'It's not *treason*, it's negotiating! It's asking for help! Anyway, it's not like she's asking to rule over the Free State or chop off the queen's head or anything, she just wants to *talk* to Steed. Even so-called enemy nations should have an open dialogue.'

Jupiter raised an eyebrow. 'Your words, or hers?'

Morrigan ignored the question.

'Maud wants to change things. She was actually really – I mean she seemed . . .' Morrigan faltered. She couldn't say the president was *nice*, exactly. There was something far too intimidating about her to be called *nice*. 'Real.'

He made a sceptical face. 'I know many Wintersea Republic citizens who would strongly disagree with that statement.'

'She doesn't have to be a perfect person, Jupiter, she just has to help us save our friends!'

'Morrigan,' he said, squeezing the bridge of his nose, 'I don't believe for a *second* that the Wintersea Party wants to help any Wunimals, let alone ours. It's *their* laws that keep Wunimals in the Republic downtrodden and make their lives so dangerous, they're the *reason* smuggling rings exist. It's been that way for Ages.'

'But what if she really does want to change things? The Wintersea Party found a cure to save their Wunimals, didn't they? I'm *sure* that was her doing. How can she change anything if we don't give her a chance?'

He seemed to consider that. 'You realise this is a minefield, Mog. We can't just jump in and—'

'Jupiter, this morning Sofia—' Morrigan's voice broke and she found herself unable to finish the sentence. But it was clear from the grieved look on his face that he'd already heard Sofia was in hospital. 'How many Wunimals have to suffer before we *do* decide to *jump in*? If you could just *talk* to Prime Minister—'

'All right! Just . . . give me a minute.' He heaved an overwhelmed sigh, leaned back in his desk chair and stared up at the ceiling. 'I'm trying to get my head around all this. I still can't believe you went into the Republic without talking to me first.'

'Only on the Gossamer Line. I had to do *something*, didn't I?'

Jupiter sat forward again, spluttering incoherently. 'Wh-what – I mean – *did* you? *Really*? Why did you? *Why* would you think that, when there is an entire task force of *adult* Society members who are currently dedicating their lives to *doing something*? Forgive me, but nobody asked you to *do anything*!'

Morrigan flinched as if he'd flung a glass of cold water over her. She had a sudden memory of something Holliday Wu had said – she, too, had accused Morrigan of *swooping in where she didn't belong*, where she wasn't *asked to be*. Of making a mess.

Hurt feelings barrelled into anger, building like a wave inside her and then crashing violently, viciously.

'And what exactly have all you *adults* done?' she shouted. 'Have *you* found a cure? Is Dr Bramble *getting closer every day*, or is she exactly where she was last week, and the week before that? You're right. Nobody asked me to do anything, but I've DONE IT

ANYWAY, on my own. I had to go outside the Free State to do it, but by some miracle I have found an ACTUAL adult who can ACTUALLY help.'

Now it was Jupiter's turn to flinch.

'Talk to Steed,' she demanded, blinking back furious tears. 'I don't care if you're not overly fond of him, just *talk to him*. Wintersea is going to ask him one more time to meet with her, leader to leader. All he has to do is finally accept her invitation, and we can have our friends back. Please, *make him understand*. If you don't, I'll – I'll have no choice.'

Jupiter had turned very pale. 'What do you mean, you'll have no choice?'

'I mean if Steed won't accept help from Wintersea, I'll accept it from Squall.'

CHAPTER THIRTY-THREE

Dear Prime Minister

Morrigan had never been on a roller coaster, but in the forty-eight hours following her argument with Jupiter, she thought she could imagine what it would feel like.

To her surprise, Jupiter seemed to have fully accepted his mission. He left immediately after their row, determined to convince the prime minister to meet with Wintersea, and was gone for the rest of the day. But when he arrived home late in the evening, he stormed past Morrigan, Martha and Fenestra in the lobby and headed straight for the glass elevator without a word to anyone. Whatever conversation he'd had with Steed, it obviously hadn't ended well.

'Weight of the world on his shoulders, that man,' said Martha, with a rueful shake of her head as they watched him disappear. 'Puts far too much pressure on himself.'

Morrigan said nothing, but she felt a twinge of guilt in her stomach. It was she, after all, who was putting pressure on him this time.

'Yeah, I noticed he's been a bit stressed,' said Fenestra, yawning widely. She was stretched out, belly up, across the concierge desk, despite Kedgeree having already shooed her off it a dozen times that day. 'So I got him a present. Left it on his bed.'

Morrigan and Martha shared a look of surprise.

'I – gosh, Fen,' said Morrigan. 'That's really nice. What did you—'

'FENESTRAAAAAAAA!' Jupiter's roar of fury echoed through the empty hotel and all the way down the spiral staircase.

Martha winced, peeking sideways at Fen. 'Fish?'

'Rat.' The Magnificat looked extremely put out that her gift had been so poorly received. 'It was a really big one, too. So ungrateful.'

Rather like its proprietor, the Hotel Deucalion was moody and frustrated. *Unlike* Jupiter, though, the Deucalion was acting out in increasingly peculiar ways.

The shutters still hadn't come back up, despite the best efforts of Martha, Charlie and Kedgeree to force them open. All the guest suites and most of the staff quarters were cold and dark now. Morrigan's bedroom was barely holding on; she'd had to relight her fireplace at least a dozen times that day, and the talon-foot bathtub, which usually filled to precisely the right depth before turning off its own taps, had overflowed and flooded the bathroom. She was *most* worried about her octopus armchair. It had barely twitched a tentacle for days.

But while most of the Deucalion went into hibernation, some of it had entered a kind of hyper-productive turbo-drive. The courtyard orchard off the south wing grew so wild, so quickly, that it was no longer an orchard so much as an edible jungle, with an autumn harvest at least seven times its usual size.

The lobby, too, was more alive than ever. It was transforming every couple of hours now, dressing with gay abandon for non-existent events Frank hadn't planned. Mood lighting and cool jazz for a fancy cocktail party at six in the morning. Then a birthday party for no one, with so many helium balloons it was impossible to move (Fenestra gleefully sharpened her claws and took care of the whole lot by lunchtime).

By late afternoon it had transitioned into a grand, glamorous wedding. Dame Chanda thought it was an awful shame to waste the thousands of tapered white candles, elaborate floral arrangements and confetti-strewn aisle. She kept telling Martha and Charlie that impromptu nuptials would be *terribly* romantic and *just* the thing to cheer everyone up, but they stubbornly refused to take the hint.

With each new transformation, Frank and Kedgeree tried to gently talk the Deucalion down from whatever strange precipice it was on, reminding it that it was a time to rest and recharge, and things would be up and running again soon enough. But the Deucalion wouldn't listen, and when the white wedding transitioned to a pool party – complete with a waterslide where the spiral staircase used to be – they decided it would be best to just go with it.

'Ah, the poor wee lass,' sighed Kedgeree, dressed in goggles and pink tartan swimming trunks, as he surveyed the very wet lobby from the end of a diving board that was once the concierge desk. 'All dressed up and no party to throw.'

It wasn't until the next morning that Morrigan worked up the nerve to knock on Jupiter's study door. She'd braced herself for bad news, and was therefore shocked to see his satisfied expression as he laid copies of Nevermoor's three major newspapers across the desk for her to see:

CURE? NO THANK YOU, SAYS PM

NOT JUST A HOLLOW OFFER?
LEAKED WINTERSEA LETTER SHOWS STEED RELUCTANT TO SAVE LIVES

PLEASE, PRIME MINISTER, JUST SAY YES

'Page two,' said Jupiter, tapping the *Sentinel*.

Morrigan flipped the front page to see the word REVEALED! in huge red letters, above an image of a handwritten letter bearing what must have been Wintersea's presidential seal: a butterfly silhouette overlaid with an ornate *W*. A glimpse inside the *Morning Post* and the *Looking Glass* showed they'd all printed the same letter.

Morrigan cleared her throat and began to read aloud.

'Dear Prime Minister,

Thank you for meeting with me today. I regret that we were unable to come to an agreement, but I fear the citizens of the "Free State" you serve may come to regret your reticence much more deeply.

Once again, I wish to express my solidarity and sympathy for the challenge you are facing, both as a fellow head of state and a human being. The danger from this disease you call the "Hollowpox" is urgent; the devastation it leaves in its wake seems impossible to overcome. I speak from experience.

However, as I told you this morning, it is possible to overcome it.

We lost a great many lives before one of our citizens found a way to end this terrible disease and shared it with the entire Republic. We are now free from the horror of this illness – Wunimals and humans alike. I wish to pass on this act of generosity to you and your people. We will gladly give you the cure.

All I ask of you in return is hope.

The hope that our two nations might one day join hands across this great divide between us. That you and I – two modern, progressive leaders with an eye to our people's future prosperity and security – might start a conversation that could lead to the healing of Ages-old wounds.

We in the Wintersea Republic have been where you are now. We have trodden this difficult path. Please let me extend a helping hand on behalf of my country, and know that I do so in the open, earnest spirit of conciliation.

Most sincerely,
President Wintersea.'

Morrigan scrunched her face up. 'I don't understand. They . . . *did* meet?'

'Mmm. Wintersea must have invited him just after you spoke with her, because the Elders already knew about it when I went to see them.'

'How'd they know?'

'Oh, the Wundrous Society's always had informants in the prime minister's office. Steed can barely go to the loo without someone reporting the event to Elder Quinn. When the Elders heard about Wintersea's invitation and that Steed planned to reject it, they summoned the Hollowpox task force. Of course, I pretended not to know anything.'

'Why?'

'Don't you see? *They* told *me* about Wintersea, instead of the other way around. Nobody knows you used the Gossamer Line. Nobody knows you made a deal. Everything's fine.'

'Oh. Um – great.' Morrigan felt that twinge of guilt again – and perhaps, if she was honest with herself, a little bit of pride at what she'd managed to bring about. Jupiter merely waved a hand, dismissing the small issue of her treasonous act.

'So, three of us went to see Steed,' he continued. 'I raged, Dr Bramble reasoned, Inspector Rivers negotiated. But nothing got through to the great nincompoop, and finally he threatened to have us thrown out . . . so we had to call in the big guns.'

'Elder Quinn?'

'Elder Quinn.' He arched an eyebrow. 'She was *magnificent*. A one-woman rage, reason and negotiation machine. She convinced him to have the meeting – and to start taking vitamins, and to get a better haircut, *and* to call his mother! She was really on a roll.'

'Then what?'

'Then . . . nothing. Steed took the meeting. They spoke via the Gossamer. We all stood by and listened. Wintersea was perfectly amiable, even *charming*. She offered the cure and only asked in return that Steed give her some indication that the Free State and the Republic might work towards achieving a less hostile diplomatic relationship. And Steed said no.'

'*Why?*'

'Partly because he's too proud; he thinks her efficiency makes him look bad. And because he doesn't want to appear weak or traitorous by negotiating with the enemy. And because he is – as I believe I mentioned – a nincompoop. The end.'

Morrigan glanced at the newspapers. 'Except . . . not the end.'

'Except not the end,' Jupiter agreed. 'Because late last night, Wintersea wrote a letter to Steed. And then . . .' He gestured broadly to the newspapers covering his desk. '. . . the letter was leaked to every desk editor in Nevermoor.'

'Holliday Wu?'

'Holliday Wu.'

Morrigan smiled grimly. 'So is she a genius this time, or a fiend?'

'Maybe both.' He tilted his head from side to side. 'Maybe neither. It's a *slightly* dirty trick, and it will expose Steed to a lot of public outrage . . . but he was asking for it.'

'Right.' She took a deep breath. 'So what next? We have to keep the pressure on—'

'Morrigan.'

'—so do we start a petition, or . . . we should protest! Right outside Parliament—'

'MORRIGAN,' Jupiter barked. 'There is no "next". That's it.'

She gaped at him. 'You can't be serious! You're just going to give up?'

'I did what you asked,' he said. 'I took it all the way to the prime minister's office, I did *everything* I could to convince him, but Morrigan . . . this was the last trick up our sleeves. Hopefully it puts enough pressure on Steed that he's forced to do the right thing, but as for your involvement or mine—'

'But we can't just—'

'—it's *over*.'

They stood glaring at one another in the world's most furious and uncomfortable silence, until they were saved by a knock on the door.

'Come in!' Jupiter shouted, and Kedgeree entered, carrying a small wireless radio pressed to his ear.

'You hearing this, Jove?' he asked, pointing at the bigger radio on the desk, and Jupiter lunged to turn the dial up high. The stern voice of Gideon Steed filled the room.

'—has proven effective in halting Hollowpox-related incidents at night, alleviating pressure on police and emergency responders. But I am afraid it simply isn't enough, as this most recent chilling attack has shown.'

Jupiter looked at Kedgeree. 'Most recent—?'

'Happened barely an hour ago,' Kedgeree replied gravely. 'It's all over the news – a lionwun professor at Nevermoor University. It was . . .' He shook his head and closed his mouth tight, apparently unable to finish the sentence.

'Any deaths?'

Kedgeree swallowed. 'Four. Two teachers, a student, and the lionwun himself. The Stealth took him down.'

Jupiter made a strangled sound. Morrigan leaned against the back of an armchair, gripping the leather to stop herself swaying. Steed's voice carried on.

'—and therefore as of today, my government is announcing new extraordinary measures to combat this disease. We are ending the sunset curfew and instating a twenty-four/seven lockdown for all Wunimals. Effective from midday today onwards, any Wunimal found outside their home will be arrested and could face up to a year in prison. These measures will continue until we are able to contain the Hollowpox. I will not be taking questions at this—'

Jupiter reached out and turned off the wireless.

'What does he mean, "until we are able to contain the Hollowpox"?' Morrigan frowned. 'Everyone must know by now that Wintersea offered him the cure! Hasn't he seen the papers?'

'He's absolutely seen them,' muttered Jupiter. 'That's *why* he's talking about curfews and lockdowns. He's taking a page out of the Wundrous Society's book – trying to distract people, to change the conversation, but it's not going to work.' He paused, gathering up the newspapers and heading for the door. 'This will only make things worse.'

Jupiter disappeared again – presumably to rally the task force and the Elders to talk some sense into the prime minister, or at least that was what Morrigan hoped. Meanwhile, she and everyone else in the Hotel Deucalion spent the rest of the day glued to the radio, absorbing a constant stream of terrible news.

The Stink began making arrests before the ban on Wunimals in public even went into effect. By ten o'clock, the news was reporting that seventeen Wunimals were already in lockup.

Everything seemed to snowball after that. In solidarity with those wrongly arrested, more Wunimals came out in protest, ignoring the lockdown order and swarming the streets.

Later that morning, there was a news broadcast live from the Senate, where Guiscard Silverback gave a surprising speech in which he urged Prime Minister Steed to put aside his pride and accept Wintersea's offer.

The prime minister responded to Silverback's mild criticism by having the police storm the Senate at precisely one minute past midday – before his speech had even ended – and arrest him for flouting the lockdown. The arrest, too, was broadcast over the radio.

Silverback went quietly, but the same could not be said for his supporters. His arrest caused outrage, doubling and tripling the numbers of Wunimals out on the streets by mid-afternoon. Soon humans came out to protest in solidarity, and to demand Steed accept the cure from the Wintersea Republic.

Marches were broken up all over Nevermoor, and some of them turned deadly. In Begonia Hills, a large dogwun turned on her fellow protestors. In Highwall, an elephantwun tipped over a carriage (nobody seemed certain whether he was infected with the Hollowpox or simply furious).

The attacks kept coming. It was as if the Hollowpox had read Nevermoor's mood and responded in kind, suddenly culminating in dozens of infected Wunimals at once, then *hundreds*, creating a citywide emergency that was impossible to contain.

Jupiter sent a messenger to the hotel around lunchtime with strict instructions for them all to stay indoors, but he needn't have bothered. Even as the lobby battled for their attention, transforming around them from hour to hour – from a miniature golf course to a casino to a three-ring circus – nobody moved from the radio.

Jack was due home from the Graysmark School that afternoon, but at Jupiter's request, Charlie went to fetch him home in a motorcar so he wouldn't have to take the Wunderground. Morrigan was relieved to see him, but she also worried about Hawthorne and Cadence and the rest of her unit. She had no way of checking on them – her door to Station 919 remained locked. All she could do was hope they were safe at school or at home, and pace around the concierge desk like a caged unnimal, and chew her fingernails down to nothing.

All day long they waited for some spark of hope, a bit of good news. What they got instead was the declaration of a citywide lockdown for all citizens, Wunimal and human alike.

'Prime Minister Steed has ordered all residents of Nevermoor to stay inside their homes on what promises to be the most dangerous night of the Hollowpox epidemic so far,' announced a grave female voice.

That was when Dame Chanda decided she'd had enough.

'That's IT!' she snapped, getting up to turn off the radio. 'No more. No more moping, no more waiting for Steed to develop a spine. We're not helping matters by sitting around being miserable. Fenestra, please take this dreadful nightmare device away and hide it from us.' She tossed the radio to Fen, who caught it between her teeth and bounded up the spiral staircase.

Morrigan felt a wrench. 'But what if—'

'If anything good happens, we'll know about it,' Dame Chanda said firmly. 'Jove will come home and tell us himself. Until then, I think there's somebody else we need to start listening to.'

She looked around significantly. Morrigan and the others perked up, shaking off a news-induced stupor to notice their environment for the first time in hours.

The Deucalion had undergone perhaps its best – certainly its *cosiest* – transformation yet. Every surface was covered with cushions and draped with soft fabrics in soothing colours, so that the whole lobby resembled one big blanket fort. There were piles of books and boardgames in every corner, baskets full of woolly bed socks and hot water bottles. Squashy armchairs, beanbags, pillows, duvets and mattresses were clustered around the big roaring hearth. Comforting smells of clean linen, hot chocolate and buttery popcorn filled the air.

'A slumber party!' Kedgeree said warmly as he pulled on a pair of bed socks. 'The dear old gal knew just what we needed.'

They all dashed off to change into pyjamas and dressing gowns. Jack and Morrigan raided the kitchen for marshmallows and made a huge pile of peanut butter and raspberry jam sandwiches for everyone. Frank finessed the ambiance with cheerful music and some artfully strung fairy lights. Dame Chanda braided Martha's hair, and Frank painted Charlie's nails, and Kedgeree read aloud from his favourite book of poems, and they played charades and boardgames all night long and if anyone thought about the terrible, frightening things that might be happening outside, nobody spoke of them aloud.

Morrigan woke from a nightmare in which she was being hunted by a pack of lions. The lions turned into foxes, and the foxes all wore Sofia's face and Sofia's burgundy jacket, and they all wanted to devour Morrigan whole.

She sat up in her beanbag, shaking a little, and pulled a knitted blanket close around her shoulders. The fire had burned down to embers, and everyone else was fast asleep. At some point in the night, Fenestra had evidently left the gigantic nest of bedding by the fireplace and curled up against the door to the service hallway instead. It was unclear whether she was waiting for Jupiter or standing guard, but the sound of her deep-sleep purring reverberating through the cavernous lobby was immensely comforting.

It should have been enough to send Morrigan back to sleep, but it wasn't. Now she was awake, she had to know what was happening outside. She crept up to Jupiter's study and flicked on his radio, turning the dial until she found what she was looking for.

'—legislation which has been very well received by manufacturing unions in the Fourth Pocket,' said a newsreader. 'More on that later in the program, but our lead story is of course the announcement made by the prime minister's office just after midnight.'

Morrigan squeezed the arms of Jupiter's desk chair, hardly daring to hope.

'For the first time since Nevermoor closed its borders to the Republic many Ages ago,' came the familiar, albeit rather tired-sounding voice of Gideon Steed, 'the Wintersea Party has extended a hand of friendship towards us, and we have accepted it with a watchful but welcoming spirit. The Free State is an independent nation, a strong and proud nation – but we are not too proud to accept help where it is offered, especially when the lives of our citizens are at risk.'

He'd done it. Morrigan could have burst into song, or into *tears*, she was so relieved and happy. This was really happening! Steed had accepted Maud's offer. Sofia was going to be all right – and Juvela, and Brutilus, and Colin and every other Wunimal in Nevermoor. They were going to be cured! She hugged the wireless radio tight to her chest, unable to contain a squeal of joy.

'This morning at nine o'clock,' Steed continued (Morrigan glanced reflexively at the clock on the wall – it was just after three), 'history will be made in Nevermoor. We will temporarily, and on a very limited operational basis, open the border between us – the First Pocket of the Free State – and the Wintersea Republic.

'On my invitation, President Wintersea will enter the Free State on a diplomatic mission, bringing with her one other representative of the Republic. This emissary from the Wintersea Republic is a philanthropist, an energy industry leader, and the creator of the only known cure for the Hollowpox.' He paused, and Morrigan's smile faltered as she felt her brain trip over those words. A frown creased her forehead.

Energy industry leader.

Gideon Steed's voice seemed to fade away, and Maud Lowry's rang inside her head. *Why in the world would a thirteen-year-old care about the machinations of the energy industry?*

A deeply unpleasant sensation crept upon her, like she was being squeezed from the inside. Heat rose from her neck all the way up to her hairline. The small room seemed to have lost all its air.

Squall was the energy industry leader. He was the emissary.

Steed was about to open the border to the Free State's greatest enemy. How could the prime minister, of all people, not have realised that? He *must* know about Squall Industries – surely he could figure out who this 'emissary' must be, *surely* he'd put the facts together!

Morrigan turned off the radio. She tugged at the collar of her nightshirt, which suddenly felt as if it was choking her.

So that's it, then, she thought, staring blankly at the wall. They would open the border and Squall would be welcomed back into Nevermoor. He'd found a way in, at last, and it was all her fault. Oh god, she felt *sick*. She felt unbelievably, unforgivably stupid.

She'd *made* this happen for him! Squall had manipulated her, he had choreographed this entire ridiculous routine, but she'd been fool enough to dance right into it. The Gossamer Line hadn't taken her to the Chancery by accident at all – he'd *meant* for her to go there! He'd made the Hollowpox, not so that he could trick her into becoming his apprentice – his sights were set much higher than that. He'd been swindling his way back into Nevermoor all along.

Did President Wintersea know, Morrigan wondered? Was she in on the plan, or had she been manipulated too? The Wintersea Republic relied on Squall Industries and its dangerous figurehead. Wunder was scarcer there than in the Free State, and as their only living citizen able to gather, command and distribute it, Squall was the supplier of the Republic's every comfort and practical need. If he wanted a favour in return, President Wintersea would surely have no choice but to grant it. Was she, like Morrigan, just another puppet in Squall's show?

Should Morrigan *warn her* somehow? Her thoughts raced, pulse pounding in her neck.

Could Steed *really* open the border to Squall? Certainly he could stand down the Ground Force, the Sky Force, the Stink, the Stealth, the Royal Sorcery Council, the Paranormal League and every other organisation that watched over the borders.

But what about the ancient magic of Nevermoor that supposedly kept Squall out? Would it still matter, would it *work* without all that other help? Morrigan had no way of knowing.

She had to tell someone, she had to tell Jupiter! Had he figured it out already? *He* knew who Squall was. Surely he'd know what to do. Where *was* he – at Wunsoc? At the Houses of Parliament? She'd never been there, but it seemed a sensible place to start. She knew Jupiter. He would remain at the prime minister's side until the job was done.

Morrigan sprinted to her bedroom to get dressed. As she frantically pulled on her boots, she pictured a map of Nevermoor in her head, trying to plot the fastest route from the Hotel Deucalion to Parliament. Snatching up her umbrella from the bony fingers of the skeleton hat stand, just in case, Morrigan ran out her door and down the dim, cold hallway of the fourth floor – and stopped.

There was a man in the hall.

He turned to face her, desperate and wild-eyed, his white face ghost-like. With his shirt half untucked and hair dishevelled, he was almost unrecognisable. But when he spoke, Morrigan could feel the lightning-crackle of his panic through the Gossamer.

'Don't let them open the border!'

It was Squall.

CHAPTER THIRTY-FOUR

The Emissary

Morrigan stared at Squall, trying to make sense of him. She felt a frenzied little laugh bubble up from her chest like a water fountain, then stop quite abruptly, as if it was stuck in her throat.

'Sorry – what?'

'I'm the emissary,' he said urgently, staggering down the hallway towards her and holding his chest like he'd just run a marathon. She could see the whites of his eyes. 'It's me, *I'm* Wintersea's emissary. You've heard, haven't you? Steed's opening the border to Wintersea and—'

'You. Yes, I know it's you.' Morrigan took a reflexive step away from him. 'I'd figured that much out.'

'You can't let – he mustn't – *are you listening to me?*'

He lunged forward, arms outstretched as if to grab her by the shoulders, but of course his hands fell straight through her.

The back of Morrigan's neck prickled. There were things about Squall that frightened her, but nothing so much as this.

Nothing he'd ever said or done was as terrifying to Morrigan . . . as seeing *him* so frightened.

What scared you this much, if you were the evillest man who ever lived?

'But this is exactly what you wanted,' she said, drawing back in revulsion. 'You planned it this way!'

'No. Listen to me—'

'You made the Hollowpox so you could be the one to come into Nevermoor and *unmake it*. You risked thousands of lives, you *killed* people, killed Wunimals, just so you could worm your way back—'

'I made the *so-called Hollowpox*,' he raised his voice above hers, 'because I was *asked to*. Because I was compensated handsomely for it. And because when the most powerful person in the realm asks for a favour, even I don't refuse.'

Morrigan's head was spinning. 'The most powerful – what are you *talking* about?'

But even as she asked the question, a memory came to her of a conversation she'd had long ago. On Bid Day, in the Jackalfax Town Hall, before she'd ever come to Nevermoor or met Jupiter, or any of it. He had told her that he, Ezra Squall, was only the *second* most powerful person in the Republic. Second to—

'President Wintersea?' She laughed again, although there was nothing very funny about it. 'You expect me to believe that President Wintersea *asked* you to create the Hollowpox?'

'It was an extermination,' he said. 'It wasn't supposed to be for Nevermoor, it was for the Republic, but she saw an opportunity to use it to force her way into the Free State. That was never part of our deal. *She's* the one who sent it in there – bundled an infected otterwun into one of her spy vessels and launched it into the River Juro. He thought he was escaping life under the

Wintersea Party, but he was their weapon.'

Morrigan's stomach seized. 'An extermination of Wunimals? She asked you to help her *exterminate* an entire group of people . . . and you did? Just like that?'

'Yes.'

'Why?'

'*Because I could,*' he snarled, flinging his arms outwards in frustration. 'And because I had to. Because I am a Wundersmith, and that is what we do. We say yes. We do the ghastly things that are asked of us by people in power, and we do the good things, and we take none of the credit and all of the blame. It's what we *do*.'

'Speak for yourself,' she snapped back. 'And if you were so happy to exterminate Wunimals in the Republic, why do you suddenly care about Wunimals in the Free State?'

'I don't!' he said. 'I couldn't care less whether they live or die. I have *no* feelings about them *whatsoever*; that's not my fight, it's Wintersea's. I *only* care about Nevermoor. But I can promise you that once Wintersea crosses that border, there will be no cure for the Hollowpox. She doesn't want to help you.

'The Wintersea Party wants to take Nevermoor, and they will. They will take it just as they reached out their iron fist from Great Wolfacre and took Prosper, and Southlight, and Sang. I know, because I helped them do it. They will crush Nevermoor the way they crushed those places. You think you're going to save your Wunimal friends? No. The Wunimals will be the first to go, and they won't stop there. Anyone who opposes them, anyone who presents the *slightest* threat to the party will be destroyed, imprisoned or enslaved. If you think that doesn't mean you and every single one of your Wundrous Society friends with their very useful knacks, you are tragically mistaken.'

'But you're a Wundersmith.' Morrigan was utterly baffled. 'Why can't you just stop them if they're such a problem? I don't understand!'

'Do you THINK I HAVEN'T—' Squall shouted, then cut himself off abruptly. He clamped his mouth shut and stared at her, breathing fiercely through his nose. When he spoke again it was in a tight, barely controlled growl. 'Let her in, and the Wintersea Party follows. All you need to understand is how catastrophic that will be.'

Morrigan thought about what Jupiter had said about Squall. *We can't stop him from entering Nevermoor on the Gossamer, but we must stop him from getting into your head.*

Was this all just an elaborate mind game?

She shook her head. 'I don't believe you!'

'It doesn't matter whether you believe me, your predicament remains the same. If Steed doesn't keep the Free State border closed, there will no longer *be* a Free State.'

'And how exactly am I supposed to convince him to do that?'

'You can't. The only thing you can do is strike first. Make his solution obsolete. *You* have to destroy the Hollowpox yourself.'

She let out a short, incredulous bark of laughter. '*How?*'

'I'll help you.'

'Oh, of course,' she said, scowling. 'Let me guess, you want to make a bargain? You'll cure the Hollowpox for the low price of me becoming your apprentice? Pretty sure I've heard this somewhere before—'

'No bargain.' His face was solemn. 'No price. I will give you everything you need to obliterate the Hollowpox. You will owe me nothing in return. All I want is for that border to remain closed.'

Morrigan squeezed her eyes shut. Her brain ached from the

416

effort of trying to understand him. 'But you . . . you *want* to come back into Nevermoor! You told me it was *agony* to be apart from it.'

'I want it more than anything,' he agreed. 'I want it more than life itself.'

She watched him warily. This was undoubtedly the strangest conversation she'd ever had. Ezra Squall wanted her help . . . to keep him *out* of Nevermoor and to cure the Hollowpox, with no demands, no negotiations, no strings attached?

'Let me be very clear.' Squall's jaw tightened. His voice was low and ugly, his face twisting with hatred, but in his black eyes there was a cold clarity. 'I would do anything to return to Nevermoor. I would raze entire cities, end civilisations. My body may be on this side of the border, but every other part of me – my mind, my heart, my *soul* if I have one – every bit of me worth *anything* is there, in Nevermoor, and I would kill every living creature in the Republic if I thought it would bring me home.

'So when I tell you not to let me in, when I tell you you'd be welcoming a far greater threat than I, you might do me the favour of taking it seriously. I would rather stay out in the cold for ever than grant *her* even a moment of its warmth.

'You think I'm the dangerous one,' he continued in a whisper, 'and you are correct: I have done terrible things. I am a ghoulish man, a maker of monsters. But Wintersea *is* a monster. Always hungry. Never satisfied. If you let her into our city, she will devour it.'

Morrigan shivered. Her breath made clouds in the cold, dim hallway.

'Why should I believe you?' she asked finally.

'I've never lied to you, Miss Crow.'

'All you ever *do* is lie!'

'I have never lied . . . to *you*.'

And to Morrigan's profound surprise, she realised that once again, she *did* believe him. An Ezra Squall experiencing a sudden, benevolent change of heart, ready to gift her a cure without asking anything in return, was not remotely convincing. But an Ezra Squall motivated by deep-rooted hatred and a spite so strong it thwarted his own ambitions? That she could believe.

'How do I destroy the Hollowpox?'

He gave a short whistle, low and eerie. The Hunt of Smoke and Shadow instantly appeared, swarming the hallway and wrapping around them both like a thick, black fog, until all she could see was Squall's eyes, gleaming in the darkness.

'By doing every single thing I tell you.'

CHAPTER THIRTY-FIVE

Summoner and Smith

'Wunder is everywhere.'

Almost a year had passed since the last time Morrigan found herself standing on the rooftop of the Hotel Deucalion with Ezra Squall. She felt only slightly better equipped to handle it this time around.

'. . . *Eventide's child brings gale and storm*,' she sang under her breath. Threads of gold swam through her fingers, quick and curious, shimmering with light.

'And when you call some of it,' Squall continued over the top of her song, 'you are calling all of it, because everything is connected. You're activating it, signalling it to be ready – like turning a key in the ignition of a motorcar and letting the engine idle.'

'. . . *where are you going, o son of the morning?*'

Morrigan frowned in concentration. Wunder bristled in the air around her, drawing close, more of it than she'd ever allowed herself to deliberately gather at once. With it came the familiar feeling of abundance, undercut by the uncomfortable knowledge that she was standing right at the edge of her ability and could topple off at any moment. She squeezed her hands tight around her umbrella, clutching it to her chest as if it might anchor her.

Nevermoor stretched out for miles all around. Towards its centre she could see great pockets of light pollution from Old Town, Bohemia, and the never-sleeping industrial hubs of Bloxam and Macquarie. In the opposite direction, the darkened city rolled out like a map of the night sky, black and dotted with specks of light, streets like constellations.

'*Up with the sun where the winds are warming . . .*'

'Stop working so hard,' Squall warned.

'But you said—'

'I said you need to gather more Wunder than you've ever purposefully gathered before. I didn't say you had to force it up out of the ground like oil. You already *have* its attention. Look – it's dying to please you. See?'

'No.'

'Pay attention,' he said. 'Remember: *summoned Wunder shows itself to summoner and smith.*'

Morrigan had to fight the urge to roll her eyes. She tried to relax them instead, and when they were almost closed, she could see it. Traces of Wundrous energy coiling through the air, swarming to her from every direction, lighting up the sky around her like the sun. She took a deep breath and opened her eyes wide again. The brightness eased.

'You see?' said Squall. 'When you call some, you call all. Everything is connected.'

Morrigan held out a hand to steady herself against the balustrade.

'Now imagine there was a map of Nevermoor,' he continued, 'that could show you where the greatest density of Wundrous energy was gathered at any point in time. Imagine it looked like this – like the city at night – but each of those lights represented a measure of Wunder. There would be millions, *billions* of specks of light everywhere you looked, but some places would be much brighter than others. Where would those places be?'

Morrigan thought for a moment. 'The Wundrous Society.'

'Where else?'

'The Gobleian Library.' He nodded for her to go on. 'Um. Cascade Towers, Jemmity Park . . . The Museum of Stolen Moments?'

'Before you demolished it, certainly,' he said. 'And the Lightwing Palace, the Nevermoor Opera House, the Hotel Deucalion, and so on. There are hundreds of places like these, dotted all over Nevermoor, each producing and consuming vast amounts of Wundrous energy on a constant cyclical basis. On this imaginary map of Wunder density, those places would shine brightest most of the time.

'But at certain times of year, there are others that outshine them. Old Town, for example, every Friday night during summer.'

'Because of the Nevermoor Bazaar?'

He nodded. 'Courage Square on Christmas Eve. Bright, blazing beacons that cast every other Wundrous source into shadow, if only for an evening or an hour.' He paused for a moment, gazing out at the skyline. 'Tonight, *you* need to be the brightest beacon in Nevermoor. A lightning rod. This is how we will draw the Hollowpox out of hiding.'

'What do you mean?'

'You understand the Hollowpox better than most,' he said. 'It isn't a disease; it's a monster that behaves like a disease. It feeds

421

off Wundrous energy, and Wunimals have quite a lot of it. That is how it destroys them: it's a parasite, invading its hosts and consuming everything that makes them Wunimals instead of unnimals. Bleeding them dry until all they are is scaffolding. When all that Wunder has been consumed, the parasite moves on to new food sources, multiplying all the time.

'Sometimes it might sense some greater source of Wunder nearby, some living creature it doesn't quite understand. And it can *feel* the immense volume of energy surrounding that creature. It wants to invade, wants to consume it, but it can't.' He turned to look at her directly. 'Because you're a Wundersmith. Wunder doesn't just passively surround you, it actively *fights* for you. It will protect you viciously from external forces that wish to harm you. Such as the Hollowpox.'

'Oh,' said Morrigan slowly. 'That's why it kept happening to Wunimals around me.' Her heart quickened as she grasped that it was probably because of her Sofia was lying in the hospital. The realisation added a sudden, crushing guilt to the sadness and worry she felt for her friend, and she pressed a hand to her chest as if to keep it all in.

Squall leaned over the balustrade and peered down on to Humdinger Avenue. 'The Hollowpox is intelligent, but only to a degree, and you confuse it. On the spectrum of Wundrous energy, it knows you are somewhere between a Wunimal . . . and me, the person who made it and could therefore unmake it on a whim. Which means you are either an object of prey, or a predator. Now, look down at the street. What do you see?'

Morrigan peeked cautiously over the edge of the rooftop, keeping some distance between her and Squall. 'Nothing. It's dark.'

'Mmm. Now do something Wundrous. Anything.'

She breathed a tiny spark of fire into one hand and let it grow into a flame. Then, recalling her last lesson with Gracious Goldberry, she transformed it into the image of an unnimal – a horse this time – and sent it galloping into the sky. It blazed brightly for a moment against a backdrop of stars, then burned out to embers and floated away.

She'd been showing off, of course, and was secretly gratified by the tiny arch of Squall's eyebrow that hinted he was impressed. But then he tilted his head down towards the street, and when Morrigan looked over the balustrade again, she jumped backwards in fright.

Several dozen pinpricks of green light blinked into view on the street below. Shadowy figures from the surrounding streets began moving towards the Hotel Deucalion, gathering in the forecourt. They were looking up at her, she could feel it.

Morrigan heard a deep growl. A harsh, screeching cry. She hunched her shoulders, feeling a sudden chill on her neck. A cluster of silhouettes moved beneath a gas lamp; she could just make out something dark and hulking with huge, spiralling horns, and the unmistakeable slither of an enormous snakewun as it crossed the pool of light.

'They know you're not me. They can tell you're nowhere near as powerful,' said Squall. There was no smugness about him; he spoke matter-of-factly. 'But you do have a whiff of something familiar. The monster inside perks up when you're around, like a sleeping dog that doesn't know if it's caught the scent of its master, or the scent of a rabbit. It's desperate to figure you out, and so it fights to be free of the prison it's taken for itself – the body it possesses. Tell me, do you have your umbrella?'

Morrigan nodded, lifting her brolly absently. She'd been holding on to it since she met him in the hallway. 'What now?'

'Now we let them hunt you.'

And with that unsettling declaration, Squall held out his arms, leaned forward and fell straight through the balustrade as if it wasn't there at all. Before he could hit the ground, he was caught by a formless black cloud of shadow and smoke that, as if echoing Morrigan's earlier creation, resolved itself into the shape of a horse and galloped off into the night with Squall at the reins. When he was a block away, she saw him turn and look back at her expectantly.

Morrigan felt panic tightening around her throat. What was she supposed to *do*, exactly? Follow him? Open her umbrella and jump off the rooftop, like on Morningtide? What then, would she just . . . float down into the forecourt and be attacked by a bunch of rampaging Wunimals? This felt very much like a trap.

Clutching her brolly tight, she whispered to herself, 'I don't know what to do.'

And the Hotel Deucalion answered.

Morrigan watched as a long, shimmering golden cable grew from the edge of the balustrade, stretching out into the streets so far that she couldn't see where it ended, or if it ended at all.

That decided it, Morrigan thought. She didn't trust Squall. But she trusted the Deucalion.

She pulled herself up on to the balustrade, heart thumping wildly, and swung her legs over the side. She reached out to hook her brolly on to a loop hanging from the cable, tugging it to test that it was really there, that it was *real*.

Then she heard the door to the stairwell crash open, and the cry of a familiar voice behind her.

'Morrigan! There you are, what are you – NO! STOP!'

She turned to see Fenestra emerge from the doorway, wide-eyed and fearful. Fen reared back and then pelted across the rooftop towards her. Holding tight to her umbrella, Morrigan closed her eyes, leaned forward, and let herself fall.

CHAPTER THIRTY-SIX

Courage Square

There was always something thrilling about riding the Brolly Rail. Soaring across the skyline, dipping low and sailing through streets, then climbing high above rooftops, bracing yourself to jump off when the right moment – and the right landing spot – arrived. It was a peculiarly Nevermoorian experience, hitting just the right notes of exhilarating joy and absolute terror.

There was something extra terrifying about it, however, when you were gliding along a rail that didn't exist five minutes ago and was building itself as you went, and you didn't know where or when or indeed *if* you would ever land.

Morrigan tried to keep her eyes focused on following Squall and hoped he wasn't leading her to her death. But she couldn't resist a peek back at the menagerie of green-eyed Wunimals gaining speed behind her. They came out in numbers greater than she could have imagined, running and slithering and flying and galloping. It was just as Squall had described – she was a beacon guiding them onwards, drawing out the Hollowpox and leading its victims towards . . . towards what? Were they hunting her, or was she trapping them?

Only Squall knew.

She could at least take comfort from the fact that if his plan was to kill her, this was a spectacularly inefficient way to do it.

They sped through the city for a long time. Morrigan felt the strength in her arms start to give, and was just wondering how much longer she could hold on to her brolly when it became suddenly clear where they were headed.

Chasing Squall through the West Gate into Old Town, she flew past the Nevermoor Opera House and right down the middle of Grand Boulevard towards the centre of the city. Up ahead, Squall reached the golden fountain in the middle of Courage Square, alighted from his shadow horse and let it vanish into the Gossamer.

Morrigan dropped from the Brolly Rail with much less grace, her legs jolting painfully when she landed on the cobblestones. She stumbled a few steps but managed to stay upright . . . until she looked back the way she'd come, and her knees buckled.

Countless specks of green light were blinking into view, emerging from every street, alleyway and avenue that fed into Courage Square. Hundreds of them, hundreds and *hundreds* . . . an army of horns, hooves, talons and fangs, their glowing eyes all fixed on Morrigan as they closed around her and Squall.

The closer the infected Wunimals came, however, the warier they seemed. They snarled and snapped, slavered and growled, inching forward and then jumping back, each apparently waiting for some signal from the others.

Squall was right. She confused them.

'What do I do?' she asked him, shaking.

'You destroy it,' he said. 'Mercilessly and without hesitation.

But most of all, *thoroughly*. If Nevermoor is to be rid of the Hollowpox, truly rid of it, it must be finished off all at once. If you allow even one particle to survive, you give it permission to flourish. You *must* get this right the first time.'

'Yes, but *how*—'

'Wait,' he said, holding up a hand. 'Let them come closer.'

Slowly, they came near enough that Morrigan could see them as individuals. She thought she even recognised a few of them. She was sure she knew the great white bearwun who worked as a doorman at the Hotel Aurianna, a few blocks over from the Deucalion. And the lizardwun who played the upright bass in Frank's favourite band, Iguanarama.

'Think of them as one being,' said Squall, as if he'd read her mind. 'One enemy, one monster in many bodies. You can command all by commanding one. Do you understand?'

Morrigan swallowed. 'Not really.'

What had Squall led them here for, exactly? When he talked about destruction, did he mean – did he expect her to *kill them*? She was supposed to be *helping them*, not luring them to their deaths.

A huge, brightly coloured birdwun swooped down on her head. Morrigan screamed and batted it away, trying to protect herself.

'Wait,' said Squall warningly.

'Wait for *what*?' she shouted. 'Wait for them all to attack me?'

Squall kept his eyes on the circle of Wunimals rapidly closing around them. He seemed perfectly calm.

Of course he's calm, she thought. He could disappear into the Gossamer at any moment. But not her. She'd followed his instructions blindly, laid herself out like bait and walked into what might still turn out to be the most obvious trap in the world. And now she was stuck.

Morrigan's pulse beat loudly inside her skull. Her lungs

heaved as if she couldn't take in enough air. She felt like an utter fool. Was she really going to die here, in Courage Square? Nobody would ever know why she was there or what she was trying to do. She would forever be remembered as the idiot who defied a citywide lockdown to go outside on the most dangerous night of the Hollowpox and consequently got herself murdered. People would say she deserved it.

'All right.' Squall drew closer to her, speaking loudly over the din of roaring, shrieking, cawing Wunimals. 'It's almost time. Wait for my signal.'

'Your signal to do *what*?' Morrigan yelped, jumping backwards as a huge, mottled green snakewun opened its jaws wide and hissed, striking out at her.

'What do you do when you are being chased by a bear?'

Having recent experience in this field, she could answer definitively. 'Run.'

'No. You make yourself bigger than the bear.'

'How am I supposed to—'

'It isn't just Wunimals you've been gathering,' Squall interrupted, with a nod to the encroaching horde. 'Look around you. *Focus*.'

Once again and with great effort, Morrigan let her eyes relax until they were nearly closed . . . and Courage Square lit up. The shimmering white-gold Wunder she'd gathered on the rooftop had travelled with her, just like the crowd of Wunimals – and like the crowd, it had grown exponentially. It was blinding.

'What do I do with it?'

'Something big. Use what you know, what you're good at. It doesn't have to be perfect, it only has to be *big*. Enough to draw the Hollowpox out of every single Wunimal here, all at once. Like sucking the poison from a wound.'

Something big. Something *big*.

Morrigan racked her brains and came up with nothing. Squall had been right about her. She was light years away from where she ought to be.

She felt frozen to the spot. It was as if her fear had grown roots and dug down into the ground. 'I – I can't do it. I haven't learned enough yet, you said so yourself.'

Squall's face snapped towards her quite suddenly, eyes flashing.

'Now is not the time to be small!' he roared. 'Where is the Morrigan Crow who reignited the dead fireblossoms? The girl who brought down the Ghastly Market, who conducted a glorious symphony of death in the Museum of Stolen Moments? Where is *that* Morrigan Crow? Bring her back!'

'That was different! I didn't plan any of that, it just *happened*, I can't—'

'MORRIGAN! MORRIGAN, I'M COMING!'

Morrigan turned towards the frantic, distant voice, looking over the jungle of green glowing eyes.

She hadn't imagined it. There on the horizon, impossibly, was a gigantic grey blur bounding down the centre of Grand Boulevard towards Courage Square.

'FENESTRA!'

Her heart jumped up into her throat as Fen reached the square and without hesitating, leapt right into the throng, pouncing from space to space and leaping over the backs of the Wunimals to get to her. Morrigan had never been happier or more worried to see anyone in her life.

'Fen, BE CAREFUL!' she shrieked as a flock of birdwuns circled above the Magnificat's head, taking turns to dive-bomb her.

But Fenestra barely seemed to notice them. She landed deftly in the space in front of Morrigan, turning to bare her fangs

430

at the Wunimals with a ferocious yowl.

Without stopping to think, Morrigan stooped low and ran a line of fire across the ground between Fenestra and the Wunimals and all the way around, enclosing the three of them – her, Fen and Squall – in a bright flaming circle.

'What are you doing here?' Fen snarled at her. 'What were you *thinking*, running off like that, *jumping off the rooftop*, you could have been—'

'I had to!' Morrigan said in a rush. The flames surrounding them grew higher and closer. Sweat ran into her eyes, making it difficult to see, and the Wunimals became a blur beyond the wall of fire. 'I'll explain later!'

'If your idiot mates hadn't broken down that door in your room—'

'My— Who are you talking about?'

'That obnoxious boy and the other . . . there was someone else with him . . . I forget—'

'Cadence! Hawthorne and Cadence broke down my station door?' Morrigan didn't think she could be more afraid in that moment, but her fear somehow spiked, sharp and cold in her heart. 'Are they okay, has something happened?'

'They're fine; they were worried about *you*,' Fen said in a rush. 'Came running into the lobby shouting your name, said some other friend had seen you in a dream or a vision or something . . . *surrounded by fire and teeth*. They tried to make me bring them to find you, but—'

'Lam,' Morrigan whispered.

And in the middle of the madness, she felt a peculiar moment of peace. A weight lifted from her shoulders that she hadn't even known she was carrying.

Squall had been right about Wunsoc '*flipping the script*'. He'd been right that Dr Bramble wouldn't find a cure. But when he said Wundersmiths didn't have friends, he couldn't have been more wrong.

Morrigan had friends. *True* friends, friends who worried about her, and who she worried about in return. Not the long-dead ghosts of Sub-Nine's history, but *real, living* friends who would break down a door to reach her when she was in danger. Friends who were *family*, who would defend her against anything, like Jupiter, and run through a horde of crazed Wunimals to protect her, like Fen. And she knew she'd do the same for them, no matter what.

That was what made her and Squall different. She wasn't him. The sudden certainty of it made her feel buoyant and brave.

'Miss Crow, we are *running out of time*,' said Squall urgently. Fenestra, noticing him for the first time, jumped so high she just about left her body. 'You can't hold them off for ever. If you don't do something now—'

'I know! Shush, I'm thinking.'

'Squall,' growled Fenestra. Her fur stood on end. It looked like she'd been electrocuted.

'He's helping me destroy the Hollowpox,' Morrigan told her. Fen's mouth fell open in shock or dismay or possibly both. She appeared to have lost the power of speech.

'Miss Crow – *now!*' shouted Squall.

She closed her eyes, shutting out the external noise, trying to pretend she was alone.

Use what you know. What you're good at.

Inferno, she thought. *I'm good at Inferno.*

Everything is connected.

Morrigan opened her eyes and looked down at the ground, at the pattern between the uneven cobblestones.

She knelt down and reached towards the ground, taking a deep breath – and squealed as she was knocked sideways by a giant grey paw.

'Ow! Fen, what—'

'MORRIGAN, GET DOWN!'

The great white bearwun was rushing at her through the flames, bellowing like a wounded giant. But Fenestra was easily twice the size of the bearwun, and when she roared back at him over the top of Morrigan's head, it was so loud it hurt her ears and vibrated through her entire body. The bearwun flinched away, but quickly recovered and lunged for Morrigan again. Fen stepped in just in time, and the bearwun's jaws closed tight around the Magnificat's neck, twisting and bringing her head down on to the cobblestones with a resounding *CRACK*.

'FEN!' Morrigan screamed.

And suddenly – as if this was the cue they'd been waiting for – the Wunimals set upon Fenestra like a swarm of book bugs. Within seconds, nothing of her could be seen but one enormous paw grasping blindly, its sharp claws drawing blood wherever they made contact.

With a raging, wordless shriek, something like a battle cry, Morrigan pressed both her palms to the ground. Channelling every scrap of fear and fury inside, she unleashed it in one pulsing burst of fire that surprised even her. It spread instantly across the whole of Courage Square, in a pattern of interconnecting cracks and spaces between the cobblestones. The square lit up like an electrical grid struck by lightning. It was more than just fire, it was energy, bright and burning, and it lifted every Wunimal in Courage Square metres into the air, rising like heat itself. They paused there, suspended, for just a moment, until the fire burned itself out and went dark.

The Wunimals dropped to the ground with a sound like a forest of trees being cut down, all at once. Just like at the Sunset Gala, the nebulous green glow of the Hollowpox left their bodies, rose up into the air and hovered there uncertainly.

Morrigan swayed on the spot, ears ringing as she watched the eerie display. The sudden silence in Courage Square was like a blanket, heavy and soft. It felt like they'd entered the eye of a storm.

She'd done it. She'd done something *big*.

'Now what?' she asked, in a hushed voice that didn't *quite* convey her inner panic. This was the moment, she could feel it: if she didn't destroy the Hollowpox now, each one of these hundreds of fragments of it, these *parasites*, could split apart and disappear into the night. Zoom away to who-knew-where and infect hundreds, maybe *thousands* of new Wunimals.

The lights flickered around her like little emerald fireflies, swarming together and splitting apart, but keeping a respectful distance. Waiting.

Morrigan turned to Squall, who was watching them with a detached curiosity.

'It thinks I'm you.' She felt her legs give way a little. She was so tired. 'Doesn't it? It thinks . . . I'm its master.'

He tilted his head to one side. 'So, then. How do you unmake it?'

She made her brain stretch back to what he'd told her earlier. The Hollowpox was one enemy, he'd said, one monster in many bodies. *You can command all by commanding one.*

'I have to . . . tell it to do something?'

'Clearly and unequivocally.' He looked at her. 'You have to *mean it*, Miss Crow. If it doubts the will behind the words, it won't listen.'

Some of the Wunimals were stirring. She could hear them murmuring to each other, dazed and bewildered. The great white bearwun grumbled mildly as he heaved himself into a sitting position.

Morrigan felt something soft, warm and furry come to stand beside her, propping her up just as she felt she might topple over with exhaustion. Fen's enormous grey head bumped her shoulder gently.

'I can't do it,' she whispered.

'Yes, you can,' said Fenestra and Squall in unison.

The lights came closer, watching her. Waiting.

She'd thought it would feel good to destroy the Hollowpox once and for all, to know she'd helped prevent Nevermoor's total devastation. She didn't anticipate the strange undercurrent of guilt. It hadn't asked to be created, after all, but now this thing – this disease, this monster, this *whatever it was* – was waiting for her judgement.

'You have to go,' she said quietly. 'I want you to go.'

'Clearly and unequivocally,' said Squall.

Morrigan thought of Sofia and turned her voice to steel. She felt a rush of power, at once sickening and intoxicating. It was the best and worst feeling she'd ever had.

'You have to die.'

The Hollowpox listened. Hundreds of green lights blinked out all over Courage Square, one by one. Everything turned black.

CHAPTER THIRTY-SEVEN

Bed Rest

'Did you have any idea?'

'What, that she was capable of—'

'Yeah.'

'Gosh, no. I don't think anybody knew. I don't even think she knew.'

The conversation came to Morrigan through a haze of sleep. Just sounds at first, like tiny little taps on a window, demanding her attention. Formless whispers resolved into words before she was fully awake, and suddenly without meaning to, she was eavesdropping.

'What about that mad patron of hers?'

'If Captain North knew, he's done an awfully good job of pretending. Hey – how do you have *this many* library books out at once?'

'Perks of the job.'

Morrigan's eyes cracked open, just a little, and she saw

Miss Cheery bustling around a neatly made bed across from her own. On the end of it sat Roshni Singh, holding on to a pair of crutches and watching Miss Cheery's movements, a bemused smile on her face.

'You don't need to do that, Maz. I can—'

'You can sit exactly where you are and hush up about it. And stop wriggling about so much, they won't let you go home today if you pull at your stitches again.'

'I'm barely moving!' Roshni said, laughing. She reached for Miss Cheery's hand and pulled her closer, straightening up to plant a quick kiss on her mouth. 'Fusspot.'

Morrigan was still feigning sleep – she didn't want them to know she'd overheard – but it was hard not to grin when Miss Cheery dropped the bossy matron act and swooned theatrically on to the bed beside Roshni, the pair of them giggling like children.

That felt like the right moment to 'wake up'. Morrigan made a show of stirring, stretching and yawning loudly before fully opening her eyes.

Miss Cheery leapt up and rushed over to Morrigan's side.

'Oh my days. You're awake! You're actually awake.' She dropped her voice to a whisper, glancing over her shoulder at the only other occupants of the ward – a lady who was asleep and violently snoring, and an older gentleman who was deep into his crocheting. 'How are you feeling? Are you all right? Talk to me. Morrigan, say something!'

'Maybe try letting her get a word in, Marina?' Roshni suggested.

'Hi.' Morrigan's voice was dry and croaky. 'I'm fine. Just tired.'

'No doubt! You've been asleep for two days,' said Roshni.

Bursts of memory came to Morrigan, filtering through her fuzzy, freshly woken brain.

'Fenestra!' she said suddenly, trying to sit up and failing (her muscles hadn't quite woken up either). 'Where's Fen? Is she okay? My friend, our housekeeper, she's a Magnificat—'

'Oh, you mean that GIANT FLOOF?' Roshni's eyes lit up. 'She's the one who brought you here! You could tell the hospital staff didn't want her hanging around because she's not a Society member, and because she's bigger than the doorway, and – well – does she always have that attitude problem?'

'Yeah. Is she okay?'

'She threatened to eat Dr Lutwyche, so yes, I think she's fine.'

Morrigan was almost too afraid to ask her next question. 'And – and the border, did they – Prime Minister Steed didn't open the border?'

'No, he didn't,' said Miss Cheery, and Morrigan felt cool relief instantly wash over her. Wintersea hadn't come through. Which meant Squall couldn't come through. He'd kept his word. Miss Cheery cast a baffled sideways look at Roshni, and said in a slow, halting way, 'Well, there was . . . no need, in the end. Was there?'

They both watched Morrigan, as if waiting for her to pick up the cue and tell them what had happened, but she looked away, pretending not to notice.

'Have you seen my clothes?' She was wearing a pair of hospital-issued flannel pyjamas – not ideal for the trip home. Taking stock of the items surrounding her, she could see a small forest of Get Well Soon cards, two boxes of sweets, several posies and one enormous, luxurious bouquet of peonies and roses in a vase (the little card attached to them bore Dame Chanda's handwriting). But no clothes except for her cloak, hung over the

438

back of a chair. 'And do I still have shoes, or—'

'Whoa, whoa.' Miss Cheery put a hand on Morrigan's shoulder, guiding her back to the pillow. 'The doctor said once you're awake, you'll need to stay at least another night for observation.'

'But I don't want—'

'One more night! It won't kill you.'

Morrigan slumped against the pillows with a sigh. She just wanted to go home. This hard, narrow hospital cot could never compare to the nest of blankets Room 85 would make for her.

'Where's Jupiter?'

Miss Cheery hesitated. 'He was here. He's been here just about every minute since you arrived, but . . . well. Roshni says Nurse Tim kicked him out last night and told him he could only come back once you'd woken up.'

Morrigan could feel their eyes on her as the silence stretched. Finally, Miss Cheery asked in a careful voice, 'What happened in Courage Square?'

'I don't—' she began, then stopped. 'I can't really . . . I can't tell you.'

Miss Cheery's face flickered through several emotions very quickly, but Morrigan caught each one – confusion, then hurt, then worry, then a reluctant sort of acceptance. But all she said was, 'Of *course*, you don't have to talk about anything until you're ready. It must have been really frightening.'

'It's not that, it's just . . .' She paused. How to say, *I can't tell you how I destroyed the Hollowpox because you'll quickly realise I didn't do it on my own and that will lead to more questions that I won't be able to answer without admitting I acted in league with Nevermoor's greatest enemy and a man widely regarded as the evillest who ever lived . . . without really saying it?* In its fatigued state, her brain came up with nothing.

Best to take the path of least resistance. She nodded, ducking her head and hoping she looked distressed rather than guilty. 'Yeah. It was really frightening. I'm just not ready to talk about it yet.'

'Take all the time you need,' her conductor said gently. 'I won't let anyone pressure you. Not even the Elders. Promise.'

'Thanks,' said Morrigan, relieved to have bought herself some time to come up with a story more palatable than the truth. She cast around for a change of subject. 'How is Sofia?'

Miss Cheery's face fell. 'Sofia is, well – she's still asleep.'

Morrigan frowned. 'Still? But you said it's been two days.'

'Two days?'

'Since we – since I destroyed the Hollowpox.'

The two young women glanced at each other, looking troubled.

'Morrigan,' said Miss Cheery. 'Are you saying . . . do you think the Wunimals were all cured?'

'They must have been. The Wunimals in Courage Square were all right,' she said, sitting up straight. 'I saw them. They woke up. They seemed—'

'Most of them were fully recovered,' Miss Cheery agreed. 'But not all. Dr Bramble said the Hollowpox had progressed to different stages in each of them. Some haven't woken up.'

'And the ones in the hospital? The ones who were already in quarantine, are they still . . .' Morrigan couldn't bring herself to say it. *Still hollow.*

'We honestly don't know,' said Roshni. 'Nobody's told us anything yet.'

Miss Cheery gave Morrigan a quick squeeze and said, '919 popped in this morning. They're anxious to see you, especially Hawthorne and Cadence. Should I let them know you're—'

'FINALLY AWAKE, ARE WE?'

'Never mind, then,' she finished, as Hawthorne's voice reverberated across the ward.

Cadence whacked him on the arm. '*Shush*. Are you trying to get us kicked out again?'

Morrigan's heart leapt at the sight of her friends. It'd been less than a week since she'd seen them, but so much had happened it felt like an eternity.

'Thought you were planning to stay asleep for the rest of the year,' Hawthorne said at a *slightly* moderated volume, plonking down on to the end of her bed with a grin. 'Lazy.'

Miss Cheery left soon after that to take Roshni home, with a stern reminder to Hawthorne that *a bedpan is not a hat* (Morrigan didn't want to know what had happened while she was sleeping). The three reunited friends held a hushed, fast-paced debriefing of the past few days' events, interrupting and talking over each other and unravelling every last detail. When Morrigan described what had happened in Courage Square, she left nothing unsaid, even as Hawthorne's face turned ghost-like and Cadence gripped the edge of the blanket tight in both hands. It was one thing to keep the truth from Miss Cheery and the Elders. This was different. Cadence and Hawthorne were her two best friends in the world, and she would have no secrets between them.

'And what you said at the Gobleian, Cadence,' she said finally, bracing herself. 'Maybe you were right. Maybe I have been weird lately. Sub-Nine, the other Wundersmiths . . . it's strange, but . . . they feel so *real* to me sometimes. I'd started to consider them sort of . . . friends. I think I *was* getting a bit obsessed.'

'Well, yeah,' said Cadence, with a shrug. 'So what? Don't you think we'd all be obsessed if we got to hang out with dead

441

people and learn forbidden magical arts in our own secret school? Sounds brilliant.'

Morrigan smiled ruefully. 'Thaddea said it's all I ever talk about.'

'*Pfft*, who cares what Thaddea says?' Hawthorne piped up. 'She's only jealous. I think we all are, to be honest. I wish *I* could see the ghostly hours.'

'Me too,' Cadence admitted.

Morrigan's eyebrows shot up. 'You can! I mean . . . we'd have to time it right to avoid Dearborn or Murgatroyd finding out, but I bet I could sneak you both down to Sub-Nine!'

They spent an exciting half-hour planning the clandestine mission, which Hawthorne *insisted* on treating like an elaborate high-stakes jewel heist with lookouts, surveillance, and grappling hooks (he didn't yet know how the grappling hooks would fit into their plan, but he was *determined* to work them in somehow). They didn't talk once about the Wunimals still in quarantine, and Morrigan was glad to be distracted from her nagging worries.

She had one more thing she needed to say to Cadence, though, before the moment passed her by. She seized her chance while Hawthorne was drawing up a wonky, very detailed blueprint of Proudfoot House on the back of one of her Get Well Soon cards.

'I'm sorry I made you lie for me,' she said quietly. 'About the book.'

'Hilarious you think you could *make* me do anything,' her friend said with a shrewd smile.

'You know what I mean.'

'Yeah. It's okay. You still owe me.'

'Yeah.'

It was a moment or two before Morrigan realised Hawthorne had grown bored and quietly disappeared from her bedside.

'He's gone to find a bedpan to wear as a hat, hasn't he?'

Cadence nodded. 'Oh, almost certainly.'

Nurse Tim had a few grievances to air while he checked Morrigan's vitals.

'. . . and suddenly all eight of them are here, taking up all the oxygen in the room. Hanging homemade banners all over the place! Playing the fiddle! *Challenging elderly patients to an arm wrestle!* I said excuse me, this is a hospital, not me Uncle Clive and Auntie Trudy's ruby wedding anniversary bash at the Clodspoole-on-Sea church hall. Spare me the shanties.' He shifted his stethoscope from her middle back to her upper back. 'Another big breath in and out, that's the way.'

Morrigan breathed in deep through her nose and out through her mouth.

'I mean *you're* no trouble, pet, but can I just say? Your friends are a proper nightmare. Not being funny, but please don't come back again.'

'I'll try not to.'

'And then all that hoo-ha last night with Captain Dramatic and the Elders! *Oof.* One more big breath for me.' Again he moved the stethoscope, and again Morrigan's chest rose and fell.

'What hoo-ha?'

'Going off like firecrackers, they were, all four of them. Shouting! In a hospital! Grown adults, mind.'

'What were they shouting about?' Morrigan asked, though she had a fairly good idea.

'Oh, who knows. Elder Quinn said she wanted to be here when you wake up to ask you some questions, and then Elder Wong says let's bring in one of them lot from the Public Distraction Department to prepare a statement for the press about something-or-other, and that sent the mouthy ginger off on one. "*None of you lot cares about what's best for Morrigan,*" he says. "*You would have thrown her to the wolves if I hadn't fought you every step of the way!*" I thought Elder Quinn might smack him in the jaw, but he's not half stirring when he gets on a roll, is he? He should join an amateur theatrical society.'

He is *an amateur theatrical society*, Morrigan thought, taking another big breath in and out.

'I'll admit it did liven up my dinner break, but once I'd finished my cheesy lentil pie I had to kick them all out, I'm afraid. Poor old Mrs Purkiss can't take that sort of excitement, not with her blood pressure,' he said with a nod to the lady in the corner bed.

Morrigan felt dread settle in her bones. The thought of raking over the night's events, of carefully concealing certain incriminating details and crafting a repeatable lie that the Elders would believe and accept, was positively *exhausting*.

'Here, hold this under your tongue for three minutes.' Nurse Tim popped a glass thermometer in her mouth and went to fetch the clipboard from the end of the bed. 'What happened this time?'

'Oh, you know,' she said around a mouthful of glass. 'Jumped off a building, got chased by Wunimals, set Courage Square on fire.'

'Oh, aye, what are you like?' he said absently as he checked his wristwatch and made a note on the clipboard. 'And Mr Schultz is back with his ingrown toenail again— I'M JUST TELLIN' 'ER ABOUT YER TOENAIL, MR SCHULTZ,' he added in a raised voice. The gentleman waved his crochet hooks from the other end of the ward, smiling. 'You're all in the wars, you lot. Cup of tea?'

'Yes, please.'

'And I suppose I'd best let the shouty one know you're awake.'

'Yes, please.'

Despite her fatigue, Morrigan couldn't help smiling a little at the thought of Jupiter telling off the Elders. Captain Dramatic always had her back.

'More water? More juice? Doesn't look very nice, this juice. Shall I bring you some fresh juice from home? Now we're ready for the grand re-opening and the kitchen's running again, I can bring you just about anything! What would you like – pineapple juice? Grapefruit? Dragonfruit? Winterberry? Lemonberry? Rippleberry? Tripleberry? Peachy sunset? Unicorn surprise? Whimsical springtime slush?'

'No, thank you.' Morrigan sighed. 'And I know you made at least three of those up.'

Jupiter had rushed into the teaching hospital mere minutes after Tim had sent for him, and he'd been fussing around her like a nervous butterfly ever since. One minute he was checking her forehead for fever, the next fetching extra blankets she didn't need. He'd asked her three times if she wanted to move to a better bed ('The beds are all identical,' she'd told him), and twice if he should find her a spot with a nicer view ('There are no nicer views,' she'd said. 'There are no windows. We're three floors underground'). It had moved beyond amusing into tiresome, and finally graduated to maddening.

The only time he *wasn't* fretting was when they'd discussed the Courage Square events – a brief, serious, whispered conversation.

As expected, Jupiter had already heard most of the story from Fen, but Morrigan filled in the blank spaces. He'd listened to her version carefully – *twice* – interrupting only occasionally to clarify a detail here and there, then had her repeat the story to him a *third* time, erasing all mention of Ezra Squall and stitching the gaps together with mild untruths. Together they concocted a believable enough reason for her having been in Courage Square that night (cabin fever – she'd been cooped up in the Deucalion so long, she decided to hop on the Brolly Rail for a quick zip around the city before safely returning home – only she fell off in Courage Square), and a believably patchy memory of having *somehow* used the Wundrous Arts in ways she hadn't realised she was able, to destroy the Hollowpox by means she didn't fully understand. It was all *mostly* true, which of course made it an excellent lie. After a couple of practice runs, Morrigan felt confident she could convince the Elders.

Now if only she could convince Jupiter to chill out.

She watched him pick up the chart hanging off the end of her bed, then put it back. He'd already read it twelve or thirteen times – excessive, Morrigan thought, considering all it said was 'BED REST' in large capital letters.

'Jupiter,' she said firmly. 'Sit down, please. I want to ask you something.'

He came over and yanked her pillows out from behind her head to fluff them up for the millionth time. 'Of course. Just let me fix—'

'SIT. DOWN. PLEASE.'

She said it so loudly that even hard-of-hearing Mr Schultz at the other end of the ward jumped with fright, his crochet hooks clattering on to his lap.

Jupiter finally, reluctantly, dropped into the chair beside Morrigan's bed, looking as if he'd quite like to leap back up again and rearrange her many flower-filled vases. She gave him a pointed look, and he sat on his hands.

'By all means,' he said magnanimously. 'Ask away.'

She looked him in the eye. 'The infected Wunimals. The ones here in the hospital. They haven't recovered, have they? They weren't cured when the Hollowpox died. They're still . . .' She lowered her voice. 'They're still *unnimals*, aren't they?'

He rubbed the back of his neck, taking a moment to respond. 'Dr Bramble is—'

'Don't say it,' she snapped. '*Don't* say she's getting closer to a cure every day, Jupiter. Not unless you mean it. Not unless it's true.'

She glared at him, waiting, while his face transitioned through the argument inside his head. It was clear he wanted to stick with defiant optimism, but he seemed to realise that wasn't going to fly any more.

'They're . . . Yes. They're still unnimals,' he conceded. 'The ones that are awake.'

'And the others?' she asked, thinking of Sofia. She curled her hands into fists around the blankets. 'What will happen to them when they wake up? Will they be . . . hollow?'

'We don't know for certain.'

'But if you had to guess?'

Jupiter didn't answer that. He didn't need to. They sat quietly for a while, feeling the weight of the conversation settle.

'I wasn't lying to you,' he said at last. 'Those other times. Dr Bramble really *was* close. Or at least . . . she thought she was.' He paused, looking up at the ceiling for a moment, collecting himself. 'We're not giving up, Mog. We're going to bring them back.'

When he met her gaze, his bright blue eyes were wide and earnest, but she could tell he was trying to persuade himself as much as her. She nodded and gave a small, tight-lipped smile that she hoped was convincing.

'I have something for you, too, by the way,' he said, glancing at the things surrounding her bed. 'Not quite as extravagant as Dame Chanda's bouquet, but I think you'll like it. I had to become a burglar to get it.'

Morrigan raised an eyebrow. 'You what?'

'Mmm.' He ruffled up his hair and shrugged, obviously trying to look casual. 'Decided to try it last night. Something different.'

'You decided to try . . . becoming a burglar,' Morrigan repeated, and she couldn't keep the scepticism from her voice.

'Yeah, just this one time. Won't be making a habit of it,' Jupiter said, sniffing, then added, 'Mind you, I was *exceptionally* good.' As he spoke, he hopped up lightly and ran to fetch his coat, reaching into an inner pocket and retrieving something Morrigan had thought she might never see again. He held it out to her.

'Emmett,' she whispered, taking the old, battered-looking toy rabbit with both hands.

Something squeezed in her chest.

Emmett. Her *friend*.

Morrigan looked up at Jupiter. 'You went all the way to Jackalfax. And broke into Crow Manor.' Her voice cracked. It was hard to swallow past the lump in her throat. 'Just . . . just to steal him for me?'

Jupiter smiled a little sheepishly. 'Well, technically I didn't *steal* him. He belongs to you.'

Morrigan was silent for a moment. She stared at the rabbit, blinking fiercely, and cleared her throat. 'Thank you.'

'You're welcome. Dear old thing, isn't he?' Jupiter reached out to tug at one of Emmett's floppy ears, but stopped when Morrigan instinctively snatched the rabbit away. He held his hands up. 'Sorry.'

'No, it's fine, it's just . . .' She floundered for a moment, suddenly embarrassed. 'He's so old, that's all. He's falling apart.'

'May I have him for a moment?' Jupiter asked, and hastily added, 'I'll be gentle.'

Morrigan hesitated. 'Um . . . all right.'

Jupiter took Emmett from her with tender care. He cradled the rabbit, studying its seams and stitches, the patches where his yellowing white fur had been worn away by too much love, the orphaned thread of cotton on his backside where a fluffy tail used to be, before it came off in the wash and disappeared who-knows-where.

'Can I tell you something?'

'What?'

'You love this rabbit.'

She rolled her eyes. 'I already know that.'

'You don't, though. Not the full story.' Jupiter sat down again in the chair beside her bed, still holding the rabbit as gently as if it were a real unnimal. 'You *think* you love him because you've had him since you were a baby. You think you love him because he listened to eleven years of your secrets and stories. And because he was always just the right size for tucking into the crook of your neck as you fell asleep, for hiding on the seat beside yours at the dinner table.'

Morrigan smiled. She *did* used to sit Emmett next to her at dinner sometimes. Nobody knew because nobody ever sat on her side of the table, and of course if Grandmother had spotted 'that dirty old thing' in the dining room, she'd have pitched a fit. But it made Morrigan feel like somebody was on her side to have him there, even if he couldn't speak up for her.

'You think you love him because of his soft floppy ears and his dear little waistcoat.'

Emmett wasn't wearing a waistcoat . . . but he used to. Just like he used to have a fluffy tail.

But Jupiter, of course, could see the missing waistcoat. Just as he could see Morrigan's bad dreams and worries, and the hollowed-out Wunimals, and Dame Chanda's perpetual kindness.

'And because of his button-black eyes,' he continued. 'Because they remind you of your own black eyes. And because he's the only friend you had when you were small. But that's not why you love Emmett so much.'

Morrigan shivered slightly, though the room was warm.

'You love him,' Jupiter continued in a soft, low voice, 'because every fibre of his fur, every stitch in his seams, every fluff of his stuffing is infused with – is positively *glowing from* – the love of the person who owned him before you. His very first owner.'

Something in the back of Morrigan's brain clicked, like a key turning in a lock.

Jupiter held the rabbit closer, examining every inch of fur, a frown deepening the crease between his eyebrows. 'Her handprints are all over him. Cloudy silver smudges. Big hands, little hands. Hands a bit like yours. Twenty-odd years of them, layer upon layer.'

Morrigan held her breath, so reluctant was she to miss a single whispered word. Jupiter at last lifted his eyes from Emmett's dusty little face to her pale one.

'Mog,' he said quietly. 'I think, perhaps, this rabbit belonged to your mother.'

Somehow Morrigan knew instantly that he was correct. A feeling of warmth spread from her chest all the way out to her fingertips, and she reached for Emmett, smoothing down his ears gently.

It really was a most extraordinary knack.

Morrigan didn't sleep that night. She wanted to. She could have happily spent another week unconscious. But her mind wouldn't turn itself off.

Thoughts of her mother had turned to thoughts of her family here in Nevermoor. The family she'd found at the Hotel Deucalion. The friends she counted as sisters and brothers, and the new friends she'd made in unexpected places.

She couldn't stop thinking about Sofia, and about Jupiter's face when he'd admitted there was no cure in sight. Even with everything she'd tried to do these past few days – taking the Gossamer Line to Ylvastad, negotiating with Wintersea, arguing with Jupiter, everything that happened in Courage Square – so many Wunimals were still in danger. Her *friend* was still in danger.

Mostly, though, Morrigan was thinking about what Anah had told her. After visiting hours were over and Jupiter went home, Anah had crept on to the dimly lit ward to visit her.

'Morrigan,' came her whisper in the dark, then a quiet, 'Ow!' as she bumped into something.

'Anah?' she whispered back, sitting up in bed. 'What are you doing here?'

'Shhh,' said Anah, tiptoeing over. Morrigan scooted sideways to make room for her. 'I heard Nurse Tim telling your patron you'd woken up, so I volunteered to stay late so I could come see you. Normally junior scholars aren't allowed to be on duty past six o'clock, but I think they're getting desperate. Can I have a bit of your chocolate? I'm *famished*, haven't eaten a thing since breakfast.'

'Help yourself,' said Morrigan, pushing the half-eaten box into her hands. 'Is everything all right?'

Anah didn't answer at first. She nibbled at a strawberry whip, looking anguished. Finally she whispered, 'I'm glad you're awake.

451

We had a little party here for you, hoping it might wake you up, we were all so worried. What you did . . . it was really brave. And things are better now, without any new Hollowpox patients coming in. I just wish . . .' She paused to take a bite of a peppermint cream. In the dim light, Morrigan thought she saw tears shining in her eyes. 'I wish there was something we could do for the ones who are already here.'

'I know,' Morrigan said darkly. 'I thought—'

But she didn't quite know how to finish that sentence. *I thought I'd cured them?* Or worse – *I thought* Ezra Squall *had cured them?* It seemed outrageously foolish now, to have believed he would keep his word.

'Jupiter said they're not giving up,' she went on. 'They're still looking for a cure.'

'I'm sure they are,' said Anah. 'I'm sure Jupiter and Dr Bramble will keep looking for as long as it takes. But Dr Lutwyche wants the Hollowpox task force to disband. As far as he's concerned, the threat is over. He's furious about all the space and time and *resources* the unnimals – I mean the Wunimals – are still taking up. Sorry.' She winced a little at her slip of the tongue. 'He wants things back to normal, and Morrigan . . . you *know* I want the Wunimals to be all right again, but . . . they're just not. Almost three-quarters of the teaching hospital is a quarantine zone now. More of the infected are waking up every day and it's overcrowded and *unhygienic* and . . . well, it smells like a—'

'Don't say it—'

'—*zoo*, I'm sorry, but it does!' Her face flushed but she met Morrigan's glare defiantly, continuing in a fierce whisper. 'Listen. All the medical staff and assistants were called to a meeting this afternoon. This is strictly confidential, but . . . it was about what happens next.'

'And? What happens next?'

'*Please* don't tell anyone I told you. There's nothing you can do, I just thought you'd want to know in case . . . in case you wanted to say goodbye to your friend. The foxwun, what's her name?'

'Sofia.' Instantly, Morrigan's eyes prickled. 'Is she awake? Is she . . .'

She couldn't finish that question, but Anah nodded miserably, and she had her answer. Not a foxwun any more, then.

She swallowed painfully. 'What do you mean, say goodbye?'

'They're going to start moving them tomorrow, so we can begin a deep-clean and get the hospital fully operational again. The Wunimals Minor are all still asleep, they'll be moved to their own special ward until we know exactly how they've been affected. Dr Bramble is putting together a small team to care for them.'

'And the Majors?'

'Some of them will go to the unnimal husbandry facilities in the Practicalities Department here on Sub-Three—'

'*What?*' Morrigan shrieked. Anah's hand shot out to cover her mouth, but Morrigan pulled it away and whispered, 'Like *farm unnimals*?'

'—and some will go to the Nevermoor Zoo to be cared for by professionals who can – Morrigan, sit.' Morrigan had jumped out of bed and was pacing up and down, breathing hard. 'We're not unnimal carers here, we don't know how to give them the best—'

'Then they should go to their *families!*'

'And some of them will!' Anah paused, biting on her lower lip. 'To the families who . . . who want them back. If they can provide adequate care. That's what Dr Bramble said.'

That made Morrigan stop pacing. *The families who want*

453

them back. She pressed a hand to her chest, squeezing her eyes shut tight.

Would some of their families not want them back?

Who was Sofia's family? Morrigan felt suddenly wretched. She'd never asked.

'Where is Sofia now?'

Anah sighed. She seemed to regret having told Morrigan as much as she had, but it was clear she was in this now. 'Still in the quarantine wing. Ward 4A. Now listen carefully, because if you want to see her, you'll only have a very brief window.'

Morrigan had memorised Anah's instructions for sneaking into Ward 4A without getting caught, and her friend had crept back out into the hallway to go home, and ever since then she'd been counting down the hours until her *very brief window* arrived.

She'd used the time well. She'd vowed revenge on selfish Dr Lutwyche. She'd fumed silently about Dr Bramble the hypocrite, who supposedly *wasn't giving up* on finding a cure, but was happy to ship a bunch of inconvenient Wunimals off to the zoo in the meantime.

But most importantly, she'd crafted a plan. Lying in the dark, staring up at the ceiling and listening to the hours tick away – Emmett tucked under her arm, just like when she was little – Morrigan plotted her next move as patiently as a chess grandmaster.

She closed her eyes, waiting for the softly padding footsteps of the evening nurse on her midnight rounds, and once they'd disappeared into the distance, she sat up in bed and whistled.

A short whistle, low and eerie.

There was a moment when she doubted it had worked. Then she heard it, cutting through the wheezing and snoring: a deep, reverberating growl.

It came from the shadows under her bed.

'Come out,' she whispered, trying to make it sound like a command rather than a plea, while a primal fear tiptoed delicately down her spine.

The shadows took the shape of a wolf, and the wolf slunk out from beneath the bed. It brought its enormous face close to hers – teeth bared, red eyes glowing. Morrigan squeezed Emmett tighter, summoned all of her courage and addressed the dark, monstrous thing in a voice that didn't shake.

'I want to speak with him.'

CHAPTER THIRTY-EIGHT

Opening a Window

The wolf seemed to appraise her for a moment, then disappeared in a swirl of black smoke.

Was that it, Morrigan wondered? Surely it couldn't be that easy. She'd thought she might have to do something to convince it to obey her, perhaps a demonstration of the Wundrous Arts. But sure enough, the wolf vanished in one instant and returned the next, bringing with it the rest of the wolf pack. And their master.

'Don't go getting ideas about *summoning* me,' Squall said quietly. He stood at the end of her bed, cloaked in shadow. 'This won't work every time, you know.'

'It worked this time.'

'Because I was expecting it. Though you certainly took longer than anticipated.'

'I've been asleep for two days.'

His eyes flicked briefly upwards. 'Of course you have. Your stamina is abysmal.'

She ignored the insult. 'You said you'd fix the Hollowpox.'

'And so I did. Have you brought me here to say thank you?'

'You *didn't*,' she insisted. 'The Wunimals are still hollow. They're still *unnimals*. You promised—'

'I promised the destruction of the Hollowpox, and that is what I delivered.'

'You promised a CURE!' Morrigan raised her voice, then flinched as Mr Schultz in the far corner of the ward spluttered in his sleep before settling back to his steady wheezing. 'You promised a cure,' she repeated in a harsh whisper, leaning forward. The shadow wolves growled a low warning, but she didn't stop. 'On the rooftop, that day at Proudfoot House. *Do you think I would make something I couldn't unmake?* That's what you said.'

'But curing something and destroying it are two entirely different matters.' His face was inscrutable. 'I *told you* I would provide a cure to the Hollowpox if you became my apprentice. I don't recall offering to do it out of the goodness of my heart. What happened in Courage Square was a fair and mutually beneficial arrangement. I wanted to keep Wintersea out of Nevermoor, and you wanted to stop the spread of the Hollowpox. That's our business concluded, as far as I'm concerned. If you want something *more*, you need to offer something in return.'

'*Fine.*' Straightening her spine, Morrigan pushed off the blankets and got out of bed. She slid her feet into a pair of warm slippers Jupiter had left for her, gathered up her coat from the back of the chair and buttoned it over her pyjamas. 'Fine, I agree. I'll be your apprentice. Now let's go.'

There was a long, tense silence between them, broken only by the snoring from across the ward. She waited for Squall to react, but he was as still as stone, his black eyes glassy in the dim light.

'I don't believe you,' he said finally. 'Why would you do this?'

Morrigan wanted to throw her hands in the air and shout at him, but that would have brought the overnight nurse running.

'Why do you *think* I would do this?' she asked in a hoarse whisper. 'And more importantly, why do you *care*? You're getting what you want!'

'And what if I've changed my mind?' he asked. 'What if it's not what I want any more? Perhaps I've decided you're not a good enough Wundersmith, that you'll never be—'

'You haven't,' she snapped. 'So don't pretend. This is what you've wanted since the first day we met, *Mr Jones*. You've never given up. You keep coming back to Nevermoor, keep trying to persuade me. Well, congratulations! You've finally offered me something I want more than I *don't* want to be your apprentice.'

'And what's that?'

'I want Sofia back!' Morrigan cursed the break in her voice. Cursed him for hearing it. 'I want to talk to her. I want Dame Chanda to get her friend back and be happy again. I want Brutilus Brown to go home to his family, and Colin to go back to the library, and every other Wunimal in this building to just . . . to be *Wunimals* again. This isn't fair. It's grotesque. They're in *cages*, for goodness' sake. It isn't RIGHT.' She put a hand over her mouth to stifle a sob. Squall stared at her, emotionless. 'Just . . . just tell me how to f-fix it.'

'You?' He frowned, seeming genuinely confused. 'You can't fix it.'

'I couldn't destroy the Hollowpox either,' she said. 'But I did. I can do this too. Tell me the steps and I'll follow them, just like in Courage Square.'

Squall chuckled as if she'd just told an excellent joke, then stopped abruptly. He made a strange little noise in the back of his throat – somewhere between pity and disgust – that made

Morrigan feel approximately two feet tall.

'Miss Crow, destroying the Hollowpox and curing its victims are two very different tasks, requiring vastly different skillsets. You are . . .' He waved a hand up and down, casting her a disdainful look. '. . . a blunt instrument. Your performance in Courage Square was the equivalent of taking a hammer to a teacup. Destruction is *easy*. It didn't really take much in the end, did it, for all that built-up frustration and anger inside you to explode outwards?

'But this is different. Only an extremely skilled Wundersmith could restore those Wunimals to their former state, and I wouldn't even describe you as a moderately skilled Wundersmith. At this point I'd hardly call you a Wundersmith at all.'

'I have the Inferno imprint.' She held up her left hand. 'I've met the Kindling. I brought the fireblossoms back to life. I *am* a Wundersmith.'

'Bravo,' he said dryly, giving her a tiny two-fingered clap. 'You can burn things.'

Morrigan gave an impatient huff. This wasn't what he'd said in Courage Square. *Where is the girl who brought down the Ghastly Market? Bring her back!* What was it he'd said about not being *small*?

She tilted her chin upwards, determined to stand her ground. 'Just *tell me how*—'

'Set that bed on fire.'

'I – what?'

'The bed,' he repeated. 'Set. It. On. Fire.'

Morrigan glanced at the door, suddenly uneasy (someone would surely come running the instant her bed caught ablaze), but nonetheless she took a deep breath, and—

Nothing.

She tried again.

Nothing. Not even a spark.

'You see,' Squall said softly, his face twisted in disgust. 'The "how" is irrelevant. Even if the task wasn't far, *far* beyond your abilities, just . . . look at you. You're a dead battery. Too depleted – *two days later* – to accomplish even the simplest task. Any Wundrous energy swarming around you now is very hard at work helping you to not die.'

Morrigan checked the clock on the wall. The brief window Anah had promised her was drawing nearer; she didn't have time to argue. 'Then how long will it take me to—'

'*You are not listening to me,*' he said, raising his voice. 'It would take days of recuperation, *years* of study and practice. These Wunimals will waste away and die before you become the kind of Wundersmith who might be able to save their lives. You have neither the energy nor the skill—'

'But you do,' she said. 'You have both.'

'And?'

'And . . . last year, you said I gave you a window into Nevermoor, that you were leaning on me through the Gossamer and that's how I could do all those things that I'd never learned how to do. You said that once I started to learn the Wundrous Arts for myself, once I was using all the Wunder that gathers around me, there wouldn't be enough of it to lean on any more. The window would shut.' She took a deep breath, hardly believing what she was about to say. 'But what if I wanted to open it?'

Morrigan kept to the shadows as much as she could, but it turned out shadows were hard to come by in a brightly lit hospital. 'My friend is a hospital assistant; she told me we'll have a window of maybe five minutes during the changeover. The quarantined wards are all kept locked, but there's a key in a drawer in Dr Lutwyche's—'

'We are not sneaking around, and we'll take as long as we need,' Squall said, with more than a hint of contempt. 'We are *Wundersmiths*. Here, hold up your hands like this.' He removed his black leather gloves and tucked them into a pocket, then held up his own pale hands, palms facing Morrigan. He had two imprints identical to hers – a shimmering golden W on his right index finger, and a tiny flickering flame on the left middle. Of course he had the same imprints. (Logically, he must have others that were invisible to her; Morrigan knew you could only see someone else's imprint if you had the same one of your own.)

Her hands remained by her sides.

He raised an eyebrow. 'Do you wish to be my apprentice or not?'

So this was it, she thought, dread and curiosity doing battle within her. Some kind of Wundersmith ceremony that would bind them together. No going back from that.

She held up her ever-so-slightly shaking hands, mirroring him, then snatched them back. 'Wait! Just to be clear: I'm agreeing to be your *apprentice Wundersmith*. That means you can teach me the *Wundrous Arts*, not . . . evil lessons.'

'Very droll.'

'I'm not joking. This doesn't make me your puppet, or your proxy, or your partner in crime! I'm not agreeing to conquer Nevermoor on your behalf, or do your bidding, or *anything else* except learn how to use the arts in the normal, non-evil way that Wundersmiths are supposed to. Is that understood?'

'Perfectly.'

'And as long as we're clarifying things: your side of the bargain is a complete, permanent, no-strings-attached *cure*. For every single Wunimal victim—'

'Miss Crow, enough. Time is short. I have no wish to renege on our deal. Nor have I any interest in keeping Wunimals hollow; that isn't my fight. And besides,' he said, holding up his hands again and looking vaguely offended, 'when I give my word, I *keep it*.'

Morrigan took a deep breath. She had no idea whether she could trust him. But she had no choice. The Wunimals would be moved tomorrow, and who knew where most of them would end up? If they were doing this, it had to be done tonight.

Before she could talk herself out of it, she held up her hands again. Their fingertips met through the Gossamer, and suddenly – without even moving – he was rushing towards her, they were rushing towards each other, cold and black, two oceans pouring into one.

In that second, Morrigan felt a chilling flash of clarity.

She'd made a terrible mistake. It was like Golders Night all over again, but this time it wasn't water filling her lungs, it was something else.

Chaos. Madness. Power.

Whatever it was, she was going to drown in it. She wanted to pull her hands away, but she couldn't. They felt magnetised. *Danger*, her heartbeat said. *Danger. Danger. Danger.*

'Stay calm.' Squall's quiet voice broke through her panic, like a flare in the dark.

'What is this? What's happening?'

'We're building a tunnel. A temporary bridge across the Gossamer. *Stay. Calm.*'

After what felt like a long time but must have only been moments, the two oceans stopped pouring, and were still. Morrigan had the strangest sensation of peaceful, passive certainty. She felt like she was captaining a ship that already knew where it was

462

going. She was still in command, but she barely had to steer.

She imagined it was a bit like how an actor in the theatre must feel, perhaps how Dame Chanda felt when she put on the elaborate costume and mask of the villainess Euphoriana. She had the unsettling feeling that she'd stepped inside Squall's skin, or he had stepped inside hers.

'*Little crowling, little crowling,*' she heard herself sing, '*with button-black eyes . . .*'

Wunder gathered, and it was nothing like when she gathered it on her own. Squall had scarcely sung a note through her when Wunder bristled all around, like a thunderstorm was in the air.

She'd expected, when he leaned on her through the Gossamer, to feel her sense of self encroached upon, somehow *lessened*. But this wasn't that at all. Instead she felt her personhood ballooning and stretching, as if she had finally been granted permission to take up space in the world. There had been nothing frightening about it, not the way it was before. Her powers weren't being hijacked without her knowledge; this was a collaboration.

A crackle of electricity charged through her veins. It felt like she could stare down the sun if she wanted to. She was unstoppable, unbreakable, unmessable-with.

And she finally understood the canyon that existed between Squall's ability and her own. Was this how he felt . . . *all the time*?

Was this truly what it meant to be a Wundersmith?

As they walked down the empty hallway, side by side, Morrigan caught sight of her reflection in a pane of glass. She was shocked – and almost a little disappointed – to see herself looking just the same as always. How could she still be an ordinary girl on the outside, when an entire universe was swelling up inside her?

She didn't look like an ordinary girl for much longer,

however. Every few steps, they passed another window in which Morrigan saw her reflection. With every window they passed, she was changing.

It reminded her of seeing Dearborn transform into Murgatroyd, or Murgatroyd into Rook. She saw her body shrink until she was a head shorter, her hair turn grey and wispy, her limbs grow frail and bony.

'What's happening to me?' Morrigan asked. She felt no panic, just a vague curiosity.

'Masquerade,' Squall said simply.

By the time they reached the vast oak doors leading to the quarantine ward, Morrigan's reflection had become Elder Quinn. Yet when she looked down at her hands and body, she found they were her own. She hadn't really transformed at all; it was just an illusion.

Squall pressed through the Gossamer, and Morrigan saw her hands push on the doors, heard the click as the lock turned, felt her legs carry her into the ward. One of the nurses rushed forward to stop her, looking startled. She walked right through Squall as if he wasn't there. Because of course, to anyone but Morrigan, he wasn't.

'Elder Quinn! Forgive me but this ward is closed to everyone, even— Please, *wait*. You're not wearing the appropriate—'

'Get out. All of you.' Morrigan felt the vibrations in her vocal cords, felt her mouth form the words, felt the air expelled from her lips. But even she could scarcely believe she'd said it; the voice was so convincingly Elder Quinn's – frail, croaky and ancient, with a hint of steel. The nurses on duty didn't hesitate to obey. 'Shut the doors behind you. Don't let anyone else in.'

Morrigan felt the illusion of Elder Quinn fall away as she and Squall were left alone in the ward.

Only they *weren't* alone, of course. The walls were lined with Wunimals big and small – some in beds, some in cages – but far too many to fit comfortably in the space. Most were sedated, or at least in some half-sleeping, half-waking state that could barely be described as alive.

'Can you sense it?' Squall asked her. 'The void.'

'Yes.'

It was just as Jupiter had described. They were hollow, every one of them. Morrigan couldn't see it the way her patron could, but she could *feel* it, and it was perhaps the most deeply upsetting thing she'd ever experienced – like a nausea she felt in her heart instead of her stomach. Unnatural and wrong.

No wonder Anah had been so upset lately; if Morrigan had had to be near this all the time, she'd be constantly crying too.

She cast a curious glance at Squall and saw that he was staring at the ceiling, apparently unable to look directly at the hollow Wunimals. She could feel layers of his own fear and horror and disgust. It only made her furious.

'You did this,' she reminded him in a low, angry voice. 'Look at them. Maybe Wintersea asked for it, but *you* did it.'

He didn't respond.

Morrigan led him from one ward through to the next, and the next, in silence. Finally, she found what she was looking for.

'Sofia!' she cried, running to her friend. The foxwun cowered at the back of a small cage, making squeaky little chattering noises and scratching at the metal grille as if frantic to get away from her. 'Sofia, it's me. It's Morrigan, you *know* me!'

'She's still in there,' said Squall. 'They all are. I can feel them . . . teetering right on the edge of something. You can feel it, can't you?'

Morrigan nodded tearfully. She knew exactly what he meant.

There was something buried deep inside Sofia's consciousness – so deep she doubted Jupiter would have been able to sense it, even with his skill – a tiny familiar spark. Her friend was in there somewhere. She was standing before an abyss, ready to fall in at any moment, but she was still there.

'We can reel them back in,' Squall murmured. 'But are you certain we should? Are you certain it's what *they'd* want?'

Morrigan turned around, ready to snap at him about playing mind games, but the words died in her throat. He was staring at Sofia, a crease between his eyes.

'What is there for them here, after all?' he continued. 'A world that doesn't understand them, a society that barely tolerates their existence? We could give them a little nudge into the void. Doubt they'd feel a thing. We might be doing them a favour.'

Morrigan looked back at her small, terrified friend. She reached her fingers through the bars of the cage, and gave the order. Clearly and unequivocally.

'Bring them back.'

It was slow, complex, difficult work that Morrigan barely understood. It was bizarre to watch her own hands move in ways that seemed mechanically impossible, to listen to her own voice speaking in tones and languages she'd never heard before. She watched him thread and rethread endless strands of golden-white Wunder through and around each individual Wunimal, rebuilding them from the inside out, restoring everything they'd lost, everything that made them Wunimals.

Squall wasn't just Weaving something new, it wasn't like applying some kind of magical sticking plaster over a gaping wound. He was doing precisely what he'd said he would do: *unmaking* what he had made. Undoing what the Hollowpox had done. The slow way. Piece by painstaking piece. Like the little crystal palace Griselda Polaris had turned to sand, he was applying the Wundrous Art of Ruin to his own work – unravelling it from the inside. It was unspeakably delicate, and agonisingly complex, and Morrigan absorbed every second of it with breathless wonder.

When each one had been cured, they remained still and calm, in an almost trance-like state. But Morrigan knew it had worked. One by one she felt their minds return, the comforting weight of their consciousness settling upon the room.

She left every cage door open as they went.

'Will they remember who they were before?' Morrigan asked Squall at one point.

'They'll remember, because Wunder remembers,' he told her. 'Wunder has an excellent memory.'

They saved Sofia for last. Morrigan watched, heart in throat. When Squall had finally finished he looked back upon his work, and then turned to her. 'Ready?'

Morrigan could feel the Wunder in the room. It was standing on a precipice, awaiting its final instruction. 'Yes.'

And just like that the foxwun looked up, blinking to bring her into focus.

'Morrigan,' Sofia said at last in a small, curious voice. 'Hello.'

With those two words, the world was made right again.

All along the quarantine wing, one after another, the Wunimals came back to themselves as gently as waves returning to the shore.

Squall draped Morrigan in a veil of shadows, and they left.

As they made their way back through the Teaching Hospital, Morrigan could feel the bridge between her and Squall collapsing, bit by bit. The veil he'd created began to slowly disappear, but that didn't particularly matter – nobody was paying attention to her.

The noise of the Wunimals waking up had sent the staff running to the quarantine ward.

Morrigan paused in the middle of an empty hallway, holding up a hand to stop Squall.

'What happens now?' she asked wearily. Now that his power wasn't propping her up through the Gossamer, her brain and body felt impossibly sluggish, and she had to fight not to fall to the ground.

'Ah,' said Squall. 'Of course.'

He gave a low whistle and the wolf pack slunk out from the shadows, eyes burning. They surrounded the two of them, moving in a circle, swirling faster and faster until all Morrigan could see was a blur of black smoke and shadow and streaks of red light and then nothing, only darkness.

And as quickly as they appeared, the wolves were gone. The light returned. And Morrigan held a piece of paper, balanced lightly on her upturned palms.

'What's this?'

'Read it.'

This is a Wundrous Arts apprenticeship agreement between the Wundersmith Ezra Squall and the Wundersmith Morrigan Crow.

Arrangement to end either by mutual accord, or when the apprentice has mastered nine Wundrous Arts – including pilgrimage to the appropriate Divinities and acquisition of their respective seals.

Underneath were two blank spaces for their signatures, labelled 'Master' and 'Apprentice'.

Morrigan stared at it, blinking repeatedly. It felt like nothing – it could have been made of air. When she squinted, the space around it shimmered with energy, and sure enough when she moved her hands away, the contract stayed exactly where it was, hovering in the space between them.

'It lives in the Gossamer,' said Squall. 'Neither here nor there.'

Morrigan frowned. She'd assumed wrongly. When they'd joined hands earlier . . . that had nothing to do with beginning the apprenticeship. It wasn't some ritualistic seal that bound them together, it had only granted Squall the necessary access to cure the Wunimals. Which meant (one thought came tumbling after the other) – which *meant* that he'd fulfilled his part of the bargain without any binding agreement in place. *This* was the agreement.

The full picture resolved in Morrigan's head, giddy disbelief rising inside her.

She needn't sign this contract at all! Squall had already cured the Wunimals, and it wasn't as if he could undo it without her cooperation. She could simply walk away, having got exactly what she wanted and given him nothing in return.

In the silence, he reached out through the Gossamer, touched his Inferno imprint to the contract and swiped it across the page. The scorched trail he left behind curled itself into a signature – small, black and calligraphic.

'I've no interest in teaching a disinterested student, Miss Crow. Nor one who is merely fulfilling an obligation. I don't want a dead weight. I want an heir.

'You've witnessed the possibilities now. You've met the Wundersmith you could become. Opened a window into a future that could be yours. But if you are not enthusiastically, *fanatically* eager to climb through the window and seize that future for yourself, then . . . close it.' Squall's voice was barely a whisper. He gave a shrug that was almost practised in its nonchalance, but the black intensity of his gaze betrayed him; he didn't look away, and neither did she. 'I won't hold you to our agreement.'

Morrigan could almost have believed he was bluffing, except beneath the veneer of resolute calm he looked so . . . frightened. As if he'd fully accepted that she might do exactly as he suggested. Close the window. Walk away.

But of course, she wouldn't. She couldn't.

Someday far in the future, Morrigan would think back to this moment and tell herself she'd acted according to some unwritten code of honour, obeyed some chivalrous little voice in her head that sang, *you promised*. She'd given her word, after all, and decency demanded that she keep it.

But in that moment – in the stretch of her hand to the paper, and the burning of her name upon it – Morrigan wasn't thinking of honour. She was thinking of how it had felt to have a universe inside her. The universe was gone now, but the space it had occupied was still there. Cavernous and wanting, filled with a hunger like nothing she'd known.

And her hunger said, '*More*.'

Back on the ward, the snoring and the wheezing continued in peaceful oblivion.

Morrigan stood alone beside her bed. She picked up Emmett and hugged him to her chest. That simple action alone took so much will and effort. She wanted *desperately* to sleep in her own bed, to be cocooned in the safety and warmth of the Deucalion. She wanted to go home.

Morrigan didn't know how long it took her to get out of the hospital, up three floors of Proudfoot House and all the way down to the train station in her slippers, pyjamas and cloak. Hours, almost certainly. She felt as if she was dragging herself there, and she didn't know if it was her exhausted body pulling her exhausted brain behind it, or vice versa. She simply knew she had to keep going – one shuffling, tiny step and then another. It was dark on the path through the Whinging Woods, and the trees muttered low and deep, and somewhere in the forest something howled and she knew, distantly, that she ought to be frightened. That on any other day, walking the path through the Whinging Woods in the pitch-dark night, on her own, would have terrified her.

But Morrigan was too tired to be frightened.

And even back inside her own frail self, without the scaffolding of Ezra Squall's borrowed power, she could still remember what it felt like to truly be a Wundersmith, and she carried the memory with her like a talisman. Like the worn old rabbit held tight in the crook of her elbow. She would cling to that memory by the skin of her fingertips, for as long as she possibly could.

It would get her to the station, and then into a brass railpod, and then all the way to Station 919. It would see her through the black door, through the wardrobe, into the gently rocking waterbed her room had kindly provided, and at last into the deepest, warmest sleep she had ever slept. Home safe in the Deucalion, surrounded by her family.

Acknowledgements

My first and most important thank you goes to you, splendid reader, for coming this far on Morrigan's adventures with me. You've been patient, enthusiastic and endlessly supportive, and I hope *Hollowpox* was worth the wait.

Speaking of patient, enthusiastic and endlessly supportive . . . Ruth Alltimes, what a queen. It is truly the greatest stroke of fortune to have you as my editor, and I'm so thankful for your sharp eye and good heart.

I am incredibly lucky and for ever grateful to work with the dream team of Alvina Ling, Suzanne O'Sullivan, Rachel Wade, Samantha Swinnerton and Ruqayyah Daud. Thank you for the expertise, talent, creativity and resourcefulness you bring to publishing this series.

Across Hachette Children's Group, Hachette Australia, Hachette New Zealand, and Little, Brown Books for Young Readers, every member of Team Nevermoor brings so much passion, skill and hard work to the table, and I can't thank you all enough: Dom Kingston, Nicola Goode, Fiona Evans, Katy Cattell, Tania Mackenzie-Cooke, Katharine McAnarney, Louise Sherwin-Stark, Hilary Murray Hill, Megan Tingley, Mel Winder, Fiona Hazard, Jeanmarie Morosin, Helen Hughes, Tash Whearity, Dido O'Reilly, Katherine Fox, Jemimah James,

Andrew Cohen, Caitlin Murphy, Chris Sims, Daniel Pilkington, Hayley New, Isabel Staas, Kate Flood, Keira Lykourentzos, Sarah Holmes, Sean Cotcher, Sophie Mayfield, Caz Feeney, Jenny Topham, Cassy Nacard, Emma Rusher, Suzy Maddox-Kane, Alison Shucksmith, Sacha Beguely, Emilie Polster, Bill Grace, Savannah Kennelly, Victoria Stapleton, Michelle Campbell, Jen Graham, and Virginia Lawther.

Thank you to the very talented Jim Madsen and Hannah Peck for the amazing artwork, and to Alison Padley, Sasha Illingworth, Christa Moffitt and Angelie Yap for the brilliant cover designs. You have made *Hollowpox* so beautiful.

Big thanks as always to Jenny Bent, Molly Ker Hawn, Amelia Hodgson, Victoria Cappello and the entire, most excellent Bent Agency, and to the dreamy authors who make up Team Cooper. Publishing can be a strange, confusing world; it is indescribably nice to be on a little life raft full of people who support and cheer each other on. You are all doing such extraordinary things and you inspire me constantly.

Thank you to Catherine Doyle for the gift that is De Flimsé. (Told you it was going in book three.) I can't quite recall the origin story any more . . . a freezing train station after Cheltenham Lit Fest? A weird mishearing? I DON'T KNOW but it definitely made me laugh.

Thank you to Gemma Whelan, the voice (the many, *many* voices) of the *Nevermoor* audiobooks. I can't tell you how much joy it gives me to hear you bring this world and these characters to life in such funny, moving and surprising ways. It's honestly quite rude of you to be so talented, but please do carry on.

Thank you to the publishers and translators putting my books into children's hands all over the world in 40 languages.

I've been lucky to spend time with some of you already, and your care, skill and attention to detail leaves me speechless. Thank you so much.

Thank you, thank you, thank you to the booksellers, librarians, teachers, bloggers, bookstagrammers and booktubers who have shown such love for *Nevermoor* and *Wundersmith*, and passed on that enthusiasm to others. Your championing of children's books makes the world a warmer, nicer, more magical place.

To my family and friends, thank you for the bottomless barrel of love and support. Shout-out to Sherri Gordon-Harris, who occupies both categories and on whose various couches, kitchen tables and spare beds so much of this series has been written over the years, and also to *The* Chloe Musgrove for answering my (excessively specific) theatre questions.

My agent and my friend, Gemma Cooper – you are a lioness, a deep well of common sense and good cheer, the greatest advocate and the coolest accomplice I could have asked for. FIVE BRILLIANT YEARS we've been on this caper together, and I can't imagine doing any of it without you. Thank you for always having my back.

And finally, cheers to me old pal Sal (the genius behind 'What's That Smell?', which made us both wheeze with laughter in a deeply undignified fashion, but what's new) and to my splendid Ma, a nine-star human, the Deucalion of mothers.

Turn the page
to find out the title
for the fourth Nevermoor book,
coming soon!

THE
MYSTERY OF
MORRIGAN
CROW

'Exciting, mysterious, marvellous and magical'
ROBIN STEVENS, author of MURDER MOST UNLADYLIKE
Nevermoor
THE TRIALS OF MORRIGAN CROW
JESSICA TOWNSEND

WundeRsmith

THE CALLING OF MORRIGAN CROW

A Nevermoor
BOOK

JESSICA TOWNSEND

Wundrous Society Entrance Examination

Welcome, candidate! Entry to our esteemed Society is a privilege granted to the few and the special. To succeed you must prove your sincerity and quick-thinking by completing the following four trials. Cheating will result in immediate disqualification. Answer as honestly as you can. Good luck!

BOOK TRIAL

1. What is your favourite book?
2. Why?
3. If you could be a character from a book, who would it be?
4. If you wrote a book, what would it be about?
5. What do you like best in a book: adventure, mystery, surprise, drama?

GUESS TRIAL

1. Which of the following creatures and beings do you think appear in *Nevermoor*? Dragons, vampire dwarfs, talking cats, witches, bass-playing lizards?
2. In *Nevermoor*, the main character Morrigan is given a nickname; which of the following do you think it is: Morrie, Morro, Moz, Mozza, Mozzie, Mog, Mo, Mor?

3. Morrigan is cursed to die on her birthday. Which birthday do you think it is? Her tenth, eleventh, or twelfth?
4. To enter the Wundrous Society you must have a special talent. What do you think Morrigan's is?
5. In Nevermoor they have an unusual mode of transport. What do you think they use to travel? Umbrellas, curtains or cats?

FRIGHT TRIAL

1. What are you most afraid of?
2. What else are you afraid of?
3. Would you be willing to face your fears in order to gain entry to the Wundrous Society?
4. Do you believe in ghosts?
5. If you were trapped in a cemetery with flesh-eating zombies, how would you escape?

SHOW TRIAL

1. Do you consider yourself to be extraordinary?
2. What are you good at?
3. If you could choose one extra special talent, what would it be?
4. What is the most extraordinary thing that's ever happened to you?
5. Why do you want to join the Wundrous Society?

Turn the page to find out if you passed...

Wundrous Society Entry Examination Answers

BOOK TRIAL

1. *Nevermoor*, obviously! Although you might not know it yet . . . so we'll award 1 point for your own honest answer.
2. 1 point awarded for a well-considered answer.
3. 1 point awarded for an interesting answer.
4. 1 point awarded for an interesting answer.
5. You're in luck, *Nevermoor* has them all! 1 point awarded for any answer.

GUESS TRIAL

1. They all do! 1 point awarded for any answer, 2 points awarded if you said 'all of them'.
2. 1 point awarded if you said . . . Mog.
3. 1 point awarded if you said . . . eleventh.
4. To answer that would spoil the book! But we'll award 1 point for an interesting answer.
5. 1 point awarded if you said . . . umbrellas!

FRIGHT TRIAL

1. 1 point awarded for an honest answer.
2. 1 point awarded for an honest answer.
3. 2 points awarded if you said yes. 2 points deducted if you said no.

4. 1 point awarded for an honest answer.
5. You'd climb into a grave, obviously! But we'll award 1 point for another clever idea . . .

SHOW TRIAL

1. The correct answer is YES we are all extraordinary in our own way. 1 point.
2. 1 point awarded for any honest or funny answer.
3. 1 point awarded for any honest or funny answer. 1 point deducted for any talent which would be used for ill-gain!
4. 1 point awarded for any honest answer.
5. 1 point awarded for any honest answer.

RESULTS

If you scored 15 or more points then CONGRATULATIONS you have been granted entry into the Wundrous Society! Welcome to the family. If you scored 14 points or fewer then we're sorry you were not successful this time. Try again soon and remember, honesty will get you far . . .

Find out what your knack might be with this quiz!

1. WHAT ARE YOU SCARED OF?
a. Being alone
b. Bullies
c. Bad curses
d. Nothing

2. CHOOSE A LAST NAME:
a. Swift
b. North
c. Crow
d. Blackburn

3. CHOOSE A COLOUR:
a. Green
b. Blue
c. Red
d. Grey

4. PICK AN ANIMAL:
a. Horse
b. Wolf
c. Owl
d. Cat

5. CHOOSE A WORD:
a. Light
b. Mystery
c. Magic
d. Strength

6. PICK AN ELEMENT:
a. Water
b. Air
c. Fire
d. Earth

7. YOUR FRIENDS WOULD DESCRIBE YOU AS:
a. Friendly
b. Smart
c. Kind
d. Brave

8. PICK AN OBJECT:
a. Key
b. Book
c. Map
d. Cloak

Turn the page to find out...

MOSTLY As:

MESMERIST

HAS THE ABILITY TO GET PEOPLE TO DO
WHATEVER THEY WANT.

MOSTLY Bs:

WITNESS

HAS THE POWER TO SEE EVERYONE'S
TRUTH AND SECRETS.

MOSTLY Cs:

WUNDERSMITH

HAS THE ABILITY TO CONTROL WUNDER
AND IS EXTREMELY POWERFUL.

MOSTLY Ds:

DRAGONRIDER

IS A PHENOMENALLY SKILLED
RIDER OF DRAGONS.